Blue Belle

A Wildflowers of Scotland Novel

By

Sherrie Hansen

D1398840

Published by Blue Belle Books
Saint Ansgar, Iowa

Blue Belle Books
PO Box 205
Saint Ansgar, IA 50472

For information regarding bulk purchases of this book, digital purchase and special discounts, please contact the publisher at BlueBelleBooks.com

Cover design by Stacy Castanedo
Photo by Sherrie Hansen

Manufactured in the United States of America
ISBN 978-1676016182

Happy birthday
to Pat!

Love,
Paul & John
10-21-2023

To my friends from Gather.com and Jenny's Cherry Writers, whose encouragement, assistance and critiques I greatly appreciate.

Many thanks to Lisa Deyo, Mary Ann Olsen and Deb Rohne.

Sherrie Hansen

Chapter One

She was having a panic attack. He was sure of it. The classic signs—shortness of breath, chest pains, trembling, sweatiness, a sense of terror, numbness—were either written on her face or obvious in her gestures. What had set her off? The Blue Bell was as safe a place as he could imagine.

Michael St. Dawndalyn resisted the urge to jump up and go to her rescue. He wasn't a doctor in Scotland. He was a contractor. And not even that, if you wanted the truth. The last thing he needed was to draw attention to himself, make people wonder how a common rock layer would know so much about anxiety disorders.

He watched as one of his younger crew members approached the booth where the woman was sitting with a pot of tea and what appeared to be sticky toffee pudding. What was Logan doing in an apron? Seeing the lad's large girth, criss-crossed with strings like a trussed side of Abershire beef, was scary alright, but even that didn't account for the woman's blue mood.

He looked on helplessly as she cowered, recoiled, tried to compose herself and failed. He watched as she fought for breath after panicked breath. It was Logan—kind, gentle giant, harmless as a mountain hare, Logan Galbraith.

Doing nothing, when he knew he could help, was driving him crazy. Two Americans, both living in Tobermory, Isle of Mull, Scotland, and he'd been all but rude to the woman because he was afraid she'd Google him and find out he was wanted in Wisconsin. He wanted to help, but he had to keep his distance.

Screw propriety. He jumped to his feet and catapulted himself in her direction. At the very least, he had to get Logan away from her. Poor fool was hovering over her like Algernon with his mouse, trying to make her feel better, never in a million years guessing he was the cause of her angst.

The crowd parted instinctively as he approached, not because they knew he was a doctor, but because he was their leader. They

3

trusted him to help. He was their boss, their provider.

He nudged past Logan until it was he who filled her frame of reference.

"Isabelle, is it?" Everyone at the pub knew her name. Small town, just like Oconomowoc. He used his most reassuring, kindly voice, the one he'd been told could just as likely melt a woman's heart as soothe a patient.

He stroked the back of her hand. "Take deep breaths. Think about your favorite spot in the world, the place where you feel safest and happiest and free from any cares." He whispered so only she could hear.

Her hand trembled in his. Her shallow gasps changed to deeper, fuller breaths.

And then she lifted her head and locked her blue eyes directly on his. He felt it happen, the bonding, the imprinting, the life-altering zing of energy that passed between them.

A tall gent that he recognized as the new pastor at Parish Church came alongside him. "Pastor Ian MacCraig. Anything I can do to help?"

A woman with dark auburn curls whooshed up and wedged herself between them. "Sweetheart, it's going to be okay. I promise you, it's going to be all right."

Isabelle's eyes flickered away from his. She glanced at the other woman and then back at him, the blue of her eyes even bluer against her pale skin, pink cheeks, and soft red hair.

The auburn-headed woman smiled brightly. "Ye're too young and pretty to be having a cardiac episode, so I'm assuming what ye're experiencing is a good, old-fashioned panic attack."

Isabelle looked up at the woman, her face showing obvious relief. Michael continued to block Isabelle's view of Logan, and when she wasn't looking, motioned for his young charge to return to the bar and give the woman some space. What about Logan had set her off, he could only imagine.

"I'm Rose. Rose MacCraig, Pastor Ian's wife from Parish Church."

Michael backed away when he saw the look of relief on Isabelle's face. The important thing was that she got help. He didn't need to be the one who healed her. This Rose might not be professionally trained, although for all he knew, she had more degrees than he did. What did matter was that Rose was confident of her ability to help. Her positive approach was in turn instilling confidence in Isabelle, who appeared to trust her. Maybe another woman's touch was what she needed.

He stood quietly by as Rose took charge. Isabelle's eyes searched for his one last time. He met and held her gaze while Rose talked her down from her hysteria. When her breathing had returned to normal, he left the pub, content not to tempt fate. He needed to be in Scotland, and he needed to keep his identity a secret. There was too much at stake.

#

Isabelle MacAllister put her hand to her chest and felt her heart rate slowing to normal.

"I'm happy to listen if ye need someone to talk to." Rose tried to reassure her.

She wasn't keen on opening up to a complete stranger for obvious reasons. But then, she really didn't have anything to hide except... and if she thought about that right now she'd be in the throes of another panic attack. So she would just tell the pastor's wife enough to satisfy her curiosity and deal with the rest later. She didn't want to seem rude when everyone had been so nice to her. She looked around the room, searching for the man who had been so kind to her a few minutes earlier. Gone.

She rubbed her forehead. "I was going to ask the tall waiter in the apron if I could take his photo for an article I'm working on."

"You're a reporter then?"

"Yes. For *Insight* magazine. My office is in Roanoke, Virginia. I'm writing an article about the recent problems that have plagued the United Kingdom's farmers."

"Yes." Rose twirled a tendril of hair between her thumb and first finger. "First mad cow disease, and then hoof and mouth. The prices for wool and beef keep dropping lower and lower."

Isabelle gulped another breath of air.

Rose nodded. "Logan used to be a farmer, aye?"

"That's what the woman behind the bar said when I was looking at the day an' daily's on the board."

"So you were going to photograph the lad?"

"That was the plan. We hadn't gotten much further than 'Sae do ye fancy a wee drum?'" Her heart shivered in her chest. "That's when I turned on my camera and discovered the memory card was missing."

"Had you filled it and forgotten to buy a new one, or taken it out to download the photos on it?"

"No. I download the photos with a cable that hooks directly into my laptop. And I rarely even use this camera." Her mind flitted to Ben—the last place on earth she wanted her thoughts to travel—as the sickening truth hit her. That, and the realization Logan's large size, broad shoulders and short, Marine-style buzz made him look the spit and image of Ben, at least at a distance. She grimaced and felt a fresh batch of shame wash over her.

She looked up at Rose. There was definite empathy in her eyes. She didn't know why, but she knew instinctively she could trust her. "A man I know—knew—used my camera once or twice. He must have taken it."

"Why would he have wanted the memory card? Was there something valuable on it? Evidence that could have incriminated him?" Rose's eyes looked serious, but there was a spark of something else she couldn't quite put her finger on. "Sorry. I have a bit of a wild imagination."

Isabelle's head started to spin again and this time, her stomach followed suit. Ben had pictures of her—pictures that would leave nothing to the most vivid imagination. How could she have known Ben was… How could she have trusted him? She was smart, savvy, an investigative reporter. And she'd been hoodwinked by a two bit criminal, a conman who now had photos he could use against her.

"Are you okay?" Rose asked again. "Not to alarm you, but your face turned the slightest bit green there for a second."

"I'm fine." But she wasn't. She'd traveled to what was practically the end of the earth to get away from the man, yet here he was, stalking her electronically and emotionally.

"I'll be fine." She hoped she would be. When she'd first met Ben, she'd been proud of the fact he'd served with the Special Forces. Now that she knew he was a trained assassin and computer espionage wizard, she was scared of her own shadow. She'd done the right thing by turning him in to the police, but now she lived with the terror Ben would make her pay. The memory card gave him just the ammunition he needed.

Rose continued to try to reassure her. She looked up at the bar, but the man who had helped her was nowhere in sight. Not that it mattered. No one could help her now. Still, she was curious. Maybe it was just the fact that she'd been so out of it at the time, but she could have sworn he was an American.

#

The next day, Michael headed back to the Blue Bell as soon as they'd finished their day's work at the castle.

"Guid day, Michael." One of the farmers who worked for him called from across the room. "Bevvy up—the ale's oan me tonecht!"

Michael nodded and paused to survey the eclectic mix of people perched on stools, plopped on chairs, and straddling benches around the circumference of the Blue Bell. Both the people and the pub had a comfortable, well-worn feel about them—despite the fact that Damon Hermance, the new owner, had recently had every seat in the place reupholstered.

He accepted the frothy drink from the barmaid, settled into his seat, and swiveled into position so he could see who was there. The stools that lined the bar had been plumped with just enough padding to take the pressure off a man's weary haunches at the end of a long, hard day. The dappled tones were just right for camouflaging the ever-present muck and mud brought in by his stone layers.

No matter what the locals thought of Hermance—most of it not good—it was clear careful thought had been given to every detail of the pub's refurbishing—far more thought than Michael had given to any of the specifics involved in his own remaking. He had to give Damon credit for that.

He ran his hand over a set of age-old initials carved in the soft, smooth pine of the bar. They could have belonged to a friend of his great-grandfather's. Thankfully, Hermance's controversial efforts to pretty up the place hadn't included redoing the surface of the well-dented bar, except to buff it up a bit.

"So ye're staying out at Bluevale Castle, are ye?"

Logan Galbraith's voice carried so clearly that for a second, Michael thought he was standing behind him, asking him about Cnoc Fuar, the cottage where he was staying down in Bluebell Valley, on the far side of the castle grounds—which made no sense. Logan knew exactly where he lived.

He turned and watched as Logan handed a cottage pie with a thatched roof to the same American woman he'd been bothering the night before. And why? Logan wasn't even a waiter. He couldn't enjoy being trussed up in a too small apron cutting swaths around his middle. What was he up to?

"I'm in one of the cottages." She squirmed as though there was a stray upholstery tack sticking out from her seat. But at least tonight, she was keeping it together.

"Must be the whitewashed but and ben below the garden wall that looks down to the sea," Logan said.

Her eyes looked downright panicked at the speed with which Logan had put two and two together. She'd learn. People were no different in Scotland than they were in America. Everybody knew everything about everyone.

Why on earth had she come back if Logan bothered her so? She'd only begun to frequent the Bell and she wasn't meeting a friend. She always sat alone—by choice, if Michael knew anything about human behavior—and he did.

"So what brings ye to Tobermory and the fair Isle of Mull, if I may ask?" Logan's brogue was loud enough that Michael could hear him clearly. He had to strain to hear the woman's replies.

"The rainbow-colored buildings along the waterfront, I suppose. And the castle. The way it guards the inlet made the island seem—I don't know—safe."

Michael grunted. Probably the same URL he'd looked at back in his office in Wisconsin. Not that he was inclined to argue with her assessment of the place. He couldn't deny the island was picturesque. And it had been the perfect haven for him.

"Sae ye're not after the gold then, eh?"

"No." She looked a little less ill at ease. "But it didn't hurt that you have a chocolate factory."

Michael swiveled around to face the bar before Logan could spot him eavesdropping, but he could still hear Logan going on about the local legend that there was a sunken Spanish galleon from 1588, filled with gold coins, buried in the bottom of Tobermory Bay.

He should have realized it was the gold. Logan and his mother thought every stranger who came into the pub more than twice was involved in a plot to unearth the gold and abscond with the buried treasure.

He smiled in spite of himself. Isabelle's rosy cheeks and girlish, reddish blond curls made her look the least likely pirate he could imagine. Although there was something complex lurking beneath her careful, Southern facade. Maybe that was why he'd yet to tire of looking at her.

He tried to appear stern and aloof as Logan passed the door to the kitchen and squeezed between the edge of the bar and the liquor-lined wall behind it.

"So you've stooped so low you were willing to don an apron just to get near the lady," Michael said. He felt only a tinge of guilt about teasing Logan, though truth be known, he was the last one who should be hassling someone for pretending to be an expert at something he knew precious little about.

Logan grinned. "My Mum's the cook. Ye cannae sae I dinnae have a good excuse to be helping out."

Michael shook his head. "Your get-up has nothing to do with your Mum, and you know it." The younger man's bulky frame and elongated hands were far more suited for hefting rocks, mixing mortar and fitting stones than maneuvering around a slippery-floored kitchen or navigating the obstacle course of chairs and customers that packed the pub. If Logan had grown up in Wisconsin instead of Scotland, he'd probably be clutching a football and dodging a blitz of linebackers from whatever team the Green Bay Packers happened to be playing that week.

"The wee bit o' pride I had to set aside to accomplish my task has been weill worth it." Logan lowered his head and jabbed Michael's ribs with his elbow. "I'm the first person she's bared her soul to since she darkened the door."

Telling Logan she was staying at Dunara Cottage hardly qualified as an inside scoop—the whole town had known since five minutes after she'd arrived—but Michael didn't want to burst Logan's bubble, so he just smiled. "You're a pro at getting the ladies to open up to you, all right."

His young employee smiled broadly. "My mum thinks she works for the Spaniards who want to scour the bay for the sunken treasure."

"You thought the same thing about me when I came to the island. If I remember right, your Mum had me pegged for a sonar technology expert because of my refined mannerisms and scholarly good looks."

9

"G'wa," Logan said, with a laugh. "No one said a thing aboot good looks to the best o' my recollection."

Michael followed Logan's eyes back to the booth.

"She's eye-sweet, a right," Logan said.

The strappin' laddie was right about that. She was pure Southern belle, warm and dewy-looking as a sultry night laced with the scent of cherry blossoms—a true lady, if her shy but charming gestures said anything at all. Definitely not an agent of subterfuge. But he'd never convince Logan of it.

Michael let his eyes roam back to the booth. There was still something about the woman that was not quite right, assuming his instincts hadn't dulled too much in the last nine months. Maybe it was the way she kept clutching at her bag. He would have written it off as the jittery habit of someone who'd lived in a big city too long if she hadn't looked so stiff and... Downtrodden? Deflated? He didn't know quite how to describe it. For whatever reason, Isabelle looked as blue as the wildflowers blooming in the pasture behind his cottage.

He took a sip of ale and tried to analyze his fascination with the woman. He couldn't deny she'd set his senses singing the moment she'd walked into the pub. But then, he'd been working for almost a year with piles of unyielding, gray stones, and a randy bunch of men with heads as hard as the rocks they wielded. It was probably a natural reaction.

By the time Michael thought to tear his eyes away from her, Logan was back at her side.

"Ye've caused quite a stir with the locals," Logan was saying, cozying up to her like they were buddies from way back despite the fact she looked increasingly ill at ease. "I don't mind telling ye they've all been doing their best to find out who ye are and what ye're up to."

They've been? Michael rolled his eyes. Like you're not one of them?

She looked around the room as if gauging—no, doubting—the trustworthiness of each face. "I suppose their curiosity is understandable."

Nor did she care to be forthcoming about why she'd come to the island. Logan might not see it, but it was crystal clear to Michael that she valued her privacy just as he did.

10

Logan inched closer and topped off her water glass. "My mum's got you pegged for a barrister come round to try to persuade the town board to reconsider their decision to forbid dredging for gold in the bay. What's got them in a flap is yer six-month lease. Folks are a-clattering aboot it aright. Most goer-byes stay no longer than a fortnight or two."

Her eyes opened wide, apparently shocked to find out Logan knew the terms of her rental agreement. Might as well get used to it, Michael thought. Logan was obviously going to keep pecking away at her until she coughed up the rest of the story.

"You can tell your Mum I'm from Virginia. I'm a writer," she said in a resigned voice.

Logan's face lit up. "Aye," he said, drawing out the short word as if that explained everything. "A poet here to walk the same ground Robert Burns once trod? Or a novelist looking for your inspiration in the old haunts of Robert Louis Stevenson or Sir Walter Scott? Wait. Now that I think aboot it, you look a mite like a J. M. Barrie type."

Her? A Peter Pan fan? With that skittish look in her eyes? No way. Michael's favorite Barrie line played itself in his head like a well-worn record... *Every time a child says, "I don't believe in fairies," there is a fairy somewhere that falls down dead.* Sorry as he was to say it, her blue expression alone could slay dozens.

"I usually work as an investigative reporter, but I'm here on temporary assignment writing travel articles for *Insight* magazine. I'll be traveling all over Europe while I'm here."

See, he'd known there was something. The fact that she carried a laptop around had made him nervous from the start. Michael stifled a groan and tightened his fist around his ale. Damn. The last thing he needed was some journalist sticking her nose where it didn't belong. The slightest bit of curiosity on her part could ruin everything.

"A remote island that's only accessible by ferry seems like an odd place to settle if ye're planning on traveling aboot while ye're here." Logan said.

"I do a lot of my research online," she said. "The internet is a gold mine. My goal is to lure American travelers back to Europe, particularly the British Isles, in light of all that's transpired in the last few years."

Logan nodded. "Ah suppose you mean mad cow. Hoof and mouth."

"Not to mention airline safety concerns due to terrorists, SARS, Iceland's volcanoes, and the whole situation in the Middle East."

Logan sighed. "Aye. And rightly so. The whole hoof and mouth debacle hurt many fine folk. The restrictions they put on hiking and traveling to keep it from spreading aboot dinnae even apply to this area, but the trekkers stopped coming nonetheless."

The woman took a sip of water. She looked passionate in her desire to help—he'd give her that. "I'm sure it's been terribly hard on the farmers who had both infected animals on their land and bed and breakfasts in their homes. To lose their herds, then have tourism drop off to almost nothing..."

"Aye. Many are still in dire financial straits. That's why Michael St. Dawndalyn, the American sitting over at the bar, has been such a godsend."

Michael twisted around as fast as he could and grabbed a newspaper from the barstool next to him. He took a deep breath and tried to appear as though he were nonchalantly reading the news.

"The one right there—the tall gent with the fair hair who's wearing the wool sweater," Logan said. "I'd be happy to introduce ye."

"Maybe later," she said, in a half-strangled voice, to which Logan appeared oblivious.

"When Michael set aboot recruiting stone layers to work on the keep, he went straight to the farmers—said they're the hardest-working, most dependable gents aboot no matter what part of the world ye find yourself in."

So Logan was making him out to be a hero. The muscles in Michael's jaw clenched and unclenched as he momentarily recalled the stack of subpoenas he'd left cluttering his desk when he'd walked away from Oconomowoc. There were some who would disagree.

"Mr. St. Dawndalyn's efforts sound very admirable," the woman was saying. "I'd like to think I can help by writing articles that will put a positive slant on the opportunity to see the British Isles now, while prices are reasonable and accommodations are readily available."

"The reporters who've come before ye seemed more intent on getting the public revved up than on helping." Logan's voice sounded as wary as she looked. "They knew good and weill how rumors would gae aboot once they get people clacking about herds being burned to stave off hoof and mouth. It was tragedy enough without the muckle hash journalism that came with it."

"I've got my work cut out for me then—proving I'm different from my unscrupulous associates," she said calmly. "I value the truth above everything else. If my stories don't sell because they're not scandalous enough, so be it."

"I hae ye." Logan sounded unconvinced.

Michael looked over his shoulder as discreetly as he could. The woman was taking a bite of the steaming hot mashed potato and cheddar cheese crust that topped her meat pie. He could smell the succulent filling as she poked down through the top—pungent leeks and green peas fresh from the garden. He loved the Bell's food.

"Weill, enjoy your champers," Logan said, and "Go n-eiri an t-adh leat. Good luck in Gaelic." He extended his hand to her. "I'm Logan Galbraith, by the way. Ye might mention that the queues are blissfully short at the ferry terminals and Historic Trust sites."

"Good idea." The woman extended her hand and smiled, looking as though the effort of talking to Logan had drained her. "Isabelle MacAllister."

By the time Logan returned to the bar, he looked like a cat who'd been in the cream, lapped a little too much, and gotten indigestion.

"She cannae have come here just to write about mad cow disease, can she?" Logan asked, glancing back at Isabelle. "She would nae come all the way to Tobermory to do something she could have done from London."

Michael glanced at the blackboard on the wall behind the stools, with its neatly printed list of the pub grub that was currently available. He'd already ordered the same vegetable strudel he'd had twice earlier that week. It was hard to improve on perfection.

"She must be connected to the blokes who want to dredge the bay." Logan fumed. "There's nae other explanation for it."

"All the more reason not to be spilling your guts to the woman," Michael cautioned him. That was the problem with Southern belles—they lured you into complete and utter surrender with their sweet-as-honey voices. Then, when it was too late, you realized you'd been had by a mind as sharp and acute as a shard of fine Irish crystal.

His stomach rumbled more from nerves than hunger. Damn it anyway. He would not let some reporter ruin the idyllic life he'd forged for himself over the last nine months. He loved working with his hands again, breathing in the fresh, outdoor air, feeling the wind in his face and the cool Scottish sun warming his shoulders while he worked. Better yet, he liked seeing the immediate, tangible results of his labor, watching the walls of the keep grow higher and stronger with every week that passed.

There was no way in hell he'd risk all that. For years, he'd earned his living maintaining a psychological interest in people and still remaining professionally detached. How hard could it be to do the same where Isabelle McAllister was involved?

He let his eyes linger on her for a second longer, just to prove to himself he could do it. Her high-necked, long sleeved sweater covered her from the soft curl of fabric under her chin to the rolled cuffs that hung down over the tops of her petite hands. He could almost feel his finger slipping under the soft bit of wool, tipping her chin up a notch and lifting her face to meet his.

Fine. So there was something about her that threatened his objectivity. That didn't negate the fact she was a reporter, and as long as he was obliged to keep the confidences that had brought him to Scotland in the first place, there could never be anything between them.

"If I have to watch you mooning around in this apron much longer, I'm likely to lose my appetite." Michael scowled at Logan. "Tally up your lady-friend's tab and be done with it, will you?"

Logan pushed away from the bar and strode over to her booth just as Mrs. Galbraith appeared with his supper. The enticing aroma of steamed carrots, loamy mushrooms, and zucchini wafted out from a slit in the pastry on top. The warm steam bathed his face as he used his fork to make the opening wider.

But even with the distraction of food, he could not keep his eyes off her. When he looked back, she had picked up her fork with her left hand and her knife with her right. Not a good idea. Just because the Brits could wrestle peas and champers and tiny bits of beef onto their forks with their knives, and feed themselves with what seemed like the wrong hand, didn't mean she could.

Michael grimaced as a pea slid down her chin and fell to her lap. He watched out of the corner of his eye as she daintily dabbed at her mouth with her napkin.

"Logan?" Michael heard her say, when she'd discreetly

recovered the wayward legume.

If Logan had had a tail, it would have been wagging.

"Would you mind if I tried to snap a quick photo of you to send in with my next article?"

"Me?" Logan blushed as he reached behind his back and attempted to untangle the strings of his too-small apron.

"No, leave it on. That's the point I'm trying to make," she said. "Farmers are going to any means necessary to support their families."

"So I'm to be the sympathetic gent who's eking out a living on the wee tips I earn serving skoosh and fortifiers?"

"Something like that." She smiled.

Logan smoothed his apron and struck a pose.

She raised her camera to her eye and snapped.

Chapter Two

Dunara Cottage had a charming aura about it even without a fire crackling in the hearth to illuminate its finer points. The leathery glow of a single parlor lamp cast long, lacey shadows on the wall behind a potted pink geranium. The flower, which Isabelle had inherited with the key, perched on a rough-hewn mantle just wide enough to support the width of the clay pot wrapped around its roots. Isabelle sat within arm's reach of the stone fireplace in a deeply cushioned, slip-covered chair, her laptop computer balanced on her knees.

She typed another comment into the string of instant messages she and Gloria were sending back and forth between Scotland and Virginia. Their online names dated all the way back to a high school production of *Bye Bye Birdie*, where they'd sung a song called *The Telephone Hour* with the lyrics: *What's the story, morning glory? What's the tale, nightingale?* Isabelle, always a night owl, had been dubbed Nightingale, and Gloria, a cheery, up-at-dawn person, Morning_Glory.

Nightingale: I keep intending to build a fire, but by the time the thought crosses my mind, it's nearly bedtime, and I'm too drowsy to stay awake until the fire burns down.

Morning_Glory: You said you have a warm quilt on your bed.

Nightingale: I do. Besides, it would be pointless to try to build a fire tonight. It's been pouring since early this afternoon, and the wind is so strong I'm sure all the firewood is soaking wet by now.

Morning_Glory: Aren't you even a little nervous, being so close to the water?

She adjusted her font settings to bold face so she could see in the fading light and burrowed down even deeper into the chair's soft cushions.

Nightingale: I've been in far worse storms back in Virginia. Remember that time I was in Wisconsin researching an article on cheese when I saw a tornado? Now that was scary.

16

Gloria's words appeared on her screen after a slight pause.

Morning_Glory: I was just looking at that commentary in the archives.

Nightingale: The one I did for Food and Wine about the cheese wars? If Ronald asked you to dig up that old thing, he must be going to let me do the article I suggested about product origination suits.

Morning_Glory: He asked me to find out if Europeans have threatened American companies with lawsuits based on the premise products should only be named after a town or region if they're actually produced in the same area. I did, and it's true. Many Europeans believe they have the sole rightful claim to products that originated in and are named after their regions.

Nightingale: So, no more Swiss Cheese unless it's actually imported from Switzerland.

Morning_Glory: Right. No more Kalamati olives unless they're harvested and canned in Greece, and no more frankfurters unless they're produced in Frankfurt. And no more Dijon mustard unless I want to pay for a French import.

Nightingale: So when do I start? I can't wait to get back to writing articles with a little more meat. No pun intended.

Isabelle could hear the wind whistling around the stone walls of her cottage as she waited for Gloria's response. The glass windowpanes facing the sea rattled in their frames.

Morning_Glory: Sorry, sweetheart. I didn't know you wanted the article or I would have put in a good word for you. Ronald already asked a new staff writer to do the piece.

Nightingale: But I suggested this very topic just last week. And I'm right here in Europe.

Morning_Glory: Austin is very young. Ronald is probably just trying to get a feel for what he can do. I'm sure it wasn't anything personal.

It felt like an intentional slight, which was very personal.

Nightingale: Ronald keeps reassuring me by telling me how much he wants me back, but sometimes, I wonder.

Morning_Glory: You act like he's cheating on you with Austin. I mean, Austin does have some good ideas, but he's not you.

Nightingale: But the cheese wars were my idea.

Morning_Glory: Well, if Austin is looking through the archives and tagging your work, I would take it as a compliment. I think

Ronald's prime motivation is to have someone young on staff who can connect with our Generation Y and Millennial readers. Some of his ideas are a little on the sleazy side, but I guess these days, it's about whatever grabs the headlines.

Nightingale: You must remember how we were at his age—looking out for ourselves and trying to climb the rungs—we didn't care who or what stood in our way.

Morning_Glory: I wouldn't worry. Austin probably just sees *Insight* as a stepping stone to some big dot.com position. And you know Ronald's reputation for chewing up and spitting out interns. Austin will probably be gone in six months.

Nightingale: Sorry to be so touchy. Skype and instant messaging are wonderful, but even for a writer, it's hard when all you have are words typed on a cold, hard computer screen.

A few seconds passed. Simply trying to figure out how to broach the subject of Ben made Isabelle anxious.

Nightingale: So not to change the subject, but have you heard anything more from the police?

She took a sip of wine and pulled her sweater a little tighter.

Morning_Glory: Are you sure you want to know? You've rearranged your whole life so you wouldn't have to deal with any more fallout from Ben. Why clutter up your mind with more gruesome details? Don't you have fuel enough for your nightmares already?

Nightingale: It's that bad?

At least they weren't Skyping. Probably better Gloria couldn't see her face.

Nightingale: May as well just spit it out, Glor. You know I'll keep asking until you do.

Morning_Glory: Fine. The police said Ben's real name is Bob Simonson. Part of the reason things have been going so slowly is that he used several different aliases. The subpoena for his telephone and internet records have finally come through.

Her heart thundered in her chest while she waited to see what Gloria's next words would be.

Morning_Glory: They've located a woman in Kentucky Ben had been with prior to coming to Virginia. In fact, the cell phone he used to call you belonged to her.

Nightingale: She hadn't reported it stolen?

Morning_Glory: It wasn't, yet. He was calling you from her house, while she was at work. Since he was there when the postman arrived every day, he was also able to order thousands of dollars' worth of goods over the internet, which he charged to her credit card, again intercepting both the packages and the bills as they arrived.

Her body filled with rage for herself and for the other woman.

Morning_Glory: He even ordered her a diamond ring.

Nightingale: And charged it to her account?

Morning_Glory: Yes. What a guy.

For a second, she felt like she was going to be ill.

Nightingale: I'm afraid to ask if there were others.

Gloria's reticence was obvious given the pause that transpired before her reply appeared on the screen.

Morning_Glory: One is from a little town in Nebraska. The van he was driving when he was with you belonged to her. She was so embarrassed when he disappeared in the middle of the night that she didn't go to the police for almost a month. There's another in Minnesota whose boss bought a computer security package from Ben and paid a $20,000 advance."

Isabelle knew the answer, but she had to ask.

Nightingale: Had he asked each of the women to marry him?

Morning_Glory: Quit beating yourself up, Isabelle.

Tears streamed down her face. She brushed them aside and kept typing.

Nightingale: I can't. I've always prided myself on my ability to accurately judge people and situations. Knowing whom I can believe and what information rings true is essential to my work. How can I ever trust my instincts again?

Morning_Glory: Because your impulses will be sharper than ever before. Because you know firsthand what evil feels like. Because you'll get a sick feeling in your gut every time you meet someone who has the propensity for that kind of evil. And because you now know if he conned that many women, Ben must be horribly good at scamming people.

Was it just her, or had the temperature dropped while they'd been talking? She was suddenly chilled to the bone.

Morning_Glory: Can we please change the subject now?

Nightingale: Sure. I guess I've got enough information to digest for the time being.

That was the understatement of the year. She hadn't even started to process the fact that Ben had stolen the memory card from her camera, and who knows how many files from her computer, and what it could mean in terms of a probable attempt to blackmail her.

She looked out the window at the darkening sky. She couldn't bring herself to tell anyone about the photographs. Not even Gloria.

Nightingale: There's sleet hammering against the windows now.

She could almost hear the relief in Gloria's next response.

Morning_Glory: I didn't think the British Isles got a lot of severe weather.

Nightingale: I don't think they do down south except for occasional torrential rains. Scotland is its own little country in more ways than one. It's harsher, more desolate and far more extreme. Wow. The noise from the storm is incredible. I've always thought the sea sounded like it was singing on the rocks below my cottage, but tonight it's frightening. And the sea is usually such a pretty blue. When I peeked out earlier, it was almost black, and very deep and eerie looking. I could hear it pounding and chiseling away at the rocks.

Isabelle's fingers trembled over the keyboard. She deleted an error and retyped the words.

Nightingale: It's getting colder by the minute.

She left her laptop, walked to the bedroom, pulled an afghan from the end of her bed, and wrapped it around her shoulders before returning to see what Gloria had typed.

Morning_Glory: What time is it there?

Nightingale: I'm not even sure. It must be getting late. It's been getting darker and darker while we've been talking.

Isabelle glanced up at the short, lace-covered windows flanking the fireplace.

Nightingale: Normally, I love being in the cottage closest to the sea. I'm the last one to see the sun before it sinks into the Atlantic every night.

Morning_Glory: And the last to get morning light, I assume— sounds perfect for someone who loves to sleep in.

Nightingale: The sun rises soon after three a.m. in Tobermory this time of year. Night owls like me are barely to bed by then.

Gloria had questioned her decision to go to Scotland, confident she would be better off close to home, surrounded by people who knew and loved her. But her friends couldn't be with her twenty-four hours a day, couldn't make her sleep at night. They most certainly couldn't make her feel safe in a place haunted with the memory of intimate encounters she had entered into trustingly, only to find it had all been a lie.

She heard a horrendous noise and caught her breath.

Nightingale: Something just crashed against the side of the cottage.

Morning_Glory: Maybe you should have stayed up at the castle tonight.

Isabelle's fingers flew over the keyboard with an urgency she didn't consciously understand.

Nightingale: I don't think I'd dare try to get there now. The rocks between here and there would be treacherous with this sleet glazing them.

Morning_Glory: Sounds like you're stuck there for the night.

Nightingale: The wind is just roaring. If this kind of storm hits the coast very often, it's easy to see why it's the castle that was built out here on the cliffs, and the town of Tobermory on the secluded bay on the other side of—"

The power went out without a flicker of warning. Her computer made a hissing noise and the little box she'd been typing into froze up. No more internet. The illumination from her screen began to fade—silly thing hadn't been keeping a decent charge for some time.

Seconds later, the last tiny bit of light in the very center of her monitor went out and she was plunged into darkness. Starless, moonless, thick stone walls, miles and miles from anywhere, Atlantic Ocean darkness.

Her heart started to pound. There were two candles in brass holders on the mantle next to the geranium, but she didn't recall seeing any matches in the kitchen or in her dresser drawers. Even if she knew where to look, she'd be hard pressed to find them without light.

She clutched at the shawl she'd wrapped around her shoulders and slid her feet over the slate floor to get her bearings. Darkness in every direction.

She should have realized the lights could go out. It was already chilly and the stone-walled cottage would only hold in what little heat remained for so long. Had she thought, she could have turned on the electric convector heater and gotten the place warmed up in case something like this happened.

She'd had plenty of practice dealing with panic in the last few weeks—she should know just what to do when its icy grip started to close in on her, shouldn't she?

She groped her way to the nearest window, wiped away a thin film of moisture from the pane, and tried to peer out. She had no idea whether the storms here lasted for minutes, hours, or days, but she felt certain no one would come to reconnect her power until the wind died down. She shivered and groped for her afghan. The din of the wind and waves was thundering so loudly she barely heard the rapping on her thick, round-topped, wooden door.

Was she dreaming? The wind quieted for one short second and she heard a voice. The coffee table skidded across the floor in front of her and she tripped over the afghan as she fought her way to the door, groping for familiar objects and walls.

"Don't leave! I'm here!" She found the door, fumbled with the latch, and turned the skeleton key in its slot.

The beam of a flashlight cut a narrow swath across the face of the man at her door. Rivulets of water, shiny and pale in the light, ran down his forehead and dripped from thick eyelashes to pool under his eyes. His eyebrows were tipped with crystallized bits of snow.

She stared at him, wishing she hadn't inherited her mother's big, window-to-the-soul eyes, and hoped the light was too dim to reveal the gamut of emotions swirling around inside her.

"I don't remember your name," she stammered, feeling as foolish as she did frightened.

"Michael. You've seen me at the Bell."

The man who had tried to help her—the one working on the old keep. Standing on the threshold between the storm and the house, she couldn't seem to move. She knew who he was but she didn't know him. Could she trust him to—

"May I come in?" He tried to swat away the torrent of freezing rain with his hand.

His voice sounded irritated. The dim fact was, she was in Scotland. People she knew well and trusted were in short supply. She moved to the side and let him pass.

He outlined the perimeter of the small parlor with one quick circle of his wrist. The beam swept across the hearth, then fell to the empty firebox.

"Do you have wood in the kitchen?"

She felt like an absolute idiot, but she knew it would be even more stupid not to admit there was a problem and accept his help. "It's all outside."

She could feel his frustration even in the dim, residual light oozing from the sides of the flashlight.

He looked over his shoulder, then opened the door and shone the light to his left, along the back wall of the cottage. "I'll have to dig down a ways to get to dry wood. Get your raincoat. If you stand here and hold the flashlight, I can use both hands."

"All I have is a cardigan."

"Put your slicker on over the sweater and you'll be plenty warm."

She could feel the blank look on her face and prayed he wouldn't turn the flashlight on her again. Lord, she felt pathetic. Her mother had raised her to be independent, to take care of herself, to be in control. Letting Ben make a fool of her had been demeaning enough. The last thing she needed was to feel helpless in yet another situation, no matter how short-lived.

"Nobody comes to Scotland without bringing some sort of rain gear."

"There's no need for sarcasm. I thought my umbrella would..." She followed his gaze to a point just outside the cottage, where an eight or ten foot sapling was bent over so far it almost touched the ground.

His own oilcloth didn't appear to be keeping him all that dry, but she thought better of saying so.

"It was eighty degrees and sunny when I left Virginia."

"The cardigan will have to do." He turned and shone the flashlight in the direction of the bedroom.

"About the firewood."

"Yes?"

"You didn't happen to bring any matches with you, did you?"

"You don't have matches?" Michael's voice rose incredulously.

"Not that I know of." She toyed with the fringed edge of the afghan and tried to avoid his accusing stare. "I haven't really looked, but I haven't seen any either. I just thought I should mention it before you went back out in the storm and got even wetter."

"How thoughtful of you," Michael said.

"I did just arrive in country and it is late spring. I had no idea it could get so cold this time of year." She huffed. Risky, she supposed—letting him see how irritated she was. But she didn't seem to be able to hold it in. "So are you going to stand there wasting your batteries, or help me find the matches?"

He slammed the door shut, trapping them both inside.

"So why did you come? Better yet, why not leave?" Definitely risky. She needed him, or at least, his flashlight. But he was so infuriating.

"Believe me, if that were an option I'd be sorely tempted. I was already fool enough to risk my neck sliding down here. There's no way I'm going to make it back up the rocks until it warms up enough for the sleet to melt."

She glanced up at Michael's face.

He was still scowling at her. "Bette was worried about you. Hans is on the continent seeing to his mother."

It went without saying their frail, seventy-year-old landlady wouldn't have lasted a minute in the storm.

"I was afraid if I didn't come, she would set out to rescue you herself."

"I don't remember asking anyone to rescue me."

He shrugged in the most irritating manner she had ever seen. "Like it or not, you have been."

"Well I don't—like it. I might not be nuts about being alone in the dark in a freezing cold cottage, but I'm hardly some helpless damsel in distress. I would have been fine. And you're certainly no knight in shining armor. You're soaked to the bone."

"So what would you have me do, get out of these wet clothes and warm up by the fire?"

"Give me the flashlight. There's got to be matches around here somewhere." She grabbed the wand and turned toward the kitchen, rummaging as she went.

He made a snorting noise as he followed her through the door.

She turned and glared, "What?"

"Nothing." He shrugged again.

Damn, she hated that shrug. "What?" She repeated, louder.

"I was just going to say that from what I can see, you're definitely a damsel."

"Duh." She hoped the hostility she felt was gleaming from her

24

eyes so brightly he could see it plain as day.

"You're here alone without a lamp, firewood or matches. You seem pretty distressed to me."

"I'm a little worried. I am not distressed." She dropped a stack of London Times she'd tucked in a cupboard for recycling onto the slate kitchen floor. The pile landed with a resounding thud. "You're so wet that if you really were a knight in shining armor, your mouthpiece would be rusted shut by now. Then again, maybe that would be a good thing."

She slammed one drawer shut, jerked another open, and tried to push the image of his full lips and finely etched chin out of her mind. It must be the light—or lack of it.

He made a choppy gesture with his right arm. "Like the Tin Man in the *Wizard of Oz?*" Michael started to laugh. The sound drowned out the roar of the storm and filled the room.

Her own laugh rose so impulsively, so unexpectedly, she hardly noticed it at first. And then it dawned on her. She'd laughed! It had been so long that she thought she'd forgotten how.

Their eyes met through the beam of diffused light. Her natural instinct was to trust him. Her natural instinct had been to trust Ben. Where did that leave her? What was she to do? Demand to see his credentials? Toss him back out into the storm if he couldn't produce proof positive he was who he said he was?

He took the flashlight from her and adjusted the angle so she could see what she was doing, brushing her hand as he reached around her to move a stack of tidily folded dishtowels. The jolt of heat surprised her. He looked nearly as frozen as she felt.

She saw the tin of matches a split second after he did.

"I found them!" Their voices rang out in unison.

A half hour later, the rain turned to a thick slathering of ice and then to wet, heavy snow that would have covered the ground if the wind hadn't been blowing it sideways at near hurricane force.

They were soaked to the bone, but they had wrestled enough half-dry firewood into the cottage to build a fire. Much as she hated to admit it, she was glad Michael had come. She'd never have been able to get the door open by herself with an armload of firewood, say nothing about fighting the slippery steps while she tried to drag in wood.

While Michael stacked the logs in the hearth, she mopped up the

25

puddles that had collected on the slate floor. She'd felt something very close to camaraderie when they'd been outside, battling the storm together. Now that they were inside, facing the uncomfortable reality that Michael was stranded for the night, she felt awkward again.

A few minutes later, the fire was blazing and she was warily watching him use her towels to wipe the water from his face and fluff his hair.

It all seemed a little too cozy.

She turned away, but the image of the intimate act still commanded her vision—the short, fair locks that skimmed his face in the front, the longer, loosely curled strands inching over his collar in the back. Okay. She'd admit it. Michael's presence in the cottage intimidated her—not because he reminded her of Ben, but because he didn't.

She'd never noticed before how low the ceiling was in the parlor, but when Michael walked toward her to hand her the towel he'd just used, he completely filled her vision, making the room seem even more intimate than it was. None of the physical markers she associated with Ben were there to remind her heart that she shouldn't trust this man. This time it was up to her head.

She tousled her hair with her fingers and looked at him openly. "May I borrow the flashlight again? I don't have any men's clothing, but I have a sweat suit that's baggy on me. It's kind of a raspberry pink—nothing I can do about the color, but I think it should fit you. You'll like it. It's soft and furry on the inside."

He had removed his shirt and was crouched low on his haunches, warming himself by the fire, when she returned. She'd removed her own wet clothing and bra and put on a wide-necked, blue sweatshirt over a black lace camisole, and matching black and periwinkle blue plaid leggings.

So. His tan and the muscles they covered made it obvious he'd spent hours in the sun with his shirt off—and working hard, the prospect of which was the reason she'd avoided going anywhere near the site where Michael and his crew were reconstructing the keep.

He turned and caught her staring.

Really? She definitely hadn't needed to see the way the hair on his chest swirled around each of his nipples before scrolling down to his belly button and disappearing into the low-slung waistline of his jeans.

26

She gave him her most convincing disgusted look—the one she used to give her mother every five seconds when she was a teenager—and threw her sweat suit at him from a respectable distance, glowering at him for good measure.

Michael reached up and snagged the suit with one fluid movement.

Great. Of course she'd thrown high. Like his ridiculously tan biceps weren't enough. There would have to be too-sexy-for-anybody's-good, honey-blond hair under his arms—hair that looked as soft as downy fluff.

Stop it, she commanded her brain. But she kept watching as he stretched one raised arm at a time into the sleeves of her sweat suit. Mutinous eyes.

He pulled the hooded top over his head, turned his back to her, peeled off his wet blue jeans, and stepped, one slow leg at a time, into the dry, very pink pants she'd provided.

She tried to look away but he was wearing snug, sheer, burgundy boxers and they were hugging the best looking backside she'd ever seen. The experience of having her emotions wrung through a ringer washer had been harsh enough to kill her spirit, but the rest of her obviously wasn't dead. Raspberry pink was the only thing saving her from making a complete fool of herself.

She tore herself away and went back to her room before he turned and saw how red her face was. The noticeably colder air felt good against her cheeks until she saw the bed and felt hot all over again. She grabbed two pillows, her blanket and her quilt.

"Which do you want?" She tried her best to mask her emotions. Who knew what Michael was thinking? His expressions had gone from angry to charming to poker-faced in the space of an hour.

He shrugged. "The blanket, I guess."

She handed it to him, wrapped her quilt around herself and plunked down on her side of the sofa.

He slid the sofa, with her on it, two feet further from the fire. "If we leave it so close we'll be as steamy hot as baked potatoes by morning."

They sat in silence until it started to feel uncomfortable and she began to get cold again.

"Would you mind terribly if we moved the sofa a little closer to the fire?" She looked up at him, not sure why nobody was saying

27

anything. They'd broken the ice, hadn't they? Did he not care to know anything else about her, or why wasn't he attempting to make conversation. They were stuck together for the night. They were both Americans. They at least had that much in common.

He didn't budge. "Cold?"

"Yes. You're not?"

"You were right about the jogging suit. It is very soft. And very warm." He took his arms out from what looked to her to be the perfect cocoon and flexed his hands.

"I suppose we could angle it."

"The couch?"

"Yes. Put my end nearer to the fire."

"Or you could just come here." He reached out, unwrapped her quilt just enough to capture her hand, and swooped down to claim his prey in a movement so swift and fluid it would have made an eagle proud. She was spooned in the hollow of his mid-section, his chin on her shoulder, his arms enveloping her on both sides, before she knew how or what had happened.

Her mind insisted, for one brief second, that she struggle. But she was so cold, and Michael had been kind enough to come out in the storm to make sure she was all right—a fairly important thing as far as redeeming factors went.

She sighed as his warmth began to seep into her. So what if she took a little comfort where she could find it? She deserved that much after what she'd been through, didn't she? Maybe Michael was some sort of a knight.

She tried to think of something to say. "This whole thing, I mean, your being here, reminds me of something I learned in one of my psychology classes when I was in college."

She hadn't even finished her sentence when he went all Tin Man on her—this time for real. She'd meant to break the silence, not to make him more stiff and uncomfortable. She rushed on in an attempt to make it better although she had no idea what was wrong. "I think it was Psychology and Physiology actually. I still remember the prof saying that part of the reason women are instinctively drawn to men is biological—not in a sexual way, but because men's body temperatures are hotter than women's."

He didn't say a word. Okay, so it wasn't the greatest subject matter in the world, but it was relevant. He certainly should have been able to manage some sort of intelligent comeback, shouldn't he?

She could have asked him what was wrong, but she let it drop. She didn't know the man, didn't really even like him, but he was warm, which more or less proved the professor's point.

In the end, it was her body, not her brain, that made the decision to relax, stop thinking, and settle back into the snug cocoon of his body. And there she stayed, content to feel the blazing warmth of the fire and his strong but gentle arms around her.

Chapter Three

Damon Hermance adjusted his sunglasses and slipped noiselessly into the booth immediately adjacent to the cubicle where Morgan Baugh and Gareth Llewellin sat talking. Before taking his seat, he'd ordered and paid for his drink at the bar. He'd told the old Galbraith woman he had a briefcase full of paperwork to catch up on and would let her know when he was ready for dinner. He asked not to be disturbed.

Once seated, he could not see the men, but their hushed voices filtered through the fabric-lined seats just loudly enough that he could hear most of what they were saying. Fools.

The two men had been speaking quietly and in utterly calm tones on his approach, but the veins in the sides of their necks had looked as though they might burst if the conversation grew any more tense. The taller of the two, Gareth, who sat facing the back wall of the pub, had occasionally looked over his shoulder to make sure no one was approaching even though he knew his colleague, Morgan Baugh, had a clear view of anyone entering or leaving the Blue Bell.

Damon had timed his entrance accordingly, just after Gareth had turned. Morgan was looking down, wrapping something he'd picked from his face in his napkin—Damon shuddered to think what. While he believed Gareth had at least half a brain, his opinion of Morgan was not nearly so magnanimous.

The pair periodically lapsed into a regional dialect of their native Welsh tongue, a language uncommon enough even in nearby Scotland that it afforded them privacy, yet closely enough related to the Gaelic spoken by the old Scots at the bar that they wouldn't draw attention to themselves if overheard.

Wise move, thought Damon, giving them at least that.

"What did ye find out aboot the woman?"

Gareth's words were followed by a faint gnawing noise, probably that oaf, Morgan, chewing on his fingernails again. Damon rolled his eyes. The foul things were always crusted with dirt and bitten down to nearly nothing.

"Gawd, she's got a fine pair of milkers on her, that one does," Morgan said.

Gareth ignored the shorter man's comment. "Her story checks out, but I dinnae believe for a minute she's here just to dash off a few stories aboot the top ten tourist spots in Europe or even mad cow disease. I was able to pull up several articles she's written for various papers in Washington D.C. and they're all hard hitting exposés. Crime rings, political corruption, sex scandals, drug dealers, corporate misconduct, tax evasion. Ye name the racket and she's helped crack the case."

Morgan grunted. "What aboot him?"

Damon waited for Gareth to speak. His right hand man had several annoying habits, one of which was to split his napkin in half, tearing each resulting piece in half again, and again and again until he had a pile of fine confetti, which he then used to make designs on the tabletop.

"He's talking oot his fanny flaps, awrite—the American Builder's Association has no licensed contractor by the name Michael St. Dawndalyn registered anywhere in the United States. But that's all I can tell ye. I've checked every nook and cranny trying to get at the truth and I'm still jiggered."

"We already knew he weren't who he claims to be," Morgan answered. "As long as he keeps doing the job he was hired to do, they may never know. He's a smooth one, awrite. The man could talk dogs off a meat truck." A loud belch escaped Morgan's lips. "Did ye find anything to link him to Sonar Technologies?"

"Nae. Not one bloody thing. Just the same series of unresolved lawsuits and failures to appear that we found before."

"All filed in Wisconsin?"

"Aye. There was one new one." Gareth's familiar voice filtered through in a cheeky sounding whisper. "A warrant for his arrest on a contempt of court charge."

"Now, there's a thing." Morgan's boorish cackle infiltrated their corner of the pub. When he spoke again, his voice was louder and more menacing. "If I have to listen to that heid bummer tell me to *pick up my speed a little*, one more time, I'll be sorely tempted to call Wisconsin and turn him over to the bobby myself."

"Dinnae even think about it," Gareth snapped. "I'll nae have you blowing our covers and ruining the hale jing-bang because ye're too hot headed to move a few measly rocks. Just stop dragging yer heels and get the job done. And keep yer mouth shut while ye're doing it."

"I'd like to see ye trade places with me for a day, ye bloody airy-fairy. Ye'd be dead of a coronary before midday break," Morgan said in an angry tone. "Why do I always have to be the one to be the low-paid skivvy? It's backbreaking work, I tell ye."

"Calm down before ye burst a blood vessel," Gareth responded. "Just do what ye're told and keep yer ear to the ground. Damon says we're getting close."

"Easy for ye to say, sitting on yer arse out on the curragh day in and day out, pretending to be a fisherman while ye play with all yer fancy gadgets. I'll be so crippled up from unloading rocks I willnae even be able to enjoy my cut when the time comes," Morgan whined.

"Ye'll nae say another word aboot my arse if ye want a cut of anything," Gareth said, his voice threatening but articulate. "Damon expects we may see a few more plants from the sonar company before we've finished the mission. He wants to be informed immediately if we meet up with any other suspicious sorts who seem to be lingering in the area for longer than the norm."

"Informed immediately," Morgan mimicked in a just audible tone, enunciating each syllable in a high-pitched voice.

Damon clenched his fist.

"Shut yer geggy, will ye? We went into this with the agreement no one need get hurt if we played things right."

"Promises, promises," Morgan sneered.

The air around their booths smoldered with suppressed fury as the men paid their bill, stood, and prepared to face the storm. Damon buried his head in a newspaper and continued to look down until the men had reached the front entry. *Idiots.* Neither of them had even noticed him or checked to see if anyone was listening.

Damon slid to the edge of his cubicle and watched out of the corner of his eye as Gareth pulled his wool coat high around his neck and tucked a plaid scarf into his collar. Gareth might talk about someone getting hurt, but Damon knew without a doubt it was Morgan who was more likely to hurt someone.

#

It was the same boat she'd seen yesterday, and the day before,

32

and the day before that, either hovering just off the coast or crisscrossing the bay at a snail's pace. Isabelle wasn't trying to be nosey, but she'd hiked down to the sea several times over the course of the last week to survey the damage from the storm, and everywhere she went, she'd seen that boat.

From what she could see, the other vessels sailed out to sea or trolled far up the coastline and returned only once or twice a week. This particular ship never seemed to stray past Mishnish or Torr lochs. It appeared to be a fishing vessel, but if they were looking for pollock, mackerel or dogfish like their counterparts, they must either know something the others didn't, or be lost. Who knew? Maybe they were photographing seals or studying the golden eagle population that flew from mountain to shore along Mull's craggy edges.

Her bicycle skimmed along the left edge of the roadway until she reached the sharp downhill stretch to Tobermory's waterfront, and climbed off her bike to walk it down the rest of the way. Brightly colored storefronts filled with treasures and sweets stretched out along the bay in an arc of rainbow hues. First came the distillery, the Old Port House, Duncan's, and Mull Pottery, their shared fronts marked off in freshly painted mint green, sky blue, vanilla ice cream and rosy pink. She pedaled past the chemist's, the butcher's, and the silversmith's, adorned in pastel hues of yellow and peach. The post office, the market, the bakery and the bank came into view as she passed the pier and curved around the point, then, finally, the Blue Bell, in all its periwinkle blue splendor.

A white-breasted cormorant swooped low over her left shoulder and swept out to the bay, dipping down to nip the surface of the sparkling waters. The bird emerged with a wriggling snatcher clutched in its beak.

She was hungry too, but that was the least of her reasons for bypassing the harbor, hurriedly parking her bicycle and entering the pub.

She ran her fingers through her hair and approached the bar slowly, willing her stride to seem casual in case she was being watched. No sign of Michael. She propped her purse on the bar and ordered a glass of white wine. She was trying to do the right thing— to smooth things over. So why did she feel so stiff and weak-kneed and stressed out?

She'd avoided coming to the Bell for almost a week, anticipating the embarrassment she and Michael would no doubt feel the first time they ran into each other. Now, she just wanted to get it over with.

She'd survived the awkward moment at the cottage when they'd woken up at the foot of her armchair, still in front of the fireplace, she practically in his lap, with her hand on his... and he with his arms snuggled around her, cupping one of her breasts.

She would survive this, too.

She thought back to the night of the storm and went over the details in her mind for the hundredth time. It would have been bad enough had it still been dark and stormy when they'd come out of their sleepy stupor, but no—they'd awakened to broad daylight, both electric lights and sunshine blazing unforgivably bright around them.

Her face grew warm just thinking about it.

She'd been fussing over the best way to handle things all week and had finally decided the only course of action was to face Michael down and be done with it.

There was still no sign of him. She took a deep breath and replayed her dream scenario: Michael approached her from the rear as she stood at the bar. She acted as though the thought that she might see him had never occurred to her. He put his hand in the small of her back and leaned down to whisper in her ear, so close she could feel the shadow of his beard nuzzling her neck.

Good grief. She sat her wine down on the table so hard some of it sloshed over the side. This insanity had to stop.

She'd been away from her friends for almost a month—wasn't it only natural she was starting to experience a little people hunger? Now that she knew someone—a fellow American—it would have been nice to sit at the bar and enjoy a little companionship over dinner. That was all. Even she knew there was more to life than occasional chats on a cold, flat computer screen.

She just wanted to talk to him. She was sick of feeling awkward because of what had happened, especially since nothing had. Of course, if nothing had happened, then why had she felt so tense, and why had Michael's voice sounded so sharp when he'd said, "We were cold and tired. We warmed up and fell asleep. End of story."

Gloria claimed all men woke up with erections. When she'd gone to Ask Jeeves to make sure Gloria was right, she'd found the Brits even had their own, quaint little term for the phenomenon—Morning Glory, no less. She was still debating whether or not to tell Gloria.

She glanced at the menu, ordered Cumberland Mash, and tried to relax. So maybe Michael hadn't been attracted to her. Maybe it had just been the morning thing. Or, maybe he'd enjoyed snuggling with her as much as she had with him. How was she supposed to know?

At least she knew what she'd felt, much as she hated to admit it. Truth be known (and it never would be, to him), she'd been at least partially awake for a full five minutes before Michael had opened his eyes. The question was, had he also been awake?

If only she'd leaped from his lap the second she'd woken up. She'd tried to blame her reticence to untangle herself from her arms on the cold seeping up through the icy slate floor, but that wasn't the truth and she knew it. It had been Michael's hands, and the gentle way his fingers had felt, lazily stroking the lace of her camisole back and forth across the tip of her...

Whether he'd been conscious of what he was doing, as she suspected, or still asleep, as he maintained, there was no denying she'd liked what she felt. Even now, part of her was completely mortified about how she'd behaved—and part of her wanted it to happen again, preferably soon.

She was being ridiculous. She'd come to Scotland to get away from men, especially men she knew nothing about, and the complications and risks that came with them. She'd come here to do a job, to regroup, to heal, to prove to Ronald she should still have a job. The last thing she needed was to be mooning over the likes of Michael whatever his name was.

#

Damn. Michael had figured he would run into her sooner or later, but he'd hoped it wouldn't be tonight. He'd had a bitch of a day, starting with a surprise visit from a young new building inspector from Glasgow, and ending with one of the crew breaking his foot when a large boulder fell from twelve feet up. He was bone tired. All he wanted was a cold beer, a hot meal, and a little peace and quiet.

Pain shot down his leg as his haunches slammed against the bar stool. "You don't happen to have an Old Milwaukee hiding back there, do you?" He frowned at the young woman behind the bar.

"An auld what?" She looked at him as though he were from another planet.

"I guess a Guinness will have to do." He swiveled around just far enough to see Isabelle out of the corner of his eye. Sure enough, she was standing, gathering her courage around her like a security blanket. He silently hoped she would lose her guts, go home, and leave him be, but it appeared his wish for an Old Milwaukee wouldn't be the only dream denied him tonight.

A few seconds passed before she made her move. Michael swung around on his bar stool and watched her approach, his Guinness cocked in hand like a defense weapon. Nothing good could come of entering into any kind of relationship with her. Better to end it now before her reporter's instincts kicked in and she felt led to investigate him.

She looked at him and he could see her shoulders inching up like a cornered cat's back.

He waited to speak until she was close enough that he could rest assured it would be her alone who would hear his words. "So. I see you've recovered from the trauma of waking up straddling my lap." Better for her to hate him so much that she never gave him another thought.

He watched intently as her jaw dropped and her petite nostrils flared.

She sucked in her breath. "Shush. Someone will hear."

"Sweetheart, if anything gives us away, it's going to be your red cheeks, not my words." He hated acting so calloused, so cruel, but it was what had to be done.

Her cheeks turned a shade darker at his insinuation but her eyes met his without a shred of embarrassment. "If you'd quit being such a lout and let me talk, I'll say what I came to say and leave."

"Your party." He took a long, slow sip from his draft and tried to stay calm. His task would be easier if she wasn't so beautiful, so vulnerable, so soft, so Southern. Shake it off, he told himself. Shake her off.

She glowered at him. "I never should have let you in. I should have left you out in the storm to freeze to death when I had the chance."

"It's very questionable who would have been frozen by morning if I hadn't come to rescue you, darlin'." God help him. He had no idea why he delighted in irking this woman so.

"You did not rescue me!" Isabelle plunked down her heel. "I just wanted to clear the air after..."

"Clear? It's practically sizzling, hon. Leads me to believe you're about as good at clearing the air as you are at knowing when to bring firewood into the house."

She looked up at the ceiling as though pleading for help from above. He'd flustered her all right—probably insulted her, too. They both knew it. By this time, half the bar knew it. But try as he might, Michael couldn't find it in himself to shut up.

"Listen, mister, it wasn't me who woke up with a..."

He slid off his stool and his feet hit the ground tensed to run. With one fell swoop, he cut her off, grabbed her arm and steered her away from the counter. "Number one, when I woke up, your hand was on it. Number two, how do you expect a man to react when you come sauntering out of your bedroom wearing some slinky little get-up that's straight off the pages of a Victoria's Secret catalog, whining because you're so cold?"

Her eyes opened wide. "Last time I checked I was entitled to buy my clothes wherever I please. If you're that desperate for a peek at a pretty woman, perhaps it's time you took matters into your own hands and—"

"You know what? I don't care if you're the last American woman between here and Australia. I've had enough." He was an expert at human behavioral science. Why in God's name couldn't he control himself when he was around Isabelle MacAllister?

She stared him down, her eyes filled with equal parts of loathing and chagrin. "You're not getting anything you didn't ask for."

"There's no need to get personal." But it had, and it was his fault. He's the one who had let their words escalate into something far more than a polite rebuff.

Her eyes were a blazing sea of blue. "We got personal when you took it upon yourself to criticize my choice of leisurewear."

"You mean your choice of lingerie." Damn! He could feel the smirk on his face but he was helpless to wipe it off.

"If you'd seen me in my lingerie, you'd remember it. I promise you, every last little snippet of ribbon and lace would be etched in your tiny brain until you died."

Which couldn't be soon enough for her, if he recognized the look she was giving him.

Worse, she was right. He may not have seen her in her underwear, but he did remember. Every swell. Every curve. The feel of her bottom pressed to his, the shape of her breast molded in his hand, the way she smelled, the little smile that had toyed over her lips when he'd first touched her breast... Every single detail was irrevocably stamped in his head.

"What I wear is no business of yours." Only a little tremble in her voice belied her bravado.

"It damn well is if you're going to be crawling into my lap when you're wearing it."

He let the disgust drip from his voice even though he could see her face starting to crumble, even though he felt far more aroused than revolted.

"Crawling? Crawling! I did no such thing, and you know it!"

"You got what you wanted." Michael wished to hell he'd remembered to grab his ale when he'd steered them away from the bar. "You just didn't have the guts to ask for it, so I gave you a little nudge."

"You have no idea what I want. You have no idea about anything! Who do you think you are anyway, some sort of shrink?"

See? He could feel his face shining in the dimly-lit pub. He'd known this would happen.

"I'm sorry." His tone changed the second he saw the sheen of a tear poking out from her eyelash. "I was just having fun. You were pretty good at giving it back the other night. I just thought... Here. Let me..." Michael took a handkerchief from his pocket and took a step toward her.

She backed away from him like he had the plague.

He stopped short. What was wrong with him? This was what he'd wanted, wasn't it?

She tossed her head defiantly and glanced across the room to the staring row of faces lined up by the bar. "If you all will forgive me, I really need to be getting home." Her voice was so patchy it barely carried across the room.

"I'm sorry, Isabelle." He offered her his hand.

Her response was to turn and leave by way of the nearest exit. The disappointment in her eyes cut him to the quick.

Chapter Four

There was still a good bit of light left when Isabelle exited the pub. If she hadn't been on her bicycle, she'd have preferred the dark. She felt absolutely and totally naked.

She hated herself for crying. She hated Michael whatever his name was for making her cry. But most of all, she hated the fact that he had the power to make her cry. She was used to being in command of her emotions. Any self-respecting, Southern belle would tell you that's the way it was done. Charming and gentle on the outside. Stiff spine on the inside. Always in control.

Isabelle tucked her purse in the basket mounted on the front of her bike and swung her leg over the bar. Something in the air stank, far and beyond the usual watery smell from the harbor. She had no clue what it was, but it was fitting, she supposed—the perfect backdrop for her rotten mood.

She pointed the front wheel towards home and blinked away a fresh batch of remorse. What was wrong with her? Tears never sprung to a Southern lady's eyes unbidden. Calculated tears might be called upon occasionally to make a point or achieve a desired response, but never ever did a lady shed tears involuntarily.

She made sure she had a firm toehold on the sometimes slippery cobblestone and pushed off, throwing her whole body into propelling the bike up the steep hill that led out of town. She surged forward, pumping furiously in a futile race to escape her rage.

She had no idea why Michael's amateur analyzing bothered her so much. Even she had to admit a good shrink was probably just what she needed.

She saw the silver Astra backing out of a parking space directly in front of her just in time to avoid a collision. She squeezed her brakes hard and hopped off her bike.

What was that smell? Isabelle wrinkled her nose. Without the momentum from her bicycle to dispel the stench, the air around the pier smelled unbearably ripe. She turned and spotted the boat she'd seen earlier. Apparently it had just tied up at the wharf.

"Whit a reek off those deid fish."

She leaned on the handlebars of her bike and turned towards the voice. An old gaffer stood leaning against a post. She nodded. The faint scent of vanilla wafting from his pipe provided a little relief from the smell of the harbor.

She could see two small crates of fish being unloaded from the ship and carried up the pier. The spectacle had drawn quite a crowd. Local merchants were waving their arms and shaking their fists, some talking to the boat's crew and others arguing among themselves.

"Looks like a bit of a batherment down at the dock," the old man said.

She moved the front tire of her bicycle to one side so the old man could pass if he wished.

He shook his head. "I've amind to stay. Been a long time since I've seen the likes of a good argie-bargie. And it's nae often I get to pass the evening with a smasher like ye. Ye on Mull to stay or just a goer-bye?"

She told him about her temporary assignment, then settled back to watch the show.

The old man stroked his beard and jerked his head in the direction of the boat. "Maybe ye should be investigating them. I've been watching this haaf-boat. I dinnae why or hoo, but something suspicious is afoot. Probably a pack of fugees." He pointed at the rig. "The tall, barmy-faced fellow in the wool coat seems to be taking most of the flack."

"He looks familiar. I think I've seen him at the Bell."

"Just another badling full of bletherin. I cannae sae why, but the more dashy-looking they come, the more trouble they be."

Isabelle grimaced, thinking back to the first time she'd met Ben and remembering how immaculately he'd been dressed. Hmm. Think what she might have been spared if the old gaffer had been there to share his wisdom when she'd needed it.

The white-haired gent nudged her elbow and pointed at the tall fellow in the wool coat. "That poor daffadile is nae lookin se weel."

She had to agree. The man looked as though he might be ill, whether from the reek of rotten fish or the wrath of the inspector, she didn't know. She looked at him curiously. Even with a scarf tied around his neck, he looked sorely ill-equipped for an outing on a fishing vessel. Her eyes strayed back to the wharf. The inspector had not boarded the ship, but was leading the man toward the clock tower that housed the town offices.

"I guess I'd better be on my way if I want to make it home before dark," she said. "The excitement appears to be over as fast as it started."

The old man sniffed the air. "The stench never dissipates as quickly as the argie-bargie does."

"I suppose the unpleasant smell will probably be around for a while. That's the way it usually goes."

He tipped his hat. "Glad to meet you. You're a catchie, awrite."

She smiled. "Catchie?"

"A likable sort."

She flashed him a bright smile. Michael what's his name might not think she was a catchie, but someone else did.

Catchie. The more she toyed with the word, the more she liked the sound of it.

But she didn't like the sound of what had gone on down at the wharf. She'd pumped the old man for plausible explanations for what they'd seen, and he hadn't a one. The tall man in the wool coat and plaid scarf had not looked like a fisherman or a scientist or a photographer. Maybe he was a fugitive.

A nagging suspicion was taking shape in her head. Granted, she was probably just being paranoid. Who wouldn't be a little jumpy after the experience she'd had with Ben? She made a mental note not to tell anyone what she feared. They'd all just think she was imagining things. She'd simply keep her eyes open and continue to be on guard, exactly like she had been every day since she'd found out Ben was a cold-blooded killer.

#

It was well past midnight when Michael left the Bell and slid behind the wheel of his car. There was no denying that earlier in the evening, he'd gotten himself a wee too blootered to drive. Still, he should have seen through Mrs. Galbraith's fiddltie-fa when she'd claimed she was short a prep cook and dishwasher and needed help in the kitchen.

Michael had often enjoyed conversation with Logan's mum while dining at the pub, but he'd never witnessed her sadistic streak until she corralled him into helping in the back room. His first assignment had been to scrub pots and pans caked with dried-on potatoes in sinks filled with murky water deeper than his elbows. His second had been to scrape slimy bits of leftover food off a mountain of dirty plates into a vat of vile looking mush the cook said was destined for some fortunate, curly-tailed grunter.

When Michael had said he needed to say goodnight and get to bed, his torturous taskmaster had insisted he stay and peel onions enough to feed half of Scotland. The old biddy hadn't been satisfied until he'd had tears running down his cheeks.

He slammed his car door, not caring a whit about those who might be sleeping in the rooms above the Bell, revved his engine and tightened his seatbelt. The whole kit and caboodle had obviously been the woman's idea of a suitable penance for the way he'd treated the "fern-tickled little lass from Virginia."

Her words, not his.

Michael had been tempted to tell Logan's mum a thing or two about where the bonny lass with freckles on her nose bought her underwear, but once the effects of the whiskey had worn off, he'd been glad he'd kept his mouth shut. It was obviously a mistake to mess with Mrs. G. To think poor Logan had grown up in the woman's care.

The old ogre's voice was still ringing in his head as he nosed the car into the left side of the narrow road and headed up the brae towards Bluevale Castle. "If only your fore-folk could have a look at ye now, ye cankersome auld crabbit. Picking on a goodly lass like Isabelle. You should be ashamed of yerself."

He knew exactly what his auld-father would have thought of any man who let himself be trussed up in an apron like a grunter ready to be roasted, and forced to do dishes. Michael shifted into second gear and watched his headlights slice through the gray daylight as he rounded a corner and climbed up the brae. Okay. So he'd gone a little too far with his teasing and ended up looking like a jerk. That didn't mean he'd deserved to be treated like a villain. Nothing he'd done was bad enough to merit having to listen to Mrs. Galbraith's clattering all night.

God, his head hurt. This time of year, a soft glow of light from the north hovered over the countryside all night long. Still, his eyes were so sore from seeping up onion fumes and lack of sleep in general that at first he barely noticed the shadow jutting out from a patch of rhododendrons along the next curve in the road.

The gentle illumination shining on the hairy coo's face was so subtle it almost went unnoticed. His own headlights didn't point a spotlight on the beast's furry red bangs and widely-spaced horns until he was almost around the corner.

He slammed on his brakes. A stale glass of water in the cup holder closest to him sloshed over its edges and doused his foot. His mail and a couple of CDs flew off the seat and bounced onto the floor. The car screeched to a halt.

Michael peered out his windshield. The cow was gone. Dear God. Had he hit it? He hadn't felt an impact. He threw open the car door and crept towards the front bumper.

The beast's plaintive bellow slashed through the night air just as he reached the spot where it lay. Its soft red nose lifted with each sad moan, its dewy brown eyes looked sorely into his. The hairy coo had toppled like a house of cards. Its legs, which appeared to be unharmed, were splayed out under the grill of his auto.

Thank goodness he'd stopped when he had. He said a silent thank you to Mrs. Galbraith for detaining him until the effects of the whiskey had worn off. That small piece of good fortune aside, he still had a problem—a big, hairy one.

His heart was pounding as he tried to draw forth what limited information his brain might have filed away on cows. His family was made up of builders and a few crop farmers, not dairymen. He could converse at length about Scottish American folklore and Native American traditions he'd learned from his great-grandmother, Waabigwani, a Chippewa Indian maiden. He was ashamed to say he'd never paid much attention to Wisconsin's agricultural heritage.

Damn! Cows dotted the hills for miles in every direction around Oconomowoc. How could he not know anything about the creatures? He'd had a client once, a teenager who'd been referred to him through juvenile court after he and his friends had been apprehended for tipping cows. Michael had helped the young man realize that every act, no matter how harmless it might seem, had a set of consequences, usually anticipatable and often negative. They'd talked about the disregard for basic decency that occurs when men stoop to torturing an animal whose brief existence is already destined to end at a hamburger stand. They'd never discussed the logistics of the despicable but popular prank, or how one went about righting a cow once the deed was done.

The only other thing he could remember was a western novel he'd read once in which there was a blizzard. According to the author, cows on the open range became disoriented, ended up on their backs, and perished because they were unable to roll over and stand up of their own volition.

Michael looked down at the cow. Its soft red bangs fell over its eyes as the animal tried to swing his massive head around to look up at him.

If hairy coos could talk, and if this one's pitiful mooing meant anything, it was saying, 'Help! I've fallen, and I can't get up.' He couldn't just back away and ignore its plaintive pleas. Besides, if he left the poor cow until morning, someone who really was foaming drunk would probably come along and run the poor thing over.

He groaned and petted the cow. He assumed it would take a swarm of strong men and probably a rope to right the beast even if the big Highlander wasn't hurt. He had to get help, even if it meant waking someone. In other words, he was damned if he did and damned if he didn't. There was no way he could right the situation on his own, but if he went for help, everyone would know what had happened and he'd be the talk of the island by daybreak.

He leaned over his vehicle and laid his aching head on its roof. It was useless. There was no way to keep the mishap from coming to light. He stroked the cow's side in a manner he hoped was comforting, spoke briefly to the animal in the same voice he used to console his patients, and sprinted up the hill in the direction of the nearest farmhouse.

Chapter Five

His phone started to ring just as Michael finally walked in the door of his cottage. A call at this time of night could only mean one of two things—an emergency call from someone in the States who knew it was two a.m. in Scotland but was desperate enough to wake you, or a call from some idiot who didn't understood how to calculate the time difference.

After sprinting nearly three kilometers, braving four protective farm dogs, awakening two indignant women—each of whom looked amazingly like an angry Mrs. Galbraith—and rousting five men and boys from their beds, only to find the cow had disappeared without a trace when they returned to his car, Michael was in the mood for neither.

He could still hear the farmers' amused laughter echoing in his head as he threw his jacket over a chair and reached for the phone.

He thought he'd been humiliated at the Bell, but nothing could beat rounding the corner where he'd left his auto with a whole damn cavalry in tow, only to find his car sitting in the middle of the road, its door still flung wide, and nary a beast in sight.

"Ye just made me day, lad," the first farmer had said, cackling into his handkerchief.

"A bit o' trouble ain't nothing when the reward is this sweet," the other had said.

"I cannae sae when I've last had a ditty so rich for the telling," one of the younger men had said.

Michael made one last attempt to banish the memories and flicked open his cell phone.

"It's about time," Michael's attorney said accusingly.

He grasped the left side of his head and moaned. "Buck, if you knew what I'd been through in the last ten hours, you'd slam down the phone and run."

"No can do, Michael. Your day of reckoning is at hand. I will try to be brief, however. A little cooperation from you would go a long way toward that end."

45

Michael hated his arrogant tone. Only a twenty-four year old fresh out of law school who already owned his own firm—albeit financed with his father's millions—could sound so cocky. The thought that he had to put up with such egotism and pay for it besides was enough to make him ill. The fact that he was related to the man—even if just by marriage—made him boiling mad.

Buck, who never seemed to get what he thought of him and wouldn't have cared if he did, said, "First thing on the agenda—Mrs. Henriksen is willing to settle if you'll simply apologize and advise Stephanie to move home."

He could hear Buck's pencil tapping as clearly as if he were in Milwaukee. That alone drove him crazy. If precious Bucky hadn't been his mother's stepson, he would have fired him months ago.

"I have no intention of apologizing for anything, Buck. Stephanie is an adult. She came to the conclusion she needed to get a place of her own without any help from me."

"Her mother claims you adversely influenced her and did irreparable damage to their relationship, evidenced by Stephanie's ongoing refusal to speak to her."

"I asked Stephanie repeatedly if she'd thought through the ramifications of moving out of her mother's house. The young lady was simply determined to assert her independence. Who wouldn't be after being under the thumb of an extremely paranoid, overprotective mother for twenty-four years? That doesn't mean her actions were intended to alienate anyone, least of all Mrs. Henriksen. Stephanie is simply a young woman being a young woman."

"Telling Stephanie her mother is paranoid and overprotective will certainly be construed as libelous."

"I never told Stephanie anything of the sort. I did what I always do—listened, encouraged, helped her sort out her feelings. Nothing libelous about it. The records will bear that out."

"Was she still in counseling when she ceased communications with her mother?"

"She stopped speaking to her mother the day Mrs. Henriksen threatened to subpoena the transcripts of my sessions with her daughter and sue me if Stephanie didn't move home immediately. What would you do if your mother did that to you?"

"The case isn't about what I would do."

"No, it isn't." Michael said. "It's about backbone." Something

Buck had precious little of. "This case is about my refusal to testify against someone who trusted me with their innermost thoughts. This case is about my unwillingness to betray someone I vowed to help."

"Are you really ready to sacrifice your entire career—everything you've worked for—for the sake of a few outmoded principles? Not to mention the fact father's campaign manager is spitting nails and your mother is worried sick about you. I've pulled about as many strings as I know how to pull without you making some effort to smooth the waters on your end. Michael, I'm begging you, just come home long enough to make an appearance before Judge Rankin and settle things with the Henriksen's. When it's all said and done you can go back to Scotland and play with rocks for the rest of your life if that's what you want."

"We've been through all of this, Buck. Coming back to testify in the Henriksen case might be fairly harmless, but the second I set foot back in Wisconsin, I'll be forced to appear before the judge in the Masterson suit. We both know what that means. A. Perjuring myself, B. Risking incarceration for contempt of court, or C. Relaying information that would severely damage Carole's chances of keeping her children. If I'd been comfortable with any of those options, I wouldn't have destroyed my tapes of Carole's sessions and left Wisconsin in the first place."

"I'll make your options just as simple, Michael. A. Accept my father's offer of help. You can scorn his connections all you like, but the bottom line is your only other alternatives are B. Come home and defend yourself, C. Be fined large amounts of money, D. Lose your license, and E. Go directly to jail the next time you set foot in the United States of America."

Michael closed his eyes and tried not to give in to his fatigue. "I shouldn't have to defend myself. A. I've done nothing wrong. B. That's what I'm paying you to do."

#

One of the locals had warned Isabelle about MacGochan's Pub when she'd first come to Tobermory—most particularly in regard to the fancy chef the owners had imported from Glasgow and his unique repertoire of signature dishes.

The chef liked to thumb his nose at tradition all right. It hadn't taken her two minutes to uncover that fact. Their Sticky Toffee Pudding came with a coffee flavored sauce instead of caramel, and their shepherd's pie was a supposedly healthier version made with chicken and wild fowl instead of lamb or beef. The locals said the food was fit for tourists, and that was *aboot* it.

Still, she had taken to eating her dinner there a few nights a week. One of MacGochan's few redeeming qualities was that it was situated beneath a place called The Loft. Listening to the rollicking Celtic music sifting down through the wood beamed ceiling almost made her feel like she was a part of something social—even when she was sitting alone and had no one to talk to.

Not that she couldn't have had company if she'd wished to. Spring had officially sprung, and the bar was swarming with eager Americans, Englishmen and Danes, each in town for a few hours or the night, depending on whether they'd hired a car or taken a bus across on the ferry. A band named the Peatbog Faeries had been playing all week. They were a local group, but one that appealed primarily to tourists, just like the pub's deep-fried jalapeno poppers.

MacGochan's second redeeming quality, other than the fact that she could be reasonably sure she wouldn't be humiliated while eating there, was a section of stools set up to a bar that was wired to be an Internet Cafe. Trying to eat and type simultaneously was less than ideal, given the fact the two activities required use of the same appendages, but chatting online with Gloria while she ate was the closest thing to eating dinner with a friend she had.

She ordered a glass of white wine, logged on to the internet and found Gloria.

Nightingale: Hi, Glor. What's the word from D.C.?

Morning_Glory: Trust me. You don't want to know.

This would never do. They couldn't both be depressed.

Nightingale: Hey—aren't you supposed to be the upbeat, cheery one of this duo?

Morning_Glory: Yah, right. Don't push your luck. Besides, I've been rethinking this whole morning glory thing ever since I found out what the phrase means where you live.

Isabelle sent her a cheeky looking icon with a leering grin as big as its face.

Nightingale: I assume if you've got bad news, it has to do with Ben.

48

Morning_Glory: Indirectly, yes. One of the other women Ben was with called you yesterday and left a message on your answering machine. I called her back from your place when I stopped to water your plants.

Nightingale: Tell me what she said.

Morning_Glory: I have something I need to say first.

Isabelle set down her fork and prepared for the worst. Her heart felt like it was going to pound its way through her rib cage and pop through her skin. Now that would give the tourists at MacGochan's something to post on Facebook.

Morning_Glory: I know you haven't told me everything that happened between you and Ben. I understand some things are just too personal to talk about, even with me.

Nightingale: Personal, painful and humiliating.

Morning_Glory: The police have discovered Ben previously did time in an Alabama jail for check fraud and embezzlement.

So she'd been duped by a common criminal. And here she'd been consoling herself with the assumption Ben was some sort of genius, a Frank Abagnale sort—uncatchable, a master of thieves, a con man so cunning he could outwit even the FBI.

Morning_Glory: You didn't even know his real name at the time, so even if you had thought to see if he had a criminal record, you wouldn't have uncovered anything.

Nightingale: He bragged about the work he did in the Special Forces—kidnapping diplomat's wives, killing people the government wanted out of the picture. That should have told me something.

She'd been a nervous wreck ever since the police had confirmed the one thing she'd hoped really had been a lie.

Morning_Glory: You thought he was a hero, one of the good-guys. He led you to believe his actions were noble and brave.

He'd led her to believe a lot of things. Her hands felt icy cold, and she shook them, trying to make them wake up.

Morning_Glory: There's no easy way to put this, Isabelle. For all I know, maybe it's already occurred to you. But given the circumstances of Ben's background and his obvious promiscuity over the last two years, some of the women have decided they need to be tested for HIV.

If Isabelle hadn't desperately needed to save face after making a fool of herself in the town's only other respectable pub, she most certainly would have retched, right there at the Internet Cafe, in front of the open windows facing the town centre.

She gulped, and choked, and swallowed over and over again, desperately trying to regain her composure. Even then, she felt like she was caught in the fulcrum of a merry-go-round possessed by an evil spirit, whirling round and round until she was spinning so fast she could barely hang on. Her fingers faltered on the keys as she typed her response.

Nightingale: I don't need to be tested. I'm fine physically. Nothing we did...

Was it possible to contract HIV of the mind?

Nightingale: I'm sorry. I just can't talk about this. Please tell the woman who called that I appreciate her concern.

Morning_Glory: I'm relieved to say the least.

Gloria's reply was followed by a smiley face icon complete with pink cheeks and eyelashes fluttering joyfully about.

There were times Isabelle wanted to bash in the head of whoever the idiot was who was responsible for creating smiley faces.

Morning_Glory: The woman I talked to also mentioned counseling, and an online support group some of them had joined for victims of fraud. I'll send the link.

Nightingale: I really don't think...

Morning_Glory: You need to talk to someone, Isabelle. If I'm too close to the situation, well, there has to be a counselor or psychologist of some sort there on Mull. If not, a pastor.

Nightingale: Glor? The woman you talked to didn't say anything about Ben trying to blackmail any of them, did she?

The time that passed before Gloria's response was her first indication she was going to be lambasted. If there was one thing Gloria wouldn't tolerate from her, it was idle speculation. Like Gloria always said, "The truth is bad enough. You don't need to borrow more trouble where there is none." Except there was plenty of trouble and good reason to suspect Ben. Gloria just didn't know it.

Morning_Glory: Isabelle, I know you're a writer. You have a vivid imagination. But you've got to stop assuming the worst! According to this woman, and the police, Ben has never re-contacted anyone after he's left. Besides, what could he possibly have that he could use to blackmail you?

Nightingale: I need to go, Glor. Just keep me posted on any more developments, okay? I appreciate it. Really, I do.

She wrapped her arms around herself, hunched her shoulders and lowered her head. She'd been such a fool, such an idiot. Her utter stupidity was so contemptible that, in her mind, she was undeserving of compassion or support from anyone. Her experience at the Blue Bell, with the one person she'd thought perhaps she could trust, had certainly proved her assessment to be correct.

"Hello!" A woman with a soft flounce of auburn hair was standing beside her stool, a baby in one arm and a toddler at her side. "Isabelle, isn't it?"

"Oh. I know you, don't I?" She struggled as she always did after talking to someone from the States, to switch from one world to another.

"Yes. From the Blue Bell."

"You helped the night I..."

A flash of genuine concern settled on the woman's face as though there were a direct link from her heart to her smile. "I'd hoped next time I saw ye yer face would be wreathed in smiles, but I'm sorry to say ye still look a wee blue." She let go of the toddler, held out her hand, then evidently thought better of it and gave her a quick hug—as tightly as she could with a baby in her arms. "Rose MacCraig."

Rose beamed down at the toddler at her side and up at the little one she was holding, both of whom had the most beautiful mocha skin, curly, dark brown hair and huge brown eyes.

"I dinnae think ye've met my children—Liam is two and a half, almost three, and Luella is a little over a year."

They were adorable, although neither of them looked like Rose or her husband, who, if she remembered right, was blond and fair.

"Now ye've seen me, ye have to promise complete secrecy. My husband, Ian, claims MacGochans' haggis is so short on brains and long on grains it barely qualified as revolting, but I rather like it. So every once in a while, when he's tied up with a meeting at church, I take the children for a stroll down the hill and help myself."

Isabelle laughed.

"Please join us if ye haven't already eaten. I've thought of ye so many times since that night at the Blue Bell and wondered how ye were faring."

Isabelle stiffened a little. Rose had been a huge help the night

51

she'd had her panic attack, but besides being generally empathetic, she couldn't imagine the woman would have any idea what she was going through—or what to do about it.

Rose looked at her as though she could read her mind, motioned for her to follow, and breezed over to an open booth. "I'd love to tell ye how I met my husband and came by these beautiful little ones."

Okay. Well, at least she had someone to talk to over dinner. That *was* what she had wanted.

They ordered their meals, and Rose occupied Liam with a coloring book. Luella seemed sleepy and content to snuggle in her lap.

Five minutes later, Rose had filled her in on what was evidently the condensed version of Pastor Ian, her now husband, capturing Rose on a video, half naked, while she'd been engaging in a passionate romp under the flying buttresses with a man who turned out to be a thief. *Wow.* She never would have guessed.

Rose leaned across the table and whispered confidentially. "Oh, and if ye hear a rumor about me being raped by my kidnappers, and poor Ian having no idea I was with child when he married me—or the alternate version that's circulating on the mainland, where the only reason poor Ian married me is that I was expecting Digby Bentworth's baairn and he didn't want me to have to raise the child alone. Which definitely doesnae make sense, since Digby was as white Scots as I am. But of course, they dinnae know that. But then, neither is Theory A plausible, unless I was to have popped out a toddler nigh on seven months after my ordeal."

"But you really were kidnapped?"

"Yes, unfortunately. But I wasnae violated, at least nae sexually. Aside from a few bruises I got when they threw me out of the auto, my ego was the only thing that was battered. Thank goodness Digby and I never did anything that could have resulted in pregnancy. So ye see, neither of their theories can possibly be correct."

Their meals were delivered by a slender young woman who bore no resemblance to Ben or Logan, and they sat in silence for a few moments while they tended to their meals.

Isabelle flaked off a bite of salmon, took a bite of potato doused in green peppercorn sauce, and looked up at Rose. "And your family and the people at St. Conan's were eventually able to forget about seeing you naked... and accept you?"

Rose handed Liam some small bites of her haggis, took a bite herself, and wiped her mouth with her napkin.

"To a certain extent. There was actually a bit more to it than I've told you. When Ian had the opportunity to start out fresh in a new location, I was as eager as he was to put the past behind us and move on. Although, as I've said, Scotland is a small country. News—particularly scandalous bits like mine—skips from one island to the next faster than those new hovercrafts everyone's always clattering aboot."

"I'm sorry you had to go through all of that, but it helps to know I'm not the only one. I mean, that someone's been through something similar...

"And made it to the other side." Rose smiled easily, as though she wasn't the least bit bothered by people talking about her behind her back. "I promise ye, one day soon it will all be better and nae one will even give it a thought."

"So, how did... I mean, you're married. And the children..."

"We got Liam though a private adoption arranged by a friend of Ian's from seminary who's a missionary in Botswain. We would have been on the list for years if we'd gone through conventional channels, and at our age, we didnae want to wait. Even then, who's to say we ever would have been selected given my tarnished reputation.

"Now the baby here is family, although once again, rumor has it we adopted a second just to put people off the scent when it came to Liam. Truth is, Luella belongs to my oldest nephew, Jaime, and a pretty little girl from the West Indies who he met in college. My brother-in-law didnae want their good name sullied by a shroud of illegitimacy, and the baby's birth mother was just starting at University and didnae feel she was ready for a child. And we were, so there we are. My sister can come and visit her grand-daughter any time she wishes, and instead of being my little sweetheart's great-aunt, I get to be her mum."

Liam chose that moment to duck under the table, squeeze through their legs, and take off running. Rose leaped up, plopped Luella in Isabelle's lap, and went after him.

Where on earth did she get her energy?

Rose returned with Liam in tow and a whirl of commotion and said, "So here Ian and I are, the happiest parents on earth and blessed beyond our wildest imaginations. Of course, I had to learn to put my trust in my Heavenly Father, not anyone here on earth, since even the best of us is only human." She winked. "Although I still think Ian MacCraig is as close to perfect as any man can be."

"It's quite a story."

"And a prime example of how a person can go from rock bottom to mountaintop if ye have faith enough to turn your affairs over to God Almighty."

Isabelle doubted her own judgment when it came to men and women she could see, touch and feel. How someone could blindly accept guidance from a being you couldn't even be sure was out there was beyond her. But she thought no less of Rose for having that kind of faith. In a way, she envied her.

Rose gave Liam a few more bites. "I'm nae trying to say my skin is impenetrable. Once, when Ian and I were still in the thick of the scandal, and Ian's sister was trying to convince Ian to get our marriage annulled, and my brother-in-law, Kevin, was chiding me for being some sort of wanton woman, I said to him, 'I hope none of yer children ever does anything wrong, lest ye're forced to feel the sting of half the country censuring ye.' Which of course, I didnae really mean—I would never wish anything ill on my sister or her dear children, even if they are half Kevin's and even if..." She turned and fussed with the baby's hair, a single curl on the very top of her head. "I felt guilty I'd ever said such a thing when we found out about little Luella. But then, the good Lord worked all of that out, too. And as long as we're being completely honest..."

Speak for yourself, Isabelle thought with a smile, while Rose dashed off in hot pursuit of Liam once again.

A moment later she was back. "So as I was saying, as long as we're being truthful, I may as well admit there was some small satisfaction in seeing my brother-in-law feel the prick of scandal."

Isabelle was glad Rose MacCraig was so comfortable in her own skin that it made no difference if half the country had seen her naked, or that everyone was talking about her behind her back and imagining things that weren't true. That didn't mean that Isabelle... Rose didn't have any idea what it was like to be the only child of an old money, Virginian family like the MacAllisters, or a saintly group like the members of her home church, who were direct descendants of the first Puritan settlers, and proud of it.

Rose could jest about the prick of scandal all she wanted to, but Isabelle wore the mantle of generations of expectations that did not include being taken in by a con man and photographed in the nude, and having to flee the country in disgrace before anyone found out what an utter, abject fool you were. Rose MacCraig couldn't possibly know about any of that.

The rest of their short but eventful meal was dominated by distractions from Luella, who had started to fuss, and Liam, who was getting increasingly antsy.

When they'd each had a pot of tea and a piece of Lumpy Bumpy Toffee Pie—which was every bit as wonderful as Rose promised— Rose said goodbye and left to get the children to bed. Isabelle logged back on to the internet to see if there was any word from Ronald about the article she'd submitted about Scotland's farmers.

Chapter Six

"Eh! If it isn't the fearless cow slayer! Or should I say the fear*ful* cow slayer?" Logan laughed as Michael entered the Blue Bell and thumped him on the back as soon as he was at arm's length.

"I did not hit the cow. It merely tipped over in front of my vehicle. And I was only trying to be conscientious when I went for help."

Logan caught the bartender's eye and waved his head at Michael. "I cannae sae I know what it's like to hit a hairy coo myself, but I'm supposing this beleaguered gent needs a drink."

"If we could please drop the subject, I would prefer to talk about something else." Michael seated himself and watched as the bartender poured a mug of his usual.

"They do have cows in Wisconsin, do they nae? I thought ye said it was the dairy state?" Another farmer teased. "I only mention it in case ye dinnae know, but cheese does come from milk, which comes from cows."

The men scattering the length of the bar, many his own crew, erupted in laughter.

"Folks just cannae get over the fact ye didn't know a hairy coo can get himself up once he's toppled," Logan said. "In Scotland, our lads have been known to tip a coo or two in their day. The first rule of thumb is to run like hell once ye have tipped the bugger over, as the hairy coo is likely to be angry, spring to its feet, and charge after ye."

Michael held out both hands, palms up. "Well, I once read something in a book that led me to believe otherwise."

Logan's face crinkled up. "Let's just hope he didn't learn how to build stone walls from reading a book."

"Maybe that's what those fancy American credentials behind his name stand for—Degreed in the Art of Castle Building."

"Rumor has it Sleeping Beauty, Cinderella, and Rapunzel all gave him excellent recommendations."

Michael closed his eyes and wished to God he hadn't inherited his grandfather's fair, show-all complexion.

"Aye. For all we know, he's probably a graduate of *Cinderella's School of Glass Slippers and Cobblestone Paths.*"

Michael shook his head.

"Bet he got high marks in *Laying Floors 101—Chinking Stones So Smooth That Cindy Won't Chip Her Slippers.*"

The crowd roared.

Michael groaned. Never mind the fact half of what they were saying was true—if they kept this up any longer he'd soon be the laughing stock of every town from here to Edinburgh.

People still hadn't stopped talking about the fact that he'd spent the night of the storm in Isabelle's cottage and showed up two hours later than usual for work the next morning. Now they had his and Isabelle's infraction at the Bell, Mrs. G's humiliating torture, and the fact he had inadvertently tipped over a hairy coo to clatter about. Would it never end?

"I thought I heard ye clacking out here, ye haggis-headed auld crabbit."

Great. He'd forgotten today was Mrs. Galbraith's day to mind the kitchen.

"I know your canaptious ways are second nature to ye, ye stupid wee nyaff, but hoo ye think such bletherin would set weel with a goodly lass like Isabelle, I dinnae ken. If ye cannae see hoo..."

Sometimes Michael was glad he could only understand half of what the locals said. As it appeared in this instance he might need to defend himself, however, he thought it advisable to admit his deficiency. He looked at Logan. "What is she talking about?"

"She's unhappy with ye because Isabelle hasn't set foot in the Blue Bell since the night ye creamed the hairy coo. Says ye chased the lass away, so it is ye who should fetch her and bring her back."

"I did not cream the cow! The cow is fine! I'm sure Isabelle's fine, too. How much could she miss the place? She hasn't even been coming here for a month."

Twenty sets of eyes bored down on him accusingly.

Where had he been when this happened? Obviously, he'd blinked his eyes and missed the magical moment when Isabelle MacAllister had won the hearts of everyone in the place.

Michael lifted his hands in surrender. "Fine. I'm sorry I chased the bonny lass away. I'll be off to find her and bring her back as soon as I've had a bite to eat."

Mrs. Galbraith stood at the door to the kitchen. Looking at her now, with her broad backside blocking all but a few wafts of light from the brightly lit kitchen, it was questionable who would make the better Green Bay Packer—Logan, with his strapping shoulders and remarkable strength, or Mrs. Galbraith, who shared most of her son's girth and had a killer glare besides.

Michael sighed, then stood. "Fine. I don't mind starving. So I'll be off to find the bonny lass right now, before I have anything to eat." He walked towards the door, taking short, drawn-out steps, waiting for someone to say something or at least offer him a bag of chips. He lifted his jacket from the peg and slowly slipped in each arm.

He heard a jumble of Gaelic behind him and turned to see Logan's mother disappearing into the kitchen.

Logan gave him a cheery wave. "She saed going to find the lass right now is the smartest thing ye have done in a long while."

#

The pub's comforting clatter wrapped around Isabelle like a favorite sweater. The night was still young. Any other time, she might have lingered, listening to the music while she whittled away at her next article. But it was the fifth day in a string of days so warm and sunny it felt more like July than early June and it seemed like the perfect time to indulge her hankering to do a bit of writing outside. From what she'd heard, the air didn't get much warmer than this in Scotland.

She was midway through a story about a bathing pool built by the Celts some 1500 years earlier on a stretch of beach a short walk from her cottage. She'd been researching and writing about the influences of the Druids, Romans, Celts and Vikings on the British Isles. All she needed to put the finishing touches on the article was to scope out the place in person—what it felt like to walk where the Romans had walked, or something to that effect.

After a brief stop at Dunara Cottage to replenish her backpack, she left on foot for the Celtic Bath. Her landlady had recommended evening as the perfect time to dip one's feet—that in-between time of day when the sun had meandered westward far enough to warm the water, but when it was not yet dusk, when it got very chilly very fast.

On the way to the sea, she climbed over a fence via the cleverest little stile, walked past an ancient stone circle, and passed through two gates where sheep were grazing. Although she turned around every so often to snap a shot of the castle in the distance, the best view awaited her when she arrived and saw the sun's reflection shimmering against the still, blue water of the pool. She found a flat boulder at the edge of the water to use as a perch, and tried to imagine how the bath had looked and what the people had been like all those centuries ago.

The Celts had carefully fitted the rocks rimming the pool to catch the water and hold it at a consistent depth. Maybe she hadn't given Michael and his crew of merry rock crafters enough credit. The longer she studied the pool, the more she could see there was a distinct artistry to the way the stones were arranged.

"It's fascinating, isn't it?" The words startled her although the voice delivering them was gentle.

She glanced back just long enough to catch a glimpse of Michael, his hands in his pockets and a chagrinned look on his face. She turned back to the sea.

"My Grandpa was the one who taught me to lay stones." Michael was still some distance behind her. "In my home town, there are dozens of stone buildings built by my great-grandfather... no two alike. I can remember when I was a little boy, he would always ask me if I could see the faces of the rocks. Claimed each stone had a personality."

She could hear pebbles skittering in his wake as he came closer. Still, she stared ahead at the pool. She hadn't forgotten how horrible he'd been that night at the Bell, but then, she had wanted to put what had happened behind them and move on.

His voice grew a bit louder. "Grandpa claimed that just like a good manager of people assigns each of his men the task he is best equipped to do, a rock layer must assess the strengths of each rock, determine what they're destined to do, and place them relative to the job they're designed for."

Wow. Suddenly, it all made sense. "And here I thought rocks were just faceless lumps of matter."

His sigh floated forward on the wind.

She could hear his feet shuffling against the stones, and a few loose pebbles shifting down between the cracks in the rocks.

Michael cleared his throat. "Logan claims that when the storms come through they blow every wisp of impure air out to sea, leaving the sun to shine through virtually unfiltered atmosphere."

She said nothing for a moment. "Is that why it's been so warm this week?"

"Yes, and why the sun's rays feel so powerful. Half of my men are as red as lobsters after a week of it."

Whatever the cause, the air did seem to be charged with an intensity she'd seldom experienced. Warm, but not heavy with humidity like in Virginia. Clean. Pure. Cleansing.

"You're working on a story?"

She turned ever so slightly. "I'm calling it *Those Who Came Before, Remnants of Eras Past*—at least for now."

"Sounds interesting."

"Not really." She sighed. "I need a catchier title before I send it off to my editor. So far I've written about the Druids—Stonehenge and the like, the mosaics at Bignor Roman Villa in West Sussex, and Jorvik, the Viking village at York."

"I loved the mosaics at the Roman Villa. The workmanship is exquisite. When you think about how many thousands of years ago... It's mind-boggling."

She looked over her shoulder and flashed a smile. "Thinking about how they fit together all those little pieces into a pretty design kind of goes along with the rock laying thing, doesn't it? I'll bet you play Tetris on your computer, too."

Michael laughed. "Good guess."

The silence between them eased into a comfortable lull.

"So you're here to experience the Bath," he said.

"That, and to collect my thoughts." She stared up at the sky.

"Wouldn't it be nice if the same winds that clear the air could blow the cobwebs out of our heads while they're at it?"

She turned to face him full on, her knees hugged to her chest, her chin resting on her hands.

He crouched down on the boulder opposite hers. "Have you ever been to Germany?"

"The summer between my junior and senior years in college."

"In Bavaria, they talk about a wind called the ferne."

Her eyes twinkled at the mysterious pause he used to punctuate his sentence before rolling the word ferne reverently off his tongue.

"All kinds of strange things happen when the ferne comes a blowing. People disappear, moodiness and depression run rampant, and crimes of the heart inexplicably rise."

"So what are you saying? That whatever set us off the other night was a result of some bizarre weather phenomenon?"

He simply raised an eyebrow and held her glance.

She cocked her head and tilted her chin up a notch. "Is this supposed to be some sort of apology or are you saying it's the ferne's fault I started to cry in front of half of the Bell?"

Michael rocked back on his heels and held out his hand. "Forgive me?"

"Sure." She slipped her hand tentatively into his. "I guess I have been a little sensitive lately—don't ask. But my friend Gloria says I have a tendency to go looking for trouble where there is none."

"If it's weighing on you that heavily, it's trouble, whether real or imagined."

A butterfly fluttered between them and danced over the tufts of sea grass poking out from the rocks.

She caught her bottom lip with her teeth and looked away.

"I'm a good listener if you feel like talking."

When she finally spoke, her voice sounded timid even to her own ears. "Have you ever tried Internet dating?"

"No, not personally."

Michael obviously couldn't share the statistics with her without blowing his cover, but sadly, he could attest to the fact that nearly thirty percent of his cases last year had had some connection to the Internet... a twenty-something wife so enamored with her internet lover that she left her family, only to find out her online paramour was still in high school; a man so addicted to masturbating while watching online pornography that he couldn't make love to his wife; a teenager who racked up ten thousand dollars in charges to his parents' credit cards, gambling in an online casino...

Isabelle continued talking in a tone that was confessional. "The whole thing started when I was asked to do an article on a site called DreamDates.com. I was skeptical at first. I only posted an ad for the sake of research, but my findings revealed an astonishing number of success stories."

"On some level, any of us who are single would like to believe that finding the perfect mate is as easy as punching your preferences into a computer."

"So you don't think I'm totally nuts?" Her voice squeaked.

"We've all entertained fantasies about finding one magical person who complements us in every conceivable way."

She looked at him, her eyes searching for understanding. "The one who's meant to be."

"Yes." He caught and held her glance. "So I take it you got some viable responses to your ad?"

"Several actually." She blushed. "I'm probably a little pickier than most people."

"Unrealistically high expectations?"

"So my mother has been telling me for years."

"But you eventually met someone who seemed to meet your qualifications?"

"Well, kind of. Not really. His name was Ben."

He watched her chin tremble as she fought to go on.

"Before I met Ben, I'd received several letters from men whose basic characteristics were supposedly a perfect match to mine."

"But...?"

"Their descriptions all met the parameters I had set, but their initial emails all included allusions to—and in some cases, even the juicy details of—nasty divorces, squabbling kids, custody battles, restraining orders, bouts with alcoholism, demented mothers, ex-wives bent on revenge, bankruptcies, and careers in the toilet. As a reporter, I'm always in favor of knowing the rest of the story, but c'mon."

He could feel his face getting warm. It was a foregone conclusion he would never be chosen as a poster child for full disclosure. He was only doing what he had to do to protect his clients. He cleared his throat. "Honesty is great, but when you're totally open with someone at the very beginning of a relationship, you take a huge risk. If you wait until you've grown to care about each other before you start sharing the intimate details of your life, the same things that might have driven you apart at the start may not make any difference at all."

"Exactly. Having too much information, too early on, can kill any prospects the relationship might have. And yet, after my recent experience, I'll take that chance. I want the whole story up front, so I know exactly what I'm getting into."

Well, that ruled him out. "That's quite a conundrum." He willed himself to relax. "So I gather when you first heard from this Ben, he went about things differently. What did he do? Reel you in by being mysterious?"

Her cheeks flamed red. "I may have been stupid to fall for his line, but you needn't compare me to a fish."

"You're not stupid! From what you said, I'm just speculating he probably only divulged information after he had learned what you wanted to hear."

She lowered her head and wiped away a tear. "At first, he only told me he was a writer."

His heart went out to her. "You'd probably included that in your profile."

"Of course, I was intrigued we shared something so elemental. I remember fantasizing he was a famous, multi-published author who had just happened to stumble upon my personal ad. Of course, if that had been true, he would have had to have been secretive to protect his true identity." She looked up at him sheepishly. "Until he was sure I could be trusted."

She was barely into her story, and already, he wanted to strangle the man. "You probably poured out your heart to him, while his emails were very short and sporadic."

"Now I'm being likened to one of Pavlov's dogs."

"It's not personal. It's a proven fact of human nature that intermittent reinforcement—"

"I know. Is more effective than constant."

"You know it. I know it. Con men know it," he said.

"At the time he first contacted me, he was probably still involved with his prior conquest, so I suppose he didn't have a lot of time to spend on wooing the next. Me." Her face looked like it was melting around the edges.

Michael gently guided her. "I'm guessing he asked a lot of questions about you and revealed very little about himself."

"Yes. I was flattered he was so interested. I mentioned early on that I grew up attending a little Episcopalian church. Lo and behold, in his next letter he revealed he had been raised in the same faith."

"Each time you gave him a little more information, he would shape his story to complement your own."

"Yes—until he had me believing he was the perfect man for me."

Isabelle groaned. "I should have known better. I should have seen right through it. It's one of the oldest scams in the books."

"I'm sure you're trained to be objective, to nose out the story at work, where you have to be hard-hitting and analytical. When a person goes home, they should be free to express their soft, tender side."

"I know there are a lot of horrible human beings in the world. I see them all the time at work. But I'm a good, honest person. It's simply inconceivable to me that someone would—could—treat another person... My mind just doesn't work that way."

Which is exactly what I like about you, he thought.

She looked up at him with wet lashes. "Every time I talk to you, you seem more like a shrink and less like a stone layer."

He discreetly but quickly changed his position so she couldn't see his shoulders had stiffened.

She looked at him with a half-smile, her lashes still heavy with moisture. "Admit it, Michael. You're far more observant than the average Joe."

"I like to paint when I'm not fitting stones. People who paint have to train themselves to see things others don't—just like writers do." He had liked to paint as a child. Michael adjusted his collar and tried to find a more comfortable position.

"Oh! I'd love to see some of your work. Do you do oils? Watercolor?"

"Oils." Damn. He was so bad at this. Now he'd have to get himself to a city, buy a new set of oils and some canvases, and hope he could fashion a painting that was halfway palatable.

Her knee had drifted into his. He froze for a second and waited to see if she would move away from him. When she didn't, he let his leg relax against hers. The heat from each of them flowed into the other like they were of one skin.

He looked up. "The sun is finally starting to sink. Looks to me like you'd better be taking your dip soon, as Bette would say."

"Oh, I'm not really going in. I'll just dangle my feet over the edge."

"How's that going to teach you what you need to know? If you're going to understand the essence of the ages past, you need to get into the water and feel it." Michael pulled his shirt out of his jeans and started to unbuckle his belt.

"Have you been in before?"

"Sure. Lots of times. Bette and Hans are down here almost every evening in the summer and fall."

"I didn't bring a suit."

"Unless you don't have any skivvies on, I'm assuming your undies are as modest as the average swimming suit."

He lifted one leg and then the other, stripping out of his jeans while she watched.

He turned his back to her, adjusted the waistband of his boxer shorts and sat down on a flat rock at the side of the pool, his legs hanging over the edge. "Go ahead. I won't look."

"Yah, right."

But a few seconds later, he heard her slipping her clothes off.

"This is probably the most insane thing I've done in the name of research yet." She padded quietly to his side, stood by the edge of the pool for a second, then lowered herself gingerly beside him.

He looked at her and raised his eyebrows. "Well I can't say you didn't warn me."

"What?"

"About your lingerie."

She slid into the water until all that showed was the thin, plum-colored straps of her tiny, pushup bra and a profusion of color on the swells of her breasts.

He handed her a stick. "I've been told a person should check for snakes before getting into the water."

She was out of the pool and back on the rock before he could say boo. He watched as she curled back on her haunches, raised her knees to her chest and clasped her ankles with both hands. "The water's not as warm as I thought it would be."

"Right." He splashed the stick in the water. "My crews occasionally get out this way. I've sent them out several times looking for a particular kind of rock we use when we're mixing mortar. Maybe you've seen them out and aboot in their Nicky Tams."

"Nicky what?"

"A piece of leather with straps the men tie around their trousers, just below the knees, to keep the hairy beasties that hide in the rocks from jumping out and..."

She stood with a jolt. "If you're trying to get me back in your lap, you're doing a damn good job of it."

He grinned and held out his arms.

She stooped and pushed him. He grabbed her arms. They tumbled into the water together.

"Ouch." I think that was a rock." He complained.

"Duh." She sputtered. "Tell me you were kidding about the snakes." She splashed him with one hand while she wiped water out of her eyes with the other.

He grinned. "I was kidding about the snakes."

"And the hairy beasties?"

"Well, there are hairy beasties, but they're more afraid of you than you are of them."

"That's what my mother always said about hornets."

"And?" he said.

"I got stung."

He watched as a wild range of emotions shadowed her face, changing her features as quickly as the sun when a cloud moves across its path. She squirmed, and her thighs tensed against the sides of his legs. Michael loosened his grip. He slowly moved his hands from her waist to her hips.

Her eyes pierced his. "You have a real gift for bringing people's emotions to the surface."

He brushed his thumbs against her waist. "People's in general, or yours?"

"Mine, if you must know." Droplets of water rained from her arms as she lifted her hands and placed one on each of his shoulders.

He splayed his fingers across her back and gently massaged each knotted muscle he encountered. "And what are those emotions telling you?"

"Despite the fact that you're sometimes inexplicably rude and too damn sexy for anybody's good, you're a trustworthy sort for the most part."

"For the most part?" He laughed, and shifted slightly. Her hips slid over his legs until her position had adjusted to his.

He spent a second wondering what the hell he was doing and why he was nothing more than a flighty little moth pulled to her flame when she was around. He spent a second considering the fact he would likely get burned. And then, he stopped caring and kissed her.

She leaned away from him. "I don't care if rocks do have personalities. You're way too perceptive to have learned all you know about human nature from fitting chunks of stone together." Her eyes scanned his face. "Are you sure you're not some sort of psychiatrist?"

He rotated his shoulders until her fingers took the hint and began to move in a slow dance over his skin.

This was so dangerous. She could hurt him, really hurt him. She could ruin everything.

He tried to make himself care that getting involved with Isabelle MacAllister, investigative reporter, was the absolute worst thing he could do—and failed.

"If I were a psychiatrist, then what we just had would be called a session, and I would be acting unethically if I..." He leaned towards her and brushed his lips over hers.

Her eyes continued their search of his face. "I suppose this wouldn't be allowed either." She ran her fingers through the damp curls on his forehead and kissed him on the throat.

"No. If I were a psychiatrist and you were my patient, we definitely couldn't..." Their lips met in a tentative kiss and melded in a wet, wild, passionate... "Be doing this."

She pulled away from him, rubbed her hands over the wisps of hair on his chest. "You might sound like a psychiatrist , but you feel like a rock layer." She curved her back and ran her tongue over his left nipple. "Firm." She suckled at his right side. "Strong." She buried her face in his chest. "Hard."

"Whoa." He tried to straighten up but she ran her fingers through the curls that fanned across his belly and he couldn't make himself do anything but enjoy the moment. "You're going to have to expand your definition of hard in a minute here if you keep kissing me that way."

She lifted her head, met his glance, and smiled. Her cheeks were flushed and rosy, her hair, tousled and damp at the ends. He took a strand of hair and rubbed his fingers over her ear, smoothing the lobe between his thumb and forefinger. His hand moved down to the lace at the top of her bra.

She smiled sweetly and moved his hand back to his side.

He reached out to tickle the silky fabric on the underside of her bra, to feel the swell of her breathing, the weight of her breast.

67

She steered his hands back to her arms.

"But you touched mine. Don't men have equal rights on this island?"

She nabbed his hand. "You felt my breasts the night of the storm. I just leveled the playing field."

His laughter echoed over the landscape. "I was asleep. I didn't know what I was doing. I wasn't cognizant at the time."

She nuzzled his neck. "You knew."

"How could you tell?"

Their mouths fused in a greedy explosion of need, their hands sightlessly exploring each dip and swell.

"You're shivering." He could feel her nipples jutting into his chest. "You have goosebumps."

"I do feel chilly all of the sudden."

"We lost the sun. Let's get you back into some clothes."

He lifted her out of the water and wrapped his body around hers.

"You feel good."

"The sun's not gone. He pointed. "It's just blocked by that outcropping."

"A total eclipse."

"There's a patch of sunshine a few yards that way. Let's get you warmed up before you catch a cold." He took her hand and started for the rays.

"There's a towel in my backpack." She motioned in the opposite direction.

"You go on. I'll grab it and catch up to you."

She was smiling when he turned away. He found her backpack with a digital camera perched on top, picked up both, and turned. She was standing in a patch of sunlight, her clothes clutched in one hand, looking for all the world like the subject of a Maxfield Parrish painting. Both sky and water framed her silhouette. Sunlight glowed around her like a halo, illuminating the swell of her hips; the small of her waist; her beautiful breasts; every lush layer of hair brushing her shoulders.

He wandered closer, mesmerized by the streak of sunshine holding her in its spotlight. He lifted her camera to his face, wanting to preserve the image of her beauty for all eternity.

He could see the sun flickering across her nose through the lens of the camera as she turned to look at him.

68

"What are you doing?" He could see her mood changing as unexpectedly and instantly as if the sun had disappeared for good. "Put it down! Please! Right now." She was sobbing, pulling on her clothes in short, choppy movements, and flailing her arms as she ran towards him.

They met in the shadow lands somewhere between the bath and the sunbeam. He tried to take her by the shoulders and pull her into his arms, to explain what he did not understand. She pushed him away.

In the end, he let her have her freedom. Isabelle grabbed her backpack and her camera and warned him not to follow her.

He watched her back as she ran towards Dunara Cottage. His heart caught in his throat each time her feet started to slip on the loose bits of slate peppering the path.

She was still within sight when she fell to her knees and caught herself with palms outstretched. She did not turn to reassure him, but picked herself up and continued to clamber up the incline towards Dunara Cottage as fast as she could go.

Chapter Seven

The light from the wall sconce illuminated the table where Gareth and Morgan sat talking, knee to knee. The dainty, beaded shade mounted on the light captured the glow and directed it straight down, leaving their faces in relative darkness.

"Damon has a new assignment for ye," Gareth said, "and he does nae want this one botched up like the—"

Morgan's face was plastered with a leering grin. "Like yer little horse and pony show down on the docks last week?"

Gareth felt the red creeping across his face. He took a long draw of tipple.

"Gawd, talk aboot a stench. Ye made a hash out of that one awrite," Morgan said.

"I kept them from going on the boat, didn't I? And that's nae what I was talking aboot."

"Nothing I've laid a hand to has—."

"That's the problem. Not a single thing ye've done has told us anything we dinnae already know. Ye've been on the job for weeks and we still dinnae have a single thing connecting Michael St. Dawndalyn or Isabelle MacAllister to Roanoke Sonar Technologies."

Morgan's eyes bored into his. "There's nothing there to find on him, I tell ye."

"Lucky for ye, Damon is close to making the same assumption. For the next week or so ye're to continue to keep an eye on St. Dawndalyn." His Adam's apple bobbed so erratically he could hardly swallow. "But he also wants ye to step up your efforts to kutsch up to the woman."

Morgan's eyes narrowed to two fleshy slits. The ends of his lips curled up. A clump of nose hairs protruding from his left nostril quivered.

"Ye'll do nothing to jeopardize the mission. She's a crafty one, with her wide-eyed innocent act, but when it comes down to it, her balls are probably bigger than yours."

"We'll see aboot that." Morgan smacked his lips.

"She'd sooner claw yer eyes out than go anywhere near the likes of ye."

"Damon gave me this assignment." Morgan leaned forward menacingly. "I'll be the one to see to it."

Gareth's eyes blinked in a staccato cadence he was helpless to stop. "Just keep in mind it's facts we need. We donnea need to know anything aboot her except what she knows about the operation."

"I'll find out what she kens, awrite."

"I'm serious, you blathering fool. If ye're smart, ye'll keep your pants zipped and yer crotch out of it," Gareth said. "Use the head the good Lord gave ye for once in yer life and just do what Damon asks."

"Blah, blah, blah."

"Damon sent the spare key to Dunara Cottage and a flash drive so ye can download the contents of her laptop."

"If getting into Isabelle's MacAllister's lap is what he wants, I'll have the job done in no time." Morgan laughed at his own joke.

"Damon will not take kindly to yer scaring her off. If ye'll mind your Ps and Qs this time, all will be weill."

"Keep your nose in joint, will ye? I'll mind myself wella right. In fact, I'll think I'll bid my farewells to ye now before the sun starts to dip and take myself a stroll down to Dunara Cottage. If the lady is home, I'll say I'm there to be sociable. If she's gone, I'll have a private look-see and find out what I can."

#

Logan cursed under his breath, wishing for the first time in his life that he was half his size. He sucked in his breath and tried to flatten his body to the end of the booth behind the one where the two Welshmen sat talking. He could neither hear nor understand a hundred percent of what they were saying, but he caught enough to know Michael and Isabelle were involved with a sonar company. His suspicions had been right.

#

Isabelle tagged on an additional two paragraphs to the end of her article when she got back to the cottage, connected to the internet, and sent the piece to her editor. It was mid-afternoon in Virginia. Her timing, for once, was perfect. Ronald liked to review new articles before he went home for the day, spend the evening mulling over any foibles, and do his editing first thing in the morning.

She cursed herself for letting Michael distract her. If she hadn't come to her senses when she did, she might have missed her deadline entirely.

She checked her email before she disconnected and found a nice email from her mother full of chatty news of family friends and relatives. Good news, good memories, good cheer. By the time she disconnected, she had nearly forgotten about the whole camera incident. She felt safe being alone—because she wasn't really. She had her family, her friends, people who had known her since she was little. They all loved and cared about her and were there for her no matter where in the world she was. She stripped out of her damp clothing, stepped in the shower and let the hot stream pour over her in a cleansing torrent of water and tears.

#

Michael took the long way around to get home from the Celtic Bath so as to make sure Isabelle was settled in for the night before he went traipsing by her cottage, which was certain to have freaked her out even more than she already was. He stopped along the way to explore the ruins of Fort Dun Ara and watch the seals at the Pier. Despite the rumbling of his stomach, he lingered momentarily at the Standing Rocks and briefly enjoyed the view of Bluevale Castle from the hill above Dunara.

Unless he had been willing to cut cross country, climb fences and risk another unwanted encounter with a hairy coo—this time, with the sharp end of its horns—there was no way to get back to the castle without passing Isabelle's cottage. So he crept stealthily through the brush, keeping her front door in close sight as he rounded the slope that led past her door, ready to take cover if he needed to. Much as he would have liked to get to the bottom of whatever was bothering Isabelle, he was determined to respect her wishes.

He was rounding the last corner at the base of the hill and

wondering what he was going to tell Mrs. Galbraith about his failed attempt to get back into Isabelle's good graces so she would return to the Bell when he caught sight of a vaguely familiar looking, half-bald head disappearing behind a rhododendron bush.

"Morgan?"

"Er, sir. Hoos it goin? I see ye be out enjoying the warm air, too. Fine evening for a stroll, eh?"

The man looked as panicked as a deer caught in headlights.

"Fine evening or no, I'm not sure the residents of this cottage would take too kindly to your snooping around their windows."

"Oh. I dinnae realize this one was occupied. I was up at the castle, and uh, decided to do a little bird watching, yes, and ended up on the trail. Good thing the castle can be seen for miles around or I'd probably be lost by now and forced to spend the night roaming the moors."

"You forgot your binoculars."

Morgan lifted his hand and rotated a knuckle at the base of his right nostril. "Twas a buzzard which caught my eye. Looked right big enough without magnification. Off I went, following behind, of no mind where my feet were taking me."

Michael stood blocking the path to the sea and looked Morgan square in the eye. "Well, since the buzzard didn't choose to linger here, I'm sure you'll be on your way."

"Yes, I'd best get back to Tobermory before the light fades any further."

"Sounds like a good idea."

Morgan turned and scrambled back up the path.

Michael was not eager for another encounter with Isabelle, but he stayed put for a moment, waiting to make sure she hadn't been disturbed by their voices. A pump hummed softly in the background and he thought he could hear water running. No doubt she was in the shower.

Michael seriously doubted Morgan had been on a bird watching expedition, but he had no clue what he had been doing. He saw no sense in alarming Isabelle unnecessarily, especially when she was already upset. He decided against telling her about the incident. She might really lose it if she knew she had the likes of Morgan creeping around her cottage.

He stuck his hands in his pockets and rummaged about, looking for something to eat. He was so hungry he would have killed for a candy bar. Nada. He climbed to the top of the hill behind the cottage and watched Morgan's shuffling retreat.

Maybe it wouldn't be a bad idea to take another look at the Standing Stones, circle back and make sure Isabelle was okay. Maybe by that time, she'd be feeling a bit more hospitable.

He walked to the west, fantasizing about grilled cheese sandwiches and homemade tomato soup, chocolate chip cookies still warm from the oven, and a thick serving of Skippy peanut butter sandwiched between two soft, white slices of Wonder Bread. The sun was shining between two of the standing stones like a talisman when he approached the ancient monument. Maybe one day, Isabelle would fix him dinner. Was that too much to hope for?

#

Isabelle stepped out of the shower and reached for a towel. Her cell phone's melody was nearing the end of the song. She raced across the room, trying not to slip on the slate floor, flinging water left and right like some sort of wet dog, clutching her towel with one hand.

"Isabelle?"

The voice was familiar, but not one she'd anticipated hearing in Scotland. "Yes?" she said.

"Ronald."

"Ronald! It's good to hear your voice! I wasn't expecting—"

"You may not be so happy to hear from me once you've heard what I have to say."

Isabelle gulped and tried to pull her towel a little tighter without letting go of the phone. The terry cloth slipped, exposing one breast. "Is something wrong?"

"Not if you like getting your butt chewed."

An ominous pause followed during which Isabelle supposed it was pointless to say anything.

"Damn it, Isabelle. I hate it that you've put me in this position. I know you've been handed a load of crap, but it's been, what, three months now? We've spent half of our travel budget for the whole year getting you settled in Europe, and all I'm getting from you in return is horse-shit."

She hadn't seen any horses lately. The best she could do was to envision one of the steaming hot, fresh-from-the-cow piles of brown goop she'd learned to avoid when she was hiking. Ronald thought her work stunk. Her eyebrows creased into a pout.

"I'd like to quote you if I may." Ronald cleared his throat and began to read. "The Celts, the Romans, the Vikings. Each had a great empire. Each was a powerful leader of their age. So, where are they now? What caused the downfall of a people so prolific and advanced for their time?

"More importantly, one has to wonder if the same fate will befall us one day. What will be our demise—a cataclysmic war? A super virus or bacteria immune to all known treatments that kills hundreds of thousands like the Black Plague once did? Maybe Mad Cow Disease is more than a blip on the medical screen. Although the food supply throughout Europe is now tested regularly and proven free of the disease, rumors still abound. Several scientists claim that even after blazing hot fires were used to burn the infected animal carcasses, the remaining ashes still contained traces of live Mad Cow. It's a chilling thought.

"Maybe it won't be disease, but a bio-chemical disaster, or a dirty bomb planted by terrorists. Maybe it will be the apocalypse born-again Christians have been warning us about for years. Buzzards are a common sight on the Island of Mull. Let's just hope they won't be feasting on the remains of our civilization anytime soon."

Isabelle tried to swallow and couldn't. She tried again to no avail.

"Does that make you want to get on an airplane and go visit Europe?" Ron thundered.

Her chin started to quiver. "I guess I'm having a hard time trying to write fluff when I'm used to exposition."

"This isn't exposition. This is the inner ramblings of someone who's scared and depressed and very possibly on the verge of being psychotic."

"Well, there's a nice quote for my bio."

"I'm not kidding, Isabelle. If you don't give me something I can work with it's going to be the tag line for the reference letter you'll need to send out with your resume."

She gulped. "What about the article I did on the local farmers? I really felt like it captured the essence of why it's so important to reconsider Europe as a vacation destination." Surely it had been okay. She'd felt so proud and confident when she'd sent it off to Ronald. The photo of Logan had been the perfect illustration.

"I don't know how to make myself any clearer, Isabelle. Yes, the plight of area farmers and the dismal economy in general is why you're in Europe, but no one wants to hear about downtrodden workers. Did Germany rebuild their tourism industry with tales of half-bombed cities needing to be rebuilt after the war? Of course not. They lured people back with photos of big-breasted German women in low cut dirndls clutching mugs of Hofbrau beer."

"So if I retake Logan's photo in low cut jeans and no shirt so you can see his rippling muscles, serving me a dram of whiskey instead of a pot of tea, you'll use the article?"

"Sarcasm isn't going to help, Isabelle. You know I've always liked you, and I feel terrible about what this asshole did to you, but that doesn't change the facts. I need five good travel pieces by the end of next week. Make the pieces good and upbeat. If Sheila likes them, I'll see to it you get something juicier. You mentioned a sunken treasure in one of your emails, and an old castle that's being rebuilt, didn't you? There's got to be a good investigative piece lurking in one of those stories. Once you're back in Sheila's good graces, we'll get you going on something deeper. I promise."

"So exactly what kind of fluff does Her Highness want?"

"Sandy from *Food and Wine* suggested doing *A Chocolate Lover's Guide to Europe*. They've discovered the health benefits of the flavinoids or catechins in chocolate can lower cholesterol. Make that your first priority so we can ride on the shirttails of these new findings. And I don't want to hear anything about fat grams, understood? Don't even mention the word calories."

"I get the picture."

"That brings me to my next suggestion."

"I'm afraid to ask."

"Puffins. I want a pictorial on puffins. There are supposedly hundreds of them nesting on a little island just off Mull. And Isabelle?"

"Yes?"

"Think cute. Cuddly."

She could hear him taking a swig of coffee before he continued. She rolled her eyes.

"No buzzards. No birds of prey period. I don't want to know who or what likes to munch on puffin pie. I don't care whether or not they're near extinction—"

"Okay. I get the idea. Maybe you'd like me to write an article on cross-Atlantic cruises for those who are still afraid to fly. I promise I won't mention the Titanic."

"Be as flippant as you like, Isabelle. I'm telling you, it's time to do or die. I voted to bring you home where I could keep a better eye on you. Sheila's take was, 'Give her the new assignments. If she does a good job, she stays. If not, she's off the payroll. And she can find her own way home.'"

"She really said that?"

"Her exact words."

Isabelle's entire body was covered in goose bumps. She'd been wet, chilled, and caught in some state of undress for hours. Her well-being had been threatened, both in her imagination and in her skewed version of reality. She said goodbye to Ronald and set the phone back on its cradle. Her body felt deathly tired; her emotions, exhausted.

Still holding the towel loosely around her, she fumbled to open the top drawer of the dresser that lined one wall of her bedroom.

Her breath caught in her throat. The goose bumps sitting on the surface of her skin grew roots and burrowed into her bones. Someone had rummaged through her underwear drawer. Someone had been in the cottage. Someone had violated her private things. Their fingers had touched the fabric that touched her. What if she'd put a pair of panties on without looking?

She grabbed her backpack and started throwing socks, bras and panties into her bag. She chose her stiffest pair of blue jeans and the same baggy, sweatshirt she'd let Michael wear during the storm from the bottom drawer and slid into them with no bra or panties on underneath. She added her nightgowns to the pile in her backpack, and anything else that looked touchable. She shoved her towels into a duffle bag, pulled the drawstring shut and grabbed her purse.

She was reaching for her keys when she heard a knock on the door. She peered out the window beside the door before flipping the latch. Him.

"Michael, I thought I told you not to—"

"I was worried about you."

She looked at him and tried not to cry again. She wanted to, but not in front of him. "Someone was in my cottage. While I was gone." She took a gulp of air.

Michael's face paled, and then flushed with anger. "Is something missing? Were you robbed?"

"No. Not that I can see. I had my laptop and my good camera with me. There's little else here of value." Her voice broke. "I'm sure the door was locked when I got here." She let her eyes skitter around the room, looking for more evidence someone had been there. "How could someone have gotten in unless they had a key? There are no broken windows."

"Are you absolutely sure someone was inside? I mean, you were upset when you came home. You're not just—"

"Imagining things? No. I can tell someone's gone through my personal things." She choked back a sob. So much for not crying. She'd be doing well at this point if she could ward off hysteria. "I'm very detail oriented. I fold my bath towels a certain way, and my hand towels another. The phone rang just as I was getting out of the shower, so I almost didn't notice, but I know I had my bras and panties arranged in the drawer just so."

Her whole body felt pale and transparent. Thoughts—how? who? why?—bombarded her brain.

Michael took a step toward her with his arms outstretched, either to hug her or because he thought she might faint.

"Get away from me!" She could feel it happening all over again. Another panic attack. "It was you!" Her temples pulsed with adrenalin. "I was at the bath for a good thirty minutes before you arrived. The path from the castle goes right by here. You knew I wasn't home. Bette told you where I was. You didn't think I'd know."

"Isabelle, think," he said. "Why would I do such a thing? The last thing I want is to hurt you."

"You're always hurting me. Saying things, doing things..." She sobbed and held her face in her hands. He didn't try to touch her again. She'd told him not to, but really, she wanted him to ignore her and just do it. No she didn't. She didn't know what she wanted.

"I'd be the first to admit I can be a jerk at times, but I'd never abuse your privacy. Think about it, Isabelle. Why would I break into your home?"

"To see if my lingerie was really from Victoria's Secret. So you could tease me about it. You couldn't wait to see it for yourself after I taunted you about it."

"Victoria's Secret or K-Mart Blue Light Special—your intimate apparel holds no appeal for me unless you're in it." He smiled tenderly and reached out one hand.

Her hands were trembling, her shoulders shaking with mixed emotions. "You should go. I'm going to have to go to the Laundromat before I can wear any of this."

"I can't leave you alone like this, scared half to death."

"Having you for a bodyguard makes about as much sense as leaving a fox to guard the henhouse."

"You're one gutsy lady, Isabelle MacAllister. I'll give you that."

"You were closer to the truth the first time. I'm scared silly. And not at all sure I'm not losing my mind."

"Now that I've got an inkling about. After what you've been through, I'd be worried if you weren't panicking."

She thought about Ben and her stomach lurched.

She met his eyes and brushed away the tears from her cheeks.

"My car is parked up at the castle. Come on. I'll give you a lift into town and we'll see if the laundromat is still open. I'll guard your undies while you go down to the constable's office and report this to the inspector."

"I can't. They don't know how observant I've trained myself to be... since Ben. They'll think I'm a raving lunatic."

"They don't know anything about Ben. The possibility that you're just being overly paranoid will never occur to them. What they'll think is you're a woman who knows how she folds her underwear. They need to know what's happened."

Michael seemed seriously worried. She was grateful he believed her, but the look on his face did nothing to comfort her.

Chapter Eight

Rum truffles, creme de mint, tangerine, rose, and violet creams, each one hand-dipped in smooth, shiny wet chocolate. Row upon row of melt-in-your-mouth morsels, each signed with a subtle dash of mint green, peach, pink or lavender, the mere suggestion of which is enough to tease one's taste buds into a frenzy of anticipation. Nothing could suit Tobermory better than a colorful mélange of chocolates to match its rainbow-tinted pier.

Isabelle mulled over her notes and made a few changes to her preliminary outline. The owners of Tobermory Chocolates had been kind enough to give her an impromptu tour of their tiny but efficient kitchen. From there, she was off to Birmingham, England to do a chocolate tasting at Cadbury's state of the art facility, then, to catch a hydrofoil across the channel to have her first bites of Belgium's famous Cote d'Or and Davina Chocolates. Her interviews with Lindt, Toblerone, and Nestlés would be conducted in Zurich, Switzerland, an easy and scenic trip thanks to her Eurail Pass.

While she was on the mainland, she planned to enjoy at least one haute cuisine dining experience in each country she traveled to as well as the Medieval city of Mittelbergheim, a picturesque village in the Alsace-Lorraine region of France where Bette had grown up—all in the name of research.

This fluff stuff was turning out to be more fun than she'd thought possible.

But before she left town, she had two items of business to attend to—one on the other side of the estate, one on the other side of the globe. Isabelle looked at her watch and decided to ring Gloria up first.

Her cell phone rang before she could flick it open.

"Hello?"

"Hi, Isabelle. Ronald again."

Uh oh. "Ronald." Twice in two days. This couldn't be good.

He laughed. "Don't sound so thrilled to hear from me."

"Of course I'm happy to hear from you. Again."

"Have you been able to line up the interviews we talked about?"

"I asked the travel agent to fax you a copy of my itinerary. I'm off to meet the Cadbury Bunny first thing tomorrow morning."

"Gawd. The one who lays eggs? I hope you're kidding."

"Chocolate eggs."

"That's even worse."

"You're the one who wanted fluff, Ronald. Easter bunnies are cute and cuddly. They have fluffy tails. Hey, I think I'll visit Beatrice Potter's house while I'm down south. Nothing like the mention of Peter Rabbit's house and a few photos of Mr. MacGregor's garden to endear me to readers of travel sections everywhere."

"Okay, smarty. You can cut the crap. I get the picture."

"I'll cut the crap if you cut the suspense. Did you call to check up on me or fire me?"

"Neither. Sheila has another idea she wants me to run by you. It's a little more adult in nature than the Easter bunny."

She let this latest tidbit sink in. "Adult as in grown-ups who find multi-layered meaning in *The Velveteen Rabbit* or adult as in the *Playboy* bunny?"

"*Playboy*. Sheila wants you to write an article on Europe's nude beaches."

"You're kidding."

"Serious as a heart attack."

"I hope she doesn't expect me to visit one."

"That's why I called. Since you're going south to Switzerland, it makes perfect sense for you to swing by the French Riviera before you come home. You may want to take some notes on this next part, Isabelle. Sheila said to tell you she wants a few suggestive but G-rated photos we can use in the newspaper draft—lots of leg, shoulders, backs, maybe a beach ball to cover—"

"Okay. You can stop right there." She was speechless for a moment. "I thought Sheila wanted fluff. Nude beaches aren't fluff. What they typically are—from my understanding—is flabby, fat people and pretentious perfect people and... and... She can't make me go, can she?"

Ron sighed. "Remember the buzzards, darlin'. You're in no position to bargain."

She gulped. "So all I have to do is go there and take a few beach ball photos?"

"For the most part, yes. Sheila is hoping to sell a racier version of the article to an adult publication, so you'll need to take a few full frontal shots as well. And make sure you get releases. Gloria says it's imperative you get full names and addresses from both the subjects and witnesses."

"So Gloria's in on this, too."

"It's not like it was her idea. Anything sensitive has to be run by legal before it gets the final go-ahead."

She sighed. "I'd be willing to spring for a telephoto lens out of my own pocket."

"And get names and releases how? Use models instead of real people if you'd rather."

"Either way, I'll have to talk to naked people."

"You know how the game is played, Isabelle. Do whatever you need to do to get the story."

"It's pure sensationalism. You know how I feel about that."

"It's not. It's strategy. Think of it as a battle. There are millions of tourist dollars at stake. We all want to win. New England wants the tourists, and their money. So does Canada. So does the Rocky Mountain Tourist Association. So does the Texas Hill Country Commission on Tourism. So does Upper Michigan. So does Iowa. So does everybody. To win the war, we have to have an edge. Something we can offer that the competition can't. Your little trip has been underwritten by the tourist boards of several European countries. There are lots of parties being thrown. We have to give the tourist a reason to come to ours."

It took a minute for her to process what he was saying. "Iowa? Europe is competing with Iowa?"

"Sure. Thousands of Midwesterners travel to Europe every year. It's where their roots are. Iowa's marketing director knows it. They also know people don't have a lot of spare cash right now and they're afraid to fly. Iowa's ad campaign for the summer? *Europe Without a Passport.*"

"I'm ashamed to admit I don't know enough about Iowa to get your point."

"They've got the Dutch and their tulips in Pella, a Danish settlement with a windmill in Elk Horn, Anton Dvorak connections in a Bohemian village called Spillville, and German settlements like Schleswig and Holstein," Ronald said. "But there's one thing they don't have."

"I can think of a million things they don't have. Pubs, for one. I'll bet there's no Blue Bell in Iowa."

"There's a Victorian bed and breakfast called the Blue Belle Inn. Google it if you don't believe me. And Iowa has diners—with Maid Rites. Diners are hot right now. They have cute little sheep and big-eyed cows grazing in picturesque pastures. They have half-timbered buildings, country churches, round barns, Indian forts, Lewis and Clark sites..."

"Okay. Let me guess. Iowa has no nude beaches."

"Smart girl."

She sighed. Huffed was more like it. "Fine. I'll do the article. But this had better be enough to exonerate me. I don't want buzzards hanging over my head the whole six months I'm here."

"Agreed."

"And I want some meat. I can get some of what I need over the internet, but it would be nice if research could do some digging on the Spanish galleon in Tobermory Bay—previous attempts to locate it, advances in sonar technology, who the major players are and where their funding comes from."

"Done. Do you want research to see what they can dig up on the castle as well? Assuming you still want both stories."

"I would be interested in knowing some background on historic renovations in general. The United Kingdom's equivalent to America's National Register of Historic Places is the Historic Trust, but I'm not sure if individuals are bound to follow specific protocols and building specifications when dealing with buildings of a certain age. The contractor who's working on the keep is American. A guy by the name of Michael St. Dawndalyn. I've gotten to know him fairly well. He might be able to help me out on this end."

"I'll get legal started on it right away. And Isabelle?"

"Yes?"

"It's good to hear you sounding like yourself again."

"Remember you said that, Ronald, because when I'm done writing about chocolate and Peter Rabbit and Playboy bunnies on the beach, I really want to do an article about William and Kate and the debate over royal succession, and the ever widening cracks in the European Union, and how European cultural, religious and educational trends are different than ours in America. There are so many great stories about Europe just waiting to be written."

"Great ideas, Isabelle. We'll talk again soon, about happier subjects. I promise."

She said goodbye and ended the call. Surprisingly enough, in light of the whole episode with her underwear drawer, she did feel somewhat normal—at least for the moment. That was the reason she'd wanted to call Gloria—to apologize for being such a namby-pamby about Ben. It had been three months, and she hadn't heard or seen a thing of him in all that time. It probably was time to unfreeze her bank accounts, quit checking her credit report every week, and stop jumping every time she saw her shadow.

Gloria had come damn near to being a saint through the whole thing. Isabelle owed her a big thank you. Isabelle knew in her heart she wasn't totally over the trauma of her ordeal—not by a long shot—but even a friend as good as Gloria had her limits. It was time to buck up and move on. Any residual trauma would have to be dealt with internally, or, if she got desperate, perhaps in some anonymous online support group. If she kept letting her friends see inside her heart, they'd end up thinking she really was ready for a trip to the loony bin, or worse yet, hating her, or just not talking to her at all. And she couldn't blame them.

She probably owed Michael an apology, too. She hadn't known him for very long, but recently, he had been the one to bear the brunt of her occasional tendency towards hysteria. It would be easy to convince Gloria she was all better. Michael had seen her bra straps and bikini underwear sticking helter-skelter out of her backpack less than twenty-four hours ago. Michael knew there were moments when she still clung to the edge of rational thought by a mere thread.

\#

Michael looked over the top of his reading glasses just in time to see a deer sprinting across the picture window opposite his bed. He liked to think of his bedroom as his own private box at the theater where the long, flowing drapes on either side of his stage framed a panoply of rolling moorlands where grouse, golden eagles, and red deer pattered about in a constantly unfolding drama.

He reached back to bolster the pillows propped behind his back and pushed his quilt down around his waist. He had just re-immersed himself in the bizarre world of Stephanie Plum and her Grandma

Mazur when his cell phone jingled cheerily. Strange that the things that went on in Evanovich's New Jersey burg could seem more foreign to him than Scotland did.

"Happy Birthday, dear!"

"Mom! What a surprise."

"I wanted to catch you before you went off to work. Oh, sweetheart, it's so good to hear your voice!"

"You're not calling from home, are you? Buck said he warned you the opposing council may try to subpoena your phone records."

"I bought a phone card at Home Depot. And I'm calling from Myrtle's house just to be on the safe side. Myrtle's not one to gossip."

"That's true. I trust Myrtle implicitly," Michael said. "You know, Mom, for an old broad, you're not too bad at covert operations."

"It's not like I just fell off the turnip truck. I've got a few brain cells left."

"Don't kid yourself. You've got more smarts than most women a third your age. And your motherly instincts to boot."

"So how are you, dear? I miss you terribly. I hope you have something special planned for your birthday with your friends."

"Just business as usual, I'm afraid. I miss you, too."

"If you were here, I'd have Charles' driver pick up a half-dozen, still-warm Krispie Kremes and deliver them to you."

"You know me too well. I've had enough scones to last a lifetime. And what I'd give for two slabs of Wonder Bread slathered with Skippy's Super Chunk peanut butter. Hard rolls and hot cross buns served without butter lost their charm several months ago."

"You'll be wasted away to nothing by the time you get home. That haggis sounds just horrible."

"I manage to find plenty of good things to eat. I just miss a few of my favorite things. Not as much as I miss my favorite people though. How's my baby sister doing? I haven't talked to Barbara and the kids for months. I miss Tori so much I can hardly stand it." Before he'd come to Scotland, he'd taken care of his little niece every Wednesday afternoon while his sister, Barbara, volunteered at the hospice.

"They're all fine. They miss you, too, Michael. Tori still loves her storybooks. I took her out to your place last week when I went to check on things and she had a hi-o time in the old tire swing that hangs from the oak tree down by the creek."

"I had forgotten it was there. You're sure the ropes are sturdy enough to hold her?"

"Sat in it myself to make sure it was strong enough. She said your name the other day when we were looking at some photos from Christmas. It sounds like two words when she says it—kind of like *my-key*, but I know what she means. You'll always have a special place in her heart, Michael."

"What I wouldn't give to have one of her ooh-tight hugs."

"But other than that, you're doing well?"

His mother sounded concerned, and he didn't want her to worry, so he bucked up and made sure his voice sounded strong and confident. "I'm doing great."

"Grandpa would be so proud of you if he could see what you're up to. You and your stones. You always did love playing with rocks."

"I like to think I'm doing right by him."

"I just wish you could find a way to put all this nasty legal business behind you so you could come home."

"Me, too. But don't get your hopes up, Mom. I really thought both lawsuits would be dropped by now."

"Maybe if you talked to them one more time—I met Dr. Masterson at a fund raiser last week and he seemed like such a nice man."

"A lot of people seem really nice, Mom. You know that. Especially when they're at a political rally, on their best behavior." The implications of what his mother had said started to sink in as he spoke. "Charles didn't accept any campaign contributions from Dr. Masterson, did he?"

"You know I don't get involved in any of Charles' financial affairs, darling. Politics either, for that matter. I'm merely window dressing when it comes to our public life."

"That's not true, Mom. You're a wonderful hostess—you coordinate the menus, hand-pick the recipes, supervise the staff and the caterers, and charm everyone who attends with your gracious smile. Charles is lucky to have you."

"And I, him."

He ran his fingers through his hair, restraining the urge to yank on a handful of the longer strands. "I know you love Charles, Mom.

And God knows you certainly deserve to have a man in your life after losing Dad when you were so young, but you'll have to forgive me when I say I'd like to strangle the man once in a while. I'd bet money Masterson is a registered Republican. He's either using Charles to get to me or trying to put Buck in a compromising position. He damn near has my license. If you don't watch your backs, he'll have Buck disbarred, and Charles ousted from the Senate before this is through."

"My feathers would be ruffled if someone was trying to take my children away from me, too."

A shaft of sunlight speared the windowpane directly across from Michael and hit him square in the face. He blinked. "Please don't defend him, Mom. You know I can't go into any detail, but you have to know Dr. Masterson is not fighting for his kids because he loves them too much to let them go. This man is all about power. Power over his wife. Power over his offspring. Power over his adversaries."

"You make him sound so cold. He's a doctor."

"He's a surgeon—with a lousy bedside manner from what I'm told. Just promise me you'll be careful, okay? Nothing about this case is what it seems."

Chapter Nine

Michael couldn't have asked for a nicer birthday. The air was just warm enough to go shirtless, providing you were working in the sun and working hard, the sun just hot enough to make you sweat, the breeze just brisk enough to keep you dry. It wasn't even noon and they'd already raised the north wall of the keep by over a foot. The batch of mortar they'd just stirred up was the perfect consistency— not too sloppy, not too dry, not too grainy, not too smooth. The day had the potential to be perfect.

He shielded his eyes and looked out at the sea. Its intense blue calm was mesmerizing; its glistening, sunlit peaks and swells, hypnotic. With considerable regret, he turned his back to the water, stuck his hands in his pockets and waited for the results of his latest evaluation.

The building inspector pushed his glasses up on his nose and scribbled on a pad of paper. "Everything appears to be in order, Mr. St. Dawndalyn, except for the matter of your credentials, which remain notably absent."

"I'm sorry, about that, sir. I'll contact my secretary back in Oconomowoc and try to find out what the hold-up is." With any luck, the examiner would find Oconomowoc's pronunciation and spelling as daunting as the average American did. If any resulting confusion precluded an attempt to verify his qualifications, all the better.

The inspector handed Michael a pen. "My fax number is on the back of this inspection form. Please see to the matter post haste, Mr. St. Dawndalyn, or I shall have to file a report with the governing board of regents."

"I will certainly expedite matters to the best of my ability, Mr. MacClellan. Thank you for your continued patience. With things in such an uproar in America right now, I'm sure my request has probably been stashed on the bottom of a very deep pile of things to be attended to." It was a lame excuse and he knew it, but he was grasping at straws. There were no credentials. Hell, he didn't even have a secretary anymore.

"I'll be expecting your fax within the week."

Michael nodded. He saw the inspector glance past him, and looked over his shoulder to see who or what had caught the man's eye.

"Morgan." Michael loosened his collar. There went his perfect day. He'd seriously considered firing the man after what had happened out at Isabelle's, but he had no proof Morgan had anything to do with the break-in. After giving it some thought, he'd decided it was better to have Morgan close-by where he could keep an eye on him. "Is there something I can do for you?"

Morgan removed his hat and clutched it with both hands. "Ah, sir, I thought I should let ye know that a part of the north wall has collapsed. A man's been injured."

Michael took off running at full throttle. Morgan and Mr. MacClellan followed, but were soon left behind in a cloud of dust.

Michael burst around the corner in a rush of adrenalin, his heart pumping frantically.

Rory Anderson sat on a stump with his boot pulled off, rubbing his big toe. The other men were going about their business.

"Rory! Are you okay" Michael skidded to a halt and his work boots peeled back a foot of sod. He could feel the sweat breaking out on his forehead.

Rory looked puzzled. "I'm awrite. Dropped a fair sized boulder square on my toe. Nothing I haven't done aboot a hundred times before. I'll live."

Morgan and MacClellan burst around the corner, wheezing so loudly they sounded like a pair of novice bagpipe players.

One of the men on the scaffold pointed in their direction. The men working on ground level began to gather around in a semi-circle, their hands still gripping trowels heaped with mortar, rocks and finishing tools.

"Is this what you're in a snit about, Morgan?" Michael asked. He turned to Rory. "Are you sure you're okay? Morgan said part of the wall had given way."

"Well, I guess a part of it did," Rory held up the rock that had fallen on his foot. "I'm awrite. I dinnae know what all the fuss is aboot."

"A grim foreshadowing of what could have happened." Morgan

said loudly enough for the whole assemblage to hear. "The higher this wall gets, the more danger we're all in, I tell ye. We should be provided with protective gear. We should be working in construction cages. We need power hoists, air winches, and forklifts. These are not the middle ages, and ye're not working with a horde of expendable serfs. These men have wives and families."

A few of the men shifted their feet uncomfortably. The inspector's eyes grew big. His already rotund face puffed up until it looked like his collar would choke him.

Michael clenched his fists. "The scaffolding has worked fine so far," he said calmly. "We've had only one minor accident in the four months since we began work on the keep."

Logan stepped forward to stand beside Michael. He planted his feet squarely in the dirt and brushed a smattering of sweat off his neck. He turned to Morgan. "It appears to me it's a bit too late for you to be worrying aboot safety gear, old man. Looks like ye've already taken a rock in the head, or maybe several."

Nervous laughter erupted from several of the men. The scaffolds were bare. The entire crew clustered around them.

Michael put his hand up and stepped between Logan and Morgan. "With the exception of the accident that resulted in Donald's broken foot, which I've taken care of, and an occasional stubbed toe, we've had no recurring problems or safety worries to date, Morgan, why such concern all of the sudden?"

"Someone has to think of your men," Morgan yelled, turning to face the crowd. "Ye've had one maimed already, and now a second. If it's true he runs such a safe show, I for one would like to see some proof—have the inspector examine the safety records from the last few projects St. Dawndalyn's worked on."

For a moment, no one said a word.

"My mum tells me every night that my head is as hard as a rock," a shirtless young man he'd just hired said. "I'm not worried aboot safety gear."

A round of laughter circled the ring.

"A lot of heavy equipment would accomplish nothing but to tear up the brae and disturb the wildlife."

"If our fore-folk could build a keep that stood over three hundred years without the help of modern gadgetry, I say we can too!"

The inspector cleared his throat. "As long as a complaint has been made, I am compelled to conduct an investigation. St. Dawndalyn, since ye'll have your secretary on yer mobile anyhoo, you should not mind obtaining the safety certificates, or whatever the American equivalent might be, from your last two or three jobs."

Michael's jaw dropped.

"It should nae be a problem unless ye've got something to hide." Morgan taunted him.

Michael faced the inspector. "Sir, we're as concerned about safety in Wisconsin as you are, but I don't know if such documentation exists. If it does, I have no idea where it might be or how to get my hands on a copy."

"No need to fly-up." MacClellan said. "Do what ye can. Atween now and then, I've amind to be keeping a close watch on things anyhoo."

"Of course. Stop by any time." Michael turned to the crew. "Let's get back to work. If we can get another six inches on the wall before day's end, we'll be at the right height to frame the first of the arrow loops tomorrow morning."

He turned and tried to usher MacClellan towards the gate—preferably before Morgan had a chance to cause any more trouble. He would have words with Morgan Baugh once the inspector was gone and the rest of the men were back at work.

"I'll need your signature here and here." MacClellan pointed to a series of Xs he had marked on the inspection form.

He was scrawling his name beside the last of the marks when Isabelle appeared over the crest of the hill. Hmm. Maybe there was hope of this being a respectable birthday after all.

She smiled and waved. A surge of heat welled up from his belly—or somewhere in the vicinity.

The inspector cleared his throat. "Good day, Mr. St. Dawndalyn."

Michael nodded. "The same to you, sir. Again, I apologize about the fracas with Morgan."

"No harm done."

Well, that was yet to be seen.

"If I may give ye a word of advice, son. It seems as though ye've got a man with a bone to pick. Whilst I keep an eye on you, it would appear ye need to keep an eye on that one. Incidents like this are often a precursor to something more problematic simmering under the surface."

"I'll heed your advice, sir."

MacClellan's jowls jiggled as Michael shook his hand.

Isabelle lingered a few feet away until Michael was alone.

"Sounds like there was an incident of some sort." Her eyes were filled with concern but it didn't dim her smile.

Michael's eyes darkened. "I should have mentioned this the other night, but I didn't want to scare you, so I resolved to keep a watch out myself and spare you the grief."

"You're forgetting that I didn't ask for help and that I don't want to be rescued," she said, her face all sweetness and her voice hard as cement. "That extends to problems of any variety, not just storms."

"Touché." Guess he could forget about his little damsel in distress fantasy once and for all then. "Today's incident involved Morgan Baugh. I also caught him snooping around Dunara the other night when you thought someone had been inside the cottage."

He paused and gave her a moment to absorb what he had said. "I don't know if you've ever met him or not. He's often at the Bell. I've seen him in the company of a tall gent who wears a long, dark coat and a distinctive plaid scarf tied around his neck."

Her face etched over with concern. "As a matter of fact, he introduced himself to me one night while I was waiting for my food. Do you think he was the one who went through my things?"

"I have nothing to back up my suspicions or I would have told you before." Michael laid his arm across her shoulders and walked alongside her. "By the way—this is not a protective gesture. I just wanted to touch you and it seemed like the only appropriate way considering the general lack of privacy."

She left his arm where it was. "What did Morgan have to say for himself when you ran into him at Dunara?"

"That he was doing some bird watching—following a buzzard that supposedly swooped over your cottage."

"The buzzard connection seems appropriate enough—he rather looks like one. But the bird watcher part of the story doesn't ring true if you ask me."

"It didn't seem likely to me either. I'm not trying to scare you, Isabelle. I just think you should keep your eyes on him." He lowered his voice as they approached the castle. "After today, I'm more convinced than ever Morgan Baugh is trouble."

Chapter Ten

Michael looked at Isabelle apologetically. "I should probably find out where Morgan's gone and tend to some damage control after the ruckus he caused."

The sounds of rock meeting rock, metal scraping stone, cement mixers churning, and mortar slapping against iron went as unnoticed as background music at a restaurant.

"If you've got time for a quick picnic first, I've got egg salad sandwiches and fresh strawberry pie for two packed in my basket."

"My mom used to make egg salad sandwiches for me and my Dad when I was little."

She blushed.

He tried to wipe the pained expression off his face. Forget holding her at arm's length. Forget subtlety. Whether or not she would admit it, she needed protecting, and he needed—egg salad sandwiches and fresh strawberry pie. "Let me take the basket. It looks heavy."

"Thanks." Her eyes darted away from him and scanned the horizon.

Michael turned. "What is it you see?"

"Nothing really. Just a feeling. I'm just a little jumpy knowing this Morgan's nearby."

"I'll watch your back—if you'll let me."

"Thank you, but I'm leaving for Switzerland and the French Riviera later today." Her eyes drifted in the direction of Dunara Cottage. "That's why I came by. I hate to bother Bette with Hans still away, but I probably should have someone keep an eye on things while I'm gone."

The sun slanted to catch them in its rays. Their shadows moved in lumpy synchronization on the stone wall behind them as they slowly meandered its length.

"Actually, Hans got back yesterday, but if you trust me to take care of things, I'd be happy to keep watch for you." He watched as a smile slid across her face.

"Normally I wouldn't worry about it. I'll have my cameras and anything else of value with me. But just knowing someone was in the cottage..."

He took her elbow and steered her around a boulder jutting out of the moss. "You know, I think a little vacation will do you good. You've been walking on eggs for weeks."

"Unfortunately, this isn't a vacation. But the good news is I'm going to be eating eggs instead of walking on them—Cadbury Creme Eggs." She grinned and raised her eyebrows.

"Can I come, too?" Michael teased. "Traveling alone sounds very dangerous to me."

He saw her shiver as though she had suddenly taken a chill.

"I'll be on guard." Her eyes panned to the north, and then to the south. "With someone like Morgan, it's almost easy."

"Easy?"

"Morgan gives me the creeps. Every hair on my body stands on end when he's around. I don't know how else to describe it except I get the heebie-jeebies every time he walks by. You know what I mean?"

"Obviously not." He grimaced. "If I'd had your sixth sense, I wouldn't have hired him in the first place."

"Trust me. It's a lot easier when the villains come dressed like wolves. It's the ones who appear to be nice, harmless, and respectable who are truly scary."

Michael felt a flash of guilt. He hadn't been entirely honest with her, granted, but that hardly put him in the same ballpark as Morgan, did it? His lies of omission had nothing to do with Isabelle. "I wouldn't get too hung up on Morgan. Granted, he's got an extremely bad attitude, but I can't see it going any further than that. Both the inspector and Bette said there have been other break-ins in the cottages in years past. With so many tourists coming and going this time of year and different couples in the B&B almost every night, it could have been anyone."

"I'll probably never know for sure. I can't think of any motivation Morgan would have to do such a thing. It was probably a random occurrence."

"I'm sure you're right." Michael let his fingers rub against her back where his hand rested. "The door to the cottage is old, and a little warped from the sea air. Most likely the latch didn't catch when you left and someone was just being nosey."

"I'm sure you're right."

"No lingering worry this is connected to Ben?"

"I'm sure. Deep down, I know there's no way Ben would follow me here or anywhere else. He used me. He got what he wanted. Now he's off using my money to woo some other woman. I'm sure I'll never see or hear from him again."

Michael pulled her a little closer. "That's what your head is telling you."

"I guess there's no sense pretending my heart is following suit— at least not quite yet."

"Maybe it's a good thing you're still scared of men like Ben. Keep your guard up. You're still pretty fragile inside."

"Be afraid of men like Ben, but don't be afraid of you."

"I didn't say that."

"You thought it." She looked down.

"Yes, I did. I'm not him. I have no desire to hurt you, and I'm certainly not after your money."

Her lips arced into a smile. "So you admit you're after something."

"We're a motive-driven species. We're all after something."

"So your motive is?"

"To bring you pleasure."

"Oh, really."

The fact that he derived so much satisfaction from watching her blush proved his point. He watched as the pink splotch at her neck crept up to her cheekbones, then spread down the swell of her collarbone to the tops of her breasts.

"Really." He let his eyes roam over her and tried to shove his conflicted emotions back in the box. He cared about Isabelle. That was a given. He hoped to help her. That was who he was. But wanting her... That was far more complex.

"You make me wish I wasn't leaving."

"So don't. What do they have on the mainland we don't have here?"

"The same exact things they don't have in Iowa. Swiss chocolate and nude beaches."

He raised his eyebrows. She was making this entirely too hard.

"It's a long story. Trust me. You don't want to know."

"Does it involve cows?"

"In a roundabout way."

He laughed. "You're right. I don't want to know. Let's move on to the part about nude beaches."

"Ah. Somehow I knew you'd pick up on that one."

"I'm pretty sharp that way. I even know a little French. Are you sure you don't need an escort? Going to a nude beach by oneself sounds a little..."

Her laughter bubbled up and enveloped them like little stars twinkling in the sky at the end of a fireworks display.

"You're welcome to join me if you wish. But don't get your hopes up. I'll be the one with my clothes on."

"That's what you say now. You'll get there and you'll feel more out of place with your clothes on than you do off." He massaged her shoulder with the palm of his hand. The response that rippled through her body went straight to his heart. "You could stay home, buy a box of Tobermory Chocolates at the mercantile and meet me at the Bath after the sun sets. Think of all the money you could save."

She smiled. "Dream on."

"It's my birthday. I'm entitled to a wish."

He regretted the words the instant they left his mouth. What an idiot he was! If he expected his enemies in Wisconsin to remain in the dark about his secret life in Scotland, he should know better than to give out his birth date. Any self-respecting fugitive knew that much. While he was at it, he might as well write down his social security number on a piece of paper and hand it to her with a note that said, "Please investigate me."

"It's your birthday?" She looked up at him and flashed him a smile that could have melted all the chocolate in Switzerland. She tugged on his arm. "Over here." She pulled him several feet to the left until they were hidden behind the south castle wall. "There." She stood on her tip toes to kiss him. "Happy Birthday."

"Hmm." He closed his eyes and savored her taste. "I knew these walls would come in handy for something someday."

She leaned into him with an eager tension that revealed both her uneasiness and her desire. She was hesitant at first, but he could feel her growing confidence, then the wonder pulsing between them. Her lips were moist, smooth, full. He ran his fingers through the curls framing her face.

She pulled back just far enough to take a breath. "Who needs chocolate when I've got you?" Her lips pressed back into his with a grace as tentative and sweet as she was.

He groaned and pressed her close. "Who needs nude beaches when you've got me?"

She laughed. "I have to go. I already faxed a copy of my itinerary to my editor."

"You could say your flight was cancelled due to a bomb threat."

"Just the kind of reassurance my readers need."

He laughed. He wanted her to stay—just as badly as he needed her to go. He pulled her closer. There was no good outcome to this situation. If things continued as they were, he'd be put in the position of telling lies far more damaging than any he'd already been forced to concoct. If he cut her off now, when things finally seemed to have come full circle between them, she would be understandably curious about the cause behind his actions.

It wasn't smart to make an investigative reporter suspicious. *Great.* Now he was past lying and on to manipulation. "I'm sure you'll be fine as long as you keep your eyes open."

She looked up at him, sought his eyes and held them for a moment before she spoke again. "Speaking of eyes being opened..."

"Yes?" His heart started to pound.

"I had a long talk with my editor, Ronald, last night. He impressed upon me in no uncertain terms it's time for me to get past what happened with Ben and start dealing with the here and now."

He would have taken her hand, but he could think of no way to explain the pulsing in his wrist.

"He's right you know. Not that I haven't known I need to move on. My friend Gloria has been trying to get me to see it for weeks."

"Healing takes time. No one can do it for you, much as the people who love you would probably like to."

"I consider Ronald a friend, but the primary motivation for his concern is my worth, or apparent lack of it, to the business. I think what's really helped me is to be able to talk to you about what happened. I'm nothing to you except for the fact we come from the same huge country, yet you took the time to listen. I just wanted to tell you I've appreciated your concern and patience. You've been a great help to me."

"I did my fair share of hindering as well."

"You didn't know."

"I do now." He pulled her close and held her until she stirred.

Even then, he kept one hand on each of her shoulders. The effects of her epiphany were so clear he could see them. The sassy edge was still there, but it was twice as cute on her now that it was being fueled by spunk and not terror.

He hadn't known what he felt for her could be any more intense. "For the first time since I met you, you look relaxed."

"I can't continue to live my life in fear. If I do, I'm letting Ben have the final victory. I'm not willing to do that."

He kissed her on the top of her head. "Your new attitude suits you well."

"Thank you." She exhaled in a slow, contented sigh. "I'd better get going if I'm going to make the ferry."

He jerked his head to the left. "Let's head over to the grassy area on the other side of those rhododendrons. I'll check on the men and grab some pop from the trailer while you unpack our picnic." He took a step back.

"Perfect. I brought an old shawl to sit on and some plates— nothing fancy."

"Great." He took another step backwards. "I'll be back in a few minutes."

She was driving him crazy. He'd been attracted to her when she was skittish and resisting him at every turn. How could he possibly refuse her now that she was right here, oozing charm and flirtatiousness and femininity?

He cursed silently. He should be having lunch with his men, quelling their apprehension and reassuring them all was well.

"See you in a few minutes," she said.

"Yeah." If he could just find the resolve to leave, he could send one of the men who worked for him back up the hill with a message he'd been called into the inspector's office and been unavoidably detained. He wanted nothing more than to be with Isabelle, but he'd made too many mistakes already. He couldn't let this continue. He kissed the top of her hand and disappeared around the corner of the castle.

Chapter Eleven

When Gareth had gone above deck to greet Damon Hermance, sunlight was sparkling on the smooth expanse of water visible in all directions from the boat, and the seas had looked calm—not a ripple broke the surface. The swells rocking the men working below may not have been choppy enough to generate white caps, but the way they tossed the ship from side to side was a graphic reminder of the powerful currents lurking beneath the surface.

"There it is, I tell ye!"

"Make sure it's not another gold colored pocketbook like you found last time."

"Yeah, that was the discovery of the century."

"It was full of credit cards no one had bothered to cancel."

"All expired."

A half dozen men crowded around the monitor. A cheer went up from the crew.

"Look at the shimmer on that baby!"

"I never thought I'd see the day. How many days have we spent crisscrossing this stupid ocean, staring at the bloody resonance magnetometer for hours on end? Hell, I never thought I'd see gold. Gold!"

"It certainly looks promising," Damon said. "Turn her about and mark the precise spot."

The boat surged to port. "Now, you idiot! Cut the engine and drop anchor." Damon cursed.

The lad at the helm grabbed the controls frantically. "I'm doing all I can! We're at the worst possible depth. I think we're too far out to get a fragment with the mechanical arm. We may have all the latest underwater-detection equipment when it comes to side-scanning sonar and echo-sounders, but if the lines are too short to reach the cache, we're still screwed."

"So the equipment on this boat wasn't designed for deep sea recovery. Cry me a river. And then figure out a way to get the damn gold. I pay you to be creative."

"The flag ship was supposed to be in the bay."

"This could have been part of the bay five hundred years ago. A half a millennium is one hell of a long time for waves to roll and sands to shift."

"We'll have to get divers if we need to go any deeper."

"Wait—on that ledge just to starboard. It looks like another piece, a coin, maybe. Can you reach it?"

"Yes, Yes! It's just enough higher that I think I can."

"You've got it!"

"Woo hoo!"

Damon stepped forward to watch their progress. He turned to Gareth. "Are we far enough away from the *Thesis*? The coin could be from her."

"The lab will be able to tell, sir."

"Won't the impressions from the mint be worn down to nothing?"

"The steamer went down in 1889. Coins from that period will be vastly different from anything we find from the 16th century. I'm more concerned aboot drift from the galleon wreck lying off Duart Castle. It dates from around 1640. We're out a lot further than we should be, but with the way the currents sweep, I would be inclined to think nay."

Gareth stood to one side as the younger men gleefully slapped each other on the back. Their chortling echoed off the cramped shell of the inside of the boat in an almost deafening chorus.

Gareth cleared his throat. With Damon on board, a situation that had only occurred once before, Gareth was at somewhat of a loss as to what to do. "If we were in international waters, we could have a vessel made for deep water archeology here by week's end, and probably enough funding to find the rest of the cache to boot. Of course, the gold would still belong to the Scots."

"Scotland. Spain. Neither country would ever see a dime of the money by the time their attorneys got done filing lawsuits and bickering," Damon said.

"But the attorney we consulted aboot the sunken treasure specifically said that—"

"Just because I asked you to find out what you could about the laws doesn't mean I intend to follow them." Damon's face twisted in a sneer and he spoke quietly enough that the rest of the men couldn't hear him. "I've always lived by the rule that says 'If you know what laws you're breaking, you're less likely to get caught.'"

"Yer record certainly proves yer theory, sir." Gareth hated calling him sir.

"You don't get by with murder by thinking like a criminal, Gareth."

"Nae, sir. Of course not."

"Learn to think like an investigator, and you've got the world at your fingertips."

"Leave nae tracks. That's been yer advice from the onset."

"Now you've got the idea, mate." Damon thumped Gareth on the back.

The expression on Damon's face was as menacing a look as Gareth had ever seen. He gulped. "I'm sure the Scots will ne'er know what hit them, sir."

"Nor will the Americans."

"Sonar Technologies?"

"Don't doubt for a minute Sonar will get what's coming to them, but I was referring to our nosey little investigative reporter and her new best friend. Pity St. Dawndalyn had to get involved with the woman. I was suspicious of him to begin with, but in retrospect, I don't believe he has any ties to Sonar."

"Morgan could find naught on him."

"Pity. I've rather grown to like the man." Damon adjusted his collar. "Yes. Misfortune can come wrapped in a variety of packages—some of them very pretty."

Gareth fingered the gold ring on his left hand. "Ye're right aboot the Scots. If we can keep things quiet for a few more months, they'll go on thinking the gold is buried under tons of mud and ne'er be the wiser."

Damon's face twisted into a snide smile. "Losers, weepers."

Gareth chuckled aloud. "Head for shore, lads. The sooner we get the artifact to the lab in Edinburgh, the sooner we'll know exactly what we're working with."

"Speaking of," Damon said, "I've got two weeks' worth of news to catch up on. I want to be briefed on every detail of the operation as soon as we dock."

#

Isabelle used her fingers to smooth the shawl over Bluevale's grassy green lawn, scanned the rise blocking the castle from view, and glanced at her wristwatch for the thirtieth or fortieth time since Michael had left.

Ben had abandoned her just this way. They'd had a nice evening, the thought of which now filled her with revulsion, and settled in for some much needed sleep. When she'd awakened, he was gone. She'd lay in her big oak sleigh bed waiting for him to come back from the bathroom, or his early morning walk, or wherever he'd gone, for almost an hour, basking in the afterglow of what she'd thought was a wonderful night spent together.

She hadn't thought much about it even when she'd discovered his car was gone; hadn't really worried until noon rolled around. He'd said he needed to make some important calls and his cell phone had been acting up the whole time he'd been in Virginia. The town where she lived was known for its poor cell phone reception. She assumed perhaps he'd gotten up early and driven down to Lexington where he could get a better connection.

It wasn't until three or four that she'd grown suspicious enough to check and see if his suitcase was still in the closet in the guest room where she'd made room for his things. When she'd seen her neighbor return home from work late that afternoon, Isabelle had swallowed her pride and asked her if she had seen or heard Ben leave.

Ben had climbed out of her bed and into his car, never to return. Isabelle hadn't even heard the door close on his way out.

"Hey. You look like you're a million miles away. Your talk with your editor didn't make you homesick, did it?"

Her heart started to pound. She hadn't heard him coming.

Michael plopped down on the very edge of the shawl and stretched his legs out on the lawns. He pulled on a shoot of grass, stuck the reed between his teeth and looked out over the field.

She took the sandwiches from their wrappers and laid one on each plate. "I was starting to think you'd had another run in with Morgan."

"Sorry I took so long."

She balanced one plate on her knee and reached across the shawl to set the other near Michael's hand. "Help yourself."

He continued to look away from her.

"So tell me how you used to celebrate your birthday when you lived in Wisconsin," she said. She felt strangely disconnected from the voice that left her body and floated across the air.

Michael took a bite of his sandwich and set two cans of soda in the center of the shawl. He selected one and popped the top.

"My grandfather used to take the day off and take me out on the lake to go fishing. Every year, no matter how busy he was. As I got older, he complained farmers shouldn't be allowed to make babies from late August to early September, because spring was too busy a time to be bothered with birthdays."

"But he took the day off anyway." She smiled. "This is the same Grandfather who got you started laying stones?"

"Yes." He nodded.

"Did the two of you work on any projects together before your Grandfather retired?"

"Dozens of them. I worked for Grandpa every summer. The town where I grew up is full of stone buildings built by my grandfather and great-grandfather—the train depot, town hall, numerous pavilions in area parks, and hundreds of residences."

"And did you stay in town when you started your own construction company or did you spread out to other cities in the area?"

Michael cleared his throat. "The whole concept of building changed in the time period when I was growing up. It's extremely rare to see an entire building built of stone anymore. Partial rock faces on the fronts of homes are the 'in' thing now—a trend that's come and gone several times in the last 20 years. Stone fireplaces, fences and foundations are always popular in some parts of the country."

"It must take a pretty big town to be able to support a stone layer."

Michael tilted his head back and took a swig of pop. "To find work, today's stone layers have to be skilled in working with brick, lime rock, and river rock, and be willing to take any kind of masonry work available to them, even if it means traveling the length of an entire region."

"What was the last big project you worked on before coming to

Scotland?" She dished up two pieces of pie filled with lush red berries, spooned a dollop of whipped cream on top of each piece, and topped them off with two sprigs of fresh mint she'd found growing outside the door at Dunara.

"Are you always this curious or am I being interviewed?"

His voice sounded teasing, but there was an edginess underlying his remark that she couldn't ignore. Or was she imagining that, too?

He frowned. "You really don't want to know all the boring details of my life, do you?"

"Sure I do." She wanted to know everything about him, to peel back the layers until she could see the heart and soul of the man. Because she cared. And because she needed to know all there was to know, because of Ben.

Michael crossed his legs and leaned back. "Have I mentioned how beautiful you look when your brow isn't creased into a million little worry lines?"

"Fine. Be evasive. Lucky for you, I need to dash if I'm going to have time to run these things back to the cottage and still make it to the ferry." She took his plates, yanked on her shawl until the fringes trapped under him gave way, and glanced around to make sure she hadn't forgotten anything.

"No need to leave in a huff."

"I'm not feeling the least bit huffy. Are you?"

"No. Not at all." He stood and put his hands in his pockets. "The pie was great."

"If I'd known it was your birthday I would have packed a candle."

"You really do seem—"

"Well, I'm not. Just in a hurry."

"Can I help carry something?"

"No. Got it."

"Have a wonderful time in Switzerland."

"I'm sure I will."

"Don't eat too much chocolate."

"What's that supposed to mean?"

"Nothing. I just don't want you to have any reason to feel bashful once you get to the French Riviera."

"Bashful?"

He shuffled his feet and shifted his head. "You know what I mean."

"No. I'm afraid I don't. First of all, I'm not taking my clothes off. Second, it sounds very much like you think all it's going to take to put me over the top on the weight scale is to eat a little too much chocolate. Which means you think I'm bordering on fat."

"Who said anything about fat?"

"You did. What other reason could there be to watch how much chocolate I eat?"

"Maybe I'm worried you'll get a tummy ache and have to spend your whole time in France in your hotel room instead of the beach."

"I don't have a hotel room. I have a cabin on the beach."

"You're absolutely sure you're comfortable traveling alone?" He looked so hopeful.

"Will you stop it! How can you possibly be so sensitive one moment and so infuriating the next?" She pulled away from him and stooped to rummage through her backpack, then handed him a copy of her itinerary. "This is where I'll be in case there's any problem with the cottage while I'm gone."

"Okay."

"You might want to let Bette and Hans know you have it. Hans has the only extra key to the cottage," she said.

He wanted to send her off with another kiss so as to leave no doubt in her mind he was far more sensitive than he was infuriating, but he didn't. He was playing with fire and he knew it. This had to stop and it had to stop now.

#

"Persnickety bitch." Morgan muttered under his breath. He crouched low and moved stealthily along the inside of the castle wall. "The lassie thinks she's got the heebie-jeebies now, just wait 'til I'm finished with her. I'll give her the creeps."

He reached deep into his pocket and fingered the keys to Dunara Cottage. His fingers closed in on the smooth, well-worn surface of the key Gareth had given him two weeks earlier, and then, the sharp, newly cut copy he'd had made the day before. He'd even taken the ferry across and gone to a locksmith on the mainland so as not to arouse suspicion.

He'd look after her things while she was gone awrite. That idiot St. Dawndalyn would never know he'd been there. But Isabelle would know. She'd know the second she walked in the door.

He would have to be patient. That, or rework his plan altogether. He hadn't counted on her going away. He smiled broadly, felt a gnat fly into his mouth, and reached up to pick the bug from his teeth with a fingernail. He quivered in anticipation as he thought over his plan, making mental modifications as he thought through every contingency.

He loved his job. Not only would he fulfill Damon's wishes to the letter, he'd satisfy a few urges of his own. He had everything planned out perfectly.

He put his left hand into his other pocket and fondled the springy curl of pubic hair he'd found when he'd been in her cottage, in her dirty clothes hamper, stuck in the elastic leg band of her privies. He'd already used it once. Just laying it on his nuddy belly and looking at it while he'd gone aboot the five knuckle shuffle had given his naughty bits the best buzz they'd had in a long time.

He'd make her hair stand on end awrite. Every curly red wisp of it.

Chapter Twelve

Michael gripped his cell phone and paced the floor in front of his bed. He saw, but was mentally oblivious to the pair of squirrels frolicking on the other side of the windowpane. He'd been on hold for almost five minutes. Buck's secretary hadn't seemed impressed by the fact he was calling from Europe, but then, everyone who worked for Buck or his father appeared to think money grew on trees.

"Well, if it isn't my favorite step-brother," Buck finally drawled.

The twerp even spoke slowly. Not that he had come to expect any less when Buck was on the clock, and Michael was footing the bill.

"I'm your only step-brother, and I'm calling because I need a document. Something official looking from the State of Wisconsin, if possible."

"Have you lost your mind?" Buck said.

"Not yet. Now get your pen. I need a letter on some sort of government letterhead stating 'the state of Wisconsin has been reorganized from eight regions to four due to budget cutbacks.' Something to the effect that 'multiple offices were closed, things are in a general state of disorganization, some files were misfiled, others lost altogether,' yada, yada, yada."

He could hear Buck's pen rapping on the edge of something. The desk? His wireless headset? Was it possible the man could write with one hand and rap with the other?

"Are you getting this?" Michael demanded. "Finish it off with 'however misfortunate it may be, they regret they are unable to comply with the request that they forward safety records pertaining to Michael St. Dawndalyn, AAMFT, ABPB, MPA, APS.'"

There was silence on the other end of the line.

"Did you get all that?" Michael asked again. "I'm assuming you have my credentials on file. If not, I can repeat the acronyms. It's very important each of my affiliations be listed, in the precise order I just gave them."

"Oh I've got them all, alright. In fact, I've added one more set behind the American Psychological Society—OYDR. Off Your Damn Rocker."

The stunned silence ringing in Michael's ears nearly drowned out the clatter of birds whipping over the cottage. "Up Your Ass, Buck. That's UYA in case you didn't get it the first time."

"Michael, listen to me very carefully. To date, the only thing you've done that is actually illegal, at least in the United States, is to show contempt for the court. While people can and often do go to jail for this offense, the charges are usually dropped when the case is resolved."

"Which may never happen as long as you're representing me."

"I'll ignore that for the moment," Buck said. "Damn it, Michael. What you're asking me to do is to falsify records. Number one, it's a highly punishable criminal offense in and of itself, even more so when you're dealing with the government. Number two, I'm your attorney. I will do nothing illegal. I will defend you to the best of my ability if you persist in doing illegal things, but I will not, and cannot knowingly break the law myself."

"I've seen you look the other way dozens of times when your father has shredded one set of documents and manufactured others in the name of politics. Why is it okay for him to twist the truth to suit his purposes and not me?"

"My father is his own keeper. So are you. You can do exactly what you wish, Michael, and I won't say a word. Just don't ask me to do it for you."

"I would if I had a piece of letterhead to copy. But I can't. I'm half a world away in case you've forgotten."

He hardly heard what Buck said next, except for one line, and it was a zinger, considering the source.

"What you do is between you and your conscience."

"What did you say?"

"What you do is between you and your conscience."

Had he been less flustered, it would have floored him to think Buck, whose ethics had always been in question, was giving him a lesson on morality. But he was on the clock, and he really didn't need to go into that now.

"Okay. Let's think this through," Michael said. "What if you write a letter on stationery from your law firm, stating, 'at the request of your client, Michael St. Dawndalyn, AAMFT, ABP—'"

"Enough already. I've got it."

"Fine. Anyway, 'upon St. Dawndalyn's request that you provide the Scottish Inspections Agency with safety records filed from the period immediately preceding your client's relocation to Scotland, you conducted an extensive search and no such reports were found.' No part of that would be a lie, would it?"

"I'll search my little heart out as long as you don't ask me to bring the government into it. We both know I'll come up empty handed."

Unfortunately, a little heart was exactly what Buck had. Michael could already see the list of charges on his next bill—*Time Spent Searching for Nonexistent Safety Records I Knew Didn't Exist Before I Started Searching:* 3 hours, $900.00.

"Exactly," Michael said. "Just say 'it's unclear whether such records ever existed or if they are routinely disposed of at the completion of a project.'"

"Don't push it," Buck said. The rapping intensified twofold. "I guess I don't see a problem with this approach."

"Great," Michael's brain felt like it was on overdrive. "You might also mention you 'checked the courts for any grievances, complaints, lawsuits, or liens that might have been filed in conjunction with my company and found none.'"

"If only that were true," Buck said. "You and your company have lawsuits up the wazoo."

"My construction company doesn't."

"You don't have a construction company!"

"As a matter of fact, I do," Michael said calmly. "And a highly respected one at that, fledgling company that it is. All I'm trying to do is to keep it that way without getting myself into more trouble than I'm already in. So what's the verdict? Will you mail the letter or not?"

"Tell me this. Have you had a safety problem upon which this letter will have some legal bearing, or is it a routine matter that will get filed away in some bureaucrat's file cabinet?"

"I have no safety problems. I do have one employee who's out to make trouble and one inspector who sees the situation for what it is but wants to play by the books. I can't push MacClellan any further. His patience is already wearing thin because he hasn't received my credentials."

"And never will," Buck interrupted.

"I can't keep making the same excuses over and over again every time he asks me for something. He has to think I'm making an effort to comply with his wishes and I'm as frustrated as he is that my other paperwork hasn't shown up."

"Fine. I'll mail the letter," Buck said. "But if I were you, I'd be wearing my safety goggles religiously. In my opinion, sooner or later, this is all going to blow up in your face."

Michael sighed. "Thank God you're usually wrong." His bravado faded as his thoughts went to Isabelle. "There's more at stake here than you know, Buck. All I can say is I hope your track record remains unblemished."

"Thanks for the vote of confidence." Buck snorted. "Your trust in me is particularly well-timed given the latest development in the Masterson case."

Michael put his free hand to his forehead, closed his eyes and rubbed his temples. "Mom already told me he showed up at Charles' latest fund raising event, if that's what you're alluding to. All I can say is, watch your back. I could swear the man is a Republican, so you know there's an ulterior motive if he's suddenly contributing to a Democrat's campaign fund."

Buck's pen stopped rapping. "I hadn't heard. I hope my father was smart enough to turn him down."

"If there's any doubt I'd talk to him at your earliest opportunity." Michael's brain raced ahead. "If you didn't know about the fund raiser, what recent development were you talking about? Or don't I want to know?"

"I'm sure you'd rather not." Buck sighed. The rapping started again. "This whole thing is turning into one gargantuan disaster."

#

Isabelle settled back into a feather-filled sofa cushion and looked around her room at the Fairy Falls Hotel. The charming little inn was everything Dunara Cottage and Scotland weren't. Windows sporting pristine yellow and blue chintz drapes with contrasting piping were framed by creamy, lemon-striped walls bordered in daisies and bluebells. A ruffled, marigold skirted table stood in the corner, topped with a porcelain tea cozy and a silver tray piled high with lemon tarts and just-baked biscuits.

The quaint but sparse furniture, whitewashed walls and faded quilt she had grown accustomed to at Dunara were a good complement to the one-sided, wind-beaten trees framing Bluevale Castle, the wild, tempest tossed Atlantic, and the screeching buzzards and sea gulls nesting along the coast. Stow-in-the-Wold's Fairy Falls Hotel stood in complete contrast to everything she held dear in Scotland. The inn was a feast for the eyes—the water flowing through the village a trickling stream that sang lullabies in the night, the robins and starlings outside her door tucked away in flowering bushes and libernum arches.

She could smell the roses that laced their way up and over the walkway leading to her door as she reached for her cell phone and dialed her mother's number. She hadn't called home since she'd phoned to tell her parents she'd arrived in Scotland, so it was high time she did. Tonight there were no distractions—just her, a handful of petit point pillows, a soft-cushioned couch, and a dozen other things that reminded her of Virginia.

It wasn't as though she and her parents had been out of touch. Her mother emailed her on a regular basis. But given Isabelle's discovery that the memory card from her camera was missing, the letters were less a comfort than a reminder Ben had the means to humiliate her and her parents in front of everyone whose opinion of her mattered.

She pushed the thoughts to the back of her head. Her fear that her parents would find out what had happened was the very reason she'd barely spoken to her mother since Ben had disappeared. She could hide the awful truth in cheerful sounding letters typed on a computer screen, whereas nothing much escaped her mother's perceptive ear for trouble.

Isabelle envisioned the pink princess phone that sat at the edge of the walnut nightstand on her mother's side of the bed while she waited for her mother to pick up.

"Hello?" Her mother's southern drawl was as proper at a quarter to six in the morning as it was at high tea every afternoon.

"Hi, Mom. I hope I didn't wake you."

"Isabelle! How nice to hear your voice! Royce! Wake up! It's Isabelle!"

She could hear bedsprings creaking and pictured her mother

rolling over and propping a pillow behind her head.

"I've told you to call any time of the night or day. The alarm was set to go off in fifteen minutes anyway. We're always happy to hear from you! Dear, it's Isabelle. Put your robe on and hurry downstairs so you can listen on the extension. Daddy will be on in a minute, sweetheart. What are you doing up so late? You know how run down you get if you don't go to bed at a decent hour."

This was perfect. If they stuck to topics like this Isabelle would have no trouble fooling her mother. "I'm just fine, Mom. I've been up in Birmingham visiting the Cadbury factory. My assignment is to do an article on chocolate, but I found two other great ideas for stories while I was there—one on rock music and the other on J.R.R. Tolkien."

"From the *Lord of the Rings*?"

"And *The Hobbit*. I found out Tolkien spent much of his boyhood in Birmingham. In fact, many of the images in the trilogy are based on his experiences here and in the Midlands. I'm really excited about writing a story on Middle Earth's English connections. It's a hot topic right now because of the release of the movies.

"And..." She paused for dramatic effect. "It turns out Black Sabbath, ELO, and The Moody Blues are all Birmingham bands. Stevie Winwood is from here, too. I think Ronald is going to love the article I've got planned on Europe's musical connections. Of course I'll include the Beatles and the whole British Invasion phenomenon."

"It's a brilliant idea, sweetheart. Your enthusiasm is contagious, and I don't even like rock and roll."

"If I list concerts and European tour schedules as well as points of interest, the article should be a great draw in a travel section. Ronald might even be able to sell it to one of the bigger music magazines."

"It sounds like you're doing a wonderful job, dear," her father said from the kitchen. "I'm sure your editor will be thrilled. Are you spending the night in Birmingham?"

"No. I drove a ways south so I'd be better positioned to catch the train across the Channel tomorrow. I'm sitting in a B&B near Stow-in-the-Wold, in the Cotswold's. It's totally Laura Ashley. You'd love it, Mom."

"Royce, darling. We must visit Isabelle while she's in Europe. I know I'd adore it there."

"I'm sure you would, sweet pea, but this just isn't a good time to be away from the company with the economy in shambles and our stocks the lowest they've been in years. Tell her, Isabelle." Her father's Scottish accent had softened considerably after years of being surrounded by southerners. The bit of a lilt he'd retained from his boyhood on Prince Edward Island seemed even more pronounced than usual to Isabelle now that she could trace its origins.

Isabelle laughed. "The whole reason I'm here is to lure American tourists to Europe. If I can't even talk you two into visiting me, I'm obviously not doing a very good job."

"See what you've done now, Royce? We can't have Isabelle thinking she's a failure. Of course we'll come, dear. Your father can never say no when we say pretty please with sugar on top."

"Isabelle? A failure?" Her father laughed in the hearty, full-bodied way only he could. "My little girl's never disappointed me, and I'm sure she never will. Anyone says different—well, that's just hogwash."

"You hear that, honey? We're both so very proud of you. I'm sure dozens of people were vying for this assignment. The fact that they choose you is quite an honor."

Okay. So she hadn't told her parents she'd almost been fired, or that she'd begged her editor to let her come to Europe because she was scared half out of her wits and desperate to be so far away from Virginia that Ben would never find her.

Her mother's voice softened a little. "Of course, we hope you don't stay in Europe too long. You know me! Call me old-fashioned, but I still dream you'll come home and find some nice young man to settle down with. You know, you're not getting any younger, dear."

"Now don't start with her, Shirley."

Isabelle's stomach lurched at the thought of her parents seeing photographs of their one and only daughter splayed out naked, being silly and sexy and living out a fantasy she would never have chosen to share with them. What on earth had possessed her to pose for Ben?

"Don't let him fool you, dear. Your father's not quite as eager to be a grandfather as I am a grandmother, but he misses you terribly, just as I do. You know we'll both be delighted to have you home again, whenever that is."

The sad fact was, although her parents loved her dearly, they barely knew her. Not anymore. She was thirty-two, and a successful career woman. In their eyes, she was still, and always would be, their sweet little girl. Isabelle looked at the carefully color coordinated Maxfield Parrish print hanging over her bed. The woman in the picture was half naked. Her parents, like everyone else, accepted it as art. But their daughter half naked would be considered sick. Smut. She felt sure of it.

"Don't let her get to you, honey." Her father spoke in a confidential tone. "Of course we'll be delighted if you bring a young man home someday, but we'll love you just the same, whether or not you ever make us grandparents."

Isabelle sighed. Even parents who dealt with things like their daughters choosing to pursue careers instead of getting married and having babies wouldn't want to know their precious offspring had posed naked for a con man. Even parents who accepted that their children couldn't stay virgins forever certainly wouldn't want to see pornographic photographs of their daughter distributed to every family friend, relative, and business associate in their daughter's computer's address book.

Her mother responded in a soothing voice. "We had such high hopes when you phoned about that nice young man you met at your church. Ben, wasn't it?"

So she'd lied to them about where she'd met Ben. She hadn't dared tell them she was dating someone she'd met on the internet. They never would have understood.

"He certainly sounded like he had a good head for business," her father added. "The banking field can be very lucrative for a man of integrity who has people skills. From what you told us, it sounded like this Ben had a good grasp of the intricacies of the electronic world as well."

Ben had a good grip on electronic banking all right—emptying accounts, charging thousands of dollars on other people's credit cards, intercepting bills, hacking into computers, and dodging the most sophisticated security systems.

"The military has the latest and the best when it comes to cutting-edge technology," her father said. "Anyone with a background in the Special Forces is bound to have had some top level training that would leave them well prepared for a high echelon position in the civilian world."

"It's too bad the timing of this reassignment to Europe came right when things were going so well between the two of you," her mother lamented.

No. No. No! This was not the direction she had wanted the conversation to head. Her mother could detect minute variations of emotion and mood in the voices of people she didn't even know. All Isabelle had to do now was open her mouth and her mother would know something was wrong. Isabelle had to change the subject, and she had to change it now.

"Actually, I've met a man in Scotland whose company I really enjoy," she said. One who's as honest as they come, she thought to herself. "He's from Wisconsin."

"My." Her mother said. "Wisconsin. That's almost as far away as Scotland, isn't it, Royce?"

"Oh, I don't know, Shirley. At least it's on the right side of the Atlantic."

"It's definitely out west. It's on the other side of the Mississippi River, is it not?"

"No, Mom. Wisconsin is east of the Mississippi. You know, just north of Chicago."

"Chicago. Oh. I see." Her mother paused. "Well, what's a boy from Chicago doing in Scotland? And what does his mother think of him being so far away from home?"

Chapter Thirteen

Michael stared out the picture window opposite his bed with his cell phone in his hand. A herd of miniature red deer was grazing in the field adjacent to his house. He looked at them and looked away. His forehead felt drawn and tight, his face frozen and expressionless. "Well, Buck? Are you going to tell me the bad news or do I have to guess?"

"Dr. Masterson has accused you of having an affair with his wife."

Michael's heart thudded in his chest. "That's ridiculous! I would never do such a thing. He'll only hurt his own chance with the judge if he's desperate enough to go around making groundless accusations against me."

"It's not quite that simple, Michael." For the first time, Buck sounded almost sympathetic. "I don't believe for one minute Masterson actually thinks you slept with his wife, but he's evidently got some sort of proof she's been sleeping with someone."

"And I'm the bait he's using to find out who it was."

"You're the perfect patsy. He knows you won't step forward to defend yourself, but I think he believes his wife will want to safeguard your reputation enough to tell him the true identity of her lover."

"I can't defend myself without revealing what I know."

"Exactly. At this point, it's a win / win situation for Masterson. At the very least, it's one more opportunity to defame his wife, which can only make her case weaker, assuming he's got the proof he says he does."

"And if I were to step forward to protect my honor—"

"Masterson's attorney would haul your ass to jail and keep you there until you divulged who she is having an affair with."

"Which is exactly what I've been trying to avoid all along."

"So you do know," Buck said as though suddenly everything was perfectly clear.

116

"Of course I know. I was the woman's therapist for two years. She trusted me with every last detail of her life. That's what people do when they come in for counseling."

Buck changed the tempo of his rapping to randomly spaced, staccato taps. "Having an affair in and of itself isn't sufficient cause to lose your children. There must be more to the story."

Michael had almost ceased to hear the incessant noise. The speed and intensity increased as suddenly as it had slowed. "Trust me, there is."

"Her actions must have endangered the children in some way," Buck said.

"No. She would never do anything to hurt them."

"Then she must be protecting the man she was sleeping with. It must be someone her husband knows. A business associate, perhaps. Or someone who's married."

Silence as deep as the ocean separating them seeped through the room.

Buck was the first to speak. "You're doing all of this to protect someone who's not even your client?"

"I'm protecting my client's confidences."

"Michael, no one expects you to ruin your life to save someone who you don't even know."

"I do know him, and his wife, and his children."

"Tell me, Michael."

"I swore to Jane I would never divulge his identity."

"And what if it comes to a choice of Jane losing her children or revealing this man's identity?"

Michael's mind whirled with the ramifications of what he was about to suggest. "Buck, hear me out for a minute. It's possible Masterson has inadvertently handed us the key to all of this."

"I don't see what you're getting at."

"What would be the harm in letting people think Jane and I did have an affair? She came to me because Masterson was abusive and controlling. I was everything her husband wasn't—the epitome of understanding, kindness and acceptance. Who could blame her for falling in love with me? Given Masterson's reputation, she would certainly have the sympathy of the courts."

"And you would lose your license for sleeping with a client."

Michael sighed.

"Think about it, Michael. I know you're having a ball playing with rocks and pretending you have a new life in Scotland. But the reality is you've stretched the truth to its limits. It's bound to catch up with you eventually. Then you'll have nothing."

Buck paused for a moment. "I know I don't often profess to be a fan of yours, Michael, but you're a talented doctor. You have a gift for communicating with and helping people. The real crime here would be to see your hands tied for the rest of your life. Think about it. Never able to help anyone in a professional capacity again, never able to practice your science, never able to be the very thing that defines you. Are you really willing to give up all that?"

Michael stared at the wall. "When is the next hearing scheduled?"

"There's an evidentiary hearing set for the end of the week. I was going to recommend you find a barrister in Tobermory and arrange to make a sworn affidavit in front of a judge attesting to the fact that you never had sexual relations of any kind with Jane Masterson. Are you willing to do that, or do you have another plan?"

"I don't know. I just don't know."

The silence between them was unbroken. Even Buck's rapping had come to a halt.

"Buck?"

"Yes?"

"Mom doesn't know anything about any of this, does she?"

"I haven't said anything."

"You're sure she's doing well?"

"She's fine, Michael. She appears happy and healthy. Dad talks about her grandkids coming over to the house and raves about what a wonderful hostess she is when they entertain."

Michael hesitated. "You'll talk to Charles about Masterson and do whatever you need to do to keep the asshole away from them?"

"I'll call Dad as soon as we're done. I'll get a restraining order against Masterson that covers the whole damn family if I have to."

"And Barbara? Have you talked to her lately?"

"No. Your mom mentions her and the kids every so often, but I haven't seen them in quite some time."

"I miss the kids more than anything. Especially Tori. She probably wonders why her Uncle Mikey hasn't been by to see her in so long. I'll bet she's talking a blue streak by now." His voice grew gruff, and he swallowed hard as memories of his niece flooded his thoughts. "She's two already. I missed her birthday." He sighed. "She probably doesn't even remember me after all this time."

"Knowing your mom, I'm sure she shows her your picture every time they're together."

Michael clenched his jaw. "Just promise me you'll keep an eye on all of them. If I know Masterson, he'll stop at nothing to get what he wants."

"I'll do what you ask as long as you'll think about what I said and promise not to do anything rash without talking to me first. You've got too much to lose, Michael."

#

Lightning flashed along the horizon and shimmered over the bay. The reflections of the rocky crags lining the shoreline wobbled and swayed like a drunken sailor each time the wind set the water to rippling. Gareth tightened his coat and adjusted the wool scarf around his neck to protect his face from the ocean's icy spray.

"Is there a reason ye asked me to meet you at this God forsaken place?" Morgan asked as he approached from behind. "The Bell's a might warmer, especially on a night like this."

Gareth turned slightly, but avoided Morgan's eyes. He looked back to the sea and said nothing, dreading the task before him.

"I've a new assignment for ye, and I dinnae want a scene in public." He watched Morgan as he digested his words.

"Ye make it sound as though I'll nae be relishing the task."

"Damon's been hearing rumors aplenty aboot ye since he returned from Germany. He is nae pleased at the way you managed to ruffle everyone's feathers at the castle yesterday. Ye've aroused suspicion and drawn attention to yerself—two of the very things which Damon warned ye against."

Morgan's eyes narrowed. His face twisted in an unspoken sneer. "Ye can count on me to complete the remainder of my assignment with the utmost discretion."

Gareth shook his head and clutched his scarf as a gust of wind jabbed at them. "It's too late. Ye've had yer chance and failed. He's done with ye now."

Morgan's eyes glittered in the moonlight. "Just because I've

119

been biding my time a bit does nae mean I've nae got a plan. Quitting the construction crew was the best thing I could have done. Now I can go aboot tailing Isabelle more discreetly. I swear it to ye. No one will even know I'm aboot."

Gareth hunched his shoulders and put his back to the wind. "Damon wants ye in Wales. He'll find ye there when he has another assignment for ye."

"He cannae do this to me." Morgan cursed.

"Ye did it to yourself, ye old fool. Your hot head has made ye more of a liability to Damon than an asset. And that, he will not tolerate."

"But I have a plan."

"Ye're dismissed! Do ye hear me? Go back to Wales!"

He locked eyes with Morgan, and had a fleeting image that the two of them must look like a pair of bulls facing off. "I'll need your key to Dunara Cottage."

"Bloody bastard." Morgan reached into his pocket and shoved the key at him. "Damon's not seen the last of me, and neither have ye."

"Ye're right about that. Damon has eyes everywhere. He'll be watching you wherever you go. And ye'd best nae be forgetting it."

"What Damon might see with his eyes closed, ye wouldn't know if it bit ye on the head, ye blathering idiot. Ye'd best be remembering that." Morgan spat out his threat. "Damon's nae seen the last of me by a long shot. Nor has the fair Miss Isabelle MacAllister. I promise ye that."

Chapter Fourteen

Isabelle tapped her foot on the hardwood floor of the German consulate and waited for Bette's friend, Simone, to join her. Strasbourg, France's half-timbered buildings, flower-filled window boxes and winding pathways were so enticing it had been hard to convince herself she wanted to leave. But Bette had insisted that if she was going to be anywhere in the vicinity of Alsace-Lorraine, she had to see the village where she and Hans had grown up.

She pulled out her iPad and decided to check her email while she had the opportunity to hook into the consulate's WiFi. The most recent message in her inbox was an advertisement from Travelocity. The headline was in such bold print it would have leaped out at her even if it hadn't affected her personally—AROUND THE WORLD IN 48 STATES, No Passport Required.

So Ronald was right. She scanned the subtitles. The copy was just as catchy. *Who says you can't experience foreign lands without crossing the border? With Last Minute Deals, you can travel internationally within our very own 48 states!* "*Sample dim sum in San Francisco's Chinatown, give in to the Latin rhythms in Miami's Little Havana, bask in Boise, Idaho's Basque Country, spice it up in New York's Little India, or enjoy the luck o' the Irish in Boston. America truly is a cultural melting pot.*

Depressing as it was to know Ronald had been right about something, she felt a renewed sense of justification about her mission in Europe. Not that she had anything against couples and families spending their vacations at home in America, but the Europeans she'd met whose well-being was dependent on travel really were hurting, and if there was something she could do to help—even if it meant going to a nude beach—she was happy to be of service.

The young woman who had gone to fetch Simone from the room where the archives were stored reappeared and waved her arm toward a much older woman, stooped and wrinkle-lined, following at ten paces.

Simone's face broke into a broad smile. "Bette was right about you my dear. What a pretty thing you are. Of course, Bette was no slouch in the looks department fifty years ago."

"Thank you, Simone. I'm very pleased you agreed to meet me and ride with me to Mittelbergheim."

"Oui. Such a big name for a tiny village. Did Bette tell you the name means 'the place between the mountains?' Mittelbergheim is one of the most picturesque villages in Alsace, and like so much of France, has a renowned gastronomic reputation. We will have a delightful time poking around, as you Americans say."

"Your English is flawless," Isabelle said. "Bette mentioned that you're fluent in several languages."

"One has to be when they grow up in a region that first belonged to Celts, then—until Attila the Hun destroyed it—the Romans, then the Franks, the Germans, the French, the Germans, the French..." Simone chuckled.

Isabelle smiled. "A city with a checkered past. I'm assuming the French language is dominant now?"

"Yes, the old ways are fading fast. In Alsace, a German dialect called Alsatian is spoken, but its use is decreasing. So we are Strasbourg to the French, Strassburg to the Germans, and Elsass-Lothringen to old Alsatians like Hans and Bette."

"So there are still German influences sprinkled in with the French?"

"Ah, yes. Indelibly entwined. Even Quiche Lorraine, which most people assume to be French, comes from the German word 'kuchen,' which means cake."

Isabelle smiled. "Bette mentioned Damon has a gift for different languages, as you obviously do."

"Damon?" Simone looked puzzled for a moment. "Oh, you must mean little Sigismundus."

"Sigismundus?"

"Sigismundus Damon Hermance. I had forgotten the boy's middle name."

Isabelle grinned. She'd never met Damon, but Michael had described him as tall, dark, in his late 40's or early 50's, and brawny. Not the sort of fellow she'd have associated with the name Sigismundus.

"Yes, little Sigismundus was quite the master of both language—

and theatre—by the time he'd finished his first year or two of school. He was a petite child with dark hair, a late bloomer was what Bette always said, given she and Hans were both so fair and stately.

"He was teased without mercy because of his small size—I suppose one must feel some sympathy. In the first several decades after World War II, there was still much anti-German sentiment. When Sigismundus was in his third year, a new teacher came to town, and the little scamp took advantage of her naiveté to assume a French identity. If I remember correctly, he called himself S. Deville Herman, an appropriate name, now that I think of it, little devil that he was."

"No one caught on?"

"Not until the third term, when the teacher became suspicious of a record Sigismundus had forged, and called his father."

"Didn't the other children say anything?"

"Looking back, I feel sure the lad threatened them with some horrible fate should they blow his cover. Of course, knowing what we know now, it's obvious he was capable of most anything, certainly something aberrant enough to scare a group of small children."

"Pardonnez-moi." The young Frenchwoman who had gone to find Simone earlier approached them and spoke to Simone in a rush of French Isabelle only partially understood. She caught the words 'train' and 'Mittelbergheim' and assumed from the urgency in their voices that they needed to hurry to catch the train.

"Merci!" Simone spoke to the other woman in a torrent of French, then turned to Isabelle. "We must leave immediately or we will miss the train. I have... how do you say it? Lost track of the time?"

Isabelle nodded. "Of course."

"Allons!" Simone called out to her co-worker as she steered Isabelle toward the door. "Come, dear. We can sit and chat over a carafe of Riesling when we arrive in Mittelbergheim. The Alsatian white wines have a very distinctive flavor due to the continental climate..."

#

Michael looked at Isabelle's itinerary one last time and stuck it in the flap of his backpack. Today was the day. She'd left Switzerland for Alsace two days ago, where she'd visited Strasbourg and made a brief stopover in Mittelbergheim. She'd headed south from there and spent the night at a villa in Provence. Assuming she was still on schedule, she'd checked into her cabaña on the beach at Saint-Tropez earlier that day.

His toes ground into the soft, warm sand as he scanned the rainbow of colorful umbrellas dotting the beach. Oconomowoc, Wisconsin was about as different from the south of France as a place could be. So, what was he doing here? He was accustomed to analyzing what other people did and why they did it. For some reason, he'd never seemed to acquire the same knack when it came to his own actions, some of which had been particularly asinine as of late. Having acknowledged that disconcerting bit of information about himself, he adjusted his shorts and wove his way through a wave of naked beachcombers.

He'd come to the French Riviera on a whim.

No, he hadn't.

He'd come because he wanted to be with Isabelle. It had been just a little too tempting, knowing when she would be arriving, what she'd be doing, and which cabin she'd be staying in. The fact that the last few days had been filled with one nightmarish revelation and frustrating situation after another had been all the additional motivation he'd needed to flee reality and follow her to paradise.

He hadn't stopped to reason why, how she would react, or what he would do when he got there, he had just gone—thrown some suntan lotion, a beach towel, his wallet, some sunglasses and a change of clothes into his backpack and gone.

The only glitch in the plan so far was that Isabelle's cabin had been locked when he'd arrived. When he'd seen the thin-walled, screened-in little cabaña where she was staying, he was glad he'd come. How could Isabelle feel safe, staying alone in a flimsy place like that?

He assumed Isabelle must be in town shopping or soaking up some rays while she worked on her article. Since he preferred naked people to shopping, he opted to look on the beach first.

Knowing Isabelle didn't feel all that comfortable being around nude sunbathers, he assumed she wouldn't have strayed too far. If he knew her at all, his guess was she'd head for the closest, least crowded section of beach within eyeshot.

He stepped over a pair of legs, tried as hard as he could not to look at what was between them, and set out in hot pursuit.

Man, he was good. There she was. Easy to spot. She was the only one fully clothed on the whole damn beach. It was her all right, sitting on a purple beach towel in her prim cotton blouse and crisp khaki shorts, her notebook in hand, a straw hat with pansies woven into the brim perched on her head.

He went around a sixty or seventy-ish looking couple that looked like they came to the beach often, walked a few more feet, crept around the edge of Isabelle's beach towel, and plopped his bag a few feet away from her.

Her head was down, no doubt out of fear that if she looked up, she might find herself face to genitals with a perfect stranger. Of course, better stranger than acquaintance.

He unzipped his backpack, spread out his towel and sat down beside her without saying a word. He could see her muscles tighten, preparing for flight, as she started to slowly inch away from him.

"Fancy meeting you here," he said, tipping the brim of her hat up just enough so she could see him.

"Michael! Oh, my gosh. You scared me to death!"

He smiled. "At least I left my clothes on. Think how scared you would have been had I done as the Romans do and—"

"What are you doing here?"

He wasn't sure if she was pleased or slightly disconcerted and thought maybe he didn't want to know.

"You said I was welcome to join you."

"I was being nice. I didn't think you'd actually come."

"Neither did I." He couldn't tell her what an emotional roller coaster ride the last few days had been, or how stressed out and in need of a little relaxation he'd felt. Or, that he was secretly hoping to see her naked. "I took a chance and hoped you'd be happy to see me."

"I probably will be once the astonishment wears off." She smiled just a little, then looked at him suspiciously. "As long as you don't have any funky ideas about you and I getting naked."

Michael took that as a sign anything could happen. The fact that she was thinking about it must mean she was tempted on some level, didn't it? "So, have you been enjoying the scenery so far? Having a good time?" He looked around at the smattering of bodies dotting the horizon. "Perfect day for sunbathing. Although it appears you're a little overdressed for the occasion."

"See? Now that's what I mean. The only reason I'm out here at all is that the breeze we had this morning died down and it was getting muggy in the cabin. I assumed it would be cooler out here by the water."

"You'd be a lot cooler if you'd take off some of your clothes." He grinned. "Just sayin'."

"And so it begins."

"What could be the harm in stripping down to your bra and panties? You'd be more comfortable and you'd still be wearing ninety-five percent more clothing than everyone else."

"Everyone else but you."

"The only reason I've still got my clothes on is that it seemed like the polite thing—I mean, since you're fully dressed."

"Right." A sly smile played over her lips.

"You say the word. I'll be naked in two seconds flat."

"So be naked. Who am I to stand in your way?"

"Fine. It's settled then. I'll do it." He slipped his hands into his pockets. "There's just one small problem."

"Yes?"

Great move on her part—with the disinterested voice.

She smiled. "As long as it's a small problem and not a big problem."

"Very funny." He considered his next move. "The problem is, my mother raised me to be a gentleman."

"Well, then, we'll just have to insure you're on your best behavior at all times while you're naked. My research revealed certain protocols one is expected to observe while unclothed. I'd be happy to share them with you."

He frowned. "You don't understand. When I said I was gentlemanly, I was referring to the whole ladies first thing."

"Hmmm. Ladies first." She pursed her lips like she was seriously considering his suggestion. "That certainly is very thoughtful of you, Michael."

"Thank you. I'm here to serve."

"Which is why I couldn't possibly take advantage of your considerate offer."

"No?" He shook his head.

"No."

"You're sure?

"Quite sure."

He stifled a chuckle and started to unbutton his shirt. "You were kidding about the whole Miss Manners for Naked People, weren't you?"

"I was not."

"What, like not staring at other people's private parts?"

"Exactly. No gawking allowed." Isabelle looked down and examined her fingernails, then checked her cuticles for signs of imperfection. "And that's just the start."

"What?" He laughed and stripped off his shirt.

She looked down. "No... you know... in public."

"No what?" He unzipped his shorts. "Groping under towels?"

"Sorry. Nice try, but no can do." She smiled.

"You're no fun at all."

"Oh, but it is customary to have a towel with you at all times," she added. "To sit on."

"I'll keep that in mind." He dropped his shorts and stepped out of them, shook the sand off the back and stuck them inside his backpack.

She glanced up at him and blushed. "Actually, I suppose a towel might come in handy for a variety of reasons."

"You think?" He grinned. "So what does happen if, say, a man should suddenly..."

"Get aroused? In theory, I suppose no one would notice since we're not supposed to be..."

"Looking at each other's privates. Great."

She picked up her notebook and read from her notes. "It's really not about sex. It's about being uninhibited, unconcerned with what others think of you, and unashamed of your body."

"So which are you? Uptight, worried about what other people think of you, or embarrassed of your body?" He slipped his boxers down to his ankles and stepped out of them before laying down on the beach towel he'd spread on the sand beside hers.

"None of the above." She was cool all right. Never once did she glance at the region below his waist. Not even for a second. If she tried any harder not to look, he feared she might never move her neck again.

"I wouldn't even be here if my editor hadn't forced me to come."
She sighed. "Drat. I'd almost forgotten. I have to find someone
who'll let me photograph them for the magazine." She looked at him
hopefully.

"Forget it. I'm in enough trouble already." Great—way to spill
more of the beans. "With my mother, I mean. My stepfather is a state
senator. With my luck, the photos would find their way back to
Wisconsin and ruin his bid for reelection." Stupid. Stupid. Why was
he telling her more about himself? She might be the subject of his
deepest fantasies at the moment, but she was still a reporter.

"So you don't think a poster of you relaxing in France would
boost his campaign effort?"

"Thanks, but no thanks."

"I understand. Really, I do."

"I'm sure there are plenty of people out here who wouldn't mind
posing. Some might even consider it a turn-on. You know, like a
secret discovery fantasy."

"More like a not-so-secret discovery nightmare," she muttered.

He reached down and used the edge of his towel to adjust
himself as discreetly as he could. He did feel rather—naked. "I don't
remember President Bush's approval ratings exactly soaring when
his daughter let it all hang out at that college party."

"Right. Some sleaze ball reportedly offered the guy who
supposedly had the video over a half million dollars for it."

"Wow. The kid had to have been tempted," he said.

"I felt sorry for her."

"Why? It was her choice."

"But she wasn't thinking. She was just being silly and having fun
for once in her life. She'd probably had to be a perfectly good little
girl from the day she was born. All she wanted to do was let down
her guard for a few minutes and just be herself."

Isabelle wrapped her arms around her legs and wiggled her butt
down into the sand. "Now, for the rest of her life, she's going to have
to live with the fact that she totally humiliated her mother in front of
the whole neighborhood, the entire church, and all of her friends at
bridge club, her father will never be able to look her in the eye again,
and her grandmother will very likely disinherit her for being such a
floozy. Worse yet, the guy she was starting to like probably dumped
her because he'd never want a slut like her to be the mother of his

children, and no one at work ever took her seriously again because every time they look at her all they'll be able to think about is her slightly puffy areolas, and her pouty little nipples, and the way she trims her pussy hair into a cute little 'V' just above her..." She stopped and glared at Michael.

"Go on," he murmured.

"You're doing it again!"

"Me? I've hardly said a word. What did I do?"

"That thing you do when you lay there and listen to every word I say until I've spilled my guts all over the place. You know. The incredible professional shrink act."

He made a great display of huffing indignantly. "All I'm doing is listening. You obviously needed to get some things off your chest."

"Nice try."

He had to laugh at that one. "Seriously. It appears you have a great deal of empathy for the President's daughter. What's so revealing about that?"

"Nothing. It's just that any normal guy would have interrupted me about two hours ago to tell me who won the Super Bowl, or who made a birdie, or some other inane thing, and then I would have lost my train of thought before I'd totally embarrassed myself. If none of that worked, the very least you could have done is to lean over and kiss me just to shut me up. Don't they teach guys anything in Wisconsin?"

"Well forgive me for being a good listener." He rolled his eyes, stretched his arms out and linked his hands behind his head. "Although I must admit that last suggestion—kissing you to shut you up—sounds like a pretty good idea."

"It wasn't a suggestion. It was a defense mechanism. A fake shrink par excellence such as yourself should know all about those."

He would have gone ahead and kissed her if he hadn't been naked. The way things stood, he figured he'd be better off not pressing his luck.

Chapter Fifteen

Isabelle very cautiously let her eyes drift as low as Michael's torso. All she'd done was think about kissing the man and now she couldn't keep her eyes off his... Not his crotch. Only his torso. Why was she so attracted to underarm hair anyway? It was just so soft and downy looking, the way it grew in that springy little thatch, just popping out of nowhere, begging to be stroked.

Michael smiled like a cat who'd finally caught the mouse. "I thought staring wasn't allowed."

"My eyes are nowhere near your private parts." Of course, the words no sooner left her mouth than she found her eyes straying in the direction of his... Bad eyes. It was like they had a mind of their own. She forced herself to look back at his face, which was hard, because she had to admit, she liked what she saw.

She took one more quick glance and then headed back to his face, but only after she made a few more stops along the way. She frowned. "Sorry."

He laughed. "Feast your eyes."

She rolled them instead. And told them to get back where they belonged. Immediately, if they knew what was good for them. Unfortunately, they seemed to think they knew better than she what was good for them, and kept going there—against her wishes. "Stop it! You're doing it on purpose."

"What? Lying here?

"You know exactly what I mean. You're too damn sexy for your own good and you obviously don't have a shy bone in your body, and..." Her eyes made a second slow journey to his toes and back again. This had to stop. Next thing she knew she'd be drooling on him.

Michael's eyes returned the favor. "So are you going to take off your clothes, or do you want to talk some more?"

"Well, if those are my only two options..." She sighed. "What do you want to talk about now?"

"The President's daughter."

"I was afraid you'd say that."

"I'm just supposing after what happened, she probably has a hard time letting down her guard and just being her silly self again, even if she's with someone she really cares about and wants to trust."

"You're probably right."

"Who knows—after what happened, she might even have developed a camera phobia."

"A camera what?" She clutched her ankles and didn't say anything for a few seconds. "You mean like freaking out when someone tries to take a picture of her when she's less than fully clothed?"

"Yup. That's what I'm talking about."

Michael shifted his hips, which of course, she knew because her eyes were acting independently of her brain again.

She made herself look away. "Well, it makes sense that she would be a little paranoid at first, don't you think?"

"Sure. But I would hope she'd eventually learn to trust again."

"Is that your professional diagnosis or just another fake opinion?"

"It's my sincere hope."

"Well, I hope you're right. I mean, for her sake. She's still young, and her whole life is ahead of her, and she probably dreams about settling down and having a family someday."

"You think so?"

The look on Michael's face nearly wrenched her heart in two. "Yes. I do." A tingly sensation ran up her spine. "If I had to venture a guess, I'd say the whole episode probably taught her a few things. I would think the next time she feels like getting naked in public she might choose a more secluded spot, preferably at a place where no one knows her."

"Like you did today."

"Right." The stretch of beach she'd chosen was by no means deserted, but the area where they were sitting was slightly removed from the more populated areas where drinks were served, musicians were playing and vendors were hawking their wares. "If she's smart, she'll make sure no one she's with carries a camera."

"Good idea," he said. "Want to check my bag?"

Isabelle stared straight ahead. "It would be nice if she had some guarantee she could trust whomever she might choose to share the experience with."

"If trust came with guarantees, the whole concept wouldn't have much meaning, would it?"

Damn, he was good. "I suppose not."

Michael rolled away from her and began rummaging through his backpack. "Okay, Miss Manners. What about helping each other get sun tan lotion on all those hard to reach spots? Is that allowed?"

"Sure." Her voice barely squeaked the word out. Michael threw the bottle over his shoulder and caught her square in the lap.

He folded one arm under his head and laid face down. "Why don't you start on my back?"

She looked down at his backside and tried not to swoon. "Your butt is pretty white."

"It hasn't seen the sun since one hot, July day in the late 70s when Mom said it was okay to run naked through the lawn sprinkler in the back yard."

She giggled—okay, nervously—squirted a glob of suntan lotion between his shoulder blades and proceeded to massage it in with slow, sweeping circles.

"I've always loved having my back rubbed."

"Turn this way a little so I can get the sides." She used her palms to make a crisscross motion from one shoulder to the other and continued alternating one hand after another in arcs down the length of his back until she reached his rear. Another squirt of lotion. It was time to massage his buttocks.

He spread his legs just far enough to allow her access to the insides of his thighs.

So why did she suddenly feel so timid? If it weren't for those damn rules of etiquette she'd have been sorely tempted to...

He turned his head and looked up at her. "If you're not careful, you're going to get this oily lotion all over your clothes and ruin a perfectly good outfit."

It was getting hot. Her blood felt like it was practically boiling. "I might actually do it if I had on my regular underwear." She was tempted.

"Don't tell me you left all your pretty panties at home."

"Well, most of them, yes, but that's not the problem." She tentatively touched his behind and started to work the lotion into his skin. "I'd heard French lingerie is to die for—you know, silk embroidered demi-bras and skimpy little tulle thongs—so first thing this morning I found a little shop and kind of went wild."

His buttocks tensed. "I don't have a clue what a demi-bra is, but thongs are modest enough, aren't they? At least in the places that count. Obviously there's the back, or no back, I should say. But at this point, you've seen mine, so there's no reason to be shy about yours."

She squeezed one of his buttocks in each of her hands, leaned down, and blew on his rosebud for just a second before she loosened her grip.

"Wow. Is that allowed?"

"Probably not."

"Maybe you could do it again."

"Silly boy." She squirted the back of his thighs with a generous dose of the coconut-scented cream and kept rubbing.

"So are you going to tell me what a demi-bra is?"

"No comment." She let one fingernail dangle between his legs as she rubbed lotion on the inside of his thighs, then moved to the backs of his knees.

He snapped his ankles up to meet his thighs, trapping her hands in the fold of his knees.

"Ticklish?"

"Evidently."

She laid her palms on his legs and pushed them down as gently as she could. "Let me try one more time. I'll be good."

"Oh, you're very good. That's the problem."

"I'm flattered."

"You should be. Now tell me about demi-bras."

She giggled. "Well, they're much smaller than a traditional brassiere, and they give support from beneath the breast with widely spaced straps that connect to the underside of the bra."

"Maybe you should just show me. This support lingo is confusing."

"Nice try. Bottom line, they don't cover the breast at all and your nipples are left completely and utterly bare. They're great for dresses that have wide or square necklines, and they show lots of cleavage."

"Very descriptive—if you like books with no pictures. It would be more fun to see an illustration."

"I can't show you what one looks like because that's not what I have on." She moved down to his ankles and rubbed the bottom of his feet with another dose of tropical balm.

"So here we are—me naked, you fully clothed. You privy to every freckle, and me still clueless as to something so innocuous as what your underwear looks like. Does that seem fair to you?"

"Poor baby." She laughed. "You want me to describe it?"

"Only if you won't show it to me."

"I won't."

"Fine."

"It's called a butterfly body string and I can feel it threading it's way around and about each of my more sensitive body parts every time I move."

"Wow." His back rose and fell as he took a deep breath. "Is it more or less modest than a thong and demi-bra?"

"To be truthful, I don't think the words modest and body string would ever be used in the same sentence."

"That bad, huh?"

"Yup."

"Go on."

"Well, if you were rubbing suntan lotion on my backside right now, you'd be looking at exactly 4 tiny black strings—one at the base of my neck, one in the middle of my back, one just below my waist, and the other disappearing into..." She ran her finger down the crack of his ass. "...and ending here."

He moaned. "Finally—the good stuff. What about the front?"

"The front is a little more complex. There's a string circling each of my breasts. Another string starts between my breasts and runs vertically from my sternum to my pelvis, where it intersects with a little triangle of silk with a butterfly embroidered on it."

"Mmm… That covers your..."

"No, not exactly. It's perched midway up my belly. From it come two more strings that run down to my privates and eventually meet up with the one I already mentioned that disappears..."

He rolled over and looked her in the eye. "So these strings disappear, and then reappear..."

"One on either side of my, well, you know." She could feel her cheeks turning pink.

"So if I'm understanding this right, all that's left to cover your crotch is two thin little strings?"

"Yes, except they don't exactly cover anything. They're just there, on the sides."

"Oh." His eyes got bigger.

"It's called an open thong. The sales lady said they originated in Brazil."

"I see. Or I wish I could." He smiled. "So the function of an open thong would be to...?"

"Well, the split strings more or less hold everything else together, and I guess they feel good, too." Her cheeks felt like they were on fire. She smiled and sighed simultaneously.

He looked into her eyes. "Be really, really honest. This little get-up probably set you back a good hundred Euros, and looks great on you besides. Aren't you dying to show it off?"

She squirmed. She was feeling somewhat dazed. "Well, kind of. Yes. I mean, there's a part of me that..."

"I probably don't need to ask what part."

She laughed. "Good one."

"Okay. So I'm laying here naked, and to be frank, having a very enjoyable time. You want to be naked, but for some reason, you're too shy to just do it. What can we do to make this easier for you?"

"Promise me you won't take any pictures?"

He continued to hold her glance. "Scout's honor."

"Were you really a boy scout?"

"Yes. Don't change the subject."

She focused on his face as she unbuttoned her blouse, button by tortuous button, never looking away. "Remember, this isn't about sex." Her voice faltered ever so slightly. "It's like I said before, about being unashamed of my body, and..."

Michael crouched on his haunches and rose up to hold her shoulders, which were still covered in cotton. "I can't lie about this, sweetheart. If you're feeling the slightest bit of what I'm feeling, it's very much about sex. It has to be about it, at least in part, because I'm here, and I'm very enamored with you. You know that, don't you?"

She unbuttoned the last tiny button, unsnapped her shorts and slowly pulled the zipper down. "But it's not just about sex."

"Exactly." He kissed her on the forehead. "For you, it's about trust. You trusting me."

"And feeling safe and secure enough to bare my soul again."

"Yes. That's it. God, you're beautiful."

Isabelle slipped her arms out of her sleeves and turned to face

135

him head on, her breasts standing at attention, all pouty and protruding and slightly puffy just like she'd said, but softer than he ever would have imagined, creamy as porcelain and more beautiful than anything he'd ever seen. She scooted out of her shorts, keeping her legs closed in an endearing, ladylike way, and lay down on her towel, facing him.

"Wow." He looked at her, probably with wonder written all over his face, if he looked anything like he felt. "You're stunning. And the butterfly thingy is beyond words."

They lay facing each other, breathing, taking each other in, wondering what would come next.

Her eyes went to his face, searching for something deeper than his skin. She ran a finger around each of his nipples and made a trail to his belly button. "So what is this about for you, Michael? Sex, in part, you said, honestly enough. And for me, trust. What else is it for you?"

"I'm usually the one asking the questions," he admitted, "figuring other people out."

"And you're very good at it. But I don't have your gift for presupposing what's going through someone else's head. Tell me."

He leaned toward her and kissed her lightly. "I think for me, it's caring about you so deeply I will do whatever it takes to be with you, protect you, and help you heal, no matter what price I have to pay or what consequences there are to bear as a result." He kissed her again.

She wet her lips with her tongue until they glistened in the sunlight. "I think I need some suntan lotion."

He took the bottle, squeezed several droplets onto her tummy, and plucked the strap from her belly so he could rub lotion underneath.

"You have big hands."

"And more than a few calluses after working with rocks all spring. I'll try to be gentle."

Her shoulders drooped as she started to relax. She rolled over onto her back to give him better access.

The sound of footsteps and voices approaching from the direction of the water distracted her for a second. She lifted her head. A foursome, two men and two women, all nude, stopped a few feet short of Isabelle and Michael's towels and spread out blankets and baskets filled with wine and baguettes. She tensed.

"No need to feel shy," he said. "I think they're speaking Italian. No one we know. Probably never been to either Virginia or Wisconsin."

She sighed and sank back into the sand. "I know it's silly, but I'd just die if anyone I know saw me like this."

"That's why we're here and not at Virginia Beach." He cupped her breasts and rubbed lotion on her nipples.

"You're cheating you know." She laughed. "This doesn't exactly fall under the heading of hard to reach places."

He withdrew his hand, but a lopsided smile slid over his face. "Watching you do it will be just as fun as doing it myself."

"Voyeur."

"Tease."

Something—instinct, a sixth sense, whatever—made him look over his shoulder at the Italians.

A man sat on his haunches directly in front of them, his back to the ocean, crouching so low to the sand his balls dragged on the ground. At first glance, Michael was so taken back by the man's close proximity and the size of his genitals, which he couldn't help but notice, that he didn't realize what was about to happen.

It took him a minute to put it all together. The man was situated at an angle to take a side view photograph of his friends, the three of whom were spread out on beach towels separated by just enough space to put Isabelle in the direct center of the photo.

That's when Isabelle raised her head to see what he was looking at. It came as no surprise to Michael she was startled—the telephoto lens bearing down on them was nearly as long and thick as the man's cock. Still, even knowing what he knew, he was unprepared for the anguished whimper that rose from her throat when she realized she was in the direct line of the camera.

He rolled on top of her without thinking, spreading his legs to straddle her torso, flattening his body over hers to shield her from the incessant clicking, probing lens of the camera. She froze.

Well, there was one for the family photo albums—him spread wide open and captured in living color, his asshole tipped to the sun and his balls flapping in the wind. Better he than her, but, damn it...

There was an even bigger problem. He lifted his head just high enough to look Isabelle in the eye.

Chapter Sixteen

"Houston, we have a problem." Michael shifted his weight in a futile attempt not to exacerbate the situation. "Can you see if our neighbor has put his telephoto lens away?"

Isabelle lifted her head, squirmed enough to loosen her arm, and raised herself up on one elbow so she could see over Michael's shoulder.

"You're not helping matters any," he said.

"Helping what? Oh." She lowered her head and settled her body back under him. "He's putting the camera back into the bag. They're pouring some wine. It looks like they're getting ready to eat."

Did she know what she was doing to him? "Do you think they can tell something is wrong?"

"Is something wrong?" She looked up into his eyes, then lowered her lashes.

If he hadn't already been hard, he would have been when she looked up at him, her face, calm with southern reserve, her eyes, molten heat. "You know damn well what's wrong with me."

She swiveled her hips and used her hands to brush the hair back from his face. She kissed him, a cool, wet, just on the surface of his lips kiss.

"You're teasing me."

"I'm thanking you. Getting between me and the camera is the most chivalrous thing anyone has ever done for me."

Her drawl washed over him like summer rain. He was beginning to think it intensified when she was feeling passionate. Or was it him? His senses felt so acutely tuned, every move, every word was magnified. He tried to shift his weight away from her with little success.

"So," he said, "We appear to have solved one problem and created another."

She smothered his jaw line with tender, little kisses. "I don't have a problem."

"Well, I do. I think I'm caught in one of your strings."

"Oh." She looked up at him, her eyes wide. "And here I assumed you were lingering in this position because you liked it."

"Oh, I like it all right. That's the problem." He tried to lift himself.

She winced. "Wait. The strings are all connected. It feels like you're choking me when you do that. If you hang on, I can try to..."

"Please. Don't move. Every time you move... Just try to stay very still while I..." He supported himself with one arm while he tried to reach between them and free himself. His fingers brushed against her pubic hair. "Sorry. I didn't mean to..."

"I know." She reached between them and touched his belly button as if to use it for a compass point. "I think if you lift yourself up a little higher, I can..."

"No! You don't have to..."

"I know." Her hand closed around his shaft. "Stop wiggling for a minute." If she was trying to torture him, she was doing an awesome job of it. "Here's what we'll do. On the count of three, you lift and I'll see if I can..."

He rose up on his haunches as she tried to disentangle him. Her hand guided a string up the length of his cock and slipped it over the head.

He tried to rock back on his knees.

"Wait. You're still stuck. Some of the strings that look like a single strand are actually two or three little spaghetti straps. They all fan out at some point," she added lamely.

He groaned.

"It wouldn't be so hard to get you loose if you weren't so..."

"It's not going to get any smaller if you keep doing that."

She reached down, looped one finger around the base of his cock and squeezed his balls lightly.

He could feel his face contorting as he tried not to respond to the pleasure flowing through his body. "What the hell was that?"

"It's a technique that's supposed to help a man hold back. I read about it in a book my friend Gloria has."

"Well, it's not working."

"Fine. Try to think about something that will make it shrink."

"Right."

"Seriously." She reached down for his balls again.

"Will you stop that?"

139

Her eyes grew large. "Did I hurt you?"

"No! It feels wonderful."

"It's not supposed to."

"Well it does."

"Okay." She stared up at him seriously. "You must have had to climb over the same old couple I did to get to me. The ones with the alligator skin that look like they've lived on the beach for about three decades. Saggy breasts. Droopy balls. Baggy bellies. Stretch marks."

He leaned forward on his elbows and thrust his butt a little further into the air to give her better access. He heard her sigh.

"I don't think it's working."

"Sorry. All I can think about is you and the butterfly strings." He lowered himself and waited as her hand slipped back between their bellies to try again.

"Oh." She gasped.

"What did I do?"

"Nothing. But when you moved..."

"Did I hurt you?"

Her hand grasped his penis and rubbed the length of it. He strained against the sensations that welled up inside him.

She moaned. Very quietly, but loud enough so he could hear her.

"I mean it. If you don't stop doing that..."

"But it feels good."

"It's not supposed to feel good. We're in the middle of a damn carnival and half of Europe is gawking at my ass."

Her hand still held his penis. "I didn't mean for it to feel good. It just did."

"Well, I didn't mean for it not to feel good." He shifted his weight ever so slightly. "Like that?"

She sighed. "Umm. Perfect."

"Good." He did it again, and listened for her soft moan of approval. "It feels good to me, too."

"Oh, yah. Right there." She gasped her pleasure against his neck to muffle the sound. "Do you think anyone would notice if you kept doing it for a few more seconds?"

He could feel a breeze teasing his balls. "Lord, I hope not."

She gyrated her hips under him.

He could feel it all—soft skin, wet curls, a hard nub. Her palms were moist and warm, and his skin slid in her hand as she tried to move him. "Isabelle." He moaned.

He felt another string slipping over him, a springy cushion of curls tickling the end of his cock, then moisture, then slippery, wet bliss. Tight, hot, slippery wet bliss. His cock was in paradise. "Are you sure this is what you want? Because..."

"Positive." Her breaths were short and choppy.

He could feel her body trembling, her nipples jabbing into his chest, her belly rising and falling under his. He slid in a little deeper. She was so wet it was impossible not to.

Her response was another squeeze, this one, from the inside. How did she do that? He pumped in and out of her in short little jabs, listening, and rubbing the spot where it seemed to please her the most. "What about safe sex?" God, he wanted it to be safe.

"I'm on the pill. I've always been safe. What about you?" She clutched his hair and thrust her pelvis up to meet his.

"Safe." He gasped.

She reached around and grabbed one of his butt cheeks in each hand, and squeezed.

He panted. "Was that a comment or a request?"

"A plea."

He granted her request. "I can't believe we're doing this." He tucked his knees, adjusted his angle of entry, and moaned when her fingers gripped his backside even tighter. "Can you see if anyone is watching?"

She lifted her head. "Yes."

"Yes, you can see, or yes, they're watching?" He slid into her as deeply as he could.

One of her hands was between them now, alternately rubbing her clitoris and stroking the hair growing around his cock. "Yes, but I think only the Italians can see."

"Only?" He withdrew, looked her straight in the eyes and thrust into her again.

"There might be a few others," she said.

"And they know what we're doing?"

"Oh, Michael...Yes, oh yes. Come with me."

Her body pulsed and bucked under his as he exploded inside her.

He heard a soft whimper mumbled against his chest. The rest was drowned out by the round of applause that erupted behind them.

#

Isabelle woke in a state of pure bliss—a warm bed, a cool breeze, a soul well-loved. Without getting up, she reached over her shoulder and groped for Michael's back, which had been cozily nuzzled against hers for most of the morning.

Her hand rubbed languidly over the sheet where he should have been. She reached a little further, and smoothed his pillow with her fingers. Her eyes opened wide, her heart thudded in her chest.

"Michael? Michael! Are you here?" Please be here. Don't be gone! A tiny pinprick of panic took shape in the back of her brain and rolled through her body like a snowball gathering momentum on its way downhill.

He was gone. She grabbed for her purse, flung it open and frantically clutched her traveler's checks, her credit cards, her cell phone. Where were the keys to the rental car? The keys to the beach house? She'd had them in her purse, hadn't she?

A key turned in the lock, but she was so crazed she didn't hear it.

"Looking for something?"

Her shoulders jerked taut—she looked up and felt her face growing red as she watched the realization dawning on Michael's face.

"No," she lied. One jolt of heat from his eyes and the snowball had started to melt.

"You thought I was gone." His voice was accusing. His eyes looked hurt—half perturbed, half angry.

She looked at the insulated cups in his hands and sniffed. "Hot chocolate with raspberry syrup?" She tried to slide her wallet back into her purse but it caught halfway in.

"You're shaking. You thought I'd skipped out on you."

"I didn't know... where you were..."

"You were checking to see if I'd stolen anything from your purse."

Her whole body felt cold.

"You really think I could walk out on you after last night?"

"No. No, I don't. I trust you."

He still looked skeptical.

"I was still half asleep. I was just a little disoriented." She watched as his expression changed from cynical to worried. "Just because my emotions went into panic mode doesn't mean I don't trust you with my mind. And my heart."

"Some way to show me."

"I couldn't ask for anyone more trustworthy." She moved closer to reassure him. "You've got the whole home-grown, hardworking, honest-to-a-fault Midwestern thing plastered all over your face."

His eyes darted away from her. "I'm no saint. Believe me."

"But you are. I doubt you even have it in you to lie—about anything."

"You make me sound like frickin' George Washington."

"I'm serious, Michael." She smoothed his hair back from his face with her fingertips. "Everything you are is steeped in truth and integrity and old-world values. I have no qualms about you whatsoever. You're exactly the kind of man every woman dreams about taking home to meet Mom and Dad, showing off at her class reunion, introducing to her colleagues at work."

He nuzzled her neck. "And damn good-looking besides, right?

"And extremely sexy." She whispered against his jaw.

"Learning to trust again, after a betrayal, is not an easy thing. I understand if you need time. I hope after you get to know me better..."

"I trust you implicitly." She rubbed the palm of her hand along his thigh. "If you want, next time you get out your canvas and oils, I'll pose nude for you to prove it."

"Oh, I want, all right." He leaned down to kiss her shoulder. "But you really don't have to prove anything to anyone. As for me personally, I rather like trying to solve the mystery of a beautiful woman who loves being naked but is terrified of being seen."

She looked up at him warily, feeling more naked than she had on the beach. "My exhibitionist streak peaks when I get to a certain stage of arousal. After I come, I pull the covers back up around my neck and revert to my skittish, demure self."

"Demure?"

"What happens in France stays in France, right?"

"Only if I can say the same of Wisconsin."

"I'd die of embarrassment if anyone from home had seen me last night."

"Hey. I was the one with my ass in the air."

She pulled away from him. "Titillating as I'm sure the view was, I wouldn't exactly want the pose featured on the postcards we send to our families at Christmastime."

He reached for her and pulled her back into his arms.

She sighed. "If only I had met my Prince Charming when I was twenty-two and just out of college. I'd be safely married, doing the wild thing with my husband behind locked doors like the proper, respectable Southern belle I'm supposed to be."

He kissed her again. "Personally speaking, I'm glad you're just the way you are at exactly this moment in time."

"Life would be so much easier if I was one of those women who hates sex."

"What?"

"Surely someone with such vast experience in the field of pretend psychology has met at least one or two of them. I listen to them talk about having to suffer through sex AGAIN because their husbands are so insatiably horny, like it's some sort of dreaded marital duty, and wonder why I'm still single when I'm the one who's freaking passionate, uber responsive, loves being naked, and evidently has a bit of an exhibitionist streak."

"You are somewhat of a dichotomy. I admit I'm having a hard time reconciling the naked beauty in the butterfly string I was with on the beach last night with the sad, uptight, very blue belle I met a few weeks ago."

"May I remind you I was fully clothed until you came along?"

"Wrapped up in your little cocoon, just waiting to spread your wings..."

"You know, I've humored you when it comes to this incredible shrink routine you do. Generally speaking, it's kind of cute..."

"Cute? Helpful, maybe. Cathartic, at the very least. Brilliant wouldn't be over exaggerating all that much when it comes right down to it."

"See? There you go." She sighed. "Fine. You're an exceptionally gifted pretend shrink. The thing is, we spent all night making love, and, my momentary panic attack aside, I'm basking in some pretty sweet sensations right now. So it's not a good time for another session." She ran her fingers up and down his arm, smoothing the crisp hairs in one direction and then the other. "When I think back on this day, I don't want to remember that I dredged up a nightmare. I'm trying to make some new memories here, sweet new memories I can dream about and relive when I want to feel safe and warm and sexy and loved."

"Okay. Message received." He cupped her breasts in his hands. "You're definitely sexy. Absolutely warm. Unquestionably loved." He tugged on her nipples with his thumbs and forefingers. "Safe, I'm not so sure."

Chapter Seventeen

The turbulent air that had been whipping around Bluevale Castle's rocky facade and stirring up waves on the bay was finally still. Damon reeked of sweat and saltwater. His muscles were sore from being batted about on the tiny boat where he'd spent the better part of the last thirty-six hours. He was less than thrilled to see his mother.

He could see Bette's small but regal shoulders silhouetted against a ring of rhododendrons just outside the castle door, a pillow wedged behind her back, as she sat gazing out at the sea.

"Damon," she said, still appearing mesmerized by the blues and pinks and yellows of sky and ocean merging at the horizon.

"It's been a long day, Mutter."

"Have a seat, dear." She patted the throne-like chair beside her where his father usually sat. "I've barely seen you since you returned. I sometimes wonder whether it's me you come to visit when you're in Scotland or the crew of the *Baurley.*" She looked over her shoulder and cringed.

If the way he felt was any indication of how he looked, he supposed he was not at his best, especially through the eyes of his mutter's refined sensibilities. "I'm in dire need of a hot shower, Mutter."

"So I see." She waved him away. "Join me when you're done."

He flicked his wrist to draw attention to the briefcase he carried in his right hand. "I'm frighteningly behind on my paperwork. My plan is to take over your office for the evening and have most of it caught up before nightfall."

"You're going to catch a death of a cold if you keep putting in such long hours, mein liebste, especially if you insist on refusing to wear your wet gear on the boat." She turned back to the sea. "You work harder than most men do even when you are here to relax."

He could hear the pride in her tone even as she chided him. Too bad Hans wasn't around to set her straight.

"You take care not to catch a chill either, Mutter."

His impatience to get on to the task at hand drove him to make his shower short. Neither his mother or father was in sight when he slipped into Bette's sitting room and spread out his laptop computer on her desk.

He plugged in his laptop, connected to the internet and squinted at the screen while his fingers attacked the keyboard. He could feel every muscle in his neck. His whole body felt rigid with tension. He slammed his hand against the table and cursed. He was almost in.

He kicked the stone wall at the back of his mother's sitting desk and wished he hadn't.

"What's all this ruckus about?" His mother poked her head through the door. "Is everything all right, mein liebste?"

He looked up and scowled. "Just peachy, Mutter." He tried to unfurl his brow. His father's barrel-chest and muscled arms screamed of German blood; his mother had appeared frail for as long as Damon could remember. He hated upsetting her, more so, her clinginess once she felt she had reason to worry about him. He flashed his most cherubic smile.

"If you say so, liebling."

He waited until he heard the door to the den close before he swore.

He typed in another series of numbers and letters, waited, typed a bit more, then smiled. He was in.

Just as he had hoped. Isabelle hadn't checked her email in the last forty-eight hours. He smiled, and began sifting through her mail, skimming through letters from her father, an aunt, and someone named Ronald. The next two entries originated from the same IP as Ronald's, but the sender's name was Gloria.

Damon skimmed the text. What a delicate name for such a feisty woman. And one with connections to the legal department at that.

His stomach clenched as he read the contents of the first letter— well-researched notes on each and every attempt to find the sunken treasure of Tobermory Bay, including those from his previous endeavor. His scowl deepened as he read. The information was accompanied by supporting dates, facts and telephone numbers. His fingers pounded over the keyboard as he printed the information, then paused as he prepared to delete the file permanently.

He cursed himself for being such an idiot. Isabelle had obviously requested the information. If she didn't receive the research at some point, she would question Gloria, and the information would be resent. Damon opened and copied the letter, erased the information pertaining to him, his company, and their botched first attempt, then set about the task of pasting the remaining information in a letter of the exact same format and text originally sent by Isabelle's company. When he was done, he logged into the email accounts on his computer, changed the sender information to match that of Gloria's original message, and resent his revised edition.

Thank God he'd hacked into Isabelle's computer when he did. In the hands of someone with Isabelle's reputation for ferreting out details, the information Gloria had sent would have been their undoing. A shudder ran through his body. If he hadn't taken matters into his own hands, the imbeciles who worked for him—or used to work for him, in Morgan's case—would have botched the whole deal. He hated getting his hands dirty, but this near fiasco attested to the fact that if he wanted something done right, he had no choice but to do it himself.

He felt his body convulse at the thought of what lay ahead. He certainly didn't relish the idea of having to do away with a pretty thing like Isabelle MacAllister, but if it came to it, he would do what needed to be done before he'd see the project fail again.

He'd worked too hard to lay the foundation for this operation, the least of which, convincing his parents to buy Bluevale Castle and spend their retirement in Scotland so he'd have a reason to frequent the area without raising eyebrows. Purchasing the Blue Bell and restoring it and Bluevale's keep had provided insidious ways to plant his men in the area without arousing suspicion. The only thing he hadn't counted on was his father hiring St. Dawndalyn.

He went on to the second post from Gloria. This one was about a different subject matter entirely. He read the page on Michael St. Dawndalyn carefully. His people had unearthed much the same facts, still, he checked every word. He stroked his chin. It was obvious St. Dawndalyn and Isabelle hadn't known each other until they'd met in Tobermory. If anything, this proved St. Dawndalyn's innocence of any involvement with the sonar company or the investigation.

Damon leaned back in his chair. Except for the last paragraph, it was old news. Even then, it was not the words that gave him pause, but Gloria's concern. She sounded almost motherly in tone.

I'm so sorry Isabelle. I know you didn't tell me Michael's name so I could investigate his past, but after what you've been through with Ben, I just wanted to be sure. Again, I'm so sorry. I know how upsetting this is going to be. I'm just thankful this time around you found out the man has been lying to you before you got involved with him and not after.

Judging by Gloria's words, it sounded to him like poor Miss MacAllister was about to have her heart broken. He grinned. He could think of no better way to keep Isabelle distracted enough that she wouldn't take notice of what he was up to.

Damon scrolled to the top of the letter, remarked Gloria's second letter 'Unread' and went on to the next post.

This one was from a B.S. It contained a .jpg attachment. He scrolled down slowly, his smile inching higher with every downward roll of the screen.

"Now that's the way I like to see you looking, lieb."

He nearly jumped out of his chair. His mother was mere inches away. He'd been so mesmerized by the photo on his screen he hadn't noticed her approaching.

"Mutter." He minimized the screen a second before she rounded the corner and looked over his shoulder. He spun around in his chair to face her.

"I believe I'm going to walk down to the baths for a bit, Damon. Would you like to join me? Your vater is in Tobermory, so it would be just the two of us."

"I'm sure Vater would love to go with you when he returns. Why don't you wait for a bit and go with him?"

"My hip has been aching all day." She moved closer to his screen. "MacAllister. One of the cottage tenants is a MacAllister. I think you've met her, Damon. The girl in Dunara. Isabelle. She is such a sweet girl. Are you emailing her?"

Great. He could barely read the toolbar without his glasses. His mother was so fragile a stiff wind would blow her over. How convenient that her eyes hadn't succumbed to the maladies of old age. "It's a common name, Mutter. Besides, why email a tenant? If I want to speak to her, I can walk fifty yards down the path and knock on her door." He smiled and patted his mother's arm.

"Not today, you couldn't. I believe she's on her way home from France." His mother pointed to a slip of paper on the far side of the desk. "Michael dropped by a copy of her itinerary in case there was trouble. Someone was inside her cottage last week."

"Oh, really?" He glanced at the piece of paper and feigned surprise. "How unfortunate. Was anything missing?"

"Not that I'm aware of. Still, it frightened her." His mother glanced at the itinerary. "What day is it today?"

"I'm sure Miss MacAllister did not leave a copy of her travel plans so I could hunt her down, Mutter."

"You could do worse than to spend a little time with her, Damon. She is a lovely girl."

"Fine." He smiled magnanimously. "If you feel so sure I would enjoy her company, I will make it a point to speak with her when she returns."

"I believe she will be back by the end of the week." His mother tittered in anticipation. "When I heard Isabelle was heading to Europe to write a series of tourism articles on the mainland I insisted she go to Strasbourg and look up Simone."

"You did what?" Damon's voice sounded more menacing than he'd intended it to. He instantly regretted startling his mother. "Whatever for?" he asked, trying his best to feign disinterest.

"She wanted to write about a medieval village. What better place to visit than Mittelbergheim?" Bette smiled absently.

She was good, all right. He could just imagine Isabelle MacAllister pumping his poor old mother for information. Unfortunately he could just as easily see his mother gushing on endlessly about their family history without once realizing she was selling out her own son to the enemy.

"I know you were not especially fond of growing up in such a small, remote village, but many think it is the most beautiful place in all of France," Bette said wistfully.

"You mentioned a few months ago Simone only works a few hours a week, sorting papers for the archives." Damon said, trying to console himself. "The chances are slim Isabelle will even find her there."

"That's why I phoned ahead and told Simone when Isabelle would be coming," Bette said, patting his back. "You look so tired, mein liebste. Perhaps when Isabelle returns, the four of us can have tea one afternoon so you can get to know her better. It would do you good to take a little break from your work and have some fun." Bette smoothed a strand of his hair back into place, smiled contentedly, and exited the room as quietly as she'd come.

Damon turned back to the computer screen, maximized the photo from B.S.—Ben, per the attached note—and saved the file to a flash drive, which he popped from the computer before settling back to more fully appreciate the view on his screen. Hmm. It appeared he would be getting to know Miss MacAllister much better than he'd imagined. He cocked his head. Ja, that was more like it.

"Um." He grunted approvingly. Her breasts were the first thing to catch his eye. Perfect. He loved puffy nipples. He slowly lowered his gaze. The wanton, cross-legged pose she'd struck for the camera made her look more like an American Indian at a powwow than a Southern Belle at a cotillion. He craned his neck and took her in at every angle. So, her hair color was her own. Ach du liebe Zeit! She had red hair not only on top, but where it mattered the most.

Chapter Eighteen

Michael reached up and smoothed a stray curl from Isabelle's face. His shoulder was burning hot where her cheek touched his shirt and his arm was starting to fall asleep, but he loved the feel of her nuzzled close to him so much that he didn't care.

The train lurched under them as it raced through the tunnel. They were deep under the English Channel, and Isabelle was sound asleep, oblivious to the millions of tons of water pressing down on them. Her facial expression looked so serene it almost had an angelic quality about it.

He only wished he felt so at peace. God help him. He wanted Isabelle's trust so badly. There was no way he deserved her admiration. He had to find a way to make this right. He'd wanted to tell her everything back in France, and he'd come close, especially when she'd started to wax on about truth and integrity. But she'd been so happy—they'd been so happy. He just hadn't had the heart to burst her bubble. She deserved a few flawless memories to savor in her daydreams after the nightmare she'd been through. Didn't she?

Isabelle sighed contentedly and stretched her neck against him, her lips opening and closing ever so slightly in her sleep.

He'd almost told her the truth that morning while they'd waited at the train station. He traced her jaw line with his finger. He simply hadn't had it in him to mar the idyllic glow surrounding them. He'd waited to see that look on her face since the day they'd first met. Now that it was there, he wanted to keep it there, forever.

If only he could make her understand how he had inadvertently gotten caught up in the whole charade of pretending to be a contractor without destroying the fragile trust she had finally bestowed on him. Worthy or not, he counted it as his sacred duty to try to protect her from any more heartache.

Her lips turned upward and she giggled without opening her eyes.

He whispered. "What's so funny?"

Her lash fluttered against her cheek but she didn't look at him.

"Must be some dream."

Her shoulders twitched with the laughter she was trying to hold back. "I was just thinking about those people whose photos we took at the beach."

"Ah." He smiled, remembering all too vividly.

"We must have walked four miles before we found someone who was up to your standards."

"Hey. A too-honest portrayal of what the average European looks like naked isn't going to convince anybody to hop on an airplane with someone who might have SARS, fly to a country that might be harboring terrorists, and pay ten bucks for a Big Mac that might be tainted with mad cow."

"But you can get beer with your McDonald's in Europe."

"Small comfort."

"Might as well stay home and go to the Tulip Festival in Iowa, huh?" She laughed.

"You betcha," he answered in his best Iowegian accent.

"The couple I picked out wasn't that bad looking."

"If you like pancakes for boobs instead of breakfast."

"Michael!"

"I'm serious. If anything's going to lure someone to visit the French Riviera, it's my Swedish girls. One look at Ingrid, Birgitte, and Sophia, and every red-blooded male in America is going to be logging onto the Internet to buy discount tickets to Europe."

She rolled her eyes. "I was trying to hold my journalistic standards to a higher level."

"Trust me." He tipped his head and kissed her. "Frederick and Ernestine just weren't cutting it. No one in their right mind would travel anywhere to see those two naked."

"And you're qualified to judge who's in their right mind and who's not because you're a man, or because you're a fake shrink?" Her eyes crinkled merrily.

And his heart broke, because every time she teased him about being a fake shrink, his degree in psychology chafed against his neck so painfully he could hardly bear it. "You just have to trust me on this one."

She smiled. "I trusted you to decide where we were going to eat lunch yesterday and you choose McDonald's."

"McDonald's Nouveau Monde."

She laughed. "We were within feet of some of the finest eateries in France."

"I've been in Europe for almost a year now. I was hungry for a little chausson aux pommes."

"It's still a hot apple pie, fried in oil, wrapped in a cardboard box no matter what language you say it in."

"You forgot *dipped in cinnamon sugar*."

"A fried pie by any other name..."

"Oui, mon cher." He drew himself up in his seat and squared his shoulders. "A rose by any other name... for that matter, je t'aime is just I love you, but in le French, it sounds tres romantique, no?" He bent over and kissed her neck.

She moaned low in her throat. "Don't start. With our track record, we'll end up doing it on the train."

He scanned the crowded car. "Train sex is risky business."

Her eyes were smoldering when they met his. "*Risky Business* is nothing when you just finished filming *French Kiss*."

"True." Michael laughed. "Maybe for our next feature, we should do *Rob Roy*. I've always wanted to wear a kilt."

"Hmmm. You did mention there are things about you I don't know yet. Maybe we should try *The Whole Truth*."

The train veered suddenly to the left. Isabelle clutched his arm until it straightened out and sped along its way.

Michael opened his mouth to speak. This was his chance. They hadn't known each other for all that long. Isabelle was smart enough to realize there was a whole world of things they didn't know about each other. She hadn't asked for a psychological profile, references, or a resume before they'd made love—she'd gone into it knowing she'd only seen the tip of the iceberg. That's how it was when you were just getting to know each other. Sure, she'd had one bad experience—someone had lied to her, hurt her, stolen from her. But she had to know that no one bares their whole soul all at once, that there were some things you had to wait to tell until the time was right.

A few painful seconds of silence crept by but the words just wouldn't come. "We could try *An Affair to Remember*."

"As long as we don't have to do *To Catch a Thief*." She sighed. "I've had it with *Dirty Rotten Scoundrels*."

"How about *Entrapment?*" he said. "Part of it was filmed right on the island, at Duart Castle. Have you been there yet?"

"No." Her face looked serene and trusting, her mouth, relaxed and free from tension. "I've not seen the movie either. I'd love to though. Imagine Sean Connery and Catherine Zeta-Jones right there on Mull, in the flesh. I wonder if they ever ate at the Blue Bell while they were on location?"

"We'll have to ask Mrs. Galbraith. Nothing gets by that woman."

"Excellent idea."

Michael watched as Isabelle's brow crinkled up. She suddenly looked as though she were millions of miles away.

"Speaking of the island," she said, "how well do you know Hans and Bette? I mean, besides the fact that you work for them. Do you know what Damon does for a living?"

"Bette invites me to tea at the castle periodically, usually when Hans is gone and she's lonely. Our conversations concern the keep for the most part, but she does get to reminiscing about the village in Alsace where she grew up and their years in Wales every so often. I've only met Damon once or twice. Besides owning the Blue Bell, I don't know what he does for a living. I don't know that he even works. It's possible he doesn't need to."

"Their years in Wales?"

"Hans was the German ambassador to England and Wales for over a decade. It was during that time they first visited Tobermory and fell in love with the town. Why do you ask?"

"Something I learned while I was in France made me wonder about Damon. You know, with ties to three plus different countries, it would be very easy for someone like Damon to fabricate several different identities to use for whatever devious purposes he had a mind to."

He shifted uncomfortably. "It sounds to me like your imagination is starting to run away with you."

"It was something a friend of Bette's mentioned about Damon when he was a child," Isabelle said, gazing off into the distance. "I think she used the word aberrant, but we were interrupted and she never finished her thought. When I asked her about it later, she mumbled something about 'everyone deserving a fresh start' and 'Bette not being aware of certain things' and 'not wanting to hurt her dearest friend in all ze world.' That's all I could get out of her."

"A lot of years have passed since Damon was a little boy." He stroked her hand. "Bette's friend was probably wise to leave well enough alone."

"Once I catch a scent and start following a trail, it's hard for me to stop until I've unraveled the whole mystery."

"Isn't that what investigative reporters are supposed to do?"

"I'll admit I've been overly suspicious since... I just can't shake this feeling I have about Damon. There's something about him that makes me wonder if he's really who he says he is."

"As I said, Mrs. Galbraith would be the one to ask. Nothing much goes on in Tobermory that she doesn't find out about."

She rubbed her fingers over his hand. "It seems odd, thinking about being back at the Bell. Walking in and seeing you, and—"

"Knowing what I look like naked?"

"Well, that, too. Seriously though, joining me in France— surprising me the way you did. The whole thing is like a fairy tale come true. I don't want it to end just because we're going home."

"We're not going home, mon cher. Virginia's another lifetime altogether, and Wisconsin and its woes are thousands of miles from here. All we're doing now is heading back to the castle to make a few more of your wishes come to life. Trust me." He smoothed her hair with his lips. "You and I are a dream come true. Nothing's going to end unless you want it to."

"Promise?"

The word clanged in his head like a gong. God how he hoped that day would never come. "Promise."

#

Morgan approached the door of Dunara Cottage under the cover of a veil of fog so thick he was wet simply from walking through the moisture hanging in the air. He wiped away the water beaded on his upper lip, and with one last glance over his shoulder, pressed the tip of the key to its slot. He slid it in with one smooth thrust, turned the handle and slipped in the door.

Isabelle had been gone for almost a week. He noted with satisfaction that the scents of her perfume and hairspray that had initially lingered in her wake were gone. The air inside the cottage had grown stale, even musty. The smell of his work boots and sweat had replaced her more feminine ones. Perfect. He wanted her to know something was different the minute she opened the door.

He could feel his craggy facial features morphing into a proud smile. His charge all along had been to keep Isabelle MacAllister occupied so she wouldn't notice what was going on in the bay. He was fully committed to his task. Damon's lack of trust in him only fueled his determination to complete his assignment. There was more at stake than ever before now that he not only needed to thwart Isabelle's investigation, but shimmy himself back into Damon's good graces.

He stripped off his shirt, flung it on her chair and loosened his belt. His blue jeans dropped to his knees and crinkled stiffly around his legs. He lifted his feet out one by one, petted himself through his shorts, and sauntered into her bathroom, where he used a washcloth to wipe the dirt from his face, then rubbed the cool cloth over his cock to quell the burning heat radiating from his loins.

He went to her dresser and pulled open the drawer where she kept her under things, still stroking himself with one hand while he rooted through the delicate assortment of confections spread out before him. His mouth began to drool as he poked about, stopping only to rub his fingers over the satiny strip of a thong while he imagined where it had been and what it would feel like to have his cock slide the slender piece of fabric to one side while he mounted her from behind.

He began to hum a song he'd learned at his mother's knee— Monday for washing, Tuesday for ironing, Wednesday for cleaning—substituting his own little ditty about Monday for lavender, Tuesday for pink, Wednesday for yellow, and Thursday for green. He surveyed his options like a boy gazing up at shelves full of sweets at a bakery and finally selected a matched set that reminded him of the color of Isabelle's cheeks when she blushed.

A lewd smile lingered on his lips while he went to her bed and spread back her quilt. The pungent smell of his own seed wafted up from the sheets. If he couldn't distract Isabelle with his charm... Weill, the loss was hers. His initial plan would have been pleasurable for both of them. Now, he would avert her attentions with terror. The pleasure would still be his.

Chapter Nineteen

Isabelle tightened her seat belt a little more securely as Logan careened around the corner of Tobermory's main street. The Blue Bell lay due ahead, its pretty periwinkle blue facade illuminated by a shaft of sunshine poking out from between two clouds. "Kind of looks like the pot of gold at the end of a rainbow, doesn't it?" Isabelle said, wanting to break the silence filling the car.

"That it does." Michael commented dryly from the passenger side of the front seat. "What a homecoming."

Isabelle could only suppose Michael's tone was sarcastic on Logan's account. Logan's face had turned dark as a thundercloud when she and Michael had stepped off the ferry together.

"You're sure everything ran smoothly at the keep while I was gone?" Michael asked Logan, obviously concerned something was wrong and not having a clue what it was.

"Nothing gae doun the brae if that's what ye're worried aboot." Logan's normally pleasant voice ended on a disgusted sounding sneer.

Michael craned his neck and gave Isabelle a look over the headrest. "Weather nice while I was gone?"

"Fair to middlin," Logan said in a curt voice.

"McKee's arm doing all right?"

"His airm is fine. He was out with a bellythrawe yesterday."

Isabelle smiled politely from the back seat, not because she thought either Michael or Logan was looking, but because she felt compelled to do something to try to thaw the frost that had settled over the car. She liked Logan, and tried not to hold it against him that he reminded her of Ben. It wasn't his fault he looked like her worst nightmare. But his mood today was very unsettling. He looked like a bull about to charge. She'd never seen him this way before, but her instincts told her he was ready to blow, and she really didn't want to be in the way when his temper let loose.

"You know, I've been thinking," she said. "I'm really not all that hungry. If you don't mind driving out to the castle and dropping me off, I think I'd like to check my email, send another of my stories off to Ronald, and jump in the shower."

"It's been a long day," Michael said.

"I can't wait to snuggle up in my own bed and get a good night's sleep. I'm really wiped out," she said.

Logan slammed on the brakes, whipped the tiny car around in a breakneck circle, and backtracked in the direction of Bluevale.

"You'll have to read the article on European chocolates Isabelle wrote while she was in Switzerland," Michael said, clinging to his armrest. "It's entitled *Chocolate: Sinfully Sweet or Heart-Healthy Heaven?*"

"Michael helped with the title," she said.

"It's a great piece," Michael said, beaming over his shoulder at her. "Very engaging and extremely well-written."

Maybe Logan was jealous, she thought, looking up at the stiff bend to the younger man's neck. Maybe he was repulsed by the syrupy sweet way she and Michael were acting.

"I'm sure your editor is going to love it," Michael said. "I know I did, and I must be fairly representative of your target market."

Yes, but you're also in love, or at the very least, intense lust, therefore anything you think about me is suspect. She had a momentary epiphany in which she hoped she hadn't filled her story with references to birds chirping, bells ringing, and flowers singing in the sunlight. If Ronald was still looking for a reason to fire her, he'd have all the ammunition he needed if her writing suddenly went from morbidly dark and depressed to sickeningly sweet and sappy.

She glanced at the back of Michael's head and felt a dizzying sweep of emotions. Michael obviously wasn't the only one whose feelings were currently not to be trusted. From now on until her hormones stopped surging, she should probably send a copy of every article she wrote to Gloria and have her edit out the sentimental tripe before Ronald laid eyes on it. Fancying yourself in love did strange things to a person.

Logan swung the car around in the parking lot behind the castle and applied the brakes with a vengeance.

"Are you sure you don't want to grab a bite, Isabelle?" Michael asked. "We'd be happy to wait while you shower and take you back into town once you've freshened up."

159

She reached for her suitcase and opened the door. Michael climbed out of the front seat to help her out. "What's wrong with Logan?" she whispered once they were both out of the car.

"I don't have a clue," Michael said. "Thanks for begging off on dinner. Hopefully this will give me the opportunity to find out what's bugging him."

"I thought the two of you might need some time." She used the strap on her bag to swing the suitcase over her shoulder. "Have you ever tried using the incredible shrink act on a man?" She tilted her head and looked in Logan's direction. "Because it looks like you're going to need it."

Michael took her elbow, leaned forward and kissed her. "I was hoping to have a nice, romantic dinner with just the two of us tonight. Some good food, a little truth serum..."

"That noise you hear is my stomach grumbling," Logan called out from the car.

"You'd better go."

"Maybe he's just cranky because he's hungry."

Isabelle shook her head. "And you call yourself a fake shrink."

She watched as Michael forced a resigned smile and got back into the car. It was only then that his remark about truth serum registered. What was that about? She pushed her momentary doubts out of her head and headed down the path to the cottage. She trusted him. Didn't she?

She hated that Ben had made her a cynic, but it was there, and she doubted it would ever change, even with someone as inherently respectable and trustworthy as Michael.

The rhododendrons were in full bloom along the path to the cottage, and Isabelle savored the fragrance of the delicate flowers as she hurried towards the cottage. Much as she'd loved the Alps, Germany, Provence, and the beach, it felt wonderful to be home.

She turned her key in the slot and pushed the round-topped door in with her elbow, swung her backpack to the floor, and took a deep breath. The air was stale and smelled of rocks and loam and humidity. The white-washed stone walls that had looked so cozy only a week ago shone with a thin glaze of moisture so earthy and alive looking she wouldn't have been surprised to see them sprouting moss.

She closed and latched the bottom half of the door and left the top open to air the place out. The kitchen faucet was dripping and she noticed there were dirty dishes in the sink. She didn't remember leaving them there, but she had left in a hurry after taking the picnic to Michael at the construction site. Anything was possible.

She checked her answering machine and found a message from Bette inviting her to tea at the castle with her and Hans and Damon, who was in town for a visit. She made a note on the pad beside the phone so she wouldn't forget to call and accept the invitation once she'd freshened up. She plugged in her laptop and debated whether to shower before or after she checked her email.

Her curiosity got the best of her. She'd looked for an internet cafe the first day she'd arrived on the beach in France and hadn't found one. After Michael joined her, she'd pretty much forgotten the rest of the world even existed.

She pushed aside a pang of guilt. She'd done her job, written the articles Ronald had requested and taken the photos she needed—better ones than she would have on her own, assuming Michael was right about Ingrid, Birgitte, and Sophia. And he probably was.

She groaned as her Inbox exploded with new messages—one hundred fifty-two unopened emails. She methodically deleted the junk mail—she'd already refinanced her townhouse and Michael needed neither Viagra or length enhancements—and isolated the messages bearing the names of her parents, friends and co-workers, and began to read.

Good, she thought, scanning Gloria's research on the mythical sunken treasure of Tobermory Bay. If Ronald made good on his promise to let her do investigative work again after he'd read her latest round of fluff, it wouldn't hurt to have an exposé mostly researched, written and ready for tweaking. She saved the email and resolved to read it more carefully as soon as she finished the last of the articles on her trip to the mainland.

She read a short message from her mother reminding her Aunt Edith's birthday was next week, made a mental note to send an e-greeting, then remembered she'd seen another message from Gloria.

She tried to scroll back to the spot but her pointer snagged on another message and a naked breast popped up on her screen. Good grief. She thought she'd deleted all the junk mail. She used the mouse to scroll upward and let her hand hover over the delete button.

That's when it occurred to her the nipple on her screen looked strangely familiar. She gulped in a mouthful of air, swallowed it in one unwieldy clump, and tried in vain to catch her breath until she started to choke from lack of oxygen. She scrolled to the left, then the right.

No! Please not now. Not now? So when had she preferred it to happen? Like there was ever a good time to be blackmailed.

Her worst nightmare had come to life—and right on the wake of her dreams coming true. B.S. How appropriate was that? Ben Stensrud. Bob Steckland. Whatever his name was, the picture was of her—naked. She looked at her spread legs and the graphic details of her body illuminated by the photo and moaned.

The message was brief.

Dear sweet Isabelle,

These pretty pictures weren't the only memento of our time together I kept, sweetheart. I saved your entire address book to a memory stick. So unless you want your mother and father and Auntie Edith and Uncle Herbert to see what a nice young woman you've turned out to be, I'd suggest you tell your friend Gloria to get off my tail and mind her own business. While you're at it, better get out your checkbook and see how much money you have in your savings account.

On second thought, I know how embarrassed you'd be if I showed these photos to anyone in your family. Maybe I should send them off to Ronald instead. He really doesn't pay you enough money. If he realized how extensive your hidden assets are, you might get the raise you deserve.

I'll be in touch. Love you, babe.

Ben

Oh, how she'd prayed this day would never happen. Blackmail—even the word was disgusting. How could she have gotten herself into this position? What should she do? Alert her parents? They would never understand. No warning could ever prepare them for the humiliation of seeing their daughter in such a compromising position. And that was a nice way to put it. Knowing she was going through such a humiliating ordeal would break their hearts regardless of whether or not they ever saw the photos.

The police had been on Ben's trail for over three months now and still didn't know where he was. In the meantime, there was no way they could stop him from emailing the pictures to everyone she knew.

Maybe if she wrote Ben a letter and begged for his mercy, he would feel enough remorse to give up his plan. But that was assuming he even had a heart. She feared she'd never be persuasive enough to talk Ben out of blackmailing her when she felt such disgust for him—and for herself.

Maybe she should just give him the money and be done with it. But what if he wanted more?

At least she had Michael. The timing wasn't great, but she knew he would be there for her. She hadn't exactly told him about Ben or the photos he'd taken of her, but they'd had that long talk about President Bush's daughter, and he was so intuitive he must have put two and two together.

Michael would know what to do. He cared about her—he'd said several times he wanted to protect her, and she believed him. And, he would be far more objective about the whole thing than she ever could.

Her stomach was in knots thinking about how and when she would tell Michael about the photo Ben had sent. Not a thing you wanted to spring on anyone, especially at the beginning of a relationship, when you were still getting to know each other and building up your trust. But she felt like she had to act fast—she could just imagine Ben's itchy fingers hovering over the send button, ready to ruin her life.

Gloria. She needed a little good news, and since Gloria's first email had been about business, this one was probably personal.

Hi Sweetie. Sorry to be the bearer of bad news, but I guess it's better to get it out there so you can begin to deal with it.

Great. What now? Had Ben already sent photos to Ronald? Did Gloria know?

It's Austin—the intern I was telling you about. They're asking me to research all of his stories, which is how I found out he'd been assigned a series of articles on current affairs in Europe. I know doing a story on the British succession was your idea, yet here he is doing a story on Prince William and Kate and the faction that wants to bypass Prince Charles and give the crown directly to William.

Now Ronald has asked him to do a piece on the crumbling foundations of the European Union, and the deterioration of faith and family in European culture, both of which were stories I first heard about from you.

When I heard Ronald had flown Austin to London to attend a press conference at Buckingham Palace, I just flipped. I mean, you're right there, and we both know you should be writing the articles. The thing is, Austin doesn't know you, and he doesn't care. All he cares about is what he wants, and unfortunately, he wants your job.

Ronald and I had words, and he forbade me to tell you about Austin, but I just couldn't...

Her blood would have been boiling if she hadn't just seen Ben's naked photo of her... As it was, she felt too blue to be mad. What was wrong with people? Was there no one in the world she could trust? Didn't people's word mean anything anymore?

She glanced down to finish reading Gloria's email.

So, not to heap bad news on top of bad news, but here's what I've learned about Michael St. Dawndalyn.

She read on in a state of suspended animation. She'd wanted to read a personal email from Gloria, hadn't she? This was personal all right. Too personal. Uncomfortably, life-alteringly personal. Her cheeks felt like they were on fire as she read the words Gloria had written about Michael. Her Michael. How dare Gloria accuse him of... there was no way Michael would have... he would have told her. He'd trusted her with... He would have told her! It had to be a different... St. Dawndalyn.

Tears streamed down her face. If Michael had had a name like Smith or Jones, she could have convinced herself it wasn't true. But Gloria was the best researcher she knew. She double checked and triple checked her sources, even when her research didn't reveal information that all but guaranteed her best friend's heart was about to be trounced on.

"And you call yourself a fake shrink." Her eyes stung as she recalled the words she'd said to Michael just a few minutes before. She wanted to scream. Her body quivered with rage and humiliation. He'd made love to her. He'd known how deeply she'd been hurt. He'd known what honesty meant to her, yet he'd had no compulsion about deceiving her.

She glanced at the rest of her emails in a zombie-like state—a note from Ronald saying he was pleased with her stories on chocolate, *The Lord of the Rings*, and the British Invasion, and was looking forward to receiving the rest of her work. She found no joy in his praise. How could she, when he'd betrayed her—just like Ben with his scheme to bilk her out of her money and her pride. Just like Michael, who'd lied through his teeth.

If Michael had lied about something as elemental as who he was and what he did, what else had he lied about?

Even Gloria had betrayed her in a way. She hadn't asked Gloria to go snooping into Michael's past. If Gloria hadn't gone nosing into her private affairs, Ben never would have blackmailed her and she'd be none the wiser about Michael. She wished she'd never found out about Michael's deceit.

Tears were streaming down her face when she opened the next message, this one from Ronald, telling her he'd gotten Gloria's memo, that he wanted her to proceed with an exposé on all efforts to recover the sunken treasure, past and present.

Be careful, he'd written.

And as soon as you're done with that, Ronald had gone on to say, *set up an interview with St. Dawndalyn. His story will sell millions of copies, both in the Midwest and nationwide. Being ratted out by your shrink is everyone's worst nightmare.*

Well, not quite. She could think of lots of nightmarish situations far worse than anything Ronald's little pea brain might imagine. Interviewing Michael was one of them. Disgusted as she was by Michael's lies, she'd be damned before she'd sensationalize whatever it was he was trying to hide, whatever he had done wrong, or anything else that had anything to do with a freak show like the one he was involved with.

There was a third email from Gloria inquiring about the research she'd sent on Michael and the sunken treasure. This one was personal—Gloria being Gloria, her friend—not realizing how much she'd hurt her, although, on some level she must have had an inkling, since she kept mentioning concerns for her well-being.

Oh, Gloria—what have you done? What have I done? She thought about everything that had happened and wished to God's name she could be as naively and blindly in love with Michael as she'd been an hour ago.

But now that she knew—well, she couldn't forget, couldn't ever trust him ever again, couldn't act like nothing had happened. She'd half known Ben would stab her in the back one day when she least expected it. But she hadn't expected this from Michael. Not Michael.

She was just ready to jump in the shower when her phone rang. She glanced at the caller ID. Gloria. Great. Just great. Although it could have been worse. It could have been Ben—or Michael.

"Great timing, Glor. I just finished reading your emails." Isabelle knew her voice sounded a bit sharp, and probably cynical as hell, too. That was just the way she felt.

"I was worried about you."

"So your letter said."

"So are you?" Gloria asked. "Okay? It's been a few days since I..."

"I'm fine. There weren't any internet cafes on the beach, at least none I found."

She always felt an instant closeness to Gloria, whether they were speaking in person, on the internet, or on the phone. Today, Gloria's voice sounded every bit as far away as she really was.

"Good," Gloria said. "I mean, I'm sorry you were without contact with the outside world, but I'm glad you're all right. I know the lady at the Welsh consulate was just speculating about Damon, but her concerns still made me a little nervous."

What am I going to do? She wanted Michael, wanted Michael to protect her, to tell her what to do. The pictures Ben had might shock him, but at least he'd already seen everything they had to show.

It was more than that. Michael understood her. He would know what to do, how to handle Ben. Oh, Michael, why? How could you lie to me, and keep lying to me, after we...?

"I'm fine," Isabelle said again. She hadn't heard most of what Gloria had said but she was too numb to care.

"You sound a little odd." Gloria paused. "Are you sure you're not—?"

Isabelle cut her off. "I've been away from home for over a week. I just walked in the door a few minutes ago. I'm beat, that's all."

"I'm sorry I caught you at a bad time."

"I just need a hot shower and a cup of tea. Could I call you back, or better yet, meet you online in a couple of hours when I've had a chance to relax a little?" She didn't want Gloria to suspect something was wrong and Gloria knew her too well to be fooled for very long.

"Sure." Gloria's voice already sounded worried.

"I appreciate the call. I'm just standing here half naked, ready to get into the shower, and it's freezing cold in here."

"Why didn't you say so, silly?" Gloria laughed, pacified at last. "Sure. Call me back then. I just needed to know—"

"I'll talk to you later, Glor. Bye."

Her hand was trembling as she put the phone back on the hook. A hot shower sounded wonderful—scalding hot, body-mind-soul numbing, cleansing. She fumbled with the buttons on her blouse but she was shaking so badly she couldn't get them undone. She went to her bedroom, raised her arms and lifted the fabric over her head, twisted out of her bra, and stepped out of her skirt. She had just tugged her panties to the floor and lifted one foot when she heard a noise.

The door! She'd forgotten to close the top of the door to the cottage. She untangled her feet, slammed the bedroom door shut and reached into the closet for her robe. Damn. Her suitcase was still in the kitchen, her robe still packed inside. She could hear steps now, and a faint voice calling out her name. There was no lock on the bedroom or bathroom doors.

She reached inside the bathroom door and grabbed for a towel, snatched it from the hook and wrapped it around her in one frantic second, her hands shaking like leaves caught in a wind eddy. Her knees were quaking, her palms sweating as she tucked it under her arms and pulled it tightly to her breasts.

She looked down at the towel. Her palms—she couldn't be sweating that much. The towel was soaking wet and just-been-used-clammy, and there was something sticky, white, gooey, slimy-sticky, sliding between her left shoulder blade and the towel. She screamed.

Chapter Twenty

The wood beamed ceiling of the Blue Bell seemed a good foot lower, and the air inside the thick-walled pub, at least twenty degrees cooler than it had before Michael had left for the French Riviera. The hair on his arms bristled over a fresh crop of goose-bumps, which made him wish he was back on the beach, which made him wish he was with Isabelle.

Her image—freshly showered, squeaky clean and wrapped up in a fluffy white towel—popped into his head. He looked at Logan's normally pleasant face and wished he was back at Dunara with her instead of at the Bell about to listen to a probable tirade.

"Can I buy you a drink?" Maybe a bit of ale would diffuse Logan's ire.

"Ye cannae buy me anythin'. And I cannae keep my mouth shut any longer," Logan backed him up to the wall at the far end of the pub and leaned in a bit too close. "The only reason I kept quiet aboot who ye really are for this long is that I thought ye were tryin' tae help us."

God in heaven, Michael thought. Logan knew he was a psychologist? "Of course I want to help you." He backed up a step. How could Logan possibly know? He'd not told anyone the truth. "Not to worry. Your job is safe. I'm committed to finishing the restoration project at the castle no matter what happens."

"My job? Is 'at all ye think I care aboot?"

"No. Of course not. I just assumed..." Michael hadn't a clue what Logan was thinking.

"Sae ye admit it? Ye've bin lying to us all aboot who ye really are?"

"I never set out to hurt any of you. There are reasons. There are things at stake you don't understand."

"I understand weel enough to know ye abandoned yer post tae run off with Isabelle withit a thought to what the pirates might be up tae. A bony lass bats her eyelashes at ye once or twice and ye forget all aboot yer charge to protect Tobermory."

"Pirates? Good God, Logan, have you lost your mind?"

Of course, that, he would know what to do about. But pirates? Who or what in God's name did Logan think he was up to?

"The pirates who stole yer sonar technology. The pirates who are scoorin' the bay fur gold e'en as we speak," Logan huffed. "I defended ye when Morgan made trouble at the castle, and I've tried my best to keep a calm touch, but with you running off the way ye did, I cannae stay quiet any longer. There's far more at stake here than a wee bit o' fancy equipment! God sakes, man. The people of Tobermory have a right tae the gold say naethin aboot the fact these men will stop at naethin tae get what they want. Someone could get hurt!"

Michael's mind raced from one possible scenario to another. Could it be Isabelle had happened on to something involving Morgan? Is that why he had been acting so strangely, both at work, and where Isabelle was concerned? She hadn't mentioned any suspicions about the Welshman, only Damon, who Logan hadn't said a word about. Still, if Morgan was involved with a plot to unearth the gold, Isabelle could be in trouble. His heart started to pound. Adrenalin surged through his body. If any of what Logan was saying was fact, Isabelle was in immediate danger.

"Tell me everything you know, Logan."

The younger man looked at him as though he were the one who was nuts.

"Now!" Michael yelled. "It's obvious you've been getting your information from somewhere. Did you ever stop to think you may have stumbled upon something I know nothing about?"

"All I know fur certain is that ye're here working undercover fur the sonar company whose equipment was stolen."

"I'm not working for anyone," Michael yelled.

Logan's fingers curled into a fist. "Ye jist admitted ye waur."

"I admitted nothing. Now tell me what you know!"

"I know what I told ye an' naethin' more."

"What's all the flumgummerie aboot noo, ye bucksturdie yoong fools?" Mrs. Galbraith said, roaring so loudly they could hear her clear across the room.

Michael looked at Logan.

"Ignair her," Logan said. "She's as daft as she is days auld."

169

"I'll teel ye who's daft, ye contermacious yoong bletherskite," Logan's mother raved, heading for her son.

Michael had to admit the woman did look like she needed a prescription for hormone replacement therapy. "Talk to her. She's your mother, for God's sake."

"She's aye at me. I'm sick an' tired ay it."

"She's your mother," Michael repeated. "That's what mother's do."

She stopped in her tracks and turned to Michael. "I'll show ye whit mother's dae if ye dinnae stop thes clishmackaver collieshangie."

"I tellt ye." Logan interrupted. "Michael is an undercover agent workin' fur a big sonar company that's tryin' to recover some equipment that was stolen by the pirates who are tryin' to rob us of the gold."

"Who told you that?"

"I overheard Morgan talkin' tae the tall gent who works oan the fishin' boat."

Mrs. Galbraith eyed her son, then Michael, her dishrag sopped with bubbles ready for the flinging. "Sae ye're nae a stone-layer?" she asked Michael.

He flinched. "Let's just say it's a secondary career."

"'At wood explain a lot," Mrs. Galbraith said, transferring the dripping cloth to her left hand so she could scratch her head. "Keepin' secrits, livin' a dooble life, aye havin' tae clood the truth tae avoid suspicion... It's nae wonder ye're a wee cranky at times."

Michael rolled his eyes. At least he was finally getting a little sympathy from the old biddie. "It's been a drain all right—trying to serve two masters takes a toll on a man."

"He's jist toyin' with ye noo," Logan said. "Dinnae believe a word he says."

"Nothing a scape o' the pen to America willnae clear up," Mrs. Galbraith said, and bopped Logan in the head with her dish rag.

Logan pinched his eyes shut. Michael saw his chance to leave and took it. He still didn't understand what was going on, but he knew he had to warn Isabelle.

The light outside the pub was filtered with the pinks and yellows of sunset. Damn. He didn't have his car. He crossed the street and grabbed the handle of Logan's car. Locked. He looked around and saw an ancient, red, balloon-tired bicycle leaning against the wall of the Bell. Not the kind of bike one had to worry about being stolen. Only a desperate man would stoop so low.

He ran to the building and flung the bike into the street, loping his leg over the bar as he ran down the bumpy cobblestone street.

He was desperate all right.

#

Michael could see the flashing lights of a police car in the distance as he veered away from the scrubby brush clinging to the moorlands leading to Cnoc Fuar and pedaled up the hill to his cottage. He tossed the bike on the ground, ran inside to get his car keys, and started down the hill to the castle.

Just as he feared. The two vehicles were parked in the lot closest to Dunara Cottage. He leaped out of his car and ran down the path. "Isabelle!" He screamed at the top of his lungs. "Isabelle! Are you there?" He dared not think of what might have happened to her.

His feet skidded on loose dirt and smooth rocks as he rounded the corner to Dunara Cottage. A uniformed policeman stood in his way, blocking the entry door. "Where is she? Where is Isabelle?"

"An' ye ur?"

"Michael St. Dawndalyn. A friend," he said, clutching his side.

"The victeem was given shelter until we coods complete our inspection."

"Victim? My God, is she okay?"

"Ye'll have tae speak tae the doctur aboot 'at."

"The doctor? Where is she?"

"'Er whereaboots are confidential until the criminal who did this tae her is behin' bars."

"What did they do to her?"

"I'm afraid 'at is also confidential."

"Did they hurt her physically?"

"I'm sorry, but 'at is also confidential."

Michael tried not to scream. "Did she discover some sort of damage to the cottage when she first came home or did someone break in and accost her after she returned?"

The man wagged his head.

"Let me guess," Michael said. "Confidential."

"Right ye are, lad. Noo if ye'll excuse me, I've got wark tae dae."

His body felt like it was about to explode. He struggled to focus his thoughts and tried to think reasonably. If Isabelle was hurt, she would be at the hospital. He shuddered to think about that possibility. If something had happened to bring on another panic attack, and she was just shaken up—dear God, he hoped that was all that was wrong—she would most likely have been sent off to a friend's house to calm down. He hadn't been home. Isabelle didn't have any close acquaintances on the island he was aware of besides Bette.

The castle. He took off at a dead run.

#

Rose MacCraig spoke in an utterly calm voice that sounded the exact opposite of how Isabelle felt. "Isabelle, I know you told Bette you didn't want to be disturbed, but she says Michael St. Dawndalyn is at the front door wanting to see you and I thought perhaps..."

Isabelle clutched her robe around her shoulders and turned to face Rose. She'd been relieved it was the pastor's wife who had come in response to the police's call to the area Crisis Intervention team. "No. I'm sorry to put you in this position, Rose, but I don't want to talk to anyone right now."

"Bette said he seems quite frantic. She's not sure he'll take no for an answer. She said he seems most distraught, and if I may say so, dear, so do you. Perhaps it would help if..."

The sad fact of the matter was, she could probably use a good psychologist. She could certainly use a friend. Not that she didn't appreciate Rose coming by, but Michael knew her, and his arms were so strong. If only...

She turned her back to the lamplight and faced the tightly shuttered windows lining the rear of the lofty room. "Please ask Bette to tell him I'm fine, but I've had a terrible shock and I don't want to see him."

Isabelle tried to take a deep breath and failed. Part of her just wanted to be alone. Part of her was terrified to be alone. Although she barely knew Rose, the pastor's wife did seem to have a calming presence on her. How was it that Rose could enter the stark, cold, room Isabelle had been shown to in the Castle, and in seconds, transform it to a place of warmth and hope—something sadly lacking from her life?

Rose returned a moment later. "So, tell me what's going through your head if ye can, Isabelle," Rose said in her gentle brogue. "It will help to talk aboot what happened, I promise ye."

"I'm thinking about what a Godsend you are."

Rose laughed heartily and sent more of the icicles in the room shattering. "Ye cannae know how good it is to hear that! I'm aware ye dinnae know me weill, but the more typical response to my arrival is, "Oh, it's that little dickens again.""

"No. You've been very helpful to me already."

Rose settled back into a wingback chair at the end of the bed and motioned for her to take the other. "So, what's on yer mind, deary?"

"Well, I told you about Ben, the one who used to be my... The more I think about it, the more strongly I believe it had to have been Ben who was in my cottage. He likes to intimidate people, and this sick act just fits him to a tee. My friend, Gloria, has been investigating him. That's probably what set the whole thing in motion. Gloria is merciless when she's on someone's trail. And Ben would do anything to stay out of jail."

Rose cleared her throat. "It's a long trip across the pond, and very expensive to fly to and fro. No one seems to have spotted the likes of him around town, and you know not a thing goes unnoticed around here."

Isabelle could feel goose bumps racing across her scalp, and down her neck to her arms.

"I thought I had covered my tracks when I came to Scotland, but with all Ben knows about computers, he was probably able to find out where I was just like that. It's been my greatest fear he would come back and try to hurt me. No one else believed he would because it wasn't part of his pattern. The police said, and I can see it now, too, that Ben counted on his victims being so intimidated they wouldn't call the police or press charges. By the time he finishes with these women, they're so humiliated they would prefer never seeing him again to seeing justice done."

"These women." Rose was silent for a second. "Ye mean ye. Is that how ye felt, Isabelle?"

"But I called the police, and I confided in Gloria, who's one of the best investigators in the country. I did everything I could to—"

The truth hit her like a hurricane slamming into the Outer Banks. Her very efforts to protect herself—and others—had forced Ben to

173

do exactly what she'd feared. "All Ben would have had to do to find out I'm in Scotland was to make up some lie and call my office. No one would have bothered to cover for me because no one had believed I was in danger. Now Ben is here, toying with me like a cat playing with a mouse before he kills..."

She began to tremble violently. "What next? His back is against the wall. Ben is capable of anything—even when he isn't cornered. Now that he is..."

Rose looked a smidgen more worried than she had before, but Isabelle still didn't think she had Rose convinced Ben was in Scotland. The hot tears she'd been holding inside began to stream down her face.

Rose leaned forward in her chair and Isabelle slid into her embrace.

"What happened to ye is horrible, Isabelle, but we're going to help ye get through it. And ye will be happy again, and ye will feel safe again. Ye do know that, dinnae ye, dear?"

"I'm... fine." She sobbed into Rose's arms. "It was just so awful, wrapping the towel around me, then finding it was wet and sticky with someone's semen." She started to choke. "The smell. Oh, Rose. I can still smell it."

She wanted her mother. She could trust her mother. But that was assuming her mother would understand. And she wouldn't. Not in a million years. She could never tell her mother what a mess she'd gotten herself into. She hadn't wanted to tell Gloria about the pictures, but... for all she knew, Gloria had already uncovered Ben's final deceit. For all she knew, Gloria had seen them.

Her head started to swim. She twisted away from Rose and grasped the edges of the chair.

"Now, now. Ye smell of flowers and herbs and freshness, and that's all." Rose patted her arm, "Except for a faint whiff of antiseptic. But that's a good thing."

There was a knock on the door and Bette reappeared with a pot of tea.

Isabelle stood and walked to the stone fireplace that stretched from floor to ceiling and tried to regain her composure. "Bette, are you sure you never saw anyone heading down the path to my cottage while I was gone? A big, tall man with very short hair and extremely broad shoulders?"

"I see people of all shapes and sizes. There are dozens of people around and about this time of year. The path that runs beside Dunara leads to many places."

"But you didn't notice anyone in particular?" Isabelle's mind raced as she struggled to set aside her fear and call upon her logic. Maybe Rose was right. Maybe it hadn't been Ben. There's a man named Morgan Baugh who was caught snooping around my cottage a couple of weeks ago. Did you hear me describing him to the police?"

"No. But there's no need to describe Morgan to me. I've known the boy since he was twelve years old. He is a friend of Damon's from Wales."

Isabelle stiffened and backed away.

"I cannot believe Morgan would do such a thing. He is a nice boy, you see. And I think I would have noticed him if he had gone to your cottage. No. As I told the police, I can be of no help."

"I'm sorry to put you on the spot, Bette. I just want so badly for the police to catch whoever did this so I can go back to the cottage and get back to normal." She shivered. As if she would ever feel normal again.

"Perhaps Hans or Damon can be of some help. They sat out on the portico last evening playing chess. Perhaps one of them noticed someone, or saw something unusual."

Damon. In her panic, Isabelle had forgotten the phone message she'd received from Bette indicating her son was in Scotland again. She shuddered. She hadn't thought of Damon when the police had offered to bring her to the castle. If her suspicions about Damon were correct, how could she feel safe with him sharing her sanctuary?

"Both Hans and Damon are out at the moment. Hans should be back at any time, but Damon is out on his boat, and with the days so long, it is hard to tell when he will return. If you will excuse me," Bette said, "I will walk down to Dunara and suggest to the police that they talk to Damon as soon as he gets back. He has always had—what do you call them? The eyes of an eagle?"

Chapter Twenty-One

The stale air trapped inside Cnoc Fuar was so dense it gave Michael a headache—a moot point after Isabelle's insane refusal to see him. Not only did his head hurt like hell, his shoulders felt too heavy for his frame. He walked to the sink and looked in the mirror. His face was red. No wonder, frustrated as he felt. He stooped and cupped his hands under the faucet. A rusty spurt of water and air exploded into his hands.

He sighed. Maybe his face didn't need washing after all.

He surveyed the room. At least there was no evidence anyone had been in his house. He picked up a photo of his sister's family and wiped a coating of dust off the glass. Bothered as he was, he couldn't help smiling at his sister's glowing face and swollen belly. He hoped his mother would find a way to call as soon as there was news. Her baby should be coming any day now.

Her baby. Michael's lip curled and he deliberately averted his eyes from the man standing beside his sister. Even now, he couldn't bear to think of the child his sister was carrying as Kent's—not when he knew his brother-in-law had been sleeping with another woman during the same time period the baby had been conceived. Not when he knew Kent had fathered a baby with Carole Masterson only six months earlier.

Tori's blond curls and blue eyes jumped out at him. He paused for a second and savored the memory of her chubby-armed hugs, and the toothy "I wuv yous" he had so coveted before he left for Scotland. Had it been worth it? Could he have done more good if he'd stayed behind, told the truth, and helped his sister pick up the pieces of her life?

His nephews sat square-shouldered like little men, their tow-headed cowlicks slicked into place with mousse—no doubt against their wills. How he loved them! Surely when he explained to Isabelle how much they meant to him, that they were the real reason he couldn't testify in the Masterson case, she would understand and respect his wishes to keep his whereabouts confidential.

He stooped and pulled a window open, straightened and noticed the charger for his cell phone sitting on the table. *Isabelle!* Maybe she'd tried to call him from the cottage before the police took her to the castle. If she'd tried and hadn't been able to reach him when she'd needed him, it could explain why she was refusing to see him.

He rummaged through his bag, found his cell phone, and set it on the charger. He hadn't been able to get a decent signal in France, and none at all in the tunnel under the English Channel. By the time they'd gotten back to Scotland, he'd forgotten all about it.

His heart quickened with anticipation when he saw he had messages. Maybe Bette had talked Isabelle into phoning him from the castle after he'd left. Their landlady felt badly that it was her knock on Isabelle's door that had set the whole chain of events in motion down at Dunara. She obviously wanted to help, and Bette trusted Michael like a second son.

He still didn't understand why Isabelle hadn't wanted to see him. He could help her, damn it. Didn't she trust him enough to know that? His heart swelled with pain and longing. All he wanted to do was to be there for her... to help her, to protect her, to hold her.

He punched in his password and waited impatiently only to hear Buck's voice blaring in his ear instead of Isabelle's. "Call me immediately. There's an emergency." He checked the date and time the message had been delivered—two days ago.

He dialed Buck's speed number, wondering for the second time that day if he was really accomplishing anything by staying in Scotland. He hated being so far away from his mother, his sister, the kids. Surely if one of them was... if something had happened to his sister, or the baby... the Red Cross helped track people down when... didn't they? His throat choked up with emotions that had been festering under the surface for months.

"Buck, please," he said, feeling even more wary when the secretary put him right through. He heard a sigh on the other end of the line and felt sick with anxiety. If whatever was wrong was bad enough to reduce Buck to this eerie, uncustomary silence, it had to be—his mind rushed to one worst case scenario after another.

He heard papers being shuffled and Buck finally spoke. "I take it you know an Isabelle MacAllister?"

"Yes." Michael's heart lurched, relieved the call wasn't about his

177

family. But how could Buck possibly know about Isabelle? He'd phoned Buck's office to let him know he was going to be gone for a few days, but he hadn't said where he was going or with whom.

"Last week while you were gone, Masterson's attorney got a call from a Gloria Greene, a researcher slash attorney at *Insight* magazine who evidently works very closely with Miss MacAllister. I received a call as well. So did your mother."

"Mom?" Michael croaked.

"Yes."

"You're kidding."

"Yes, Michael, I'm kidding you. I picked Isabelle MacAllister's name out of a phone book at random and asked you if you knew her to see if I would get a rise out of you."

"I knew this would happen!" He slammed his fist into his pillow. "Mom didn't say anything, did she?"

"Not about the trial. But knowing your mother, Miss Greene probably knows what kind of diapers your mother used on you when you were a baby and how old you were when you got your first tooth."

Crap. "You obviously didn't tell her anything."

"I didn't need to. She'd already heard the whole sordid story from Masterson, who I'm sure was all too happy to share his take on you."

"Great. So she knows everything?"

"She not only knows everything I know, which granted, obviously isn't the whole story, she knows everything Masterson claims to know. And I'm sure the man didn't paint a pretty picture of you. I just hope you haven't confided anything to this MacAllister woman, or you'll really be finished. This Greene woman is a hound."

"And Masterson?"

"He knows where you are. It's over, Michael."

He felt like the air was being squeezed from his lungs. "What happens now?"

"This is still a civil matter, not a criminal one, so there won't be a formal extradition," Buck said. "What will happen is that Karl Wayzinski, our good State Representative, who, coincidentally enough is a friend of Dr. Masterson's, will call the US Embassy and put pressure on the Scottish government to put pressure on the local officials on Mull to send you home. At the very least, your cover will be blown to smithereens."

He felt as though his blood had ground to a halt inside his veins. His body was frozen, not his own. "Are you sure Masterson found out where I was because Isabelle was investigating me?"

"Positive."

The anger hit him later, when he'd disconnected, and the ice in his blood had started to thaw. Damn her! Her innocent act had been just that. A game. She'd slept with him to get a bloody story.

She'd told him getting back into Ronald's good graces was important to her, but he hadn't thought she'd prostitute herself to get a scoop.

No wonder she hadn't cared to talk to him. She'd said she was going back to her cottage to send another story off to Ronald and that's exactly what she'd done. She'd gotten what she wanted. Operation Michael had been stamped 'Case Closed' the second she'd logged on to her damn laptop and pressed send.

#

"I cannae do it, Damon," Gareth said, his voice betraying the fact he was one step away from blubbering like a baby.

"I told Morgan not to draw any attention to me or the operation," Damon said, his voice seething with rage. "I told him to go back to Wales. You did tell him I wanted him back in Wales right away, didn't you, Gareth?"

"Aye. I did tell him. I told him just hours after ye told me to."

"The bloody police came to the castle to interview me," Damon raged. "Worthless, no good louse disobeys my orders and does the exact opposite of what he's told. The man may as well have given them a signed confession from all of us." Damon paced back and forth. "The police know I'm in town, know I've been out on the boat for hours at a time, and know I've got contacts from Wales in the area. I covered my tracks as best I could, but I could see suspicion written all over their faces."

"But, sir..."

"But nothing! Morgan has made all of us vulnerable. The whole operation is at risk."

"I'm sure he was just trying to help ye, sir," Gareth tried not to stutter. "No one is more dedicated to ye than Morgan. Ye know him.

Once he gets his teeth into something, he's like a bulldog with a bone. He's been that way for as long we've known him."

"He had plenty of warning. He knew what I would do if he disobeyed my orders. You did warn him, didn't you, Gareth?"

"I did warn him. But, sir..."

"What?" Damon snapped.

"We've known Morgan since he was a wee lad. I cannae..."

"He jeopardized the mission." Damon slammed his fist into his palm with such unconstrained fury that the reverberations rippled through the air. "We find the frigging gold, we finally get the equipment we need for the salvage operation. All we need is a little time and to keep a low profile so we can recover the gold and get out. All I asked was for him to give up surveillance of that damn reporter and not make any waves."

"The woman does have a way." He wasn't trying to make excuses for Morgan, but he had to say something to lighten the mood. "Morgan was right fond of her from the start. 'Twas her milkers that seemed to beckon to him. She does have a fine set o'..."

"It has to be you, Gareth. You're the only one he trusts. If I were to call him and ask to meet with him personally, after what's happened, he'd suspect my motives immediately."

Gareth watched as Damon's coloring went from red to a pale, almost translucent shade of white. His eyes took on a glassy stare; his voice, a satiny calm.

"He knows you," Damon said. "He doesn't believe you would ever do anything to hurt him. That's why it has to be you."

Gareth cowered and winced reflexively. "Now that's exactly why I dinnae think I'm the right man for the job, sir." He was shaking; shaking so hard his teeth were chattering. If Damon didn't stop, stop right now, he was going to retch right there on the street.

"Call him," Damon said. "I don't care where or how you do it as long as there's no trace of his body left when you're done."

Chapter Twenty-Two

Isabelle rifled through her backpack, looking for a sweater. It never felt as cold in the cottage as it did in this eerie old castle. She was freezing.

No sweater. Maybe she had taken it out and laid it on the table at the cottage. It could have fallen out of her pack in her frenzy to get away from Dunara. She hoped she hadn't left it on the train or in she and Michael's cabin in France. Had she even worn it when Michael was there? She hadn't felt cold the whole time he was with her.

Tears flooded her eyes. She was extremely uneasy about spending the night in the castle. Besides, she'd bothered Bette enough already. She'd been kind enough to help her through the last few hours, let her stay in one of the guest rooms at the B&B, and use her office. It wasn't Bette's fault she was lonely and unhappy. She had wanted to be left alone and Bette had done what she'd asked.

She wrapped her arms around her chest and tried to pull herself together. If Ronald knew how close she was to another full blown anxiety attack, he would demand she return home at once and probably fire her the second she walked through the door.

She had to finish the articles and send them off as soon as possible—regardless of whatever bizarre thing might happen next. And the stories need to be good, she reminded herself. Sparkling clean and humming with passion. Compelling, persuasive, witty, and gripping.

She needed to talk to Gloria, a task she normally looked forward to. She rubbed her forehead. She'd been cynical enough to expect the pretty little bubble she'd shared with Michael on the French Riviera to burst when she got back to Tobermory, but she'd never thought it would turn out to be her own best friend who would thrust in the pin and make it pop.

Gloria obviously hadn't set out to purposely sabotage the happiness she'd found with Michael. Knowing that didn't make it any better.

But Gloria was suspicious already, and no doubt waiting for her to appear online. If she wasted any more time trying to decide what she would and wouldn't say to her, she would only fuel those worries. All Isabelle knew for sure is that however she did it, she had to get Gloria to call off her investigation immediately or Ben would send her photographs to everyone in her address book. She couldn't let that happen.

She plugged in her laptop and logged in as Nightingale. No big surprise that Gloria was there waiting, as disgustingly chipper as always.

Morning_Glory: Hey, stranger! I was starting to get nervous.

It dawned on her that for someone who was such a good researcher, Gloria was totally clueless about some things.

Nightingale: Sorry to keep you waiting. A lot has happened since I got home a few hours ago.

Morning_Glory: Your voice sounded so unlike you when I called earlier. Tell me what's going on!

Nightingale: Someone broke into my cottage while I was in on the mainland.

Morning_Glory: Oh, Isabelle! I knew something was wrong! Do the police think it was a random occurrence or connected to what's happening on the island? You did call the police, didn't you?

If there was one thing she wasn't afraid to do, it was call the police. After Ben had first disappeared, she'd given the local police back in Virginia all kinds of business. Every time she'd heard a strange noise, she'd been convinced Ben had come back to hurt her. The cops had humored her and searched her townhouse for signs of forced entry each time she'd called, but they'd never found a trace.

All that had changed now.

Nightingale: The police are over there right now trying to figure how someone could have gotten in and out without being seen or destroying the lock. I told them about Ben, that his specialty is penetrating hostile embassies and drug compounds.

Morning_Glory: You think it was Ben? Where are you now?

Nightingale: I'm at the castle.

Morning_Glory: Do you feel safe there?

Nightingale: My only other choice was to call Michael. I really didn't believe Ben would go so far.

Morning_Glory: It's not Ben, Isabelle. It can't be him. He's still in Virginia, in a little town near Fredericksburg. I spoke to him just yesterday.

It took Isabelle a moment to catch her breath. Of course she felt relief. Ben wasn't in Scotland. Then the shock started to sink in. Ben had said in his email that Gloria was on his tail, but the revelation that Gloria knew where Ben was, and had spoken to him was incomprehensible. And if Ben hadn't been in her cottage, who had been? The thought that it might have been Morgan was utterly repugnant.

Nightingale: How do you know where Ben is? Is he in jail?

If the police had Ben in custody, he couldn't follow through on his threats to blackmail her, could he? Or did inmates have access to computers?

Morning_Glory: No. He's living with his latest fiancée, and I'm working with the police to arrange a sting. Ben thinks I'm Cathy Nelson, a small town sweetheart who's just lost her wealthy parents in a tragic automobile accident. I told him I've never been married, I'm so lonely I can barely endure it, and that I'm in desperate need of someone to advise me on some financial matters.

Nightingale: You've been emailing him?

Morning_Glory: Yes. And talking to him on a new cell phone I registered using my pseudonym.

Nightingale: And you're sure it's him?

Morning_Glory: Positive. He's using the name Brad Simmons, but everything else is a match.

Nightingale: Be very careful, Gloria. Ben is not stupid. He's probably figured out you're looking for him by now.

Morning_Glory: Oh, he has. He's between a rock and a hard place, and he knows it. He has no idea Cathy Nelson and I are one in the same, but he knows Gloria Greene is very close to breaking the case. I made sure of that.

Nightingale: Why? You're just guaranteeing he'll run again.

Morning_Glory: Exactly. Straight into the arms of Cathy Nelson. I'm trying to force him to take action sooner rather than later. If he's convinced the police are close to tracking him down at his present locale, he'll be forced to change vehicles and locations and move on to his next target immediately to avoid detection.

Nightingale: And you want to be the one to catch him in the act.

Morning_Glory: You sound like you disapprove.

Nightingale: You're playing with people's lives here, Gloria. You don't know what it's like to know you've been duped by a common criminal—to lose your peace of mind, your self-confidence, and your ability to trust—all in one fell swoop.

Morning_Glory: No I don't. After all you've been through, I can't believe you don't want to see Ben caught as badly as I do.

Nightingale: I do. But you don't know what he'll do to avoid being apprehended. And speaking as one of his victims, I don't think it's worth the risk. How do you know he won't hurt the woman he's with now, or take her hostage, if he senses you're closing in?

Morning_Glory: How do *you* know she won't catch him talking to me, and start screaming at him in a jealous rage—that he won't flip out entirely and kill her, which is all a matter of judgment, since I happen to think the man is wigged out already? There are no guarantees. You have to trust me when I say we're doing everything we can to insure her safety. Both she and Ben's phones have been tapped and are being monitored night and day.

Nightingale: Like he's going to get on the phone and tell someone he's going to hurt her. Look, Gloria, forgive me for saying this, but I don't trust anyone anymore. And for the record, I don't recall asking you to use yourself as some sort of live decoy to catch Ben. And I definitely didn't ask you to investigate Michael.

Morning_Glory: Michael? Is that what this is about? No, you didn't tell me to investigate him. Aren't you glad I did?

Nightingale: Not particularly.

Morning_Glory: If you could see my face, you'd know I'm stunned beyond words. You just said you don't trust anyone anymore. From what you're saying, I assume that includes me. If you can't trust your best friend, why in heaven's name would you want to risk getting involved with someone who we know has lied to you?

Nightingale: Michael may have… Michael may not be… He's my friend, Gloria. I'm sorry if you… but Michael is my friend.

Morning_Glory: Oh, Isabelle, don't tell me you've gotten involved with the man.

She thought for a moment and started to type: *Michael is different than anyone I've ever met.* She reread the words and decided she sounded like a lovesick middle school student defending her choice of boyfriends to a disapproving parent.

Nightingale: I've been aware all along that Michael probably had a few secrets—his behavior towards me has been erratic from the start. I guess we had that in common. He was as wary of me as I was of him.

Morning_Glory: And that didn't bother you?

Nightingale: No. It told me he's as unlike Ben as a man can be. Ben is cocky and arrogant. He's cold and calculating and emotionally detached in his deception, whereas, in retrospect, I can see it's been all Michael can do to keep up his charade. Michael's deceitfulness haunts him. He believes he's doing the right thing, or he wouldn't be here, yet it's all he can do to live with the repercussions of his actions. Lying goes against his very nature. What he's doing is eating away at him. Most importantly, Michael truly cares about me. In spite of what his instincts said about me—he had to have known I'd be trouble from the first time he laid eyes on me—he felt compelled to try to help me. And he has.

There was a long pause before Gloria responded. Isabelle could only guess what she was thinking.

Morning_Glory: So ignore the information. Pretend I never sent the letter and do what you will.

Nightingale: That's just it, Gloria. I can't. Now that I know, I can't forget what he did. It was fine as long as it was an unfounded suspicion. Now that I have proof he lied to me...

Morning_Glory: Listen. You don't have to write the article. It's your choice. If you want to blow the perfect opportunity to redeem yourself down in the newsroom, go ahead. Forget I ever told Ronald you had nosed out a great story. I'll tell him I was mistaken.

Nightingale: Writing an exposé on Michael was your idea?

Morning_Glory: You make it sound like I've ruined everything.

Nightingale: I never said any of this was your fault.

Morning_Glory: It's what you meant.

Nightingale: Michael may have kept a few pertinent facts from me, but angry as I am at him, I have no wish to write an article about him. I don't care how much it might help get my career back on track. Now Ben is another story. Part of me would dearly love to see Ben brought to justice.

Morning_Glory: Part of you? I can't believe this.

Nightingale: You don't know all there is to know, Gloria. Ben is... well, we know he doesn't want to be caught and sent back to prison. And a desperate man is capable of anything. You're putting yourself in danger, and you're making things very hard for me.

Morning_Glory: You make it sound like you've been in touch with him recently. Isabelle, does he have something on you? You haven't done anything illegal, have you?

Nightingale: Of course not.

Morning_Glory: What else could he possibly threaten you with?

Nightingale: Just trust me on this one, Gloria. Please, I'm begging you. Just tell me you'll back off and leave this alone. If the police catch Ben someday, that will be wonderful. Just don't let it be you who does it. And not now. Please, not right now.

Morning_Glory: You know I can't do that, Isabelle.

Nightingale: But you're my friend. What you do reflects on and impacts me. You don't know what he'll do, Gloria.

Morning_Glory: Part of the reason I feel safe proceeding with this whole plan is I know you're out of harm's way in Scotland. He can't hurt you there.

Nightingale: It's not like I sprouted a coat of indelible armor when I crossed the ocean. Ben still has the power to hurt me. You have the power to hurt me. Michael has the power to hurt me. And if Ben didn't do this to my cottage, someone I don't even know just hurt me very deeply. All I want is for this whole awful nightmare to be over with once and for all. Some psycho is stalking me, for heaven's sake. And you think I'm safe and sound?

Isabelle's mind jumped from one frantic thought to another. What would she do if Gloria wouldn't cooperate? Tip Ben off and hope he was grateful enough to destroy the photos? Write him a letter trying to talk him out of showing anyone the pictures?

She had to do something! Anything. Her thoughts whirled around d her. It was imperative she finish the articles she'd written on France and send them to Ronald. She had to persuade Ronald not to make her do an exposé on Michael. And if she really wanted to end the insane cycle she was on, she had to play sleuth, figure out Damon's connection to the missing gold, and write a brilliant article on the treasure in Tobermory Bay—if she didn't lose her mind or her job first.

Chapter Twenty-Three

Early the next morning, Isabelle twisted around and tried to smash her pillow into a shape that actually felt good. She'd spent a fitful night in a lumpy, unfamiliar bed and she felt no more rested than she had before she'd turned the lights out.

Someone was knocking on her door. She struggled to climb out of the tall bedstead, and for a moment, didn't remember where she was or what had happened. Sadly, the sordid details came rushing back when she heard Bette's voice.

"Isabelle dear, Michael is at the door again. He appears to be even more distressed than he was last night. If I didn't know better, I would swear he's angry. Whether at you or me, I don't know, but he's acting very testy."

"He's here? Now?" She hung her feet over the edge of the mattress, slid the last foot between her toes and the slate floor, and wrapped the robe Bette had loaned her around her waist.

"I feel quite sure he won't take no for an answer this time," Bette said, her voice quavering and high pitched.

Isabelle opened the door a few inches and tried to smooth her curls with her fingertips.

"I need to see you, Isabelle," Michael said from behind Bette.

Bette jumped. "Michael?"

"You followed her?"

"We need to talk."

"I'll decide if and when we need to talk." She stomped her foot against the hard slate floor. He was so infuriating. "Ouch."

"It's an unyielding old castle." Michael had no trace of sympathy in his voice. "Bette, the lady and I need a few moments alone."

"Isabelle?" Bette said.

"It's all right, Bette. I didn't want to have to deal with this problem on top of everything else that's happened, but it's obvious Michael is determined."

"So now I'm a problem?"

"I'll just slip out and leave the two of you be." Bette let Michael enter and pulled the heavy door closed behind her.

"Now look what you've done," Isabelle said. "You've upset Bette."

"I've upset her?"

"You're the one who came barging in uninvited. You're the one who put her in the awkward position of having to disregard my wishes or go against you."

"Aren't you the considerate one all of the sudden, worrying about how Bette feels."

Was this the same Michael who had been so tender, so loving, so thoughtful just one short day ago? Even his voice was different—sarcastic, demeaning. His face looked so dark and brooding it was almost unfamiliar.

Wait a minute, she thought. I'm supposed to be the one who's mad at him. "I assume you're angry because I wouldn't see you last night." She tried to sound appropriately curt, to regain her momentum, but when she looked at his face, something inside of her broke into a million little pieces. She couldn't bear the way he was looking at her. Angry, disappointed, crestfallen, heartbroken.

Her forehead was throbbing. She parted her lips to speak, and closed them again. What was wrong with him? She hadn't told Bette why she hadn't wanted to see him the night before, only that she needed some time alone.

Michael didn't look the least bit sympathetic of the ordeal she'd been through. As far as she could tell, there wasn't a trace of concern for her welfare on his face.

"So, did you get all of your articles sent?" he asked.

What in all of this did Michael have to be angry about? She was the one who had just cause. She was the one who had been duped, deceived, and lied to.

"No. I was a little too busy talking to the police."

"I'll bet it was quite the chat you had with them. Or are you going to wait and break the story to the local newspaper so you can have an international byline?"

What on earth was he talking about?

"I can see the headline now." He paced the floor in front of the footboard. "*Local 'Contractor' Extradited For Trial in America.* Nothing catchy, just another hard-hitting exposé, skillfully researched and eloquently crafted by none other than our own Miss

Isabelle MacAllister."

"What are you talking about?"

"Mrs. Galbraith will be in her glory—she was right about me all along, wasn't she? She had me figured from the moment I walked in the pub, all right."

"What does Logan's mother have to do with any of this?"

"The old biddy always did like you."

She didn't have a clue exactly what he was going on about, but he obviously knew about Gloria's research. "So where do we go from here?"

"I'm assuming back to the United States. You've got your story. I'll testify. Carole Masterson, who I'm convinced is a very loving mother and who wouldn't hurt a flea, will lose her children. Dr. Masterson will get full custody. Their children will spend the rest of their young years with a nanny and an emotionally abusive father. My sister will have her baby, find out Kent's been screwing Carole, and get a divorce. Kent will get liberal visitation privileges—all he did was commit adultery—nothing half the world isn't guilty of these days. Carole and Kent will probably get married. My niece and nephews will spend Christmas Eve with Kent and Carole and their little half-sister, and Christmas morning with their mom.

"If I'm lucky, Buck will get the charges against me dropped so I don't have to go to jail. I'll sublet my office and try to find some sort of construction work—although I have to admit the thought of installing stone facades on prefab houses in some subdivision in Milwaukee seems a little lackluster after working on the castle all these months."

"I-I had no idea." She'd been so involved in her own drama that she hadn't noticed the face she had held in her hands a few short hours ago was suddenly lined with creases. Michael's eyes were red from lack of sleep; his shoulders stooped with defeat. She stepped towards him.

"Why did you do it, Isabelle? The things I kept from you didn't hurt you in any way. My need for privacy and my decision to camouflage my true identity didn't have anything to do with you."

"Your true identity? Your need for privacy? Call things what they are, Michael."

"Fine. I lied. It was for a good reason. One I was not at liberty to share."

"It's not the things you were lying about that hurt me. It's the fact you knew how important the truth was to me, you knew how hard it was for me to trust again after Ben, and you didn't care."

"So I was supposed to jeopardize my client's confidences, ignore the oath I took when I became a psychologist, risk my sister's happiness, and spill my guts to an investigative reporter I'd just met to honor your need for total disclosure?"

"Well, not the first time you met me, and not the part that was confidential, but the part that mattered to me, yes, once you knew me, once we had—"

"I was going to."

The fact that he looked more miserable than angry started to soften her.

"But you didn't."

"Hadn't. Yet." He reached out his arms to her. "Isabelle, please..."

She wanted to. Part of her wanted to feel his arms around her so intensely she was willing to forgive him anything. Forgetting was another matter. Naively trusting him like she had in France—with her heart, soul, and body—was another thing entirely.

She tried to keep her voice from shaking and failed. "You shouldn't take it personally, Michael. Let's just say you were the straw that broke the camel's back. I used to trust people. And I got burned. I trusted again, very tentatively. But despite the fact that I was very, very careful, my tender, new skin got scalded again.

"You're the shrink. I'm sure there have been numerous studies done on the topic. We're told to stay away from the hot burners on the stove. But we're curious. We have to try it ourselves. We touch the stove. We get burned. We think, maybe this new stove isn't as hot. Maybe it was just the other stove that burns things. We touch the new stove. We get burned again. We think, maybe it wasn't the stove's fault. Maybe it was me. Maybe my fingers weren't tough enough. Maybe if I touch it again, just barely touch it, just for a second, maybe if I'm really careful, I won't get burned this time. Maybe if I toughen up my hide and spend some time conditioning myself, it will be okay."

She stopped and stared at him. "How many times does the average person have to get hurt before it finally sinks in, Dr. St. Dawndalyn?"

"None, if they just use a little common sense. You can spout empirical mumbo-jumbo all day long and it won't negate the fact that you love me. Forget your past experiences. Forget your instincts. They've failed you before and they'll fail you again. Use your head this time. Listen to what I have to say, then follow your heart. I'm not perfect, this isn't a fairy tale, and I'm certainly no Prince Charming, but I do love you, and I'll do my best not to disappoint or hurt you ever again if you'll give me a second chance."

Her feet felt rooted to the floor, which was a good thing, because she might have fallen over if they hadn't been. Her whole body was quivering.

"I haven't written any articles about you, and I don't intend to, Michael."

"You may as well go ahead and write it, Isabelle. The damage is already done. Word gets around in a town the size of Oconomowoc. Masterson knows where I am. He's smart, ruthless, and has unlimited resources. He told Buck if I'm not in Wisconsin by the end of the week, he'll come over here personally and drag me back by my balls."

She winced. "Charming man."

"If I don't go back now, he'll make trouble for me here until I do."

"I'm sorry. I never asked Gloria to investigate you. All I did was mention your name. She was worried about me. She knew how frightened I've been."

Michael looked at her so intensely that her heart almost wilted from the heat.

"So you weren't going to sensationalize my woes and publicly humiliate me for the sake of furthering your career?"

"You know me better than that."

He gave her the look—the real shrink-look that made her feel like he was in her head looking at her from the inside out. "Do I?"

"Gloria told Ronald I was the one who got the goods on you even though it wasn't true. He did ask me to write an article on the trial and what you're doing here in Scotland, but I didn't say I'd do it."

"Wow. You're the best."

She might have taken it for a compliment if his voice hadn't been dripping with sarcasm. "Listen, it hasn't been a good day for either of us. I know I need time to process everything that's happened, and obviously, you do, too."

"I know you probably already know this on some level, Isabelle, but I'm going to say it anyway. Loving someone is more than having all the facts, double-checking and analyzing them to death to make sure they're accurate. To love, you have to trust. There comes a moment when you have to let go of your fears, take a leap of faith and just go for it."

"I'm sorry, Michael. I did well to get my toes wet when we were in France, but I'm just not ready to jump."

"I hope I'm still here to catch you when you are."

She watched him walk down the hall—away from her—until he rounded the corner at the end of the hall and disappeared from sight. She wanted to scream. But she didn't. Southern belles didn't make a scene. So she sucked it in—and hoped her dreams for a future with Michael weren't destined to be one more casualty of the past.

Chapter Twenty-Four

Isabelle took one last look at herself splayed naked across the screen of her laptop and pressed send before she could change her mind. Her hands were shaking as she moved Ben's email to a folder where it would be safe in the event she needed to produce it for evidence, then reread the letter she'd typed into her laptop.

Dear Ben,

I often wonder how you can stand to look at yourself in the mirror. You're a spineless coward, and the worst kind of bully—intimidating people smaller than yourself, scaring innocent people who've shown you nothing but kindness, and preying on women who are lonely. You're a leech who sucks the lifeblood from good, honest women who have worked hard for what little money they have. I won't even go into the abhorrent way you manipulate women into trusting you, then falling in love with you, only to screw them both literally and figuratively.

Are you mad at me now, Ben? Is any part of you sorry, or ashamed, or regretful? Go ahead and send out the photos. You're despicable. I refuse to give you any more money, no matter what you choose to do to me. The thought of you using my money to hurt more women is so reprehensible that I would rather have my photographs plastered on a marquee for all the world to see than to aid you in your evil deeds. You are without a doubt the most detestable person I have ever met.

Isabelle MacAllister

She actually felt slightly jubilant as she imagined the words flying through cyberspace to Ben's in-box. She was playing Russian roulette with the last remaining shred of dignity she had left, but at least she'd had the courage to squeeze the trigger.

Standing up to Ben was a start. Ronald was next on her list—negotiating with him would require more finesse than bravery. She gave herself a pep talk as she watched her letter to Ben take its place in her outbox.

She was not going to write an exposé on Michael. If Ronald tried to fire her because of her objections, so be it. She'd done what he asked, given him her best. Now it was his turn—to trust her judgment.

She ran her fingers through her hair. She must look a fright. Working all day long and staying up half the night to finish the articles she'd been working on probably wasn't the smartest thing she'd ever done, but she hadn't been able to sleep, and she'd figured it was better to do something productive than to spend another night thrashing around her bed and fretting about Michael.

She looked at the old, cast iron clock that hung from a scrolled bracket over Bette's desk. In another hour, it would be eight a.m. in D.C., Ronald would be at work, and the articles on Alsace-Lorraine and the French Riviera she'd sent earlier in the evening would appear on his computer screen. She knew Ronald would be thrilled with her and Michael's photos of Ingrid, Birgitte, and Sophia. If her instincts were as sharp as she believed they were, he'd be equally impressed with her writing.

Much as she hurt, it felt good to be back. She wasn't sure when or how she'd begun to feel like her old self again, but she suddenly felt like Sleeping Beauty roused from a hundred year nap. Her head finally felt clear. She was as tired and frazzled as she ever remembered feeling. Still, she felt a sense of exhilaration, an alertness she hadn't felt in weeks.

There was no way she could sleep now, when she finally felt so awake. She clicked through her files and opened the email Gloria had sent on the gold in Tobermory Bay. This was the article she needed to write. A Wisconsin psychologist who refused to testify against his client was small potatoes compared to century's old, Spanish gold buried in Tobermory Bay, ripe for the taking. Ronald would forget all about Michael if she could uncover a covert attempt to smuggle the gold away from its rightful owners. That was assuming the gold was still there, and had not already been removed, as some historians speculated. She could only hope the lure of the treasure would be as irresistible to Ronald as it had been to others.

She looked over her shoulder. It seemed wrong to investigate someone in what was practically their own home, but she had a nagging suspicion Damon was in Tobermory because of the gold. She'd tried to shake off her ill feelings out of deference to Bette, but her wariness would not leave her alone—a good sign her hunch was right.

She had at least an hour to kill before Ronald got to work and read her articles. She typed Damon's name into the computer and waited for the search engine to do its work. What had Simone been referring to before they'd been interrupted to catch the train to Mittelbergheim? What had Damon done?

The first page of results sprung onto her laptop. The whole exercise was probably futile. Even with the aid of the Internet, it was hard to trace a person when aliases were involved. That was part of the reason the police had had so much trouble tracking Ben. If Damon had been crafty enough to use a nom de plume when he was still a schoolboy, she felt sure he would be doing the same now. The fact that Europe lagged behind the United States miserably in data input, especially that of archived information, wouldn't help either. But she had to start somewhere.

There were thousands of entries—baptismal records from a Methodist Church in upstate New York, a list of winners from a race called the Barking Fish 5K, an 1893 Roster of Nebraska Veterans, a page on Moravian College Athletics, and two entries that actually looked promising—an article in French with the headline Un Enfant Si Diabolique Que Seulement Sa Mère Pourrait L'aimer, and a second in German entitled Schulen Sie Mätzchen Drehungen Schändlich Ein. She didn't have a clue what the German article said, but she could make out the words child, diabolical, mother, and love in the French headline.

The keyboard rattled from the force of her fingers rapping out commands as she worked to decipher the words in the French text, copying and pasting the phrases she didn't know into an online translator. Her curiosity changed to revulsion as she began to get the gist of the article.

It had been discovered that a local nine year old, S. Deville Herman, had been forcing other children to pose naked while he photographed them by threatening to torture their dogs and cats if they didn't comply. When an eight year old neighbor girl refused to perform oral sex on an eleven year old boy in front of Deville's camera, Deville doused his own cocker spaniel with gasoline and lit the dog on fire to prove he meant business. A group of children from the neighborhood who were witnesses to the act were so horrified they ran home in tears to tell their parents. An investigation ensued and dozens of black and white photographs, developed by Herman in a dark room belonging to his father, were discovered.

The child had been granted diplomatic immunity contingent on the stipulation that the parents leave France immediately and be barred from returning.

The names of Deville's parents were mentioned nowhere in the article, but the pieces all fit. Hans had worked for the State Department. The French government had no doubt sent him to a foreign embassy, in effect, exiling him, without taking his means of livelihood away from him. It would explain why Hans and Bette had retired in Scotland instead of returning to their beloved Mittelbergheim, or anywhere else in Alsace-Lorraine.

She began a letter to Gloria immediately, although, admittedly, knowing about Damon's probable history did nothing to prove her hunch he was looking for the gold buried in Tobermory Bay. There was no doubt in her mind, but she needed cold, hard facts to make a story. Proof. S. Deville Herman and Sigismundus Damon Hermance were clearly one in the same—she felt sure Simone could verify her hunch in the morning.

But Gloria would need more to go on than that. There had to be invoices for equipment purchases, or rental agreements, or something that would confirm her suspicions about Damon.

She glanced nervously at the tall door that led to the hall. If Gloria found the email when she arrived at work, it was possible she would hear something before the week was out.

She was almost done. In a few short seconds, Gloria would know everything she knew about Damon Hermance, and hopefully she could sleep for a few hours.

Her shoulders fell a notch as the tension holding them taut eased out of her body. She was exhausted, both emotionally and physically, but it was going to be all right. Ronald would have her articles in a few short hours, and would hopefully be so impressed he would forget about the story on Michael. Michael would be free to work out his problems with the authorities in Wisconsin in his own way, in his own time, and she would vindicate herself by writing the exposé of the year—thanks to Damon Hermance.

She had just pressed send when an instant message from someone named B-S popped up on her screen. She cast a wary glance at the name. Her privacy settings were supposed to limit the people who were able to contact her to Gloria and the small handful of friends.

B-S: So what's with your friend Gloria giving me such a bad time, little lassy? Are you angry Big Ben left you for someone else?

A chill rushed down her spine. She had forgotten about Ben—a small miracle in and of itself given the fact he had haunted her thoughts for weeks.

She pressed delete but nothing happened. What should she do? Alert some sort of Cyber patrol? Signal Facebook management? Let him talk and hope he said something to incriminate himself?

B-S: You really have no right to judge me, sweetheart. What you and I do for a living isn't all that different. You con people into telling you their deepest, darkest secrets. Once you've got what you need, you disappear into the night to write your exposés and wham— all the juicy tidbits they "confided" in you are splashed on the front page of the paper.

Nightingale: It's not the same at all.

B-S: People trust you. You use the information they've entrusted you with, knowing it will be their downfall.

Nightingale: I don't steal their money.

B-S: You get paid for what you do. You get the goods on people, screw them, and pocket the profit without feeling one iota of guilt. The only difference between you and me is that you have a boss who gives you money to screw up people's lives. I eliminate the middleman and take the money directly from the people I'm screwing.

Nightingale: The police would say there's a very big difference. What I do is legal.

B-S: You tell yourself that when you can't sleep at night, sweetheart, but you'll know you're wrong. We're like two peas in a pod, you and I. We con people into spilling their guts so we can have what we want.

Nightingale: I don't con. I research. I investigate. And the people I INVESTIGATE are almost always guilty. If my work brings to light the fact they're innocent, I make every effort to clear their names. The women whose reputations and egos you destroy are innocent.

B-S: Save it for judgment day, babe. You told me yourself Gloria does all your research—that the only thing that made you a good reporter was your good, old-fashioned Southern charm. You said it was your gift... that you'd been able to charm honey from a swarm of bees ever since you were a little girl. You bragged you'd never once been stung. All I did was give you a little bit of your own medicine, honey bunch. I hate to break it to you, but I've got a whole damn beehive full of golden, sweet honey and you've been stung. Face it, darlin'. You're a liar, just like me.

Nightingale: I am NOTHING like you.

Her fingers were shaking so badly she could hardly type when she heard the hinges of the tall, oak doors to Bette's office creak. She looked up to see a tall, dark, extremely handsome stranger standing in the doorway. She jumped and clutched her robe more tightly around her.

"Don't let me frighten you." He smiled benevolently.

"Y-you must be... Sig...um, Damon," she said, quickly closing the link to Ben.

He closed the gap between them and extended his hand. "Don't tell me my mother has been calling me Sigismundus around people I've never even met."

She smiled and took his hand as briefly as possible. "Isabelle MacAllister."

"I assumed. Mother said you were lovely."

"She's very proud of you."

He grinned, looking as laid back and relaxed as a young boy watching a baseball game. "You know what they say... Only a mother..."

A light clicked on in her brain. That's what the French headline had said. *A Child So Diabolical Only a Mother Could Love Him.* Her impressions of Damon had to be correct. She felt sure of it.

Her computer sounded an alert that there was a new instant message waiting. She reached down and tried to click out of the program.

"I didn't mean to interrupt."

"It was nothing. Just a... um, someone from the U.S."

She willed herself to stop shaking and did her best to replace her jittery nervousness with a relaxed smile. If she could get a grip on herself, this could be a good chance to try to ferret out a little information. "Bette probably told you I'm from Virginia."

"She may have."

If Damon was feigning disinterest, he was doing an awfully good job of it.

"You can finish your conversation if you like."

Her stomach burned with fear-induced acid as she flashed her most convincing smile. "Trust me. We'd already said all there was to say."

"It must be hard to find time to chat with a several hour time difference between here and there."

"It can be challenging at times." She eased herself up from the chair and ran her fingertips along the back of the high backed leather chair where she'd been sitting in what she hoped was a casual gesture. "Your mother has never mentioned where you live or what you do when you're not visiting the island. I assume you work in London, or on the other side of the channel since you're not around much."

His brown eyes pierced hers. "I'm a photographer."

She could feel the pink glow of a full-fledged blush creeping up her neck and settling in her cheeks. "How interesting. Portraits, still life, scenery?"

"Nudes." He crossed the room to pour a drink from a crystal decanter on the mantle. "Brandy?"

She felt faint. Did Damon know about Ben, that he was blackmailing her? How could he? Was he telling the truth or toying with her? "No, thank you." She could have used a little alcohol to calm her nerves, but who knew what effect it might have, sleep deprived as she was.

Damon took a sip from his snifter. "My work takes me many places. I recently returned from the French Riviera."

Okay. Now, she was unnerved. If this was a calculated ploy, the man was a master at keeping the upper hand. "What a coincidence. I was just there myself."

"So Mother mentioned."

Damon circled to her rear. She hit the on off switch on her monitor and it went black just as he rounded the corner and looked over her shoulder.

She looked up at him and attempted a smile. "Have you done any photography here on the Island? The scenic areas around the castle would be a beautiful backdrop for..." She couldn't bring herself to say the word. "...any kind of photography."

Damon leaned against the printer table in what appeared to be a perfectly harmless way. "Regrettably, no. Mother is not terribly fond of my chosen profession, so in deference to her..." His voice trailed off.

"I should think she'd be pleased you find time to visit as often as she says you do."

"The Bell has required a great deal of attention since I acquired it last year even though I don't play an active role in the day to day operations."

She was forced to twist around to see his face. "Your mother said you spend a lot of time on your boat when you're home. What's she called? I do a lot of boat watching from the shoreline when I'm hiking or working on an article."

She was taking a chance by hinting she'd noticed the boat, but it was worth it. She caught a glimmer of a reaction for the first time since they'd met. He answered with such smooth, cool confidence that she had to remind herself she'd even seen a flicker of emotion in his eyes.

"Yes. Much as I enjoy photography, as Barrie was fond of saying, *It is not real work unless you would rather be doing something else.* The boat is my something else. I find it very relaxing to be on the water."

She forced herself to smile again. His close proximity gave her the heebie-jeebies. "I assumed as much. Bette has mentioned several times that she worries about you not getting enough sleep or nourishment because you spend so much time out at sea."

"Ah, yes, my mother takes great pleasure in broadcasting my whereabouts."

A tit for a tat. Maybe he would be more likely to slip up if she could rattle him by capitalizing on his feelings of frustrations towards his mother.

She ignored the waves of panic that were bombarding her and smiled warmly as she moved a step closer. "I love what you did at the Bell by the way. Knowing you're a photographer explains all the artful touches and beautifully coordinated colors and fabrics. I'm sure Hans and Bette will rely heavily on your creative expertise when it's time to refurbish the old castle."

"It will be months before the keep is ready for interior design, but yes, I have offered my assistance." He took another sip of brandy and looked her directly in the eyes. "Ironic, isn't it? It took centuries to build the castle. It will take years to rebuild it. Yet it took mere seconds to blow it up."

She got the message. Damon wasn't about to let her jeopardize years of hard work and planning with a single blow of her horn. "Silly me. I assumed it was the ravages of time that caused the old castle to deteriorate."

"Most inexperienced eyes jump to the same conclusion. In fact, it was slighted by Cromwell's armies during the Civil War."

"Slighted?"

"Slighting a castle involves blowing up just enough to make it indefensible—usually the top half. Ashby de la Zouche and Helmsly castle in North Yorkshire are two well-known examples."

"So why not just blow up the whole thing?"

"Then or now?" He smiled. "In the 1600's, it was considered a waste of time and ammunition. Once the fatal blow had been delivered, what was the point?"

How she hated his smile. It was cynical, sardonic, and smug all at once. "One would think to prevent subsequent generations from refortifying the ruins and using them to resist other invaders."

"Why would they, when the castles were their downfall in the first place?"

"I don't understand," she said.

"The castle gave its inhabitants the false impression they were safe."

She silently willed her body not to tremble or her words to stutter. "So the castles weren't rebuilt because the Cromwell's forces proved them obsolete." Think of this as an interview. Forget he's the devil incarnate. He has no reason to want to hurt you.

"Precisely." Damon twirled his brandy snifter in his left hand and looked away from her for a moment. "Forgive me for staring."

"I hadn't noticed." But she had. "Is something wrong?"

"It's your hair." He let his eyes roam over her. "Once upon a time, long, long, ago, I had a cocker spaniel named Caramel. Your hair is the same color and has the same gentle wave." His eyes took on a faraway look. "She was beautiful. I always wanted to photograph Caramel, but alas, she died before I got the chance."

She wanted to ask how Caramel had died, but unfortunately, she believed she already knew. Fear clutched at her heart. The words she wanted wouldn't come, so she chose a safer topic and ploughed on. "Renovating vintage properties has become very popular in America."

"I supposed the world would not be complete without a few sentimental fools." He smiled benevolently. "But then, who am I to talk?"

Right. As if someone who could light their dog on fire would ever qualify as sentimental. Her mind grappled for another question that would keep them on safe ground. "Have the other castles you mentioned been restored?"

"Some were, some weren't—at Studly Royal, the ruined Fountains Abby is now a garden. Some have utilized ruins by building a newer stately home within or over them."

His eyes were still on her hair. She moved, hoping they wouldn't follow. They did.

"In many cases the locals have cannibalized the stones and the lead roofs so extensively there is nothing left to rebuild."

"There's something to be said for recycling." She tried to avoid his eyes. "In America they'd have brought in a bulldozer and leveled the whole thing to make room for a new parking garage."

A glimmer of light sparked in his reptilian eyes. Why, she didn't understand.

"The moon is lovely tonight," Damon said. "Perhaps if we were to walk down to the keep and climb what's left of the old watchtower, we can recapture some sense of why it is important to Hans and Bette to renovate the keep."

She backed up as far as the wall would allow her to. She wanted to say she wouldn't be caught dead with him, but she couldn't. "I need to get to bed. I've been working all night and need to get some sleep."

"I insist," Damon said.

"No, really," she said, more assertively. "It's been a long night, and I'm exhausted."

"I promise you you'll get all the sleep you need."

She cringed as his hand glided across her back and steered her a few inches further away from the computer.

"If it means you'll be able to get to bed a little sooner, I would be happy to help you with whatever you were working on." He halted when she was just out of reach of the computer and flicked the monitor on with his free arm.

"No, really." She tried to wrench her arm from his grip. "I'm finished with what I was doing. I just need some rest."

Their eyes diverged on the screen and Ben's words.

B-S: Here's a little reminder of what your friends and family will be getting in their email if you don't get your investigator friend off my tail.

"Ah. Your friend from America. Looks like you missed his last message." Damon reached down to click on the link Ben had so thoughtfully provided.

She could feel her face turning red, her heart racing, her entire body flushing with shame and embarrassment.

"My, my. It appears your friend has either training in the art of photography or a true gift for composition. A natural redhead." Damon cocked his head and nodded his approval as one of Ben's more explicit photos filled the screen.

Damon clicked on the History tab and the article from the French newspaper she'd been reading popped up on the screen. "Well, well, well." Damon's voice was an odd mixture of amusement and pride. "It would appear we have much in common." He flicked back to her photo and watched intently as her naked image filled screen. "The mistakes of the past do have a way of catching up with us, don't they, Isabelle?"

She started to shake. This was not going well "My only mistake was coming here in the first place. To think I thought I would be safe."

"That, yes. But there have been other errors of misjudgment on your part, and as all of us know, there is always a price that must be paid when we give in to our indiscretions."

"Fine. You've made your point. If you would please be so kind as to let me go, I've suffered quite enough embarrassment for one night."

"I beg to disagree," Damon said. "Now, where were we? Ah. I've asked you to accompany me on a walk, and I've stated twice that I will not take no for an answer." His eyes lingered on her hair once more. "I'm beginning to understand why my friend Morgan was so reluctant to vacate his post. You are a beauty to behold."

"Morgan Baugh?" Her stomach clenched even tighter. "What does he have to do with you?"

He laughed—a sick, demoralizing laugh she feared she would never wash from her mind. "Morgan is an old friend of mine from my school days in Wales. I simply asked him to keep an eye on you lest you put two and two together before we completed our mission."

A new wave of panic flooded over her as she realized how strong his grip was, how far away help was, how stupid she had been. "Michael was right. It's been Morgan who's been watching me. It was Morgan who—"

"Rest assured that Morgan, too, has learned there is a dear price to pay for second guessing me." He laughed again, and the sound chilled her to the bone. "Although I must admit, now that I've tasted your loveliness with my own two eyes, I'm tempted to think I was a bit too harsh with old Morgan. A dish so tantalizing is hard to resist."

"You sent him back to Wales?"

"Morgan will no longer be bothering you, if that's what you're worried about."

Morgan was the least of her concerns. Imagining what Damon had done to him was not fun—worrying about what Damon was going to do to her was terrifying.

"Mother and Hans are sound asleep in the north wing," Damon said, as though he could read her mind. He pulled her down a long hall toward the bedroom where she'd been staying. "Michael and his crew won't be here for hours."

She was shaking so hard she could barely walk by the time they reached her room. He took a piece of paper from the wardrobe and told her what to write. The ramifications of what he forced her to do were terrifying, but at least he didn't touch her, or take photos of her, or make her touch him. She had to keep believing she would find a way to escape before he killed her.

He dragged her from the room when she was done, down the stairs and through a narrow hallway. Both the walls and the ceilings grew closer. She could have stood upright, but Damon had to crouch, and the way he gripped her hand while he stooped hurt her shoulders and her back.

She let her feet go slack and he tripped over her limp form. While she had the satisfaction of knowing she had made him mad enough to lose his composure for a second, he didn't loosen his grip.

"Such a feisty one you are. I can see why Morgan lost his heart to you, poor fool." His face was frightening. He had the same lecherous look he'd had on his face when he was looking at Ben's photos, only this time, he was angry, too. He looked like it was taking every ounce of self-control he had to keep from slapping her.

She threw herself against him with every ounce of strength she possessed but he only grunted.

"If we hurry, we might have time to take a few photos of our own before our time together comes to an end."

"I'd sooner die." If only she could throw Damon off balance and break free.

"Be careful what you wish for. Although I will say it's fortuitous we're of one mind on the subject." Damon clamped down on her wrist, pulled her through a low, rounded doorway and started to yank her up a spiral staircase.

The walls were solid rock with an occasional slit of light. The stairs were half broken, and in seconds, her ankles and shins were scraped and bleeding.

Chapter Twenty-Five

Gareth watched from the bow as the boat crept closer and closer to the craggy coastline just north of Bluevale Castle. Damon had left precise instructions to meet him at the usual rendezvous spot at four o'clock that morning, but his craft was nowhere in sight.

He lifted a pair of binoculars to his eyes and scanned the rocky section of coastline where Damon anchored the tiny speedboat he used to navigate the inlet. The small craft allowed him to meet the *Baurley* as inconspicuously as possible given the fact it was never entirely dark in Scotland. More importantly, it kept the larger boat out of the harbor, where it would arouse suspicion and be subject to periodic searches and inspections.

"Bring her around starboard. I cannae see the cove," Gareth shouted, shading his eyes from the moonlight reflecting on the waves. He peered into the murky light. Damon's boat was bobbing on the glassy surface of the cove in the same location it was always anchored. There was no sign of Damon.

Gareth paced the length of the deck and contemplated his options. They would wait, in case Damon was simply running a few minutes late. But Damon was never late, so it seemed extremely unlikely he would be today.

Gareth put the binoculars to his eyes and scanned the rocky coast from north to south looking for any sign of Damon, then retraced the area, hoping to catch a glimpse of Morgan's stout form. Morgan could be a pain-in-the-ass, awrite, but he was a friend, and he was worried about him.

Gareth hoped Damon and Morgan had resolved their differences. Gareth had roughed him up a bit and made some serious threats, per Damon's instructions, but he'd stopped short of injuring anything other than the man's pride. Damon had made it clear that if Morgan had not left the area of his own accord by the time he put into the bay, Morgan was done for. If Morgan was still in Scotland, he could only hope the two men had spoken and put their dispute behind them.

Gareth pulled his coat more tightly around his thin frame and tucked his favorite plaid wool scarf into the crease between his neck and his collar. Once he'd satisfactorily staunched the breeze, he gazed out into the night and waited.

#

Isabelle's right shoulder slammed against a sharp rock. "You're hurting me. Stop hurting me! They'll come after you, you know." Her foot slipped on a step that was half missing. She slid down two or three steps and banged her head against the inside of the wall.

"Your thinking is a bit convoluted, my dear, but I understand you must be feeling a little desperate at the moment. You make it sound as though some penalty awaits me, when in fact I have a sizeable cache of gold waiting for me. And since the only thing standing between it and me is you, I shall surely be reaping my reward very soon."

"The police have been in my cottage. They'll find your prints and DNA. You'll never get away with this."

He laughed as though she amused him. It was maddening, and she hated him for it. She screamed as much with rage as with fear. The rough edges of the stone steps leading to the watchtower cut and bit at her legs as Damon half dragged her up and around, and up and around, and up and around the narrow, circular staircase. Her feet fumbled as she tried to stand, tried to kick, tried to find a foothold so she could push away from him and run.

"I haven't been near your cottage." His tone oozed scorn. He clearly thought himself superior to everyone and everything, including the law.

She forced her mind to forget the pain and fear she was feeling and concentrate on putting the pieces of the bigger picture together.

If Damon hadn't been in her cottage, who had been? Morgan? She gasped for air and found only dust. Morgan was disgusting, but at this moment, she would have been happy to know he was alive.

A stream of sunlight pierced the tower where a rock had broken free. A few tortuous steps later, they reached the top of the watchtower. Damon clamped her wrists even more tightly. A vast panorama of peaceful blue waters dotted with green, tree-covered islands met her on one side. A vast network of brick and stone turrets and towers in varying sizes and heights surrounded her on the other. But the beauty of the view took second place to her terror. Damon wasn't here on a sightseeing expedition.

She looked up at the sky, at the yellow and fuzzy peach clouds hugging the horizon to the east. It was almost daybreak—the dawn of a day that held certain heartbreak. She felt a sudden, urgent need to look down. A crumpled body clad in a brown jacket lay on the ground below.

"Morgan?"

"I must say, given the fact that you're the reporter sent here to foil my operation, you're the most clueless little twit I've come across in some time."

She tried to pull her hand away from his, if only to wipe the tears from her cheeks. "I wasn't sent here to uncover anything. I only started to put things together tonight. You've got to believe me."

"You can cut the act," he said. "I'm familiar with your work."

"I'm here to lure travelers back to Europe. That's it. I swear it!" She kicked and strained against him.

"You're a grave disappointment to me, Isabelle. I thought you were a worthy adversary, but you are no such thing."

He was taller than she was, and so much stronger. He clamped his hand over her mouth with an airlock so tight she was forced to abandon her struggle to fight him and focus on the simple task of breathing.

#

Michael picked up his cell phone and speed dialed his mother. No need to be evasive at this point. Much as it saddened him to know Carole Masterson's whole sordid story would soon be revealed, including the fact that his sister's husband had slept with Carole and sired a baby with the woman, he was also relieved. He missed his family. Living across the ocean from them would have been more bearable if he could have maintained regular telephone or email contact, but because of the need for secrecy, he'd been completely isolated except for his occasional talks with his mother, and of course, Buck.

He spoke to his mother briefly and told her he would be coming home soon. When she asked him if there was anything she could do, he asked her if she would please call Barbara later that afternoon.

When she asked why, he gave her an ambiguous answer and said he had a feeling Barbara would need her support in the days ahead and said goodbye before she could probe any further.

His precious niece, Tori, answered the telephone at Barbara and Kent's house just as grown-up as could be.

"Hi, Tori. This is your Uncle Mikey. Do you remember who I am?"

"Hi, Uncle Mikey. I see your picture on Mommy's desk. You read me books when I a baby."

His voice choked up at the sound of hers. "I love you, sweetie. Would you like Uncle Mikey to come home so he can read you some more books?"

"I read all by myself now. I good at reading books."

"You've gotten to be a big girl, haven't you?"

"Yes, I growing very tall. Daddy say I his big girl. You want to talk to Daddy?"

"I want to talk to your Mommy. Is she home?"

"Mommy be right back. I go find her."

He listened as the receiver clattered to the ground. It was so good to hear Tori's voice—he could hardly wait to sweep her into his arms and give her a hug.

Only a second had passed when the sound of voices outside his window—a rare intrusion given the remote location of his cottage—brought him back to the reality of Scotland and his troubles. Hans and Bette were walking up the path to Cnoc Fuar.

He opened the door, held the phone away from his head and nodded a greeting.

"You haven't seen Isabelle have you?" Bette asked. "She didn't come down for breakfast this morning, so we checked her room, and she wasn't there, which seemed a little peculiar in light of everything that's been going on."

"We thought perhaps she'd talked to the authorities and been given the green light to go back to Dunara," Hans said, "but we walked over that way and it's still surrounded with police tape. So we walked around to your place to see if she was here. We're starting to get a little worried."

"Hello!" Barbara said. "Michael? Is that you? Where in heaven's name have you been all this time? Where are you calling from?" Michael pulled the phone closer to his ear and waved at Bette and Hans to wait.

"Barbara, my landlords just stopped by and it's almost time to head to work, so I only have a minute."

"It's wonderful to hear from you, Michael," Barbara said. "Although a little surprising after all this time. Is everything all right? I thought you were in a place where you didn't have access to international long distance."

Barbara always had been a little naive, which had probably made it easier for Kent to mess around on the side when he'd an inkling to. Which, unfortunately, his brother-in-law had.

"I'll call later and explain in more detail, but for now, I just wanted to tell you I'll be home soon, and to say that if you ever need anything, I'm always here for you. You do know that, don't you, Barbara?"

"Michael, is Mama okay? Do you know something I don't?"

"This isn't about Mama," Michael said. "Don't worry about her, please."

"Then tell me what's going on. You've been gone for nearly a year, with hardly a word, and now, suddenly, out of the blue, you're on the phone hinting at some life-altering event that's going to upset me. I want to know what's going on, Michael."

He could hear the click of a second receiver being picked up in the background, and since there was no extension at Cnoc Fuar, he knew it had to be Kent or one of the children.

"What's the problem, Michael? You call after all this time to upset your sister?" Kent said.

Well, that answered that question. "I just wanted to tell you I'm coming home," he said. "I'm coming back to testify in the Masterson case. Kent, you're as familiar with the ins and outs of the trial as I am in many aspects. And I really do need to go. Can I trust that you'll fill Barbara in on the rest of the details so I can say good-bye and tend to my company?"

"How would Kent know anything about the Masterson's divorce?" Barbara asked.

There was a second long silence.

"No need to figure this all out on Michael's dime, sweetheart," Kent said. "Let's say goodbye, and I'll explain everything later."

"If you say so," Barbara said.

"I'll be in touch again in a few days, Barbara," Michael said. "Tell the kids I love them, and I'll see you all soon."

Michael turned to Bette and Hans. He hadn't meant to let them know he was going back to the United States this way, whether for a long visit or short. Even Buck hadn't been able to advise him how long he'd be required to stay in the States after he testified, or if he'd be allowed to leave at all considering he'd probably be on probation. If he was free to go and lucky enough not to be stripped of his license to practice psychology, Michael knew he would have some big decisions ahead of him—whether to officially close his practice and sell the building, or to pursue a contractor's license. If the Scottish authorities allowed him to keep working on the keep, he would face the bigger decision of whether to stay in Wisconsin or return to Scotland.

He looked back at Bette and Hans. Their elderly faces were etched with worry. "If one of you doesn't mind squeezing into the back seat of my car, I'll drive us all back to the castle. I'll take a look around and see if I can find Isabelle."

Bette turned immediately and began to walk towards his car. "Last time I talked to her was last night. She'd asked to use my office for just a bit. We've never been able to get wireless to work inside the castle because of the thick walls, so if anyone needs to be connected to the internet, they have to work from my office."

Hans followed. "When Isabelle didn't come to breakfast, we checked her room. When she wasn't there, we went down to Bette's office. Her laptop was still there. We found a bit of disturbing information on the computer screen."

"It would seem that Isabelle stumbled upon an article written about Damon when he was a little boy," Bette said.

Hans cleared his throat and looked uncomfortable. "An unfortunate incident that occurred years ago when we lived in Alsace, nothing more than a childish prank really."

Bette, who looked very distressed, gave Hans a look that was heartbreaking.

"The authorities blew things totally out of proportion," Hans said. "The Ministry of Foreign Affairs transferred me to Bulgaria, and later, to Wales, just to get us out of France."

"You should be thankful you didn't lose your job," Bette murmured quietly.

"They shouldn't have been so harsh with him. He was just a boy," Hans said.

"A boy capable of despicable, heinous acts." Bette looked as though she was near tears.

"I'm sorry, my dear." Hans reached forward and took Bette's hand. "Bette prefers we not speak of the incident."

"I don't mean to interrupt," Michael said. "And I'm sorry if I'm forcing you to dredge up old memories, but if you can tell me how Isabelle's discovery of this information might have impacted her disappearance, it could help us to find her."

Bette and Hans exchanged a glance that sent inexplicable shivers down Michael's spine.

"Might she have gone to the authorities?" he asked. "She's been looking for clues that might reveal the identity of the person who ransacked her cottage."

"We called the police before we set out for Dunara. They hadn't seen anything of her," Hans said.

Michael sped across the moor, hoping he didn't meet anyone coming round the corners. "Let's cut to the chase. You're obviously distressed. What is it you're afraid of?"

"Damon flew in from Paris a couple of days ago," Hans said.

"He's staying at the castle?"

"He was there when we went to bed, but we checked and his bed wasn't slept in," Bette said nervously.

Hans looked at Bette. Their eyes met and held for a second.

"He might simply have gone out to the boat without saying anything," Hans said. "But there's also the possibility, however remote, that Damon found out about an article Isabelle seems to have been writing."

"Hans discovered some research she'd been doing on her laptop," Bette said,

Damon would not have been happy to discover that Isabelle knew about the incidents we're speaking of," Hans said.

#

Gareth clutched his side and climbed another four or five steps before collapsing against the inside of the stairwell. Morgan was dead. His body lay in a crumpled pile at the bottom of the watchtower.

Rage filled his body, and the renewed sense of energy generated by his anger propelled him up another two dozen or so stairs before he stumbled to a halt and had to kneel on another slippery, worn-smooth step to catch his breath.

He had wanted to kill Morgan himself on one or two occasions, but there was a big difference between wanting to strangle someone and actually doing it.

Hatred for Damon all but blinded him, which was a pity, because the steps leading to the top of the tower were so worn and crumbling that he desperately needed all of his wits about him if he was going to avoid a misstep.

He tried to calm himself down, but he could still feel the blood coursing through the veins in his neck, and intermittently, a strange sense of nothingness, as though his head wasn't even attached to his body. The sharp twinges of pain between his shoulder blades and the ache in his neck were making the climb difficult, but he was determined to find Damon and have it out with him.

When he'd refused to kill Morgan, he'd thought the matter was done. But when Damon hadn't been at his rendezvous point at the designated time, he'd known something was afoul. He'd had the crew bring the boat in as close as they could, then used the row boat to get to shore. Thank goodness the water had been calm or he might 'ave been as dead as poor Morgan.

He heard voices coming from higher up the stairs and kept climbing. He was sure the male's was Damon. The woman's also had a familiar ring to it—or a lack of one. He realized with horror that the second voice belonged to the American. Was Damon bringing her up here to kill her the same way he'd killed Morgan?

Damn him. He was going to get them all thrown in prison and locked up for good. The world might not be any worse off without Morgan in it, but if Damon did away with the American, they'd have the wrath of two governments, her family, her friends, and the corporation she worked for on their heads. It would turn into a major international incident. Everyone would be looking for them. They'd have nowhere to hide. What was the arrogant bloke thinking anyway? He attempted to climb at a quicker pace and set a passel of loose rocks clattering down the hatch. He stopped for a second to see if he'd been detected, but the noise from Damon and Isabelle's own ascent was so loud that what he'd added to it hadn't seemed to give him away.

He had to stop Damon before he did something so asinine it would land them all in prison for the rest of their lives.

The woman sounded like she was being difficult, and rightly so if what Damon had in mind for her was what he suspected. She was his only chance of catching up, or overcoming his foe if and when he did. Damon was almost twice his weight, taller, and much more muscular. If she could offer enough resistance until he got there, and enough assistance when he did, they might have a chance.

"Help! Help m—" He heard her yell. Her inflections were definitely American. It had to be Isabelle.

He felt a flash of sympathy when she went quiet, and wondered what Damon had done to shut her up. She started up again for a second and was cut off mid-sentence. He feared the worst. And then he heard a keening noise and a whimper—muffled—but a sure sign she was still alive.

He was close. He tried to stop huffing so the sound of his rasping wouldn't give him away. He also slowed to a snail's pace until he'd rounded each consecutive swirl in the staircase. If he could use the element of surprise to his advantage and catch Damon unaware. If the girl reacted quickly and came to his aid, he might have a go at saving her.

If he failed, not only would the girl die—he would. Damon did not tolerate betrayals.

"Please. Don't—" The girl's protests no longer sounded feisty or brave, but resigned and tired and ready to give up. He'd not have heard her at all if he hadn't been so close.

He almost stumbled on a step that was three-fourths missing and caught himself in the nick o' time. He pressed himself against the center support of the circular stair and held his breath. If he knew Damon, the man probably had a hard on from watching the girl suffer. Nothing got the sadistic bugger off like watching someone else in agony, be it man, woman or beast.

Why, oh why, had he ever gotten involved with a man like Damon?

He paused to look through an arrow slit, listen and plan his next move. The sun had to be nearly ready to rise. The mist over the sea had begun to burn off and he could see for miles over the tops of the trees.

He would wait a few more seconds to allow himself to catch his breath, and then attack. He took three or four deep breaths to gather his courage, knowing if he didn't succeed in disarming Damon, he would never see the sea or the sun or feel a breeze in the trees again.

He crept a few feet higher, half climbing, half crawling like a babe, up and up and round and round over steps disintegrating so badly that they were nearly covered in rubble. And then, he made the most wonderful discovery possible. Damon's foot, perched on the step just above his head.

He smiled. This, he could do. He might never know if he could have actually rammed Damon head on. The man had a very disarming gaze. 'Twas probably best he would never find out. But this, he could do.

He ignored the throbbing in his neck and turned his glance this way and that until he found a piece of slate with a razor sharp edge. He would ax Damon's ankle with stone, then grab his foot and pull as hard as he could. With any luck, Damon would topple over and hit his head—or something. If he over thought it too much, he might never follow though.

Isabelle let out another whimper. There was a scuffling noise and he knew the time had come.

Chapter Twenty-Six

The closer they got to the castle, the more convinced Michael was that something was seriously wrong. If Isabelle wasn't with him, and wasn't safe at the castle, then she was in danger. She wouldn't have gone out by herself when she was still reeling from what had happened at Dunara. Especially not at first light. Not a night owl like her.

"Please dial the police," he said to Bette. "It's better to be prepared than not."

"I concur," Hans said. "Whoever has her could well have Damon, too."

"Do you think they've been kidnapped?" Bette fumbled in her purse for her mobile and did as he'd asked.

They were clueless—both of them—but at least they'd alerted him to the problem. That was the important thing.

A few seconds later, they were at the castle. Michael's tires screeched as he pulled into the car park. He was out the door before the wheels had stopped rolling. Hans had suggested they check the catacombs under the castle—a thought which didn't bode well with Michael. But since the old tunnels were about the only place Hans and Bette hadn't already looked, it seemed a logical place to begin.

Hans had said the massive doors leading into the castle were open. As soon as he was inside, he took off at a dead run in the direction of the castle's kitchen and found the stairway to the cellar that would give him access to the labyrinth. Hans had described the maze of tunnels under the castle the best he could and said they joined up with the part of the keep that was still standing. Since there was no way into the catacombs from the outside, he had no choice but to try to follow his directions. The keep had been built as a fortification. Having an easy entry in a convenient spot on the outside wall wasn't exactly part of the defense plan.

"Isabelle!" He called her name as he sped down the dimly lit hallways in what he hoped was the direction of the old watchtower.

He knew every inch of the keep's layout from the outside, but when inside the castle, he'd never been past the parlor, the formal dining room, and Bette's office unless you counted the night he'd followed Bette to the room where Isabelle had been staying, and he certainly hadn't been paying attention to the floor plan on that occasion.

Hans and Bette had said they'd check to see if Isabelle had returned to her room while they were gone, and had promised to phone Michael if they found her. He didn't hold out much hope.

He came to a V and didn't know whether to veer to the left or the right. He hadn't realized how disorienting it was being below ground with no sun, no shoreline, no visual clues to help determine which way was which.

He hoped that fool Damon knew how badly the old, original sections of the keep had deteriorated. Hans and Bette had wanted him to rebuild the missing sections of the outer walls first, then to reconstruct the parts that still stood. There was no other way to have done it. Until the new sections of wall were complete, there would have been nothing stable to attach the old tower and the remaining walls to.

The thunder of rocks raining down in the distance startled him. He stopped momentarily to see if he could determine which direction the sound had come from. Overhead, yes, but more to the right or to the left? Another rumble followed, then a roar. He ran. Oh, God. Please let her be okay! What was Damon thinking? Did he want Isabelle dead?

He feared the answer so deeply that he couldn't bear to think about it. A surge of adrenalin took over and propelled his feet faster and faster until the ground blurred under his feet. He had to get to her before she... "Isabelle! Isabelle!" If there was any chance she could hear him, he wanted her to know he was coming, that he was almost there. The tunnel came to a dead end and a circular stair appeared. His only choice was to start climbing.

He could tell the second he went from being underground to above. First, green things and roots started poking through the holes in the rocks. Light streamed through chinks in the mortar and an occasional arrowslit. Thankful as he was for the little bits of light, it only served to illustrate the horrific condition of the keep. The thing was not safe. Even someone with an untrained eye should be able to see that.

He felt his cell phone rumbling in his pocket and stopped on a step that wasn't as worn as the others to give his feet a somewhat stable foothold. "Michael."

"Michael, it's Bette. We've just found a suicide note from Isabelle in her room. I'm so sorry we didn't see it earlier when we checked. I think it's her handwriting. It looks a little odd—not like it was contemplated, but as though it were written in a great hurry."

His heart squeezed and thundered in his chest so loudly he could hear it beating over the din of the rocks crashing against the outside of the tower. "Does it say anything about where she was going?" People rarely made rash decisions when it came to suicide. Isabelle had had a rough go of it lately, but he just couldn't imagine she would... It had to be Damon.

What sounded like another meteor shower rattled overhead. A stream of smaller rocks and sediment flew down the circular stair and landed at his feet. He hoped to God the ruckus meant Isabelle was still alive and fighting for her life. If she could just hold on.

"Let me know if you hear anything." He clicked his phone shut and used his hands to brace his incline. Some steps were missing altogether, others were so worn in the center that he had to flatten his body to the outside wall and maneuver the edges, a feat that did not bode well with what he knew about engineering.

How much stress could the old tower take before it collapsed and what was going on at the peak?

All he could do was climb and hope to God Isabelle was still alive when he got there.

#

For the second time that day, Isabelle was prepared to die. She'd fought it at first. Being required to write her own suicide note had actually forced her to examine all the reasons she truly did have to live, which had been a blessing of sorts.

Another section of the thick, stone-walled staircase crumbled and crashed to the ground below. Loose stones dislodged from the mortar that had held them for centuries and rained down around her.

"Sir? Are you okay?"

"Gareth. Please call me Gareth. Still hanging on, ma'am."

"Good." She was dazed from the rocks that had hit her on the head when Garth and Damon had had their tussle, but in some ways, she was seeing things more clearly than she had in a long while. Her petty fears seemed so ridiculous now. Of course, she'd have been embarrassed about her friends and family seeing the naked photos of her Ben was going to send out, but compared to being dead, being seen in the nude didn't seem too awful. At least she had a good body, and parents who loved her, and a friend or two who would stick by her no matter what. She had all that to live for. Plus, she was a good reporter, and she had Michael. Or at least she had until yesterday.

She'd been horribly hurt by Michael's lies and omissions of the truth. He'd known how important honesty was to her. But in light of everything that had happened, she realized he hadn't done anything that awful—probably nothing she wouldn't have done herself if she'd been in the same position. She only wished she could have lived to tell him how sorry she was for judging him, cutting him off and turning her back on him—say nothing about her part in blowing his cover and exposing his whereabouts to the people from Wisconsin who were after him. She really wished she'd been able to tell him she loved him before she died.

The rock she was clinging to with her right hand suddenly let loose. It would have crashed to the ground like all the others if she hadn't still been gripping it. For a second, she felt like she was losing her equilibrium and starting to fall. This is it, she thought. But at the very last second she dropped the rock, grabbed onto the jagged mortar left behind, and held on for dear life.

"Oh, Lord." She wasn't uttering it as an explicative. It was a plea. "Oh, Lord. Please save me." She thought about Rose and Pastor Ian and wished she'd paid more attention to them when they'd tried to help her. A person needed faith at a time like this, and hers was at rock bottom—no pun intended. She'd gone to Sunday School when she was a child like everyone else, but she really hadn't paid much mind to God since she'd graduated from high school. She regretted that now. If she'd ever stopped to think death could come so quickly, so unexpectedly, without the time to prepare for it that people with illnesses were granted, she might have done a few things differently. Maybe faith was a thing that should always be a part of your life, so it was right there at the ready in times of crisis.

Gareth must have been thinking along the same lines, because she could hear him saying what sounded like the Lord's Prayer in Welsh or Gaelic. She waited until he had finished, and then said, "Thank you again for risking your life to save me, Gareth. I appreciate what you did."

"Dinnae thank me for anything, Lady Isabelle. I cannae bear it."

She remained silent. Gareth probably was guilty of bringing more bad into the world than good, but then, who was she to judge? All that mattered to her at the moment was the fact that he'd disarmed Damon and saved her. She'd watched Damon fall after Gareth had attacked him and the wall on his side had broken away from the castle and started to crumble. All she'd felt was relief that it wasn't her.

Another round of rocks shattered away from the rim of the tower and rumbled to the ground below.

She clung to her perch as the tower shuddered beneath them. "Do you think we should try to climb down? I'm afraid if I even shift my weight, the whole thing will collapse."

"My leg is broken. I can see the bone." Gareth's voice broke and she thought it sounded like he was crying.

"I'm so sorry."

"Isabelle? May I call you that?"

"Of course, you may. I owe you my life."

"I'm sure Morgan is dead. I'm assuming Damon met the same fate when he went o'er the edge. I fear I'm done for. Maybe ye are, too, but on the chance that I should die and ye should live, there are some things I need to tell ye."

She was in no position to receive his confession, but she was all he had. "I'm listening."

"We've been searching for the gold from the Spanish galleon that sunk in Tobermory Bay in 1588. Last week, we sent a coin that we found on a reef to be analyzed at the lab in Edinburgh. The results should be coming in soon. Someone will have to let the men on the boat know what's happened. And lest ye should think they're all pirates and as guilty as we are, they are nae. As far as any of them knows, the sonar equipment we're using was legitimately purchased, and our mission sanctioned by the Spanish government. We explained the need for secrecy by telling them the Scots were nae so keen on the idea of searching for the gold as the Spaniards."

For a few minutes, she was a reporter again, and not a woman very probably about to die. If she lived, she would have the story of her life. If she died, well, she could at least be grateful the last few moments of her life were filled with enthusiasm for her next big scoop.

And then, the world started shifting around her and rocks started flying and she thought about Michael. As excited as she was about writing the story of the year, she wanted her last thoughts not to be of subterfuge or duplicity or greed, but of love.

#

"Michael, can ye hear me?" Logan's mangled bits of the Queen's English and local brogue had never sounded so welcome.

"Yes! I'm right here!" Michael couldn't see a thing except for the dappled splotches of light filtering through each oddly spaced interval in the thick stone walls. But he could hear Logan's muffled voice.

"Then listen and listen good. Stop right now and stay where you are. Or more accurately, get the hell out of there!"

"I'm looking for Isabelle!"

"Well, we've found her, and I'm here to tell you if you ever want to see her again, you need to get out of the tower. Now!"

"She's safe?"

"Not exactly, but probably more so than ye."

He had no intention of going anywhere until he'd rescued Isabelle. "Where is she?" If she was further up the watchtower, then that's where he was going. The steps inside the tower were the only way to get to her.

Logan's voice was deadly serious and full of dread. "She's near the top of the tower, or what's left of it. The whole thing's nearly separated from the castle. It looks like it could topple at any moment. If you dinnae get out of there now, you'll soon be buried under a thousand ton of rock, and squished flat as a piece of shale."

"But there's no other—"

"We've got this one, Michael. You have to trust me. Get out of there. Now."

There was silence for a second.

"You're making it worse, ye silly eejit. Can't you see how far the whole kit and caboodle is listing to the right? The higher you climb, the more stress ye're putting on the walls, and the more likely it is to collapse before we get her off the top."

He started to descend immediately. He had no choice but to let go of the reins and listen to Logan.

He half scrambled, half slid to the bottom of the tower and took off running the second he hit solid ground, retracing his steps through the maze of catacombs at the bottom of the keep as fast as he could run.

Chapter Twenty-Seven

The flashing red lights circling and swirling in the early morning light gave the keep an eerie look that made Michael's stomach a frantic knot of worry and fear. The sound of sirens fading into the distance assaulted his ears. Was he too late?

"Over here!" Logan waved him towards the outside edge of the castle wall, the side opposite of where they'd been working. Several police cars, two more ambulances and the coroner's van littered the grass around the perimeter. There was a noticeable gap around the base of the tower. His gut clenched even tighter. The turret looked more like the Leaning Tower of Pisa than a once proud Scottish castle. The distance they were keeping made it obvious they thought it was going to fall.

Logan stepped over to meet him. "Morgan is dead. Damon is alive, but barely so, and only because he landed in a hedge of gorse instead of a pile of boulders like Morgan did."

So Damon was at the root of this. Suicide note, my foot. He thought of the sharp, two inch thorns that grew on gorse and didn't feel one iota of sorrow the man had endured a little torture. A quick death would have been too good for the bastard.

His thoughts turned back to Isabelle as Logan wrapped a hefty arm around his shoulders—a harbinger of bad news if there ever was one. He braced himself. Logan's arm felt like it weighed at least thirty pounds.

"Gareth is badly injured."

"Gareth?"

"A friend of Morgan's—tall, thin gent with a plaid scarf. He's been working for Damon. He's lucid. Says his leg is broken, with the bone protruding."

"Serves him right if—"

"He saved Isabelle's life. He attacked Damon before he could push her over the edge."

A shudder ran through his body. "So she's okay?"

"For now. Gareth said she's pretty bruised and battered up, and that she's taken some hits to the head from falling rocks. She's fading in and out of consciousness. She's been asking for ye when she's been awake."

The lump in Michael's throat was so big he could barely swallow.

"Is there a plan for getting her down?"

"Well, we cannae use a ladder or anything that would put more stress on the structure for obvious reasons. I tried to get them to let me move the scaffold around to this side of the wall and get at her that way, but they said it was too dangerous. They want to get in and out again as quickly as possible so as not to endanger the men on the rescue squad. Besides, there's barely a big enough spot to set it on, say nothing aboot a level one. I could have made it sturdy enough with some time, but that, we dinnae have."

The base of the castle on this side was perched close to the sea, on a steep incline rimmed in jagged boulders. One misstep, and they could all end up in the Atlantic. "Could a helicopter pluck her out?"

"They fear the wind from the blades would make the whole thing crumble before they could get to her."

"And that leaves us where?" He racked his brain for another solution.

"The firefighters are putting together the rescue net."

"They want her to jump?"

"There's no other way." Logan pointed to a cluster of emergency personnel stretching out a piece of netting flanked by tubes and hand grips.

"They want her to jump. With a probable head trauma, and who knows what other injuries. You said she's not even fully conscious." All valid concerns, but that wasn't the crux of it, and he knew it better than anyone. Jumping from two or three stories and believing the people below were going to catch you would be difficult for the most trusting of souls. His heart sank into the pit of his stomach. Impossible. She'd never be able to do it.

"What about a crane? They could sit on the level ground on the other side of the wall and still get to her."

"Already checked on it." Logan's eyes kept darting to the tower like he was afraid he'd miss its collapse if he looked away for even a second. "They're on their way. But the nearest portable crane is on the other side of the island, and you know what the roads are like between here and there. The shortest route is the road to Calgary Bay, and that's impossible with a large vehicle."

The road inched along the side of a cliff and was barely wide enough for an auto with the exception of a rare passing place. On his one and only excursion to see the basalt columns on Staffa and the puffins on the Treshnish Isles, his comment had been that golf cart paths in America were wider than the roads on Mull.

"So they're coming the long way around?"

"Yes. But even on the main road they'll have to halt traffic to let a crane pass. They'll not be here anytime soon."

What Logan wasn't saying was if the tower collapsed before they got Isabelle, they could still use a crane—to lift the boulders off the bodies in a recovery effort.

"The police would like you to try to talk her down. She knows and trusts ye like no other."

That was the problem. She didn't. He'd lied to her. He'd destroyed the first, fragile trust she'd placed in another person in months.

"You said she's been asking for me."

"Aye. Here's a hard hat for ye. Not that it'll do any good if the thing goes." Logan motioned to a sloped spot near the sea and hurriedly walked in that direction. "That's where she seems to be able to hear us the best. She says she's perched on some steps that are mostly broken away, hanging on to the mortar on what's left of the wall. If she's going to jump, she'll have to steady herself enough to hoist her body up and over without toppling down what's left of the stairs."

"Assuming she's even conscious." He followed. His insides felt like someone was using a whisk to whip them to a froth.

Logan lifted an arm to quiet the men standing around the perimeter. "Isabelle? Michael's here now. He's going to go over what ye need to do once more to make sure ye understand."

The wind whistling around the keep moaned like a little boy blowing through a gap in his teeth. He heard nothing from Isabelle.

"She hasn't said a word in a few minutes now." A man's voice with a heavy Welch accent called out from the top of the tower. "Isabelle? Wake up, darlin'." Silence. "Isabelle?"

"Isabelle?" Michael took up the chorus. "Isabelle?" He waited, listened. "Isabelle?"

"Michael?" He broke into a smile—a huge smile—which quickly faded when he realized how weak, how afraid, how hurt she sounded. "Yes. It's me, sweetheart." Another clattering of rocks cascaded down the outside of the keep, rolled, skipped, and plunked into the sea.

"Isabelle, this is very important. The men have prepared a nice soft landing for you here on the ground, and they need you to jump before the keep crumbles any more. Do you understand, and can you lift yourself up enough to get over the edge?"

Silence. Was she weighing her options, or had she slipped back into unconsciousness?

"I can try."

"That's perfect, sweetheart. All you have to do is try."

Silence. "Michael? I don't think I can..."

"Isabelle, you're very brave, and I love you so much." His voice splintered into a million droplets of sound. He hadn't wanted to break down in front of her. He was supposed to be instilling her with confidence, wasn't he?

"I love you, too, Michael."

"Isabelle? Just take one step at a time. One tiny step up, and then another, and another." He was trying to make the task sound easy, but no one knew better than he what horrible condition the steps were in.

A second later, he could see the top of her head, her soft, sweet auburn curls.

"That's it, Isabelle. Don't look down. Just swing your leg over the edge and push off a little. You can do this."

"I'm afraid. Won't I crash into the wall on the way down?"

"The tower is leaning so far to the right that you'll have a clear path down once you clear the edge."

He could just make out her eyes, peering over the jagged stone edge. "What if I hit the net and bounce off?"

"The men are trained for moments just like this, sweetheart. They won't let you fall."

"Could they put some pillows around the edges, just in case?"

"Get some pillows." Two of his men took off running towards the front of the castle.

"Done. But I don't think it's wise to wait, Isabelle. Every second counts."

"What about Gareth?"

He turned and whispered to Logan. "What about Gareth?" He didn't honestly know—or care—but she obviously did, and he didn't want to answer her with anything less than the complete and total truth.

Logan lifted his head. "Isabelle? We've spoken to Gareth and he insists that as the lady, ye must go first. So ye see, the sooner ye come down from there, the sooner he'll be safe."

He patted Logan on the back. He couldn't have said it better himself.

Her voice was soft and empathetic. "It's going to be awful for him. His leg is hurt very badly."

"We have medical personnel here to help as soon as we get ye down," Logan said calmly.

She inched her head up a little higher.

"You can do it, sweetheart. Just a little further. Try to relax. Just let yourself go. The men are all ready for you. Just jump."

"I don't think I can, Michael." She whimpered. She had to be terrified. "I—I want to. But I don't think I can. It's like I'm paralyzed. I can't move."

He hoped and prayed she meant her nerves wouldn't allow her to jump, and that a spinal injury hadn't presented itself now that she'd moved. "Try moving your pointer finger. Can you do that?"

"Yes."

He sighed with pure relief. "Look up at the sky, Isabelle. Aren't the clouds pretty? Let's talk about something that helps you relax. You like music, don't you?"

Silence. "Maybe you could sing to me."

"Sure we can. Men? What's your favorite song, Isabelle?"

"You're going to think I'm completely loony, but the only song I can think of is *Jump*."

"*Jump For My Love*? The Pointer Sisters?" Leave it to Isabelle. If she got down from the tower alive, he swore he'd dance to it with her on their wedding day.

"Yes." Her voice sounded so small and tired and alone.

He waved the men from his construction crew over to where he and Logan were standing.

The rescue squad members who weren't hanging on to the net came, too, buzzing with questions. "Who are the Pointer Sisters?"

"I don't think I know—"

"'Girls Aloud' did a remake back in 2000 something. It went to the top of the charts in the UK."

Several of the men nodded. "Awrite. We know it." They lined up and waited for someone to begin.

"Somebody pull it up on You Tube."

Someone shouted, "The pillows are here." He could see the paramedics fluffing them around the edges of the net.

"I'll start singing the parts I know," one of the men said. "Jump in when ye can."

A round of laughter followed. That was good—diffusing the tension was exactly what they needed. Michael could see Isabelle's chin now, and even a little bit of her leg curling over the top of the keep. Please hold the thing together until she gets her courage up, he prayed.

He nodded and their newly appointed lead singer started to sing.

"You are the one, you are the one, and heaven waits here at my door. And if you want more, if you want more, more, more."

He cringed at the reference to heaven—not that he wouldn't love to spend eternity with Isabelle in the great castle in the sky one day, but he certainly hoped neither of them would be going there anytime soon.

He started to sing. *"Then jump for my love, jump in and feel my touch. Jump. If you want to taste my kisses in the night then, jump, jump for my love."*

The men crouched down and started doing some sort of crazy dance with their legs spread wide while they bounced up and down and walked sideways. The chain of them looked like an Egyptian hieroglyphics come to life. It reminded him of the Jingle Bell ad Kmart had been playing before he left the States.

If there was any chance it would make Isabelle relax enough to jump... He glanced sideways and got with the groove.

"Jump, I know my heart can make you happy. Jump in, you know these arms can feel you up. Jump, if you want to taste my kisses in the night then, jump, jump for my love."

He was so busy singing and dancing he didn't see the exact moment when Isabelle lifted her leg, pulled her body over the edge and jumped. He did see her flying, arms outstretched in a magnificent leap of faith. He saw a cloud of pillows reach out and

228

envelop her at precisely the right moment, the blue sea a glittering backdrop to her bravery.

"We have her!"

He took off at a run while the others kept singing. From there on, everything happened in a blur. Two paramedics lifted Isabelle onto a mesh board; others hovered over her, checking her vitals. Some of the singers rushed over to grab on to the handholds of the rescue net. Gareth jumped a moment later with an agonizing scream.

Michael followed Isabelle and watched as they loaded her into the ambulance. She was unconscious, but she was alive. He asked if he could ride along. The paramedics shook their heads, saying they needed what little extra space there was to do their jobs. He was told to meet them at the clinic in Tobermory.

The second ambulance was just pulling away with Gareth when a roar filled the air.

"Run!"

Dust and debris, chunks of mortar and an explosion of boulders rained down on them from the keep, choking their lungs with particles of old plaster and mold. Thank you, Lord. Too close for comfort, but he would take it.

When the air had cleared enough so they could see, Michael did a quick head count of his men. All safe and accounted for. Hans and Bette hovered in the distance. He probably should have gone to them, tried to console them—the knowledge that Damon was responsible for all this had to be haunting them—but he just didn't have the words.

All he cared about was Isabelle.

Chapter Twenty-Eight

The half-raised walls of the portion of the keep Michael's crew had been working on all but blocked the pile of rocks where the west turret used to be. Blue sky illuminated every craggy spire and sunshine shone down on the crowd gathered at the base of the castle when Michael's car rolled to a halt.

If it weren't for the police tape roping off the path to the far side of the keep, you never would have known a tragedy had just occurred. The crowd might have been there for a birthday party or a wedding. Instead, they waited expectantly as Michael helped Bette from the front seat, then reached back to close Hans' door behind him,

Bette looked up at the stone crafters in the front row of the assemblage, then turned to look at Michael. "I'm so sorry, but I just can't..."

Michael stood aside as Hans, shoulders bent with defeat, helped Bette through the main door of Bluevale Castle.

"Damon is in critical condition with multiple bones broken and a spinal injury that has rendered him paralyzed. Gareth insisted on making a full confession to the authorities about Damon's plot to recover the gold in the bay, which included the theft of over five million dollars' worth of sonar equipment—before he went into surgery, in case he should die on the operating table."

"What aboot the lass?"

"Isabelle is in serious condition. They're trying to assess the extent of her injuries. Thankfully, no bones appear to be broken. A helicopter will be transporting her to Glasgow in a few minutes where they can do more tests. Once she's stabilized, she's asked to be medevaced to Virginia. I'll be accompanying her and then, once she's settled, going on to Wisconsin to take care of some business. Unless the tests reveal something far worse than they suspect, she's likely to make a full recovery."

A murmur of relief rumbled through the crowd, echoing his own jubilation that Isabelle was going to be okay.

He tried to search out Logan and finally caught a glimpse of him walking to the front of the crowd.

"Logan, both Isabelle and I want to say thank you for coordinating the rescue efforts. To all of you who helped in any way, please know I'm eternally grateful."

He reached out his hand, expecting to shake Logan's hand or even give him a hug, but when Logan stepped out from the crowd his face was clouded with anger.

He stepped square in Michael's path. "So, tell us, Michael. Are ye even a Scot?"

What was this about? "You know full well I'm a Scot. Half the town remembers my great-grandfather."

"If ye really are his kin." Logan fired back at him. "In light of what we know now, it would seem to me everythin' ye've said up until this point is suspect."

Inspector MacClellan stepped out from behind Logan. He held a clipboard in his arms, and a pen in his hand. "I should have closed down this little operation of yours months ago. Now, we've had an incident and a man is dead."

The shock he felt must have registered on his face. It had never occurred to him that he or his workers might be blamed for what happened. "It's Gareth you need to talk to, MacClellan. Morgan's death had nothing to do with our renovation, nor did the collapse of the tower."

"It would also seem that some new information pertaining to your credentials—or lack of them—has come to light, Mr. St. Dawndalyn. You give me no choice but to shut down the whole kit and caboodle until you're able to certify that you're a licensed contractor."

A moan rippled through the gathering, probably a result of his men assimilated the fact they were suddenly without jobs.

"I've not broken any laws. The men are all employees of Hans and Bette, as am I. While I do supervise the men on their behalf, they hired me only as a home repair person, not as a contractor."

"It's not for me to determine if ye've broken the law, but the authorities. Regardless, I must be able to verify this project is done according to our safety standards and in keeping with the renovation mandates set forth by the Historic Trust."

This day had been nothing but one suckerpunch after another. "Hans and Bette are fully committed to completing the renovation of the keep. More so now than ever. They feel it's one way they can give back to the community to compensate for the damage Damon has done."

He took a deep breath and plowed on. "Surely you've seen enough of our work to know we're doing an excellent job of it. You've seen the plans I've drawn up. You know what construction methods I'm using. You know my men are safety-minded and committed to excellence."

The inspector looked unconvinced. "It comes down to this— billing yerself as a home repair person may cover yer butt, but ye're acting in the role of a contractor. So the fact remains I need to see some proof ye're qualified to do the job—perhaps a full listing of your family's credentials, Mr. St. Dawndalyn, since that would appear to be the one and only thing on which ye've been basing your expertise."

"It's a little difficult to round up copies of a license for a man who's been dead for over two decades." He looked around at the circle of men watching and listening and tried to enlist their support. "You all know who my great-grandfather and my grandfather were. My mother's name is Carolyn. She married Charles-Louis St. Dawndalyn, who was French Indian, and had two children, my sister, Barbara, and myself. My father died when I was six years old. For all practical purposes, I was raised by my grandfather, who worked for my great-grandfather, laying stones. Their homestead was near Oconomowoc, Wisconsin. Google anything to do with Oconomowoc and you'll see all kinds of stone buildings built by my ancestors. I've told you all of this before."

"And ye claim yer great-grandfather and yer grandfather were certified brick layers and stone masons?"

"Yes. Of course I do. Why would I lie about that?"

"That's a very good question, lad. A very good question, indeed," MacClellan looked over his shoulder. "McClintock? Are ye still here?"

"McClintock?" Michael asked.

"Someone who knew your great-grandfather."

"Is this an inspection or a trial?" Michael tried to keep his voice from sounding as testy as he felt.

"I knew yer sinn-seanair from the time I was a wee lad. I was in the crowd that lined the bay the day he left to seek his fortune in America," McClintock said, in a voice as wizened as his stooped, bent, old body. "And I'm here to testify yer great-grandfather was no stone layer. He were a farmer."

Michael sighed. "A farmer who built stone fences, houses, bridges and barns when he wasn't planting or harvesting crops." He scanned the group until he saw Logan's head over the top of the crowd. "Logan!" he yelled. "Would you come over here for a minute, please?"

"I'd rather not, if you don't mind," Logan yelled back.

"Well, I do mind," Michael said. "I thought we'd put this ridiculous spat behind us. Obviously, we've not. If you'd please set aside your feelings for a minute and help me clear this matter up, I'll be happy to explain everything."

The crowd parted and Logan moved to the front of the pack.

Michael tried to put his hand on Logan's shoulder but he jerked away at the last moment. *Good grief.* "Logan, tell the man how you came to be so talented at what you do."

"Which o' my many talents are ye speaking o'?" A ripple of laughter wove its way through the crowd.

"You know what I mean."

"I followed me pa around the farm when I was but a wee lad. He taught me everything I know."

Michael grabbed Logan's hand and shook it. "Thank you. My great-grandfather may not have been a certified stone layer when he left Scotland, but when he got to Wisconsin, there were fields full of rocks and a town to be built, and like any good Scot, he knew what to do."

An exuberant round of applause rang out, and a few wolf whistles pierced the air.

"Fine," MacClellan said. "So ye think ye know what ye're doing. We'll soon find out."

"What exactly does that mean, sir? Do we have jobs or do we not?" Logan asked.

A hush fell over the entire group. "My supervisor reckons if the job's been done properly up until now, he'll award Mr. St. Dawndalyn temporary certification papers until such time as they can settle the matter between themselves."

"So we can keep working?"

"Provided ye pass the rigorous inspection I'm aboot to subject ye to."

A cheer swelled up from Michael's crew.

"I said," MacClellan reiterated in a pompous voice, "there is to be a thorough inspection of all work that has transpired to date, and if, and only if..."

"The work will pass muster all right," Logan yelled. "Ye could search the whole of Scotland—nay, the whole world—and not find a better built keep."

In all his years as a psychologist, Michael had never felt such a rush of pride.

A few minutes later, when the crowd had dispersed, he turned to Logan and tried to explain.

"Logan, you have to know I hated having to lie to you—and the others—about anything. I was counseling one of my clients back in Wisconsin when she told me something that would very likely have destroyed my sister's family. About the same time, the estranged mother of another one of my clients, and the wealthy husband of the woman involved with my sister's husband, sued me. I chose to walk away rather than testify against the people who had put their trust in me or to risk ending my sister's marriage."

Logan looked a little befuddled, which he guessed was to be expected. "So you really are a psychologist?"

"I only meant to take a short vacation—just long enough for everyone to calm down. Staying on and restoring the keep was something that just happened after I got to know Hans and Bette. I really did learn to lay rocks at my Grandfather's knee. Letting everyone believe the string of abbreviated credentials behind my name meant I'm a licensed contractor in the United States was all unplanned. The joke was on me when I realized how much I was enjoying my new profession and my new life. Will you forgive me?"

Logan shook his hand and gave him a look that was half grin and half grimace. "But what'll happen now? If ye're going back to Wisconsin, what'll happen to us, and the keep?"

"I'll be back in two weeks if all goes well. I'd like to put you in charge while I'm gone."

When Logan nodded, he continued. "You can start by cleaning up the cave-in and securing the adjacent walls to prevent any further collapses. When that's done, you can resume working on the east wall. I'll leave a number to call if you have questions or concerns."

"Will ye be bringing back Isabelle when you return?"

"I hope so." He couldn't imagine Scotland without her. "It'll be up to her, of course, but I hope she'll return."

"Maybe the two of you will end up together in Wisconsin." Logan winked like it was all settled.

He smiled back and acted the part. Logan obviously thought it was possible. He wasn't so sure. There were so many wounds to heal. Isabelle had said she wouldn't write the story her staff had been researching when they revealed his whereabouts to Masterson, but the story was bound to come out now that his cover had been blown. There was still a lot to sort out, between he and Isabelle, and with half of Wisconsin.

Logan looked him in the eye then. "Do I have your word ye'll return? Once ye get back to Wisconsin, you may find ye think differently about things. What weill ye do if Isabelle needs ye? The men willnae like it if ye leave them in the lurch."

"I give you my word. No more secrets. And I'll be back. I promise you that."

Chapter Twenty-Nine

"But if they sedate me, I won't know what's going on, and I'll be at the mercy of whomever…" Isabelle squirmed as much as the straps on the gurney would allow, winced, and laid back on her pillow.

By the looks of things, her attempt to get more comfortable hadn't worked.

Michael stood and massaged her shoulders ever so gently. "I promise I'll be with you every second."

"But I could be working on the story about the gold. Yes, they granted me exclusive rights, but the longer I wait, the more likely someone will leak something and I'll lose my chance to break the news. I told the people at the Associated Press I'd have my copy to them by tomorrow morning."

"The doctor said you need to rest. You said you hadn't slept in almost 48 hours when Damon kidnapped you, and the only time you've closed your eyes since then is when you've been unconscious."

"I can't help it if I'm a little wound up. Once I fall asleep, I could sleep for days. What then? If I get the story done before I go to sleep, I'll be able to rest easy, which is just what I need."

"But the doctor—"

"If they'd let me sit up, I could get started. Please, just get me my laptop. I can use my voice recognition software so I can rest my arms."

"Isabelle, we've been through this. You have a concussion. Recommended treatment includes no television, computer use, or smart phones, all of which stimulate the brain. You've got severe bruising of your neck and shoulders. If you don't relax and let the inflammation and swelling go down, you could do permanent damage. Your brain needs to rest. The more you fight me on this, the more I'm convinced you really aren't thinking clearly, which leads me to believe you really do need to be sedated. If you won't listen to the doctors in Glasgow, being a doctor of psychiatry gives me the authority to prescribe sedatives, and I will not hesitate to do what needs to be done."

"You wouldn't."

"I would. I have two lawsuits pending against me already, and I'm probably going to lose my license anyway. What have I got to lose?"

"You of all people should understand what's at stake here, Michael. This is my chance to get my old job back. You didn't know me before this whole thing with Ben. I was a completely different person. I lived for the next big story. I never took no for an answer. I always delivered. My boss could count on me 100 percent of the time. This weepy, scared, skittish little wimp I've become since Ben absconded with my money and destroyed my instincts isn't me. If I do this story, and do it well, Ronald will know I'm back. Please. I need to win back his trust. I need to get my confidence back."

He did understand, but...

She sighed, swept her half-opened baby blues across his face and turned her southern drawl up a notch. "Just let me get started while we wait for the airplane. If you let me dictate a few things while they're fresh in my mind, I promise you I'll sleep all the way across the Atlantic."

His resolve was slipping and she knew it. Instincts. She might think hers were off kilter. He begged to differ.

As if on cue, she started again, sweet and smooth as honey. "Wouldn't it be therapeutic for me to get it all out? Think of it as journaling. You psychologists love it when people write down their thoughts. What could be better for me after the trauma I've been through?"

"Sleep." He grabbed her laptop and opened the top. "Fine. But only if you let me set up the voice recognition and only if you promise to give in and go to sleep the second we're in the air."

He could hear her cell phone ringing out the song *Inside Story* from somewhere deep in the bag of personal belongings the hospital personnel had given him when they'd checked her out.

"Get it. It could be Ronald."

"Or your parents, worried sick about you." He rummaged through the bag.

"Get it before it stops."

"I'm trying."

"Open it. Quick. And pull my pillow away from my head. If it's Ronald, I don't want my voice to sound muffled or he'll know I'm lying in bed."

"Which you are."

"I don't want him to know. Just pull it out from under my neck."

"I'll do no such thing." He flipped open the top of her phone and handed it to her, against his better wishes.

Either her cell was set on speakerphone or Ronald had an extremely loud voice because he could hear every word the man was saying.

"AP needs the news clip for the buried treasure story as soon as possible—I know it will be big news in Europe, but the story I want is the psychologist from Wisconsin. Our readers will eat it up. Like I keep saying, everyone's worst nightmare is being sold out by their shrink. His coming back here to testify against his clients—now that's a story that will grab the national headlines."

He stiffened reflexively and stared her down.

"I don't think that's exactly what..." She turned her head ever so slightly and gave him a look—like don't worry, I've got this. "Ronald, I think I'll pass on the Michael St. Dawndalyn story and put my money on the gold in Tobermory Bay. The whole St. Dawndalyn thing is really nothing more than a family squabble that's gotten a little blown out of proportion."

"Are you kidding? Have you watched television lately? Three fourths of what's on is couples and families airing their dirty laundry for all the world to see. Besides, once you're done with the story, it will be about much more than that. Your job is to slant the story in a way that gives it mass appeal. Or have you forgotten what it is that reporters do?"

Oh, brother.

"Of course I haven't. I know what my job description is." Her tone had gone from sweet and southern to clipped and businesslike. "However, I don't believe I have the necessary objectivity required for this story, and for that reason, I need to pass."

Michael sighed his relief. That settled it then.

There was a moment's silence from Ronald.

Isabelle smiled at him reassuringly and whispered, "See? I told you I would handle it."

"I don't think you understand, Isabelle." Ronald's tone had also changed. "You have a choice here."

Michael cringed. Ronald was saying she had options with his words, but his voice was telling her she had no choice at all. He glanced at Isabelle. It was clear she was drawing the same conclusion.

Ronald continued. "You can write the story, or I can give it to Austin. And Austin is chomping at the bit, so I wouldn't dally too long. The truth is, he's doing an excellent job. He's young and has a lot to learn, but he's eager and he has his finger on the pulse of what our younger readers want."

"You make me sound like some sort of dinosaur."

"With this generation, a decade is the new century. The world is changing that fast. The internet is killing us, Isabelle. Our whole industry depends on luring in younger readers. While you've been gone, Austin has been leading a transition team to move *Insight* toward an online magazine format—and doing a fine job of it.

"I like you, Isabelle. I really do. I've stalled and covered for you and done everything I can to save your position at *Insight*. But if you pass on a story that has the potential to be this big, I'll have no choice but to give Austin the story—and your job."

Michael's heart went out to her. It was bad enough he'd lost his clients, his battle to protect his sister, and probably his license, too. He had hoped, after all Isabelle had been through, she would have a different outcome.

He tried to catch her eye to lend a little moral support, but her head was down.

"Fine. I'll do it." She had turned her head away from him and her voice was muffled by the pillow, but he could still hear her.

"When do I need to turn it in?"

His first reaction was shock. What had happened with her friend, Gloria, was one thing. It had been inadvertent. He could forgive her for that, no matter how damning the consequences had been for him. The damage had been unintentional. But for her to fall at Ronald's feet and save herself at the expense of his family and career... to purposefully and knowingly gain from his misfortune... She wouldn't.

She clicked her cell shut and looked at him with her eyes full of shame. "I really thought Ronald would be so excited about the gold he would forget all about what was going on in Wisconsin. Maybe he's right. Maybe my instincts are off."

"It's not just 'what's going on in Wisconsin.' It's my life. And my sister's family's life. I can't believe you would..."

It was a full five minutes before he could even look at her again. When he did, she was asleep. They'd given her a sedative earlier. It hadn't seemed to do any good. Maybe it had finally kicked in. Maybe the trauma of the last few days had caught up with her. Maybe Ronald's ultimatum had been the straw that had broken the camel's back.

No matter. He was done. He checked her vitals and continued to do so during the flight. What else could he do? He certainly wasn't going to wake her up so she could start writing her story—about him.

When they arrived in Virginia, her parents were there to meet the plane. He briefly introduced himself—why go into detail when they would soon be able to read all about him? He was sure Isabelle's next big story would fill in all the gaps, both past and present.

When the airline personnel arrived to assist her parents with Isabelle's transport—she was still fast asleep—he signed off on her paperwork and boarded his flight to Chicago, whereon he would catch a hop to Milwaukee. Buck was going to have a car waiting for him. At least there was someone who cared.

Chapter Thirty

Isabelle stood on the deck of the ferry and watched as the lighthouse off the coast of Oban came into focus. She snapped a few photos of the crisp white tower, and several minutes later, Duart Castle rising from the rocky shores of the Isle of Mull. She certainly didn't feel like a tourist—she was coming home. But the sky was a brilliant blue and made a magnificent backdrop for the crisp white of the lighthouse and the mottled patchwork of stone that made up the castle walls.

Seconds later, Torosay Castle came briefly into view as they approached the dock at Craignure. In all the time she'd spent at Mull, she'd not yet taken a tour. Maybe she and Michael—if there was a she and Michael—could go have a look one day. There were so many things she still hoped to learn about the island, to see and experience and talk about with Michael.

Her face started to flush as she thought about the talks they'd had on the French Riviera. In the month that had passed since she'd seen Michael, she'd tried to forget the tension and awkwardness that had erupted on the flight home and concentrate on the good things they'd shared.

"Isabelle!" Rose MacCraig was standing at the edge of the dock, waving at her.

Five minutes later, she stepped onto the gangplank, walked its length, and threw herself into Rose's arms. "Thank you so much for coming to get me. I really appreciate it."

"I booked a room for you at Cuidhe-Leathain B&B on Breadalbane Street just like yeasked. But I still say ye could have stayed with us."

"I don't know how long I'll be and I don't want to impose. I think Dunara is open, but I just couldn't go back."

"Of course nae. It's time to move forward, start out fresh and make new memories."

"Maybe I shouldn't even have come back. Michael hasn't

responded to any of my calls since I arrived in Virginia."

"Ian and I ran into him one night at the Bell. When I asked about ye, he said something about being sure ye were busy writing articles for *Insight*. Word has it that he's had a rough go of it—we tried to get him to talk about what was going on in his life, but that's all he had to say."

"I'm going straight out to see him once I've checked in at the B&B. If I don't find him at the keep, I'll try the Blue Bell this evening."

"I've not seen him there lately. Damon still being the owner has been a bur under some people's seats. Others 'ave said they're more concerned aboot supporting Mrs. Galbraith and the rest of the staff for fear they'll lose their jobs if traffic drops off too much. Ye know how people are."

An involuntary rush of fear rippled through her body. "Has Damon been released?"

"No—and he willnae be for a good many years from what I hear. Of course, they've had to tend to his injuries. They say he'll never walk again." Rose helped her load her luggage into her auto. "Greed has its price."

"I'm just glad it's over." How she hoped her relationship with Michael hadn't already suffered the same sad fate.

#

Michael didn't often second guess the men, but when he had an opinion, he wasn't afraid to express it. "The stones you're using are too big. The closer you get to the top of the wall, the smaller they need to be to set squarely on the base of the foundation you've already built."

"But it's a perfect fit."

He could see that. The men had gotten to be experts at picking rocks with the precise shape needed to fill the space where they were about to be set. Even he loved the feeling of finding the right shape rock for the right spot. It was like putting together a jigsaw puzzle— each rock destined for a specific spot, and all that was needed was the right eye to see which went where. "Nonetheless, it's too big. How thick is the wall where you're working?"

"A little over two feet."

"Perfect. Just keep the circumference of the rocks down a

smidgen and you'll be fine."

The stiff wind they'd been fighting since dawn gusted to what felt like thirty miles an hour. He reached for his hat to make sure it didn't blow away.

That was when he felt—yes, felt—her eyes coming to rest on him. He turned so sharply he nearly twisted his neck.

Isabelle. He almost smiled. Gut reaction. She was a bonny lass, all right. And then it all came back, the avalanche of boulders raining down on his shoulders all over again.

Except it had been her shoulders the first time, not his. Did the fact that his pain had been emotional rather than physical diminish what he felt? Of course not, you dolt. He may have switched professions on paper, but a psychologist he would always be.

"Hello, Michael."

He really hadn't thought she'd come. Maybe to Wisconsin, if he'd stayed there a little longer. But not all the way to Scotland.

"Isabelle." He held his ground, but it didn't take a shrink to know there was no escaping the stash of emotions he'd been so careful to keep under lock and key.

She glanced around at the mishmash of men and rocks and tools and clutter and said, "Is there someplace we could talk?"

How many patients had he told, 'avoidance is no solution.' Still, his instinct was to run.

"I've missed the sea. Would you walk down to the Celtic bath with me?"

His answer was to start walking. It was as good a place as any. Bette and Hans wouldn't be there this time of day. Not that they'd need privacy for anything other than the words that had to be said. And in his mind, they'd be done talking before they got to the standing rocks. Maybe even the stile over the fence at the end of the pasture.

She scurried to catch up with him, and once she had, matched his stride with a confidence he hadn't known her to possess.

"It's obvious you're not happy to see me," she finally conceded, when he slowed to climb the steps over the fence.

"I thought that would be clear from the fact I didn't return your calls."

"I don't understand why you're so... Please, Michael. I need to understand."

He struggled to find the right words. He should have known this moment would come, and rehearsed what had been clanging through his head since the moment on the airplane when she'd made it clear where her priorities lay—or didn't.

"I gave up everything for you. My career is in shambles. My sister's life is destroyed. If you hadn't come to Mull, if I'd stayed away from you like I should have... I know the life I built here in Scotland was a house of cards. Maybe if you hadn't made it crumble, something or someone else would have. But the fact is, you're the one who toppled the whole jingbang."

He watched for her reaction but she didn't try to defend herself. She just let him vent. She'd said she'd taken a few psych classes back in the day. Maybe she'd paid more attention than he'd assumed. "You had a choice, Isabelle. You chose to bow to Ronald's demands—a man who'd been unreasonable and unsupportive and antagonistic from the start. Yet you chose him."

For once, he couldn't read her.

"Do you know what Austin would have said about you if Ronald had let him write the article instead of me? You know I didn't want to write it, but I thought it was better to do it myself than to stand by and watch another reporter crucify you."

The wind that had been battering him and his men and the keep all day suddenly let out a sigh and died down to nothing.

Her eyes lit on him and flamed, roaring mad. It didn't take a psychologist to figure that out. "Did you even read what I wrote?"

He hadn't. Maybe he should have. His sister had told him it wasn't half bad, and considering the mood Barbara had been in at the time, maybe he should have taken her words for praise.

"I made you out to be a hero, both in Wisconsin and in Scotland. I enumerated the sacrifices you made to protect the people you loved. Do you really think any other reporter would have taken that slant?"

He sighed. So he should have read the article. But did it really change anything? Ultimately, she'd still chosen her career over him. "Fine. So you have your precious job back. Ronald thinks you're the greatest and everything's hunky-dory again. And this concerns me how?"

"Are you kidding? Ronald said if I'd done a decent job of playing up the scandal, the story would have sold ten times as many copies. I eventually did get my old job back, but not for the reason you think." Her eyes still blazed.

This was not the same Isabelle who had cowered and cried every time she was threatened. This was not the same woman who'd been so uncomfortable in her own skin that she couldn't trust anyone or anything.

"My friend, Gloria, set up a sting that finally led the police to Ben, but not before he forwarded a very explicit nude photo of me to Ronald. I was mortified, but I figured being a little embarrassed was better than being dead. I got over it.

"Austin, being the ever eager young reporter he is, saw a story in my misfortune and wrote an article—illustrated—about internet dating gone wrong. You can about imagine. 'If someone as savvy and street smart as our lead reporter could be taken in, then it could happen to anyone.' Totally riveting. When Ronald refused to publish it, Austin went past legal and tried to leak the story—and the photos of me, nude—to a rag. Only then did Ronald fire him and reinstate me in my old investigative post, probably because he thought I'd sue if he didn't."

Well, she had his attention now. "So what did you do?"

"I quit. I've been in touch with several publications who have published my pieces before and it looks like I'll be able to get at least enough freelance work to pay the bills."

"Which gives you freedom to write the stories you want."

"No more kowtowing to Ronald's whims. And, I can live where I want to live."

He held out his arms and she was there in two seconds. "I'm so sorry, sweetheart."

"I love you, Michael. And if you weren't in love with me, then none of what happened would have hurt you the way it did."

He kissed her, and kissed her again. "I do love you. More than anything."

"What happened with Ben changed me, Michael. Scotland changed me more. What happened between us changed me most of all. When I first came to Mull, I had totally lost myself. I've loved you for a long time, but I guess I had to find out who I really was before I could trust you. It started when we were on the French Riviera, and then when we came home, and everything started going haywire..."

"It's fine, sweetheart. I loved you from the beginning. I'll love you even more now that you're yourself again."

"So do you think there's room in Tobermory for a stone layer who does a little counseling on the side and a free-lance writer who likes to relax at nude beaches every so often?"

"Do you think your friend, Rose, could talk Pastor Ian into marrying us? How about next spring down in Bluebell Valley?"

"I think anything is possible."

He laughed. "Maybe you'll follow in Barrie's footsteps after all. You could write a novel."

"Sounds perfect." She caught his hand and swirled into his arms. "'Cuz boy, do I have a story."

Read on for an excerpt from Sherrie Hansen's next Wildflowers of Scotland novel

Shy Violet

1

She had to get away from him. She didn't care what kind of trouble she got herself into—anything would be better than being with him. She had to find a way to escape. Violet Johansen's legs pumped under her as she raced over the drawbridge, across the moat, toward the parking lot. She tugged at one door handle after another—someone must have left their car door open. It wasn't like she was in East St. Louis or downtown Detroit. This was small town Scotland. There had to be one person who was trusting enough to leave their auto unlocked.

The wind buffeted her face and the chilly air tore at her lungs. Had he realized she was gone? How much time did she have to get away? And why hadn't she done this when they were in Edinburgh, where she could have dashed into a store, ducked down an alley and disappeared into the throngs of people wandering up and down the Miracle Mile? No. She'd chosen to try to make her escape at a castle surrounded by water on three and a half sides, accessed by one east west road squeezed between a mountain and a loch. She'd chosen to make a break for it where the best and only place to hide was a stupid parking lot full of locked cars.

But Alexander hadn't let her out of his sight the entire time they were in the city. The man rarely even slept. Still, she wished she'd tried to leave before it came to this.

The wall of stone to the north of the castle taunted her. There was no way she could climb the sheer face of rock even if she'd been wearing tennis shoes or hiking boots. She had on Birkenstocks and no socks.

She never should have come to Europe with him in the first place. But it had seemed like such a dream come true at the time. The man had been knighted by the Queen. Didn't they do background checks on people before they knighted them into an age old position of trust and honor?

She could try to shift the blame, but she knew what was happening to her was no fault of the Queen's. She should have known things were going to end badly. They usually did when she blew off the advance plans, went off-road, and acted on impulse.

But if she hadn't followed her instincts this time, she might have been dead by morning. She didn't know it. She felt it. Alexander's abuse had started out with minor things, like promising her the world, then not letting her use the ladies room. But these last few days, he'd been so crazy mean to her that...

A tour bus. Certainly the bus driver would leave the door open in case someone had to use the loo. Right? Locked. Of course. The passenger's belongings were in their seats.

Panic laced with adrenalin surged through her veins. The tour had to be coming to an end.

The tea house. The girl with the red hair who'd been taking their money when they went through the line had seemed nice. Intelligent, too. A bit naive. She'd giggled like a schoolgirl when Alexander had flirted with her and given her a big tip. Hell, she probably was a schoolgirl.

Violet had to trust someone. Asking for help was not something that came easily to her, but she couldn't do this by herself. The only security guard she'd seen had been inside the castle. There was no place to hide.

She raced back to the tea house, ducking from vehicle to vehicle. Still no sign of anyone exiting the castle. She made a run for it across the open expanse of grass that led to the eating area.

She was halfway there when the lilting strains of a lone bagpipe wafted across the water. Maybe he'd been playing all along, but suddenly, the sound was so clear and true she could almost see the notes rising to the deep blue heavens over the Isle of Skye. She wanted to turn, to see the person capable of making such a sound. Her heart, breaking, her tears, flowing, her gut, wrenching—it was all there—each note a teardrop, each pause, a sigh, each lilting change in the direction of the melody, a gasp.

But she didn't have time. She clutched her side and kept running. She—had—to—get—to—safety.

"Help." By the time she threw open the door and located the girl, she could barely find her breath, say nothing of her voice. "It's a long story, but I've nowhere to go. I need a place to hide. He'll come looking for me."

The red-headed girl's eyes darted to the castle.

"Please! Is there a cellar, or a walk-in freezer, or an old shed? Anywhere." Her voice rose a notch. "He'll be here any second."

"Tour won't be done for another five minutes. That's where he is?"

"Yes."

The girl turned to a young man who was washing dishes. "Are the pirates in the bay today?"

"Last I knew."

"Come with me." The red-headed girl reached for her hand and tugged her out the back door.

They ran across the grassy ring around the moat, away from the entrance to the castle, until they reached a dragoon moored in the blue waters of Loch Alsh.

"I've a passenger who needs transporting," the girl said to the pirate at the stern of the sailboat. "She needs to go far, far away and stay there until everyone is gone."

The girl didn't appear nervous, but Violet was. The man didn't look like a tour guide. He looked like a real pirate. His hair hung in long, matted dreadlocks around skin stained dark from too much sweat and sun.

"Will ye do it? We have precious little time."

"For the price of the rest of the day's tours." The pirate used his fingers to scratch his skin under the greasy headscarf tied around his forehead. "Lost revenues, I cannae afford. Much as I'd like to help the lass."

"I have no money." Violet blinked away tears for the first time. She'd been so close.

The man must have sensed her desperation. "Climb on board. We'll take ye for a spin in the loch and find a way to work things out."

A stream of tourists spewed out of the mouth of Eileen Donan castle and began to cross the moat. She ducked, then crawled to the deepest part of the boat, her legs crossed under her, her head bowed.

"Ahoy, mateys." There was a clatter as the anchor was raised and ropes cinched and drawn, then a creaking noise as the boat left the dock. The waves hit with a jolt, swell after swell, a roller coaster ride of fear and regret and wonderment and terror.

"What's yer name, fair lassie?"

She dared not look up for fear Alexander would see her. She let out a deep breath. He was more likely checking the bathrooms, consulting the authorities, or asking around to see if anyone had seen her. Would the red-haired girl be able to resist his charms? He was a knight with a thick pocketbook. He had ways of getting what he wanted and wasn't afraid to use them, especially on young women who giggled at his good looks and swooned when he wooed them. She'd been such a fool.

"Violet. My name is Violet. Violet Johansen."

A wave splashed over the gunnels and doused her. She tried not to cower—it was just water. Water couldn't hurt her. But it was bad enough, being scared silly and at the mercy of a bunch of marauding pirates who were complete strangers. She did not want to be cold and soaked besides.

The pirates talked among themselves, a half indistinguishable mishmash of conversation and sailing lingo in Irish brogues and the lyrical cadence of Scots.

The sea calmed, and she resisted the urge to sneak a peek at the water, the heather covered hills and the blue mountains in the distance that she'd glimpsed from the castle.

"So, you're not really pirates, right?" She didn't dare lift her head for fear Alexander was eyeing them from the dock or using the binoculars he always traveled with to scope her whereabouts.

"Depends on how ye define pirate."

She still couldn't see their faces, but the voice that spoke was deep and husky.

A second voice spoke, softer and gentler. "So if I be a pirate, does that mean ye be the cooking wench from me fantasies, come to feed us delectable morsels and pleasure us on our long voyage, far from land?"

"Um. No. Sorry to disappoint you."

"There be a group of prospective passengers waiting in line at the dock," another voice said. That made three. She'd barely looked at the motley group when she'd jumped on the boat, but thought she remembered five or six total crew members.

"What's this gent look like—the one ye're hiding from? If he has a defining characteristic I could pinpoint with my eyepiece, perhaps we can determine if it be safe to swing back and pick up some paying passengers."

Okay. She got the point. She'd always hated being a nuisance. She swallowed her pride. What choice did she have? "He's wearing a black sports jacket with an ascot around his neck. Red, I think. He was wearing sunglasses and carrying a satchel over his shoulder for his camera, Kindle, and binoculars."

"Ye were dating a man who carries a purse?"

"It's not a purse. It was designed for men. Kind of like a backpack only smaller." Why was she defending him? The man was a blimey bastard. Let them think what they would.

"I'm afraid I've lost all respect for ye now. Ye know what they say aboot women who love men with purses," said the pirate with the deep, husky voice.

"Got him in my sights," the gentler voiced pirate said. "No way we can turn back now. He's got his binoculars trained right on us."

Her fear meter soared off the chart and she jerked involuntarily. She felt like her lungs were being crushed.

"Stay down, lass. He can see twice what I can at this distance. Take a look, Joe."

"Do you think if we returned her, all nice like, he'd give us his binoculars as a reward?" a gruff voice asked.

Great. Untrustworthy pirates. Just her luck. She mustered her courage and tried to sound intimidating. "More likely he'd have you charged with kidnapping and hauled before Scotland Yard."

"It weren't us who kidnapped ye. It were ye who commandeered our ship and made us do yer bidding." This one had a thick brogue.

"I'm sorry. I didn't mean to drag anyone else into this mess. As for the money you're missing out on, I'll make it up to you somehow."

"Oh, we'll find a way to extract it from you sooner or later."

A new voice. Was it the chill in the wind, or did this one sound more menacing than the others?

"What say we head over to Loch Alsh and pick up that shipment we had slated for later today?" the gruff one spoke.

"In broad daylight? A bit risky, aren't it?"

"Anyone sees us with this pretty lassie here, they'll think we're out for a picnic."

"We have to earn some money somehow. She obviously hasn't got two haypenny to her name."

What nefarious plans were they yammering on about now? As long as they weren't planning to get their goods by turning her in for ransom, and it took her further from shore, beyond the scope of Alexander's binoculars, what did she care?

That was when the weather turned. She felt the cloud cover the sun as her neck and shoulders went from being warm and cozy to stiff and cold. Her stomach lurched as swells began to pitch and toss the boat.

"Looks like we got a bit of a squall headed our way."

"Batten down the hatches."

She cowered in her corner and tried to stay out of the way of ropes, jib, and most of all, their clodhoppers. She didn't want to get stepped on.

When the first crack of lightning split the sky, she was scared half to death, but never once as scared as she had been when Alexander had been at the helm of her life.

#

Three hours later, she stepped off the pirate ship, still in one piece, although just barely.

She couldn't exactly say she felt friendly toward the pirates. It was obvious they viewed her as one huge pain in the butt, but they'd all made it through the storm and besides being soaked, she'd suffered no harm.

She'd thought she might ask to be let off at whatever village the pirates docked at to pick up their cargo, but they'd fetched it from a remote, uninhabited bay and she'd seen no other towns along the route they'd taken back.

She was thankful to have been redeposited on solid ground and could honestly say she appreciated their sailing skills and what they'd done to help her. All was well, except she had no clue what to do or where to go.

Nothing felt safe or solid as she crept up the hill at the back of Eilean Donan, trying to walk off her sea legs and make sure that Alexander wasn't still skulking about.

She thought about stopping at the tea house to see if the red-haired girl was still there, but decided to keep going when the knot in her stomach took shape and tripled in size. There were only a few cars left in the parking lot, none of them Alexander's. Had he really gone, or had he gotten the truth out of someone who worked at the tea house and parked the car elsewhere so he could lie in wait, ready to nab her when she reappeared?

She took a few more steps. She could see people securing the castle for the night and a man getting ready to close a gate that stretched across the drawbridge.

She wondered if Alexander had returned to their hotel in Inverness, moved on to Fort William, or found a room somewhere nearby so he could keep looking for her. She guessed the latter, which meant she needed a place to hide. The time she'd spent on the pirate boat had given her a chance to think—at least when she wasn't convinced she was going to die at the bottom of Loch Alsh — but she still didn't have a plan.

She looked both ways to make sure there was still no sign of Alexander and crested the rise.

For a few seconds, she felt almost safe. She was back on familiar ground, at least as familiar as it got in Scotland. She retraced her steps. The bagpipe player was still at his post, and the melody he was playing was one she'd heard before, somewhere. Maybe it was an omen that everything was going to be fine. Lord, she hoped so.

Her legs had almost readjusted to dry land by the time she was close enough to see the details of his kilt, the blues and greens and blacks of the plaid, and his face. Oh. My. The edges of her world shimmered and wobbled like a mirage fresh off the pages of Lawrence of Arabia, except that she was in the middle of a watery, wet land just off the Isle of Skye instead of a dessert in the Sahara. It had to be an illusion. The bagpiper looked so exactly like Nate Moore at twenty-two that, for a second, as she looked at the century old castle with its mossy, ivy-laced buttresses, and the timeless, heather-covered hills, she wondered if she'd been transported back in time. Except that she'd known Nate halfway around the world, in

Colorado Springs, in college, about as far from Scotland as a person could be.

And then he smiled at her, his lips curling around the gooseneck-shaped mouthpiece of the bagpipe with a burst of sound so enthusiastic she could feel his passion. She tried to right herself, to stop the chaotic balance of time and place and emotion that swirled around her. Is this what it felt like to tesseract? Had she stumbled across some magical wrinkle in time, or stepped through the back of a wardrobe to some alternate existence?

And then the music took her, and it didn't matter where she was or when it was or even what she was. The lilting, haunting beauty of the melody was all that mattered.

Someone dropped a quid in the open case beside him. She heard a car door close, but she was so enraptured with his music that for a moment, she forgot to check and see if it was Alexander coming for her. He couldn't have taken her anyway, not with her feet rooted to the ground, her spirit soaring high above the earth, her body linked inexplicably to the bagpipe player who looked so like her first love.

"Can I help you?" His voice reached through the haze.

The music had stopped. The sun was fading. She'd been standing on the grassy knoll outside Eilean Donan for who knew how long.

He wasn't from Scotland then. His voice was a unique mix of distinctively Southern paired with at least a few month of living in Scotland—Nate's face and stance with a stranger's voice.

"I'm not sure. It's been a very stressful day." I've nowhere to go, she thought. And if I tell him that, I could end up in a sticky wicket as bad or worse as the one I've just gotten out of. "I was here earlier for a tour and out on the pirate boat when the storm hit."

His eyes took in her bedraggled hair and still damp clothes. "I'm afraid you've missed your bus then." He looked so concerned, so caring.

"I was going to speak to the red-haired girl at the gift shop to see if some accommodations could be made..."

"Lyndsie."

She'd panicked. Alexander would have retraced their steps—spoken to the tour guide, the gatekeeper, the security staff, the bathroom attendant, the red-headed girl who had served them lunch, then helped her escape—anyone who might remember her. Who knew what he had told them. He was so utterly charming, so beguiling—until you knew what he was made of. She'd seen it time and time again—people so memorized by his smooth manners and dazzling smile that they rushed to do his bidding and scrambled to please him like puppy dogs knowing they were about to be given a bone.

Only now did she realize that if the red-headed girl had ratted her out, Alexander would have been waiting for her when the boat docked, more likely, called the Scottish equivalent of the Coast Guard and had her plucked from the boat and returned to him mid-Loch. She hoped this meant that Lyndsie had kept her secret and that there was at least one person she could trust.

"I'm done playing for the night. I can walk up the hill with you and show you where Betsy's B&B is if you like. It's just up the lane."

"My purse—everything I had was in the car."

"You were in an auto?"

"Yes. I have no money, no ID, no anything."

She watched his face as the obvious dawned. Whoever she'd been with—in the car—had left her, abandoned her, driven off without her. What conclusions the bagpipe player was drawing, she had no idea. Whatever it was, it was probably less humiliating than the truth.

"Wait a minute!" Had she put her safety pack on before they left the hotel? Mornings were a blur—the time when she was least alert. Her grandmother had given it to her years ago, warning her of pickpockets, flimflams, and big-city life in general. She reached under her shirt and groped beneath her breasts. Thank God! Her passport, a credit card, and a $100 bill swaddled against her skin in a contraption so soft she'd forgotten it even existed—thank you, Grandma, thank you, God.

She froze for a second's time, waiting instinctively for the bagpiper to push her to the ground, rip her body billfold from her midriff and make off with the only money she had left in the world. Nothing. Okay. She sucked in a deep breath. Two people she could trust. Of course, she didn't know his name. Then again, she knew all five of Alexander's and he was the worst liar she knew.

That was when she realized she couldn't use the credit card. Alexander would have alerted the police by now, and almost certainly asked her credit card company to flag the card. If she checked into any sort of boarding house and tried to pay with her credit card, she'd be apprehended by morning.

"I have a few American dollars, but it's all I've got." How long would a hundred bucks last in Scotland? Alexander had been paying for everything, opting for the best there was to offer, and showering everyone who helped them with lavish tips. No help there. A book she'd seen on the ferry to Mull jumped to the forefront of her mind— *The British Isles on $100 a Day*. Was it just her, or did the title imply that the chore was some super-savers feat that could be accomplished with a minimum of suffering if one really tried to be frugal and followed a few miserly little tricks along the way? It didn't bode well for her.

"I hope you don't think I'm being forward, but I have an extra bed at my place if you want to crash there temporarily."

Her skepticism must have shown.

"My roommate left for the States last month. We both came over on a ten month contract, but I had the opportunity to stay on to teach summer school and play my pipes at the castle. I opted to extend my visit—much to the consternation of my fiancé."

Talk about trusting. Youth. He reminded her of herself five or six months ago—before she'd met Alexander.

"Lyndsie—the girl from the gift shop and lunch counter—can vouch for me. I'm a decent sort. Trustworthy as they come."

"Okay." Her mind groped for an alternate plan and came up blank. "If you don't mind, I'd feel better about it if I could talk to her first. Not to imply that you're not telling the truth. I mean, you're very kind. I just..." Who else did she have to turn to?

"I understand." He knelt, scooped the coins and bills in his case into what looked like a miniature treasure chest, and laid his pipes down as gently as could be.

"You play beautifully. I'm sorry I don't have any coins." She wanted to say that if she's paid him an amount commensurate with the pleasure he'd given her, his box would be overflowing. But she didn't. She made herself look away from the way the hem of his kilt fluttered against his thighs when he moved. "I like your treasure chest. Speaking of... the pirates I was with earlier..."

He made a face that indicated he could go either way on the subject. "Nobody really knows."

"Well, they're not real pirates, are they? I mean, at first, I thought they were just actors, but their sailing skills seem pretty sophisticated for a group of gents just playing a role."

"Oh, they know what they're doing alright. A good thing, the way that storm came on."

"So what did you mean—nobody really knows?"

"I've heard some rumors, that's all. They evidently like their whiskey—like most who're from Skye." He tucked the edge of the biggest pipe in the case and zipped it shut. "Rumor has it they may be smuggling some precious cargo, but no one's been able to nab them in the act."

"Oh." Her head started to swirl again, but she didn't mention the suspicious bits she'd overheard. What had she gotten herself into?

The piper hoisted his bag over one shoulder, touched his free hand to the small of her back, and led her over the knoll toward the cafeteria and gift shop. "I'm Nathan. And your name is?"

"Violet." Her knees nearly buckled under her and he reached for her hand as though he sensed she felt unsteady on her feet.

It couldn't be. If it was Nate, he hadn't aged a day in over a dozen years. "Nathan?"

"Nathan McPhearson."

She tried to camouflage her shock. So it wasn't him. How could it have been? But she could have sworn he was Nate Moore.

He clasped her hand more tightly and they ran down the hill, through the grass, hand in hand, just like...

Who knows how much of her reaction registered on her face? She had no looking glass, and thankfully, he was watching the ground for potholes and roots. She would have to sort it out later, when she'd climbed out of the rabbit hole she'd fallen into and made her way back from Wonderland.

The door to the gift shop was locked, but the staff was still visible through the glass door, mopping the floor and counting out the money in the cash register.

Nathan—the new Nathan who looked just like old Nate, who couldn't possibly be the same Nate she'd known all those years ago because he was Nathan McPhearson, not Nate Moore—got Lyndsie's attention and mouthed "Let us in."

Lyndsie turned the deadbolt, whooshed them to the far corner of the dining room and relocked the door. "That guy was here for almost an hour, describing ye to the constable and asking everyone who works here if they'd seen ye. I can't believe I ever thought the creep a wee bit good looking."

"You didn't say anything?"

"No way. I believed ye. I hate to lie even to a jerk like him, but ye seemed pretty desperate when ye came rushing in, so I figured ye had to be telling the truth aboot him."

"Thank you." She wanted to hug Lyndsie but thought she might scare her if she came lunging at her when they'd only just met.

"Lyndsie, tell Violet I'm on the up and up so she's not afraid to come hide out in my spare bedroom for a few nights."

"Nathan? Totally awesome dude from Kentucky. A music teacher on exchange from America."

Of course he would be a teacher. Just like Nate.

"He's a mean guitar player and sometimes a drummer in addition to playing the pipes. Gives lessons to children in his spare time and is trusted by parents and grandparents all across the Isles. His only flaw is that he's already engaged and is supposed to be married at the end of next month." Lyndsie smiled shyly.

Supposed to be? What did that mean? Was there some doubt? Not that it mattered. "I'm a schoolteacher, too."

"Cool! What subject?"

"Fourth grade. I also teach two periods of art three days a week."

"So you've got the rest of the summer to sort things out."

"I guess I do." Her look must have tipped Nathan off to her mounting inner hysteria, because he was studying her with renewed concern. She was starting to freak out over the enormity of things that needed to be 'sorted out'.

"We can talk more when we get to my flat."

"If ye guys don't mind waiting a few minutes, I'll walk with ye," Lyndsie said.

"That would be great." Her shoulders started to relax and for the first time in a long while, she felt a sliver of hope peeking out from behind the wedge of clouds that had become her heart.